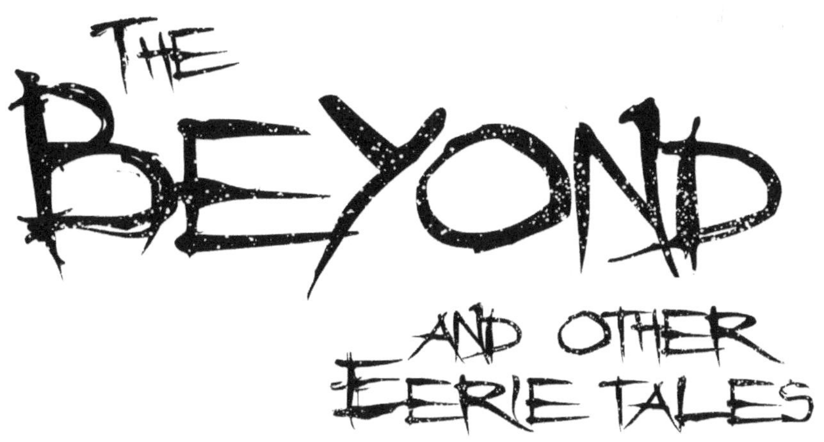

E. Tayloe Wise

Fiesta Publishing
PO Box 44984
Phoenix, AZ 85064

www.fiestapublishing.com

The Beyond is like a Window at night.

Standing inside the lit house and
looking out into the Darkness,

One can see Nothing.

But from Outside in the Darkness

Everything within is bright.

Megan Morrison

To Donna for all your
encouragement and patience during
the writing of this book.

In memory of Cyndy Conte (1952-2021)
who always believed I should
pursue my writing.

TABLE OF CONTENTS

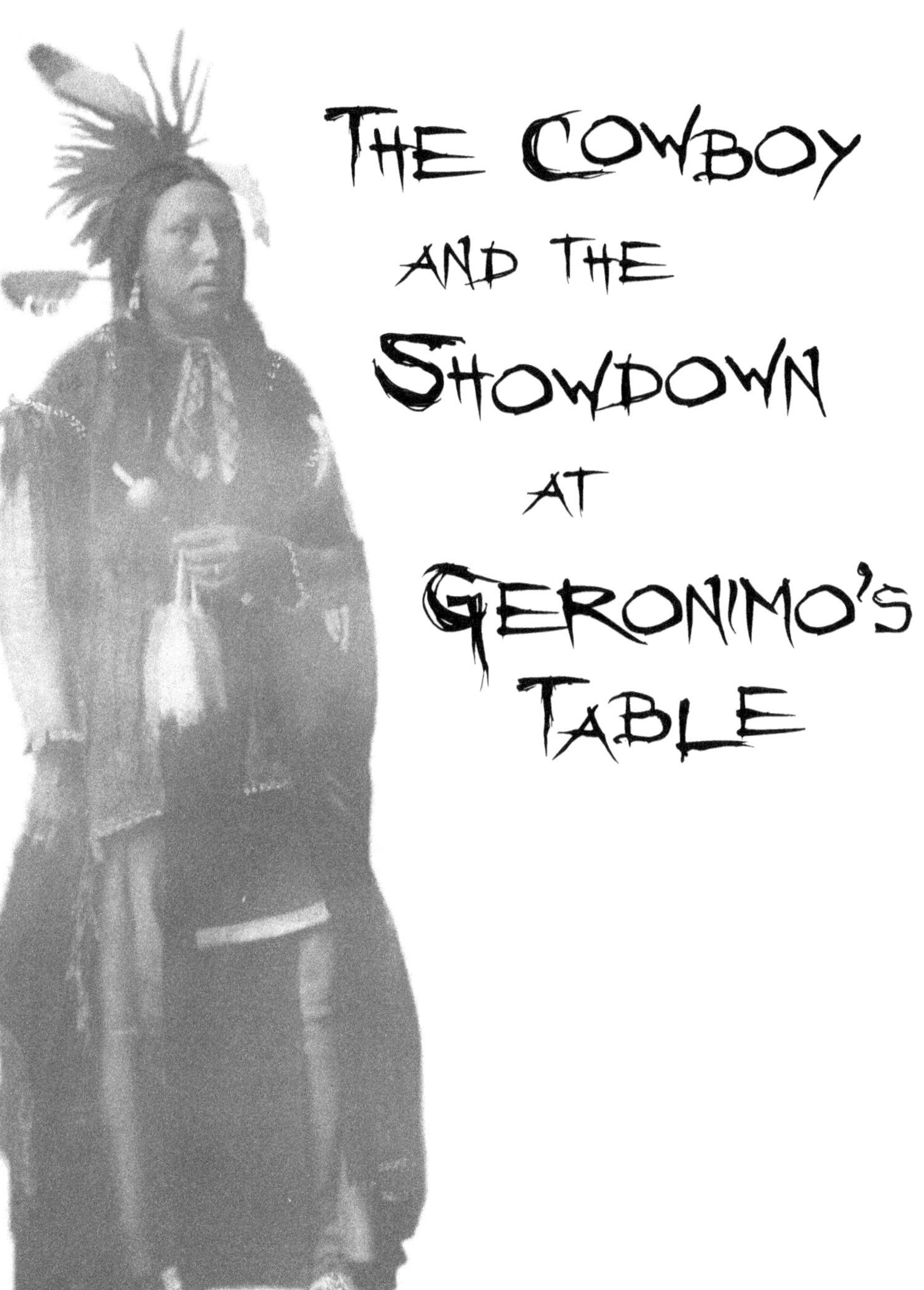

The Cowboy and the Showdown at Geronimo's Table

INTRODUCTION

The shadow of the steel grey clouds drifted slowly across The Cowboy's leathery, wrinkle-lined face, making it difficult for him to pick out distant objects as the far-off curtain of darkness approached and slowly descended across the barren desert floor. After riding hard for the last few hours, he was bone tired and thirsty. The warm water in his canteen was almost gone, only a couple of drops remained.

Sitting uneasily in his saddle while his chestnut brown mount nibbled on some dead sagebrush, he silently dragged on the cigarette he had just rolled. The silence of the desert and coming nightfall crept across the land as a cool wind out of the west began to pick up and blew the smoke back into The Cowboy's face. Scarred by time, wind, and rain, The Cowboy's countenance told the tale of many pains out on the distant trail. A week's growth of greyish beard hid the features of his weary, tired-looking visage.

His horse suddenly perked up its ears, gave a startled neigh, and shied uneasily as a scraggly coyote emerged from the brush about twenty yards away. It quickly and quietly slinked off into the shroud of coming darkness as the sun's last golden ray faded slowly into the night and died.

"Whoa! Boy! It's alright—just a scrawny no-good-*fer-nutting* coyote!" The old man soothed and petted the horse's neck with his left hand to reassure the steed that all was well. "Won't be long now, boy, and we'll be *comin'* up on that there spring I know about," he continued. "*Don'* worry, *ol'* son," he said as he kept petting the uneasy animal. "We'll be *gittin'* there soon enough even though it's *gonna* be dark."

The once hot desert began to rapidly cool and the wind picked up at a steady pace. *Well*, the old man thought, *at least it'll partially cover our tracks by morning.* He looked back with some trepidation, watching the sheet of darkness obscuring the desert behind them. He knew someone, or perhaps more, were tracking him. He'd deliberately led his chasers into a harsh and unforgiving land of no return, known as the Jornada del Muerto.

He picked up the split reins he'd been holding in his left hand, gave the horse a little nudge with his spurs, and it started to amble slowly forward. The steed moved off toward a downhill slope leading into a six- to eight-foot-deep arroyo. At the bottom, he turned his mount to the left and they continued along the bottom of the sandy and lava-lined thirty-foot-wide dried watercourse. Darkness now completely descended, making it difficult to see. Man and horse picked their way gingerly across the gully's sandy and lava-ridden floor as dust rose in little puffs behind them from their passage.

Both man and horse plodded along for several miles as they slowly ascended a gradual slope before the arroyo began to narrow. While they continued on their uphill journey, the dark clouds above them slowly moved eastward and the full moon emerged shining down into the gulch they were traversing. A medium-sized moonlit mesa, which The Cowboy nicknamed Water Hole Ridge, loomed up in front of them. The Cowboy knew he was nearing the end of the dried watercourse because its sides were now only two to three feet high.

"Well, *ol'* fellow," he said quietly to his mount as he gave the horse's neck a friendly pat, "won't be long now. That seep's just another few hundred yards away."

On the right side of the narrowing gully, a natural ramp emerged in the moonlight. He guided his horse over to it and they easily climbed out of the lava-strewn ravine. Water Hole Ridge, a low-lying dark black volcanic tableland, about twenty-five feet high sloping north to south, now loomed over them as they plodded alongside its ebony face for a few hundred yards until the horse nickered at the smell of water. The Cowboy dismounted, grasped the split reins in one hand, and walked another ten yards until a small pool of water emerged in the moonlight snuggled next to the butte's rising face.

The old man dropped the split reins, and using one of them as a rope, tied the weary animal to a thick bush. Taking both of his canteens, which were tied to his saddle, he untied and gulped down the remaining water in one of them before he refilled each cloth-covered metal water container from the seep. Next, he pulled his Winchester .30-30 from its leather sheath on the left side of his saddle and propped the weapon against a nearby rock. Uncinching the saddle, The Cowboy pulled it and the saddle blanket off the steed's back and placed both items on the ground next to the small pool of water. After untying the rein, he gently pulled the bridle off the animal's head, removed the bit, and led the animal over to the water which it immediately started to drink.

Untying his rolled-up blanket from the saddle, he spread it out on the ground in front of the seep. Next, he rolled the saddle blanket up so that he could use it as a rough pillow. Retrieving his Winchester, he placed it on the left side of the blanket. He didn't expect his followers would be tracking him at night, *but*, he wisely thought, *a man can't be too careful*. After all, he knew they wanted him to lead them to the gold where they would try to take it and kill him. He, in turn, had other plans for them.

He fixed himself a quick meal of beef jerky along with a small can of peaches. His horse, now finished drinking, stood nearby. Removing hobbles from his saddlebag, The Cowboy put them on the steed's front feet. It wouldn't wander too far now. Plus, he knew the horse would probably drink some more water during the night. Sitting cross-legged on the ground, The Cowboy rolled himself another cigarette, then cupping with his left hand, lit it and calmly smoked until it had burned down to within an inch of his fingers. He spit on the butt, then placed it on a thin rock ledge next to the seep. Lying down on his blanket, The Cowboy quickly drifted off to sleep.

When he awoke around dawn the next morning, the sun was barely peeking through the clouds. Pulling out his watch from a small pocket in the front of his vest, he saw that it was close to 5:00 a.m. An ominous dark sky obscuring the sun hovered over him. The distant sound of thunder off to the west reached his ears. In the distance, he could see a solid sheet of rain approaching like an undulating window curtain when wind rushes through an open window.

It was time to break camp. Laying his Winchester against a nearby rock, The Cowboy quickly gathered up his blanket, shook it out, rolled it up, and slipped a waterproof cover over it. Unrolling the saddle blanket, he placed it on his steed's back. Next, he lifted the saddle with its attached rifle sheath and set it firmly on the horse's back. He then tightened the cinch. After gently placing the steed's bridle over its head, he inserted the bit into its mouth and coiled the split reins over the pommel. Next, he picked up the rolled blanket in its water-resistant sheath and tied it down behind the saddle. After installing the horse's tack and double-checking it to ensure everything was firmly in place, he removed the hobbles and stuck them in one of the saddlebags. Finally, The Cowboy grabbed his .30-30 and slid it into the sheath. Taking a broken branch, he then brushed out all the tracks around the spring. *I hope*, he thought, *those coming rains will wash everything away. I sure don' wanna make things easy fer those fellas trailing us.*

Mounting his steed, The Cowboy leaned forward, petted his horse's neck, and said, "Okay, *ol' fella*, time *fer* us to move on. *Tha rains ah comin'*, which is good *fer* us as it'll wash our tracks away."

Off in the distance, he saw lightning and then heard the loud sound of thunder roll toward and over him. He kept close to the ninety-degree wall of the ancient mile-long lava tableland. The downpour hit him and the horse with ferocity as the wind-driven drops lashed both man and horse. The rain constantly dripped off the wide brim of his hat, but The Cowboy ignored it as he and his horse plodded onward. In fifteen to twenty minutes, as suddenly as it came, the storm abated and blew past them on its eastward march. Minutes later the sun reemerged as he finally rounded the southern end of Water Hole Ridge.

Off to the southeast, about twelve to fifteen miles away, he espied a familiar massive reddish-black tableland. The Cowboy had now left the wide lava field that he had traversed the previous day. To his front lay a desert with thousands of scattered lava pieces dotting the landscape. He turned his horse toward a distant monolith—aptly named Geronimo's Table. The famously elusive Apache chief had holed up close to the mesa's flanks during the U.S. Army's futile search for him. Geronimo had finally given up in 1886 becoming the last American Indian leader to formally surrender to the U.S. military.[1] He died in 1909 as a prisoner of war at Fort Sill, Oklahoma.

The Cowboy's final battle would take place somewhere in the environs close to the massive rock plateau located southeast of his present position. He knew that his pursuers would have much difficulty picking their way across the Jornada del Muerto. But eventually, he surmised, they would pick up his trail. Still, The Cowboy knew he had a couple of days to prepare. Some twenty-five years previously, he discovered the dark reddish-black butte, lying southeast of the Jornada del Muerto lava field. He knew the butte

---

1 https://www.history.com/topics/nativeamericanhistory/geronimo

intimately, which he explored and climbed when he camped next to it on numerous occasions.

On his second trip to Geronimo's Table, he circumvented the reddish-black lava tableland and stumbled upon a hidden two- to three-foot-wide flume, with footholds carved into its sides leading upward to the top of the black monolith. *Perhaps*, The Cowboy thought, *Geronimo used the tabletop as a lookout to glimpse the approach of his implacable enemies—the white man and his army?*

As he moved away from the hidden crevasse on his second excursion to the butte, The Cowboy noticed that several hundred yards away birds were flying into the bushes next to the butte's reddish-black sides but weren't reemerging as quickly as they had disappeared. He wondered, might there be some sort of water source from a seep that they might be frequenting? Slowly walking toward the area, The Cowboy observed that birds appeared to be emerging right out of the cliff face. Wading carefully through the brush, so as to avoid stepping on a rattlesnake, he quickly discovered a fold in the rock hiding a three-foot-wide entrance to what turned out to be a lava tube leading deep inside the mesa. Some fifteen to twenty feet inside the entrance to this volcanic cavern, he found, to his amazement, a seep, and along with it a small ten-foot-round pool about eight to twelve inches deep. He immediately realized the volcanic tube would be a perfect place not only to camp but also to hide his mount. The steed would be safe inside while he further explored the butte. On subsequent trips, he and his horse always camped just inside the cavern's entrance.

The grotto's walls and floor were smooth. A few days later, after this unexpected discovery, he decided to explore the nether regions of the volcanic tube. Fashioning a makeshift torch of creosote branches and twigs that he tied tightly together on an inch-thick, three-foot-long tree branch, The Cowboy moved further back into the cavern's dark recesses. Moving slowly and stepping carefully, he followed the ten-foot-high tube as it sloped imperceptibly downward. About fifty yards from the cave's entrance, he spotted a small opening in the rock on the left side of the cave. Out of curiosity, he stooped down to examine it further. The small offshoot appeared to be just big enough for a man to crawl through.

Bending further down, he eyed its black depths for the first time and he could feel a slight breeze of air exiting from the mouth of the opening. About eighteen inches inside the opening, The Cowboy was surprised to espy a small painted figure of Kokopelli on the right side of the volcanic offshoot. He knew that the flute-playing deity was a venerated fertility figure for many of the Southwestern American Indian tribes. Kokopelli, he had been told, was also known to preside over agriculture. The Indian god was known to be a master braider who also represented the spirit of music. But, most importantly, Kokopelli had a reputation for being a trickster.

Hmm, The Cowboy contemplated, *I think this opening needs further exploring, but is Kokopelli's figure luring me into some sort of trap? After all, he does symbolize the trickster. I had best be careful.*

Deciding he would need a second torch just in case the first one burned out, he returned to the cave's hidden entrance, ventured outside and replenished his first torch with some creosote tree branches and twigs which would burn more slowly. He also fashioned a second similar type of torch. Returning to the crawl space, he held a torch in front of him, while he dragged the second one behind him. The Cowboy inched forward into the small two-foot-high by three-foot-wide tunnel. After a slow crawl of twenty to twenty-five feet, during which he carefully scrutinized the walls and ground for traps, he emerged into a small, rounded chamber about fifteen feet across and ten to twenty feet in height.

Standing up, The Cowboy held the torch over his head. On the black volcanic rock walls were over a hundred painted human figures in all sorts of beautiful—but faded—reds, blues, and yellows. Some of the figures were dancing, while others were seated and stared out across the darkness at him. The eyes of those seated figures seemed to bore right through him, making The Cowboy somewhat uneasy at this surprising discovery. There were also pictures of animals—buffalo, antelope, rabbits, and one or two animals that were totally unfamiliar to the astounded man. One such animal looked somewhat similar to an elephant. But how, he wondered, would Indians know anything about elephants which, he knew, didn't inhabit America? On the other side of the tiny chamber there were fifteen to twenty clay pots lined up against the wall. Each piece of ancient pottery had intricate designs on its surface which, for the most part, were black and white in color. Walking over to them, he stooped down to look more closely at the pots, but he knew better than to touch these fragile relics.

The Cowboy realized he had discovered some sort of sacred Indian chamber. He immediately decided that he would never mention this discovery to anyone. After all, this secret subterranean room had to be some kind of sacred ceremonial site! Glancing upward at the dark obsidian-colored ceiling, which his flickering torch illuminated, he silently prayed, *Please, Almighty God, protect me while I keep this beautiful and sacred site secret.* After all, as a last resort, this chamber would make a really safe hiding place!

When he returned to civilization from these trips, The Cowboy never divulged the butte's or the cave's location to anyone. Plus, on subsequent visits to the black mesa, he never reentered the sacred chamber, but every time he stayed in the grotto, he checked its entrance. So, today, upon his latest arrival at Geronimo's Table, he led his horse into the cool chamber. With the time available to him, The Cowboy knew he had time to set up an ambush in the vicinity of the hidden secret chute with its footholds to the tabletop that he had previously discovered.

Before now, he hadn't wanted to kill his pursuers, but as they continued to dog his tracks, The Cowboy knew he had no other choice. The men had, at times surreptitiously, and then quite overtly, tracked him for the last three months and would continue to do so in their unfounded belief that he had a cached gold treasure somewhere. There had to be a showdown. He needed to put a permanent end to their dogged and misguided pursuit.

He seated himself at the end of a twenty-five-foot-long immaculately polished mahogany bar in Bisbee, Arizona Territory, so that he had a clear view of the front door and anyone who walked through it. He'd been sipping on a beer when a young guy, about twenty-one or twenty-two years old with noticeably bowed legs, walked into the bar, gave him a fleeting glance, and took a table at the front of the saloon next to one of the two large frontage windows. The Kid, as The Cowboy came to call the wet-behind-the-ears, smooth-faced youngster, had a shiny new Colt in a left-hand holster with the butt reversed for a right-hand draw.

As The Cowboy sipped on his beer, he noticed The Kid look out the window and give a not-too-subtle nod and tip of his hat with one of his right-hand fingers. The Cowboy's curiosity was immediately aroused by this obvious signal to whoever was waiting outside. A minute later, two hard-case unshaven men entered. Both gave a quick furtive glance to the right where The Cowboy was seated, and nonchalantly ambled over to The Kid's table. The two newcomers sat down in such a manner so that all three men had an unobstructed view of both the street and the bar.

The older of the two hard-cases had a nasty red scar on his right cheek that not even his dirty brown beard could hide. The younger man had a scraggly unkempt greyish beard. The Kid signaled the bartender for drinks with three upraised fingers. The bartender, grabbing a bottle, walked lazily over to their table and set the whisky down along with three glasses. While they drank, the three men spoke in hushed tones, nothing The Cowboy could hear or discern. Oddly, every so often, one or the other of them would take a hasty surreptitious glance in his direction.

The Cowboy immediately realized that the three men knew who he was. The question was, he wondered, what kind of high jinks were they up to—or about to do? A lot of people knew his real name and how The Cowboy had obtained his reputation as a "fast gun." His pseudo fame hadn't bothered him. Most men who knew The Cowboy avoided him, not wanting to tangle with such a well-known gunfighter. After all, there were eighteen men who had gotten on his bad side and not lived to tell the tale.

So, as he continued to idly sip on his beer, he thought about the second reason as to why they might have been interested in him. Some twenty years prior, while he was riding shotgun on a Wells Fargo stagecoach from Las Vegas, New Mexico, to Santa Fe, they were ambushed just before topping a steep incline. The attack came with no warning. The driver went down first, and The Cowboy took a bullet in his right shoulder and fell to the ground. The lone passenger immediately jumped out of the coach, tried to run, and was cut down by a fusillade of bullets.

The stagecoach was rumored to be carrying $50,000 in gold. In fact, it was a decoy while the real shipment left secretly three hours earlier along a little-used route to Santa Fe. The Cowboy played dead while the three desperados looted the stagecoach, ripping up its interior seats as they frantically searched for a hidden compartment that presumably held the shipment of gold bars. Assuming they had killed all three stagecoach riders, not one of the desperados paid any attention to the presumably dead men. With his back to the robbers, and blood not only streaming from his shoulder but also covering the back of his denim jacket, ever so slowly The Cowboy eased out his pistol. He flipped over, catching all three men inside the stagecoach still looking for what they believed was the hidden gold.

The Cowboy's first bullet caught the man standing just inside the stagecoach's door. As that now dead man fell backwards, the other two men half turned wondering where the shot had originated and looked at The Cowboy in surprise. He didn't let them think for long, as his second, third, and fourth bullets killed the other two men.

Struggling off the ground, The Cowboy swayed as he walked toward the open stagecoach door. Grabbing a half-open portmanteau, formerly belonging to the dead passenger that the outlaws had rifled through, he found a shirt. He painfully removed his jacket. Next, he tore the shirt into several strips and used those pieces as a bandage. He tightly wound the strips over his shirt and around the front and back of his now burning shoulder. Once tied off, The Cowboy reached in his front jeans pocket, withdrew a small pocketknife, opened it, and cut two six-by-six-inch pieces off the remains of the shirt. Wadding up each piece, he shoved one under the makeshift bandage now covering the bullet's front entry point, and then, with much difficulty and pain, he reached behind his shoulder and inserted the second wad underneath the cloth strip covering the bullet's rear exit point just below his shoulder. It was difficult and painful to re-button his jacket but he knew it would keep the shirt and bandage in place.

Then he turned his attention to the three would-be thieves. With his left hand, he dragged the first bandit he'd shot over to the edge of the road and pushed the body with his foot into the adjacent twenty-five-foot-deep arroyo. He then did the same for the other two, dragging them out of the coach and then kicking each corpse down the slope. Such work was exhausting, but he had one more difficult chore—putting both the driver's and passenger's bodies into the stagecoach's passenger compartment. After that difficult chore, he climbed up to the driver's seat and managed to get the horses moving. At times he dozed as the pain numbed, but it never disappeared. Every jolt of a wheel kept him awake and made him wince in pain.

It took him eighteen hours to reach Santa Fe. By the time he entered the main street he had begun to hallucinate. The Cowboy managed to stop the horses in front of the sheriff's office. Dropping the reins, he fell over on the side of the hard wooden driver's seat and passed out.

Over the span of the last twenty years, since the attempted robbery, the rumors had swirled and abounded around The Cowboy. Some said he killed everyone, hid the gold, and then deliberately shot himself in the shoulder. After all, there were no witnesses. But the Santa Fe sheriff sent out four men to survey the scene of the robbery where they found the three dead men at the bottom of a ravine. Leaving the three rotting corpses that the varmints had started to ravage, they returned and confirmed The Cowboy's story.

Several weeks later, the company shipping the gold later confirmed that it had secretly transported the bullion and that it arrived at its Santa Fe destination unmolested. Yet, skeptics still believed The Cowboy's story was false. Over the years, several people called him out on the story but hadn't survived after they challenged him. Nevertheless, over the past two decades, he continued to live humbly and unpretentiously while he roamed around the Southwest making a living playing cards. Surely, people believed The Cowboy stole the money; after such a long while he ought to be living a more affluent lifestyle. A few people, mostly greedy ones, simply failed to consider that fact.

Leaving Bisbee, The Cowboy drifted northeast to Silver City in the Arizona Territory where he played cards for a couple of weeks. Although he was a good card player, he never won too much from any one player, sometimes even folding when he had a good hand so someone else could win the pot. Still, he made a good living playing poker. It was during one such poker game at the Silver Ingot Saloon that he spied one of the two hard-cases from Bisbee—the one he had nicknamed Grey Beard—drinking at the crowded bar.

He didn't see the other two men but, he realized, they might deliberately be keeping out of sight so as not to arouse his suspicions. His suspicions were confirmed a few days later while The Cowboy was playing poker inside Milly's Saloon. The second hard-case—whom he'd nicknamed Scarface, due to the red scar on his face—slipped in among the crowded saloon and had a drink at the bar.

Well, The Cowboy thought, *time to mosey out of town again.*

He wanted to avoid any confrontation so, at three in the morning, he slipped out of town and headed southeast to Las Cruces. He quickly and quietly moved through the small New Mexican town before continuing forty miles south until he arrived in El Paso. The Texas town was large enough that he could easily stay lost and avoid any inquisitive eyes.

He had a few friends in El Paso, and after describing all three men, also put the word out that he immediately wanted to know if any of the three pursuers were seen in town. A month or more later, as he was playing poker inside an El Paso saloon, he noticed a young Mexican kid, maybe ten to twelve years old, enter the bar and whisper something to the dark-skinned Mexican barkeep, whose name was Lorenzo. The barkeeper reached into his pocket and slipped the kid a coin before whispering something to him. The kid was hurrying out of the bar when The Cowboy, looking up from his hand, caught Lorenzo's eye who then imperceptibly motioned with his head toward the rear of the saloon. The Cowboy quickly folded his hand, excused himself, and walked slowly toward the back of the room where the bartender was waiting.

"You asked me to keep a lookout for *tres hombres, señor*," Lorenzo said in a voice just above a whisper to The Cowboy before continuing. "One of my little spies has just reported that three dirty and dusty *hombres*, one with a big red scar on his face, just rode into town. I've sent him to round up some friends and keep an eye on the *hombres*."

"*Muchas gracias*, Lorenzo. I do appreciate it!" The Cowboy reached into his vest pocket and gave the barkeep a ten-dollar silver coin.

"But . . . but, *señor*, this is too much!" Lorenzo mildly protested.

"No, not really, Lorenzo. You can give more *dinero* to *los niños* who are keeping an eye on the men," he replied. "But," he paused for a few seconds before adding, "tell your watchers to stay in groups of two, so that if any of the *hombres malos* start to come near your saloon, they can send *un niño* to warn you and me."

"*No problemo, señor,*" Lorenzo replied as he nodded. "I will make sure they keep an eye out all day and night!"

"*Muchas gracias*, Lorenzo," the grey-haired cowboy said as he turned to go back to his poker game.

Two days later, a pair of young boys slipped into the saloon and approached Lorenzo. The Cowboy, sitting with his back against the bar's wall, was again playing poker and saw them enter. He figured something was up when Lorenzo took them aside, led them to the back area, and whispered something to them before passing each boy a coin. Looking at the bartender, The Cowboy saw him nod. A few minutes later, he finished his hand, left the table, and headed towards Lorenzo.

"*Señor*, the *hombre malo*—the one with the scar—is approaching," Lorenzo informed him. "He is in another saloon just down the street and has been asking people about you."

"Okay, Lorenzo, *muchas gracias,*" The Cowboy appreciatively said as he slipped a gold twenty-dollar Indian head coin into the bartender's hand. "I'm going to take a position at the front table about ten feet from the door. When the *hombre* enters, I'm going to talk to him, but be ready for gunfire."

"Sí, sí, señor," Lorenzo said as he walked slowly back to the bar as if nothing was wrong. He picked up a shot glass, pulled the dishrag off his shoulder, and started polishing it with the cloth.

The Cowboy walked nonchalantly to a table between the bar and the saloon's two swinging front doors. As he settled into his chair, which he tilted back against the bar's front wall, he drew his pistol, keeping it unseen in his lap.

Lorenzo walked over and brought a beer that he set down in front of The Cowboy, who nodded a silent thanks before the bartender returned to his position behind the bar and started polishing some beer glasses. The Cowboy knew that Lorenzo kept a fully loaded 12-gauge shotgun underneath the bar's tabletop. He, too, would be ready to draw down on Scarface, if necessary.

About ten minutes later, Scarface pushed through the saloon's swinging doors and immediately stopped dead in his tracks when he saw The Cowboy sitting about twelve feet in front of him. The Cowboy was staring directly at him. The two men silently eyed each other for a few seconds. The saloon mysteriously and suddenly quieted down to a deadly silence as every customer quickly intuited there was some sort of trouble brewing.

"Don't even think about drawing that pistol, mister," The Cowboy warned as he brought his pistol up from his lap and pointed it at Scarface. "I'm getting real tired of you and your other two pals *doggin'* me." He continued waving the pistol at the hard-case. "People like you never learn. You just listen to and believe the rumors about me and the gold. Well, you better stop following me in hopes of taking it because I *ain't* got it. Never had it! The only gold I got is the few coins I pick up playing poker."

"You think you're a tough *ol'* bird," Scarface said. "Well, me and my pals, we are *gonna* show *yew* one day sooner than *yew* expect! Plus, some *ol'* fart like *yew coulda* never *kilt* eighteen men!" he sneered. "*If'n yew* don't got no gold," Scarface continued, "that *doon* matter none. One of us three will surely draw down on you and end your string and make one of us more famous than *yew*."

"I wouldn't count on that, Mr. Scarface," The Cowboy firmly spoke as he replied. "You *an'* your three pals are *gonna* be in *fer* a surprise," he said as he stood, still pointing his weapon at the scruffily bearded hard-case. "You and your two buddies better leave El Paso today or else I'm coming for you all. Now, unbuckle your holster and let it drop to the floor."

"*Whadda yew gonna dew,* you mean old *bastid*? Kill me in cold blood?" Scarface smirked and sneered at The Cowboy before continuing, "You'll swing *fer* that *fer* sure."

BANG! The sudden loud ear-splitting noise of The Cowboy's pistol shot made everyone in the saloon jump or duck beneath the tables at which they were sitting.

The Cowboy had put a bullet right past Scarface's right ear. It nicked the grubby and unwashed man's ear and blew the hat off his head. The hard-case quickly put his hand to his bleeding ear.

"You motherf-cker!" he screamed at The Cowboy.

"No, I don't think so," The Cowboy calmly replied. "Now, drop your holster to the floor. I'm not *gonna* ask again. *An' don'* you put your hands anywhere near your pistol when you do so. The next bullet won't nick your other ear—it'll be buried in the undersized pea brain you got between your ears! And move your hands slowly or I'll think you're trying to draw down on me."

Scarface lowered his arms ever so slowly, undid his buckle, and let the holster and pistol drop to the floor.

"Now, put your hands behind your head," The Cowboy ordered. "Lock the fingers, turn around, and walk out of this saloon and don't come back, or even think about sending one of your friends here. You got that?"

Scarface nodded.

"Now, *git!*"

The hard-case walked over to the saloon doors, hands laced behind his head, pushed them open with his body, turned right, and started walking away quickly. The blood from his ear continued to trickle down his neck and stained his shirt.

The Cowboy turned to Lorenzo, who brought his 12-gauge up from underneath the bar and laid it on the flat surface during the confrontation, saying, "Well, Lorenzo, I thank you and your scouts." He flipped a twenty-dollar gold piece to the barkeep. "Now, I *gotta* vamoose!" The Cowboy turned and walked to the back of the saloon, opened the rear door, peeked out, stepped into the alley, and closed the door. The alleyway twisted and turned behind the various buildings including the ones from the next street over that also backed up to it.

He had previously scouted the alley in both directions, noting good places to take shelter in case of an ambush, and checked out the narrow passageways between the storefronts that led to the streets. He ambled along, taking his time as he warily walked down the alley, keeping to one side before hastily stepping over to the other, especially when he approached any of the passageways to the street. Finally coming to a side street, he peeked out, looked both ways for a minute or two, then swiftly crossed the street, turned left, and walked fifty to sixty yards to the stable where his horse was kept. Entering the coolness of the stable, he espied Joe, the owner, mucking out a stall.

"Hey, Joe, I *gotta* leave town around two in the morning. Would you be willing to move my *ol'* horse to a front stall so as I don't disturb any of the others when I leave? I'll pay *ya* for the extra day."

"Sure can," the ostler replied. "*An' don'* worry no matter about them extra two hours."

The Cowboy then told Joe about the three men, described them, and asked the old man to keep an eye out but not tell anyone that his horse was stabled there. He then paid the stable keeper, gave him an extra ten-dollar silver coin, which was more than a week's worth of stabling his horse. The man protested but The Cowboy was firm about his gift.

"Hell, mister," the old man said. "I'll stick around and make sure everything's ready to go. I'll get your *hoss* some water just before you come."

The Cowboy nodded, thanked Joe, and left the stable via its back door leading into another alley. He walked about one hundred yards, found his boarding house, and entered through the alleyway door.

He found Mrs. Fitzsimons, his landlady, sitting in her front parlor knitting. She looked up as he entered the room and sat down across from her.

"Missus Fitzsimons," The Cowboy began, "I'm *gonna* have to leave right quick. You sure have been nice to me *an'* I do *'preciate* it. Something's come up and I need to go cause there's three bad men *lookin'* for me. I don't want to be no cause *fer* any trouble to you *if'n* they was to discover I'm *stayin'* here. That could maybe put you in some danger *an'* I won't have that. So, I'll be *slippin' outta* here around 1:00 to 1:30 this morning, if that's okay with you. I'll try to be as quiet as I can when I leave and hope you don't mind that I'll be using your back door to leave."

"Why, thank you, mister," she replied as she stood. "It's been my pleasure having you as a boarder all these past weeks. And yes, I understand, so it's perfectly fine for you to slip out the back door. If you ever make it this way again, I'd be mighty happy if you stayed here another time," she said and smiled as she took his right hand in hers and patted it with a motherly touch.

"I'll do that, Missus Fitzsimons, if I return. But right now, I've got to get my stuff ready so as I can leave early and catch a few hours of shuteye." The Cowboy rose as he was speaking and took both of Mrs. Fitzsimons' hands in his and gently squeezed them. He leaned over and gave the old lady a kiss on each cheek before turning to go upstairs to his room.

She smiled again and touched her cheeks. *Why,* she thought as The Cowboy tramped up the stairs, *I haven't been kissed by a good man like that in a long while!* She continued to smile wistfully before sitting back down and continuing her knitting.

The Cowboy awoke around 1:30 in the morning. He'd packed up his meager belongings into his saddlebags after leaving the landlady. Dressing quickly, he crept down the stairs and exited through the rear door into the alley. On the steps he paused, letting his eyes adjust to the night and watching for movement, or the glow of a cigarette down either end of the alley. Waiting two to three minutes, he stepped down the stairs into the darkened passageway and headed toward the rear of the stable, which he entered about two minutes later. There was a dim lantern about halfway down the stalls and he could see that the ostler was up and had his horse ready.

"Why, thanks, Joe," The Cowboy said, as he approached the stableman.

"No problem, mister. My pleasure!" Joe answered as he gave The Cowboy a big grin in the dim light.

The Cowboy secured his saddlebags and checked the cinch, reins, and bridle. The horse was ready.

"Joe, if anyone comes looking and describes me, don't hesitate to tell *'em* I was here." The Cowboy then again described each of the three men before continuing, "If they ask you what direction I took out of here, just tell *'em* I turned left and went down that street like I might be heading for the Rio Grande and Ciudad Juárez. *Jus'* don't sound too eager to tell them anything. Act like you're *guessin'*. I need at least a three- to four-day head start."

"Okay, mister. I *dun* this before. So far, *ain't* nobody caught on, so *don'* worry none," the ostler said.

"Thanks, Joe, and here's five dollars more for you," The Cowboy extended his hand with a silver coin in it. Joe tried to protest that he'd already paid him too much, but The Cowboy insisted, so the old man took the money, tucked it into his denim pocket, and thanked him again.

The Cowboy withdrew his watch from his vest pocket and looked at it in the stable's dim lamplight before pocketing it again. *Hmmm,* he thought, *five past two. Guess I better git movin'.*

The Cowboy mounted his horse, guided him out of the stable, and turned right onto the darkened street. He figured it would take the three hard-cases a day or two in Juárez to figure out he didn't head down into Mexico. They'd probably return to El Paso, then spread out to ask any travelers approaching the city if they had seen The Cowboy. He figured his little ruse might give him five or six days of a head start before they would be dogging him again. With that amount of extra time, The Cowboy figured he'd be able to lure them into his trap, and then ambush the three henchmen.

The Cowboy guided his horse north, paralleling the Rio Grande. There was plenty of grass alongside the languidly moving river. He hoped that in four or five days, if he pushed his mount hard enough, he'd be about one hundred or so miles north of El Paso. At that point he would arrive at Elephant Butte, a rock formation that resembled an elephant. Along the way, he met thirty to forty people traveling south. Usually, he stopped to chat with them before moving northward. They would remember him and be able to describe him to his three nefarious followers.

Late in the evening of the fourth day, The Cowboy reached Elephant Butte and camped beside it. Rising early the next morning, while his hobbled horse nibbled at some meadow grass, he removed a pair of binoculars from his saddlebag and surveyed the territory to the north and east. He was looking at an incredibly forbidding landscape filled with ancient lava. The blackened rock-covered area was known by the ominous name of the Jornada del Muerto, or more widely known as the "Route of the Dead Man."[2]

The Jornada del Muerto volcano erupted some 760,000 years ago. It spewed forth a lava flow that stretched over one hundred miles from north to south and was approximately ten to fifteen miles wide. The black molten rock had covered an area of 160 to 180 square miles. The volcano's eruption produced a type of lava which left a rough surface making travel across it, if not impossible, exceedingly difficult and tortuous. The lava field became known as the *malpaís*, or "Bad Country."[3]

The Spanish conquistadors, on their fruitless quest for the Seven Cities of Cíbola, that were rumored to be piled with gold, discovered the area in 1598 when they made their first crossing of the Jornada del Muerto on foot along with a few ox carts. The Spaniards discovered pueblos with ordinary walls, but not the mystical Cíbola. Reaching the first pueblo, they found peaceable and friendly Indians who had developed a sophisticated agriculture alongside the Rio Grande. The Puebloans gave the Spaniards food and water. The conquistadors had then named the pueblo *Socorro*—Spanish for "help" or "assistance." The trail the Spaniards made through the Jornada del Muerto, which they referred to as "ninety miles of hell,"

---

2 https://en.wikipedia.org/wiki/Jornada_del_Muerto
3 ibid.

was later named the Camino Real.[4]

Crossing the *malpaís* was extremely dangerous and many perished trying to traverse the lava wasteland. But if one was an experienced traveler like The Cowboy, the grueling expanse had its hidden pathways along with few seeps known only to the Indians, or men who were familiar with the area. The Cowboy was one of those intrepid men. And now he intended to spring his trap by luring the hard-cases into the Route of the Dead Man.

Judgment day was fast approaching his pursuers. That is, if they had somehow successfully managed to cross the *malpaís*. The Cowboy figured that the lure of his supposed gold cache would drive them onward, not suspecting a trap, although they would be somewhat cautious and on edge. He deliberately left little hints of his passing along the way—dropped cigarette butts, a scrape on a rock as if from his horse's hoof, and once an empty peach fruit can. These clues, dropped every few miles, would be the bait for his trackers. He hoped these small insignificant clues would trick, or lull, his nefarious pursuers into believing he had relaxed his guard. With such information, the three outlaws would perhaps become a bit less careful and make hasty mistakes that would cost them later.

The desert started at the eastern edge of the ancient lava flow. Now he had to navigate twelve to fifteen miles to arrive at Geronimo's Table. His pursuers would have no trouble finding his horse's tracks. As he made the crossing, the desert's landscape became thicker with small creosote bushes and struggling plant life among thousands of scattered pieces of lava. A few lone and widely separated saguaros began to appear. Their ghostlike figures arose from the desert's floor standing as silent sentinels guarding something unknown. A slight westerly breeze washed over the desert and The Cowboy could smell

---

4 ibid.

the freshness of the undergrowth as it began to thicken when he finally neared the flat-topped large monolith.

✗✗✗

Whenever he had wanted to be alone for four or five weeks, The Cowboy returned and holed up at Geronimo's Table; six or seven times over the past twenty years. Some twenty-two or so years earlier, The Cowboy was passing by Fort Bowie in the Arizona Territory, which was established in 1862 to fight the Chiricahua Apaches and Geronimo.[5] He befriended an old Apache who was being beaten and kicked by a much larger and stronger man in his early twenties. The Cowboy told the youngster to stop.

"Fuck off, old man!" the would-be bruiser snarled at The Cowboy as he continued to kick and pummel the old Apache. The Cowboy walked over, grabbed the back of the now unlucky man's shirt and hurled him seven to eight feet away, such that he rolled over a few times before landing sprawled out on the ground. Infuriated, the young man reached for and pulled out his pistol at just about the time The Cowboy put a bullet into his forehead. The bully's pal had been standing by during this confrontation and started to draw his pistol. The Cowboy's next bullet blew off several fingers of his gun hand.

"Now, son," The Cowboy said, motioning with his pistol, "get on your horse and leave, before I change my mind and kill you, too. I don't approve of anyone picking on someone much older and weaker than they are no matter what *tha* reason."

The young man, wincing in pain and looking terrified, quickly walked over to his horse, and with great difficulty, mounted it and galloped off.

After The Cowboy helped the thankful Apache stand up, the old Indian, brushing the dirt off his sleeves and pants, asked his rescuer

---

5 https://en.wikipedia.org/wiki/Fort_Bowie

what brought him to the area. The Cowboy told the elderly man he was searching for a remote place to hole up for a few weeks away from any civilization so as to get some uninterrupted peace and quiet.

"For saving me, I will tell you of a secret and distant place where you will find the peace you need," the old Indian said. The Apache then described the mesa and Geronimo's connection with it. By using a stick and drawing a picture on the sandy ground, the ancient Apache described to The Cowboy how and where to safely cross the labyrinthine *malpaís*, where to find seeps, and then locate the hidden spring at the eastern edge of the lava field. The wizened Indian told The Cowboy he had been to the black butte with Geronimo, who had holed up there on several occasions when he fled from the white man's army.

The Cowboy set off in search of the mysterious black butte. It took him several weeks to locate the desolate monolith, as the old man's stick-drawn map had been somewhat vague. But a few weeks after he had arrived at the Jornada del Muerto, his search for Geronimo's Table was successful. Once or twice on his return trips to the reddish-black mesa, The Cowboy saw a wraith-like, somewhat obscured figure on top of the lone rock monument close to the top of the flume and secret pathway he had discovered. The vague figure quickly vanished after a few seconds. The Cowboy had simply put that strange phenomenon down to heat waves shimmering off the flat rock.

Each time he had holed up in this desolate place, he was careful to meticulously clean up after himself. On one of his trips across the Jornada del Muerto lava fields, The Cowboy brought a shovel that he left in the cave for use on future trips. Since he had carried some of his food in tin cans, before leaving his secret hideout, he always burned any labels from them. Then he carted the empty cans several hundred yards out into the desert where he buried them in a two-foot-deep hole located next to some of the hardened black lava rocks which were thinly scattered across the desert floor. The Cowboy always made sure to bury each set of cans at least several hundred yards distant from his previous burial site. He even took the ashes from his fire pit and flung them up into the constant winds that blew against the black monolith, as he wanted to keep this area as pristine as possible and not leave any trace of his passing.

Traveling at a moderate pace, it took The Cowboy and his steadfast mount five hours to cross the desert and reach Geronimo's Table. Guiding the horse to the left, they walked alongside the looming mesa for about a mile until they reached the deep and dark cave where, on his second trip to the tableland, The Cowboy located the hidden spring. Entering the dark cavern, The Cowboy tied his horse off to an iron C-shaped tie-down that he'd brought on one of his previous trips and hammered into the rock close to the seep so that the weary animal could drink whenever he needed it. Next, The Cowboy stripped off his saddle along with the saddlebags and rolled-up sleeping blanket. He then proceeded to set up his meager campsite.

Even though it was late afternoon, The Cowboy decided to take a look from the butte's top to see if he could spot his pursuers. Grabbing his .30-30 and binoculars, he filled a half-empty canteen with water and slung it over his shoulder. Then, he ambled several hundred yards to the hidden entrance of the secret staircase he previously discovered during his second trip to the black monolith. Along the way he tried to walk on the rocks so as not to leave any boot prints. The Cowboy decided that later on he would erase what prints he could with a tree branch.

While scaling the rocky black staircase would be arduous for most men his age, it certainly wasn't that difficult for a physically fit man in his fifties. Testing every spot where he placed his boots, The Cowboy made sure not to slip. After all, a fall down the chute would result in a crippling broken leg or more, which could well lead to a slow, certain, and agonizing death in the desert.

Fortunately for The Cowboy, at some distant point in the past, someone—Geronimo or one of his followers?—had chipped out three- to four-inch-deep toeholds every two feet or so. Plus, the upward passageway was confined enough that he could easily brace his hands, or legs, against its rough sides as he ascended to the top. After carefully scaling the flume in seven to ten minutes, he arrived at the top of the mesa. The ascent winded him, so he sat on a nearby rock and paused for a few minutes to catch his breath.

Standing, he stretched his back and legs to loosen them up from his climb. Next, The Cowboy carefully walked around the butte's rough surface until he found a somewhat shallow place near the rim where he could observe the desert to the west. By lying prone, The Cowboy knew the small indentation would partially conceal his body as he looked out over the desert he had traversed.

Settling into the rounded and curved hollow, he took his field glasses and brought them to his eyes. He spent about ten minutes surveying his back trail looking for movement or a sun flash from some piece of equipment, like a rifle barrel or a tin canteen or bridle hardware. Nothing jumped out at him as he scrutinized the arid landscape. While he had a good view, his binoculars were only accurate up to two or three miles because the desert's shimmering and undulating late afternoon heat waves obscured his vision. Yet he hadn't spotted anything to suggest his pursuers, if they had chosen to cross the *malpaís*, were anywhere close, as they would now have to cross the open desert to Geronimo's Table. As sunset was fast approaching, he decided to leave his perch and return to his cave encampment.

The next morning, he awoke early as dawn was barely creeping across the sky. He wanted to ascend back to his tabletop perch and look for his pursuers. He doubted, if they had indeed traversed the *malpaís*, that they would then try to cross the desert in the dark, much less rise this early, while much of the desert was still in shadow. They would want bright sunlight to wend their way across the daunting desert terrain now before them. After stepping outside the volcanic tube's mouth, he cut a thick branch from the rear side of a large Palo Verde tree, so that the cut would not be visible to anyone facing the mesa. The bush was located about twenty-five feet from the cavern's entrance and he used it to erase his boot prints all the way to the hidden staircase.

After arduously climbing the volcanic rock flume and then settling in at his observation place, The Cowboy took his binoculars and again scanned the desert. With the sun behind him and the desert's nighttime cooling, there were no heat waves this early in the day, so he had an unobstructed view of four or more miles to the west. He spent another ten to fifteen minutes scanning his back trail but saw nothing. Looking at his pocket watch, he saw it was just a few minutes after six.

Placing his field glasses on the rock beside the hollow, The Cowboy stood and stretched. He still hadn't decided how he was going to put an end to his pursuers. He hoped they would be tired, or, perhaps, lost a horse while crossing the *malpaís*. The loss of a mount would cause each horseman to load up and carry the extra food, water, and ammo, which would quickly tire out the more heavily laden equines. A man on foot would slow them down further. Still, the loss of a horse might force them to turn back. Yet the "smell" of a supposed gold payday would probably entice them onward where, tired and worn out, they would start to make mistakes with dire consequences. At least, The Cowboy mused, he hoped that scenario might happen.

As he was looking out over the lava-strewn desert, The Cowboy felt some sort of a presence. He slowly turned and saw a shimmering and wavy cloud behind him.

Damn! He thought. *It's way too early for heat to cause this! What tha bejesus . . .*

Within the misty white cloud, a specter of a person began to materialize. Standing, The Cowboy stepped back a few feet from the monolith's edge.

Damn! Am I going insane? Is this real? Or am I imagining this? Did I die last night in my sleep and I'm on my way to . . . ? He wondered with some amazement and curiosity.

The Cowboy pinched himself on his hand. The pinch seemed real enough!

The misty cloud began to fade and disappear. The figure of an Indian holding a Winchester .30-30 emerged and stood in front of him. The Cowboy immediately identified the man. It was Geronimo! He knew it could be no one else because he had seen an etching of the Apache chief in a Tucson newspaper when he had traveled through that Arizona town a few years earlier. The etching had been based on a famous 1898 photograph taken by German American Frank Rinehart, who specialized in capturing pictures of Native Americans and Western scenes. Rinehart had taken the picture during the 1898 Indian Congress in Omaha, Nebraska.[6] The Cowboy even saw more pictures of the famous Indian in a traveling photo exhibition that stopped in Phoenix seven to ten years earlier. Now, here, in front of him, mysteriously and unexplainably, stood that famous warrior.

How could this be? The Cowboy wondered. *Geronimo died last year in Fort Sill, Oklahoma. How could he still be alive? What in the hell's he doing here?*

"Do not be alarmed, Mr. Cowboy. I am not here to harm you, but only to help you," the Apache chief stated. "First, I want to thank you

---

6 https://en.wikipedia.org/wiki/Frank_Rinehart

for watching over the sacred shrine of our ancestors to ensure its location is not discovered. You have deeply honored our ancestors with your watchfulness during your many visits. I know there are three bad men on their way here to harm you and perhaps desecrate this sacred place with your blood. In turn, I am here to assist and protect you."

The Apache turned, motioning with his hand, and said, "Come with me; we must prepare. They will arrive in a few hours and we must be ready for their arrival."

Geronimo turned, walked over to the stairway, and quickly descended to the sandy desert ground at the bottom. The Cowboy, staring down the flume at the Apache's descent, couldn't believe how quickly the older man arrived at the bottom. Following the Indian, he touched down a few minutes later.

"First," Geronimo stated, "you are going to dig a four-foot-deep pit in front of this hidden stairway. Please get your shovel from the cave, bring it here, and start to dig the hole. I will hunt for some rattlesnakes, which we will place in the hole."

The Cowboy started to ask how the Indian chief would avoid being bitten by the rattlers, then thought better of it as he figured the snake's bite wouldn't affect the ghost—if, indeed, that's what Geronimo really was!

Instead, The Cowboy queried the chief, "Where do you want me to put the sand I dig up?"

Geronimo pointed to a nearby Palo Verde with thick overhanging green tendrils of branches. "Put it next to that tree's branches and leave your shovel stuck in the pile," the old Indian instructed as he pointed. "Your pursuers will think you have dug up the gold and will start looking for a pit to see if you left anything. They will be hasty in their search, until it's too late for one or two of them. I will ensure that whoever doesn't fall into the hole will not escape."

The Cowboy quickly returned with the shovel. The sand was easy to move, and within ninety minutes, he had a square three-by-three-foot hole that was four feet deep. No sooner had he finished moving all the spare sand, which he had piled up under the Palo Verde's overhanging branches before jamming his shovel into the top of the excavated sand, than Geronimo approached holding three four-foot rattlers that seemed almost docile. Squatting down, he carefully slid the snakes into the hole before standing.

"I need two more," the Indian chief said, "and will be back soon."

Fifteen minutes later he returned with two displeased and angrily hissing rattlers, both as big as The Cowboy's forearms. Geronimo slid the protesting serpents into the hole. The Cowboy noticed that each time the old Apache slid the snakes into the hole, none of them attempted to bite the weather-worn chieftain. Next, The Cowboy helped the Apache leader gather fallen branches, which were strong but pliable. Geronimo then tightly wove each branch into a thick cover for the hole. With that final job accomplished the two men placed it over the hole and covered it with sand.

Upon completion of this task, Geronimo turned to The Cowboy and spoke, "It is an old way to trap a man, but it will work because they will be tired, careless, and low on water." He continued, "So, now we need to brush away all of our tracks and leave just one set of your tracks as if coming out of the desert"—he pointed to the lava-strewn field which started some sixty feet away from the butte—"leading to the stairway. They will find your tracks and cross over the trap as they head towards the stairway. Whoever falls in will be bitten so many times, they will not survive for long."

The Cowboy and Geronimo spent the next hour brushing away all the tracks, including any leading back to the cave. When finished, they both stood at the edge of the lava field.

"Now," Geronimo said, "walk in a stagger toward the rock chute, climb it, and wait for me there."

How's he going to get there without leaving any tracks? The Cowboy idly wondered.

As he turned to ask the Indian, the man vanished into thin air. The Cowboy whirled around but Geronimo had disappeared. Taking off his hat, he scratched his head in puzzlement and wiped the sweat off his brow. Looking down, he saw no tracks where Geronimo had last been standing. A vague flash and movement caught his eye. He looked up. Geronimo was standing on top of the black-rocked mesa beckoning him to climb up to the tabletop.

How in the hell did he do that? The Cowboy thought to himself as he shook his head in awe at what he was seeing.

So, assuming a staggering walk, as if he was on his last legs, The Cowboy crossed the sandy area stepping perilously close to the edge of the trap, and ascended the flume to the tabletop. Geronimo was waiting for him.

"We wait," said Geronimo. "They are coming. We will lie down over there"—he pointed to the rock hollow The Cowboy has previously used—"and wait. They will not see us."

So, both men settled into the depression next to the tabletop's edge and waited as they looked westward. After an hour, The Cowboy noticed buzzards circling high in a circle about five miles away, or more.

"Looks like something happened out there," he remarked to Geronimo.

"Harumph!" the Indian chief grunted. "Yes, the Spirits have been good to us. I think we only need to worry about two men now."

The Cowboy stared at the Apache chief and nodded his head.

"Yes," he commented and then asked, "perhaps one will be on foot?'

"No," Geronimo replied, "these are bad men. Looking for gold. They would not be slowed down by a man who's lost his horse."

The Cowboy nodded in agreement. After another hour The Cowboy checked his watch. It was late morning and the sun was beaming down on both of the patient watchers. Closing the pocket watch, The Cowboy's eye caught an imperceptible movement several miles off to the west. Raising his binoculars, he zeroed in on the spot where he saw some sort of motion. He barely made out two riders.

"You were right," he commented to Geronimo. "Only two men."

The chieftain smiled and nodded his head before replying, "Good! They will be tired."

After another hour of watching, the two outlaws emerged from the desert's heat waves. Picking their way slowly through the *malpaís*, they appeared to be about a mile away. The Cowboy checked his pocket watch and noted that it was still late morning.

"It is time for us to move to the top of the flume and take up our positions," Geronimo firmly declared. "We will observe them as they come into sight and discover your footprints."

Several feet from the flume was a low spot in the tabletop. Nearby were four to five ten-pound sandstone rocks. Both men picked these up and placed them on the rim of the reddish-black monolith just in front of the low point. With small spaces between each rock, both The Cowboy and Geronimo could easily view what was below them. The height of the sandstone would ensure that their heads would be hidden. When tracking someone, the tired hunters would hardly be looking up, and if they did, all they would notice were several rocks—something that was a normal sight on buttes.

An hour later, both The Cowboy and Geronimo heard the

distant sound of horses' hooves along with the hard-cases talking. Both watchers quickly checked their Winchester .30-30 rifles and chambered a round. Several minutes later both pursuers came into sight. It was Scarface and Grey Beard. The Kid was missing. Within a minute Grey Beard spotted The Cowboy's footprints coming out of the lava field and headed in the direction of the reddish-black mesa. As the chute's entrance was hidden, it appeared The Cowboy's prints vanished into the mesa.

Both hard-cases dismounted and tied their horses to the Palo Verde next to the pile of sand.

"Hey!" Scarface said. "Looks like he found the gold!"

"Yeah," replied Grey Beard. "But where's the hole?"

"*Mus'* be here *sumwher'*," Scarface commented.

"Maybe he's hauled it somewhere," Grey Beard speculated. "But where in the hell is it? Let's look where those footprints lead. There's *gotta* be a cave back there."

He walked over to the mesa's slope and just narrowly missed stepping into the covered trap. "Hey! There's some sort of a chute with footholds in it! I bet the son of a bitch is somewhere up on top, probably in a cave or *sumthin'*."

Scarface started walking up behind him, but he stepped onto the camouflaged hole. "Oh, God!!!" he screamed. Grey Beard swiftly turned around at Scarface's scream and looked at him in horror.

"Snakes!!" Scarface screamed at the top of his lungs. "Rattlers! They're biting me all over! Help!"

Grey Beard stood there and watched. *Well,* he thought gleefully, *that's more gold for me!*

"You *fuckin' bastid,*" Scarface choked as his mouth allowed a stream of spittle to drool out of it. He glanced down and tried to draw his pistol but, instead, suddenly his body violently trembled and shuddered. He fell backwards onto the sand, his legs still in the pit. His mouth made a final gurgle along with a death rattling gasp. He didn't move, but his open and yellowish dead eyes stared eternally at Grey Beard.

Grey Beard watched as each rattlesnake used Scarface's body to crawl up and over the pit's lip before slithering silently away. He made no move to get closer to the pit, not knowing how many rattlers might still remain in it. Instead, turning toward the chute's hidden entrance, he stepped inside and started his ascent. Going was hard. He was bone-tired, but the will to find the gold drove him upwards.

As soon as Grey Beard started his upward climb, both The Cowboy and Geronimo silently rose from their hiding place and noiselessly moved over to the top of the flume. They each stood on either side of it, looked downward, and pointed their Winchesters at the climbing hard-case. Grey Beard ascended about half the way up and paused to rest. Both Geronimo and The Cowboy could hear his gasping and wheezing for breath.

Still holding his rifle downward with one hand, The Cowboy motioned to Geronimo that he was going to speak to the hard-case.

"Well, Grey Beard," The Cowboy half-shouted, "looks like you've reached the end of the trail."

Grey Beard looked upward and tried to reach his pistol when he saw the two men looking down at him. But his body was jammed up against the smooth side of the chute and he felt unbalanced as he tried to move away from the wall.

Both The Cowboy and Geronimo opened up on the trapped man. Each fired three bullets within six seconds. Grey Beard's body went limp and then fell downwards bouncing off the flume's walls on its slow descent to the bottom where it lay unmoving.

Geronimo and The Cowboy descended down the shaft, both stepping on the dead man's body at the bottom before exiting.

"Now," Geronimo spoke, "we must bury both of these bodies in the pit you have dug."

The Cowboy just nodded. He approached Scarface's body and rolled it into the former snake pit. Stepping into the pit, he arranged the dead man's body in a tight curl. Next, he climbed out of the hole and dragged Grey Beard's body over to the pit before unceremoniously dumping it on top of Scarface. In like manner, he arranged the second body in a coil-like position. He then stood up, walked over to the sand pile, grabbed his shovel, and started to throw the sand back into the pit. Since the pit was more than half full, it didn't take The Cowboy long to cover up the bodies. All the while, Geronimo stood silently by. The two men exchanged not a word while The Cowboy filled in the more than half-full pit. When he finished, he jammed the shovel into the leftover sand, wiped the sweat off his brow, and looked over at Geronimo.

"I'd better strip their horses of their equipment and turn them loose," The Cowboy said as he walked over to the two horses which were still tied to the Palo Verde. He quickly stripped them of gear, which he tossed underneath the Palo Verde, and then slapped each one on the rump. Both horses trotted off into the barren wasteland surrounding Geronimo's Table.

The Cowboy, wiping his brow, returned to where Geronimo was standing.

"It has been a good day," the Apache chief said as he walked over to The Cowboy, grabbed his arm, and then shook his hand. Both men smiled before Geronimo continued, "You are a good man, Mr. Cowboy, especially in your care of this sacred spot. I must depart, but before I do, let me tell you a secret.”

“Thank you,” The Cowboy replied. “I have tried to be true to your traditions and sacred relics, while I know other white men would, if they could find it, desecrate this holy place. I have kept this sacred spot untouched and unknown to anyone else other than myself. If I ever return, I will continue to watch over your sacred ground. But,” he resumed somewhat meekly, “I really haven’t done anything for you that merits your telling me any secret.” He looked at Geronimo in a puzzled manner.

Geronimo nodded before speaking, “I know you have been true. And all the Spirits who reside here, including myself, appreciate what you have done in guarding this sacred place. You are a man of tradition, and we, in our Spirit World, who inhabit this place, are grateful for your stewardship and guardianship of our past. Now, you need to know this before I depart.”

I wonder how he’s going to do that? The Cowboy thought.

“After I am gone,” Geronimo continued, “I want you to return to your grotto and horse. Before you leave, reenter our sacred cavern. Go to the pottery and move only the third vessel from the left. Look under the sand it stands upon. You will find something of interest that is yours to keep and do with as you choose. Return the pot to its original location. After you have left our sacred place, find a boulder and cover the entrance with it.”

Not really knowing what to think, The Cowboy simply nodded. “Geronimo, thank you for help with these hunters of gold. I never had any gold, but many think I stole it many years ago.”

Geronimo nodded and said, “Do not be worried from now on. My Spirits tell me that you will never again be approached by anyone searching for that stagecoach’s gold. Now, my friend, it is time for goodbye.”

Geronimo clasped The Cowboy's arm and held it firmly. The Indian's body started to change right before The Cowboy's eyes. It slowly became translucent and then the Apache's corporeal presence seemed to slowly vanish. He felt Geronimo's hold on his arm disappear and then the Indian chieftain was gone, leaving only a whisp of smoke which quickly dwindled into nothingness.

The Cowboy stood there speechless. *Have I*, he wondered, *been in a dream, or what?* He shook his head as if to rid it of the imaginary cobwebs he believed it to contain. He walked slowly back to the hidden grotto. Upon entering, he checked his horse to make sure it was in good shape. Prior to the events of the past day, The Cowboy had cut some Palo Verde limbs with lots of leaves. Plus, he gathered up two handfuls of the Palo Verde's pea-like fruit. He also found bunches of some sort of desert grass growing under the trees which he pulled up. His mount would have enough food for the short time The Cowboy planned to be here. He petted the horse's neck. The horse rubbed its head on his shoulder. *Well,* ol' fella, he thought, *I guess that means you're okay.* In silent reply, his mount shook its head up and down.

By this time, it was late afternoon. Removing his watch from his vest pocket and opening it in the dim and fading afternoon light filtering its way through the grotto's entrance, he realized it was five o'clock. The Cowboy closed his watch and decided to eat an early dinner. *Then,* he thought, *I'll get some sleep.* It had been a long day. He would do his exploring in the morning and then leave as early as possible.

After eating and then cleaning his Winchester, The Cowboy was ready for bed. As he lay down, he realized how tired and mentally exhausted he really was. He fell to sleep recalling the strange events of his day. *Did this really happen?* he wondered, before he dozed off.

He rose early the next morning having slept well during the night. Early morning light crept through the grotto's entrance. The Cowboy checked the time. It was 5:30 a.m. *Well*, he thought to himself, *time to do some exploring.* He rose, washed his face, withdrew some food from a saddlebag, and ate.

Exiting the grotto, he collected enough creosote branches and twigs for two torches that he would use to explore the sacred site. He soon had his makeshift torches. Lighting one and holding the other, he moved to the back of the cavern quickly locating the small tunnel he had previously discovered. Crawling in, he soon arrived at the sacred room. Standing, he slowly moved his torch in a 360-degree circle as he observed the room, its beautiful pictographs, and contents. Next, he walked over to the line of pottery and stopped in front of the third vessel from the left. About three feet above it was a small hole in the volcanic rock. Inserting his burning torch into the wall, he then knelt before the pot.

Gently touching the ancient vessel, he felt the rounded surface. He carefully gripped both sides at the bottom and gently pulled the pottery away from the chamber's wall, moving it only a foot or so to his right. Looking at the sand underneath it, he didn't see anything. Using his fingers, he carefully moved the sand. After three inches, he felt something hard. He scraped away the sand surrounding the object. He was shocked and amazed to see that it was a gold ingot! He slowly removed the six-inch-long ingot and placed it to the left in front of the second pot. Next The Cowboy filled in the hole he had dug, using extra sand from the cave's floor to fill the void he had left after removing the heavy ingot. He tamped the sand down as much as he could and then replaced the pot to its original position.

Placing the ingot in his pants pocket, The Cowboy crawled out of the sacred room and into its entry tunnel. After arriving at the grotto's main passageway, he looked around with his torch. Off to his right was a large piece of volcanic rock. It was just about the size of the tunnel he had just exited.

Hmm, he thought, *I'll need my horse to move that stone.* So, he laid the lit torch against the wall just behind the basaltic rock. He then lit his second torch, planted it on top of the lava tube's floor, put a few loose rocks around the wooden shaft's base and leaned it so that it would touch the wall just to the right side of the sacred tunnel's entrance. The Cowboy returned to the front chamber. He dug the heavy ingot out of his pocket, and without further examining it, he buried it next to his bed about six inches deep into the soft sand that had shifted in from the grotto's entrance.

Next, he leaned down, picked up his saddle and placed it onto the horse's back where he secured it, making sure the girth was tight. Then The Cowboy retrieved his lasso which was lying next to his bed and hung it from his pommel. After untying his trusty mount, he led the horse back into the gloomy tunnel. Once he reached the illuminated area, he removed his lasso, uncoiled it, and tied it as tightly as he could to the black volcanic stone he had previously spotted. Having tied the rope to the pommel, he gently turned the horse around. The Cowboy carefully guided his steed up the slight incline until the rope was taut. Calmly petting his horse's neck, he spoke to the animal.

"Okay, *fella*, let's just go nice and easy." The horse moved slowly forward dragging the heavy stone until it was even with the sacred chamber's entrance. "Whoa! Boy. Good horse," he said as he petted it on the neck again. "Now, let's back up, so the rope isn't tight, okay?" With some nudging and hesitation—and a few more pats—the horse backed up about a yard until The Cowboy commanded, "Stay, *fella*." He untied the lasso from the pommel and dropped it onto the lava floor.

The Cowboy walked back down to the rock and untied the other end of his rope. The small boulder lay about two feet from the sacred cave's entrance. Sitting down on his butt, he took both feet and pushed the stone until it was about halfway into the small tunnel opening. He moved forward and kept pushing until the stone was totally inside the small mouth of the shaft.

Dusting his hands off as he rose, The Cowboy returned to his horse, which had been placidly standing by as he shoved the rock into its final resting place and guided the loyal animal back to the front of the grotto where he secured it to the embedded C-shaped tie-down.

By now, as he noted after withdrawing his watch from his vest's pocket, it was drawing close to noon. *Too late*, he thought, *to leave today. I'll just get up really early tomorrow and leave.* So, The Cowboy sat down, dug up the gold ingot, and examined it. It had identical numbers—160—stamped on the top and bottom. *Well, I'll be damned*, he thought, *that's one hundred sixty ounces of pure gold! 'Cause this hunk feels like it weighs ten pounds!*

He also noticed two similar stamps on either end of the ingot. *Hmm, looks like some sort of royal crest*, he surmised. Then he noticed the word *"España"* in extremely small letters underneath the crest and his jaw dropped open. "Good Lord, this is a Spanish ingot!" he exclaimed somewhat in shock. "I wonder," he again audibly mused as he lifted the bar up into the air and rotated it with both hands, "just how old this bar really is? Must be a couple of hundred years old!" *Gee*, he pondered, *how in the hell did the Apache come across this?* He slowly replaced the ingot in the hole he had dug and covered it up.

The next morning, after a good night's sleep, he woke up early. Dawn was barely creeping over the distant horizon. After a quick breakfast of pork and beans, he filled all his canteens with water from the spring, then packed and saddled his horse. He ensured his horse drank as much water as it could. Finally, The Cowboy cleaned up the camp site, some of which involved him taking the shovel and tossing the horse's manure outside about fifteen feet away from the grotto's hidden entrance. Lastly, he unearthed the ingot and stowed it in a secret compartment on the underside of one of his saddlebags.

Time to leave, he thought, looking at his watch to see it was 5:30. *I've got a long day ahead.* He groaned as he mounted his steed and turned it toward the grotto's entrance.

Rounding the edge of the mesa, he set out to the west. With luck he would reach his first night's camp along with its seep some twelve to fifteen miles away. He moved his mount into the scattered lava field that stretched out before him and traveled slowly onward as they threaded their way through it. It was another hot day, and The Cowboy used his neckerchief sparingly to mop the sweat from his brow before he took a small sip from his canteen.

The Cowboy and his mount had been traveling for about two hours when he noticed buzzards circling off to his left about a mile away.

Petting his horse on the neck, he spoke to it, "Time for a little detour, *ol' fella*. We *gotta* check out what's causing *dem* buzzards to circle off yonder."

Forty minutes later he was directly underneath the circling birds. It wasn't a pretty sight, and the stench of death assaulted his nostrils. Placing his handkerchief over his mouth, The Cowboy dismounted. About fifty feet in front of him lay a dead horse, which numerous buzzards and crows were devouring, while paying little attention to him and his horse.

In front of him lay the eviscerated body of The Kid, which two buzzards were ripping apart. Scarface and Grey Beard had stripped the body of clothes and boots. Some of The Kid's ribs had been exposed to the sun by the greedy vultures. The birds glanced up at The Cowboy, then ignored him and continued to feast on The Kid's entrails, which they had pulled out of his intestinal cavity. A Gila monster was gnawing away on the body's left foot.

The Cowboy ambled over to the fetid body and stopped about five feet away. So horrid was the smell, he was forced to pinch his nostrils through the handkerchief. The two buzzards looked up at him, gave a warning *"Caw!"* and continued eating. They, along with hundreds of flies, weren't going to let any old man take away their dinner. Looking down at the body, The Cowboy could easily discern that The Kid had taken a bullet between the eyes.

Shaking his head, The Cowboy turned and walked back to his horse. "Well, *ol' fella*, we're done here," he said with some finality in his voice. "*Nothin'* more for us to do. So, off we go!" Man and horse turned to the northwest and resumed their trip.

As The Cowboy rode along, he recalled the words to a hymn he had once heard. They seemed rather apropos to him.

When I'm found in a desert place . . .

On the road marked with suffering . . .

Though I walk through the wilderness . . .

When the darkness closes in, Lord . . .

Blessed be your name.[7]

The Cowboy was seen in various towns, usually at a poker table. No one ever approached him. It was as if he had some sort of magnetic field surrounding him that invisibly pushed people away. Although it was known that he did, from time to time, frequent a bordello or two. But the gilded girls never offered any information as to whether or not he visited their place of employment. Their lips remained mum as to relating any pertinent information concerning the famous gunfighter. And then, one day, The Cowboy simply vanished into the mists of the far West. Rumors abounded as to where he might be, but no one really knew. It was rumored he was living somewhere in Montana in a cabin he had constructed near

---

7   Song by Matt Redman/ Songwriters Matt Redman & Beth Redman. ©2002 Thank You Music. Album "Top Christian Songs of All Time (2015)." Song #3798438. Also "Blessed be Your Name: The Songs of Matt Redman. Vol.1 CD (2006). EMI Music.

Flathead Lake. The sighting, or much less the cabin's location, was never confirmed.

In the early 1930s, a grizzled old man with a thousand lines on his face and a cough that never seemed to leave him approached the pastor of a church in Green River, Wyoming, and made funeral arrangements with him. The preacher was quite disturbed when the octogenarian told him he wanted no headstone and desired to be buried in an unmarked grave.

Two years later on a quiet spring morning, as the sun rose into a clear blue sky, the oldster passed over heaven's bridge. The minister followed the unknown man's wishes and buried him as instructed. A week later, the president of the local bank contacted the cleric and asked him to come in for a meeting. The banker told him that the old man had a left a will with no identifying name—just his "X" mark— witnessed not only by the banker, but also two other bank employees. The president informed the preacher that the old man had left $75,000 to the church. When the banker asked if the minister knew the old man's name, the man of the cloth said he didn't.

No one knew who the elderly man was. Could it have been The Cowboy?

The Sniper, the Loner, and the Spirit Bear

INTRODUCTION

My name is Jesse Holder. At one point in my life, I became a loner. My choice. The story I'm about to relate to you is true although you probably won't believe a single word of it. When I look back upon what happened on Friday, August 13, 1976, I can hardly give credence to what occurred. Now, some forty-five years later as I write this story, it almost seems like a dream. Yet I know it wasn't.

To start out as to why I became a loner, you need to know a little about my backstory. I'm a Vietnam combat vet. Did time in 'Nam for almost two long years before a "million-dollar wound" sent me back to the U.S.A.[8] I saw a lot of bad sh-t. I did a lot of bad sh-t and I had a lot of bad sh-t happen to me. First off, I VOLUNTEERED to go to Vietnam! Where I came from—backwoods Kentucky—there was no way out unless you went off to college or joined the military. Otherwise, you became a coal miner, a poor dead-end sharecropper tilling some rich guy's land for peanuts, or a moonshiner.

There was no way I was going to end up in a coal mine and get black lung disease like my father. If I was a sharecropper, I'd be poor all my life and probably not be able to put food on the table for my

---

8 A "million–dollar wound" was a combat injury to a soldier that enabled them to get out of combat. It sent them back to a Veterans Affairs rehab facility near their hometown in the U.S.

family, if I deigned to have one. Lastly, there was no way I would get into the bootlegging profession. Too dangerous and I didn't fancy getting shot at by some other *'shiner* or some government *revenooer*.

My sister, Jill, got banged up at age sixteen, dropped out of high school, and married the father, Robert, another high school dropout who lost his two front teeth in an auto accident—I think he was driving drunk. He was also only twenty years old and a coal miner, plus a pack-a-day smoker. She moved out and went to live with him and his parents in a four-room dwelling barely five hundred square feet in size. With little or no education, they were both doomed to a life of poverty. I never knew if they actually got married proper-like and didn't ask.

At eighteen, I knew living in coal country wasn't the kind of life I wanted. My dad, then in his late forties, had been a coal miner for over twenty-five years, but then developed black lung disease and lived off some sort of government money for his ailment. He didn't have long to live. My Ma, who was about a year younger than Pops, was right poorly in health, always coughing from the twenty-plus cancer sticks she smoked daily. Later on in life, I hoped I wouldn't be affected by all the cigarette smoke I was exposed to while growing up in my ramshackle hovel of a home.

The dilapidated shack where I lived was built on the side of a nameless mountain. The mountain probably did have a name, but I never heard it called by its actual geographical designation. Everyone just called it "The Mountain." Our shack was located way back up a six- to seven-mile winding dirt road barely twelve feet wide. The switch-backed, barely paved gravel track led up to what was called Shifflett's Hollow, which also contained three other dilapidated shack-like houses in addition to our hovel. As one looked at our tar-papered house from outside, it seemed to be leaning back into the mountain. Perhaps it was.

Pa built the wooden house right after he and Ma got hitched

in their mid-twenties. It consisted of all kinds of wooden pieces of timber which he'd scrounged up over a period of several years. Since he was working in the coal mine, it took him almost eighteen months to construct the four-room house (along with an outside privy!!). In the meantime, they lived down the road with Ma's parents where they slept on the floor of the front room.

After Pa finished building for what passed as a home, Ma got pregnant and birthed me in the bedroom of their house with the help of Miss Amelia, a local midwife. My sister, Jill, was born the same way. Ma later told me they paid Miss Amelia with a bushel of potatoes for birthing each of us.

Both Jill and I didn't have our birth certificates, which would cause me some real paperwork problems after high school. In those days, the mid-1950s, the mountain people in my area didn't much care for official documents. Mostly, they avoided whatever looked legal, as no one trusted anything to do with government-type paperwork. So, there wasn't any record for me or Jill as to the actual day we was *borned* on the straw mattress in my parents rickety corn-husked bed.

There were practically no health services where we lived in eastern Kentucky. My folks had to travel sixty to seventy-five miles to Huntington, West Virginia, to see a doctor—or even get to a hospital. Their car was a beat-up and rusty 1957 Dodge Lancer, which was broken down most of the time. So, my folks didn't go most *anywheres* for their health needs.

I knew they both had little time left. I needed a way out—I had to escape somehow. I didn't like being poor and knew I had to do something drastic to get away from the ubiquitous coal country or else I'd be swallowed up. I aspired, however, to a better life beyond these dirt-poor eastern Kentucky hills.

My high school history teacher, Miss Eula Sims, was a sixtyish-year-old spinster who wore her grey hair up in a beehive. Once she found out I could read four hundred to five hundred words per minute, she started loaning me lots of extra books from her home to read outside of class. I lost myself in learning about geography, the Civil War, World War II, ancient Chinese kingdoms, international cities like London, Calcutta, and Sydney, and lastly, art by painters like da Vinci, O'Keeffe, or Matisse. Thanks to Miss Sims, not only did I turn into a voracious reader, but I also became a lifelong reader of books. She even gave me a small paperback dictionary to look up words I didn't know or understand.

This "extra" education opened a window and gave me the inspiration to want more, and I realized backwoods Kentucky wasn't going to cut it. It would drag me down and swallow me up. I'd end up a coal miner and eventually get black lung disease that would gradually choke the life out of me. From my outside reading I knew life had to be better than this. Thanks to Miss Eula—that's what we called her behind her back—I knew there were other horizons out there waiting for me to learn about and experience. I was also determined to master how to speak proper English, but my hick words, as you can figure out from the beginning of this story, creep in a little bit every now and then.

PART I

THE SNIPER

I saw my chance to escape from Kentucky when an Army recruiter, a tall black man dressed in a wrinkle-free khaki uniform, showed up at my high school a couple of weeks before graduation. My way out! Grabbed it! Volunteered! After all, I had already been to a couple of funerals of older guys from my high school whom I hardly knew, but they hadn't managed to make it back alive from Vietnam. I'd been hunting my entire life, so I knew a little bit about stalking prey in the woods. Could the jungle be much different? By age fifteen I had become a marksman *par excellence* (which is one of them fancy phrases I learnt from Miss Eula's books). So, hunting gooks probably wasn't going to be much more different than hunting a deer, or a really wily turkey.

I graduated in June 1968 in the top 25 percent of my high school class. With such a high ranking, I probably could've gone off *somewheres* to college but there weren't no funds available. My Ma and Pa were *dirt poor,* and in those days, universities weren't interested in giving scholarships to poor, backwoods hicks from coal country. I guess they figured we'd drop out in the first semester and all their paperwork getting us into college would be wasted.

Within three weeks of graduation, I was in the U.S. Army. There was just one snag before I was allowed to join up. I was delayed for two days because I didn't have a birth certificate and couldn't prove I was eighteen years old. The recruiter, a tall Negro Sergeant E-7 named Tobler, who served in both the Korean and Vietnam wars, personally drove down to Shifflett's Hollow, picked up my Pa and Ma and drove them back to the recruiting station.

They both had to sign some sort of affidavit with two other

witnesses, attesting to the fact I was, indeed, eighteen. Pa inked it eagerly while he coughed up blood specks when signing the official paper with an "X" as he couldn't read or write. I guess Pa was happy to do so *'cause* he now had one less mouth to feed on his thin government black lung disability check. Both he and Ma couldn't remember the actual day in June I was born, so the army sergeant suggested the fifteenth and they both readily agreed.

Obviously, due to what happened in South Vietnam during Tet on January 31, 1968, Tobler wanted to make sure he could make his June enlistment quota. Thousands of new recruits were now needed to throw into the insatiable maw called the Vietnam War machine resulting in more young American men (and women!) being ground up, spit up, and placed into government-paid coffins for their final trip back to the states.

After all, having poked the bear, the powerful United States was now *gonna* teach them big bad gooks not to ambush us again like they had during Tet. During my eight-week basic training course at Fort Benning, Georgia, in the humid summer of 1968, and then continuing later in the fall at the six-week Advanced Infantry Training (AIT) course at Fort Lee, Louisiana, I had the highest target scores with both the M-14 and M-16.

After AIT, I was sent back to Fort Benning to attend the four-month Non-Commissioned Officer (NCO) school where I not only received an award for scoring the highest target grade with the M-16 but also earned my Sergeant E-5 stripes. Then, after a thirty-day leave back home, I was shipped off to Vietnam.

As soon as I arrived in Vietnam in June 1969, the Army assigned me to a thirty-day sniper school. I had just turned nineteen.

I learned a lot more about hitting long-distance targets with the Springfield Armory XM21 sniper rifle which had a twenty-round magazine. It weighed eleven pounds without the telescope. The scope was a 3-9x Redfield Adjustable Ranging Telescope (ART) for day use and weighed seven and a half pounds. The ART combined range finding and bullet drop compensation features. I also was issued a PVS-2 starlight scope for night operations that weighed six pounds.[9] So, I was carrying a lot of weight in weaponry—not counting the ammo!

After sniper school they assigned me to a small and exclusive company made up of only snipers. Our unit consisted of eight three-man teams. The other team members were trained snipers, like me, making our jobs interchangeable. As I quickly learned, the reason our positions were interchangeable was due to the fact our line of work as snipers was incredibly dangerous and fatal. Sniper teams like ours tended to take heavy casualties. In some cases, the teams simply vanished and were never heard from again.

Due to my skill set and rank as an E-5, I was assigned to the number one slot in our team. Our company operated in an area of the jungle known as "The Fishhook." It was located in an area northwest of Saigon in Tây Ninh Province. The unusual name came about because we were situated right on the Vietnam/Cambodia border line which had a configuration that looked like a fishhook.

The Fishhook, like much of South Vietnam, also had another problem that affected where we were able to hunt for "Charlie"— our VC or NVA prey.[10] Agent Orange, containing dangerously high amounts of dioxin, had been sprayed over great swaths of the jungle defoliating the trees and killing underbrush. While we were on the hunt, we tended to avoid those areas because we too were exposed.

After Agent Orange killed the trees and underbrush, elephant grass, which grew to a height of six to seven feet, reclaimed the chemically tainted area. Walking through the tall six- to seven-foot elephant grass

---

9   https://en.wikipedia.org/wiki/M21_Sniper_Weapon_System
10 "VC" is a derogatory reference to Vietnam Con San, or Vietnamese Communist. "NVA" is the name for the North Vietnamese Army, or a North Vietnamese soldier.

was extremely dangerous as you couldn't see more than four or five feet ahead so we might have easily stumbled into Charlie also making his way through the grass. In many ways, we Americans, who operated in those denuded areas, were exposed to a deadly chemical, dioxin, which had long-term effects on our bodies. At the time, we didn't realize even indirect exposure to the deadly toxin might affect us later in life, or the children we begat after the war.

Our team, named Tango Six, like all the others, had a primary sniper (me), plus my two backup men. One teammate was named The Frog, and the other guy went by the name of Eagle Eye. The Frog, whose real name was Jim Gordon, had a rank lower than mine as he hadn't gone to NCO School. He had already spent two months in 'Nam and was the last surviving member of a three-man sniper team the NVA had ambushed. A few weeks previous, The Frog barely escaped by using techniques the Army had taught him during a three-week Escape and Evasion (E&E) course in Panama.

The Frog had two important jobs. The first was to constantly survey the area around our position to ensure Charlie hadn't spotted us and wasn't silently slithering up on us through the tall elephant grass. The second, and in many ways, the most important job, was as our *commo* and map man. In addition to several topo maps, he carried the radio and made contact with our base every time we set up in a new ambush position. If we got into trouble, it was up to him to use his E&E (escape and evasion) skills and get us to an extraction point as quickly as possible. The Frog informed us his nickname came about because he was also in charge of leading our hasty retreat by zigzags plus leaps and bounds, and as he had a predilection for watery escapes, we often ended up wading in the fetid jungle's innumerable creeks.

Our number two team member was our spotter, who was nicknamed Eagle Eye because he was a member of the Salish Indian tribe from around Flathead Lake, Montana. His real name was David

Ironman and he was integral to my success in the slot as the number one sniper. Eagle Eye had been in Vietnam about a week longer than me. He was the guy who, with an ART of his own, double-checked my scope's calculations like distance to target, along with wind direction and speed.

After I checked the altitude and bullet drop with my ART, Eagle Eye and I confirmed the numbers. Then, all I had to do was dial in the info on my ART, zero in on the target, take a deep calm breath, and let it out slowly as I zeroed in and calmly squeezed the trigger. Since we all had nicknames in 'Nam, mine was Kentucky—I guess my hillbilly accent gave me away. After my shot, Eagle Eye used some high-power binoculars, which had a special film over the lenses so as not to reflect sunlight and confirmed whether my shot was a hit or not. Sometimes we just didn't know the target's status, so it was counted as a "probable."

Whenever we made a quick withdrawal from our previous setup and kill position, we usually found the nearest creek and either walked up or downstream so as, if possible, not to leave any back trail. There were a plethora of brooks and slow-moving creeks in our operations area and we were constantly wading through them after which we always checked our legs for leeches. If we found any, we burnt them off with our cigarette lighters. When we were forced to move through water above our waistlines, we always checked our torsos for the slimy bloodsuckers.

On several occasions both The Frog and Eagle Eye had to use their M-16s to take out some NVA who got too close to walking right on top of our setup location. When that setback happened, our position was now blown due to the unexpected contretemps (another fancy word I learned from Miss Eula!) with Charlie. It caused us to immediately and hastily relocate, lest there be more NVA following close behind them. That's why the rivulets became highly important to our withdrawal strategy.

My first kill was at 375 yards. Looked like an NVA platoon leader. Hit or miss, after every kill shot, I scooped up my spent bullet case. We didn't want Charlie to know what type of weapons, or ammo, we were using against them. After my kill shot, we immediately evacuated the area and redeployed to a backup position. We knew the enemy would search for and find our setup position. They would then try to trace our escape route.

Usually, our backup position was at a minimum three-quarters of a mile away from where we had set up for our kill shot. We were forced to move swiftly and quietly to cover that type of distance. Our heavy backpack loads made such a difficult trek hard on our shoulders and backs. But we had to move fast! Leaving our kill site, we always tried to use a creek or watercourse to cover our hasty escape route as we headed toward our backup position. The NVA were good trackers, so we knew we had to obfuscate—another Miss Eula word!—our retreat as much as possible, despite at the same time having to move quickly through the water or the jungle.

I used my XM-21 with its special scope as the kill weapon, but I also carried a shortened lightweight version of the M-16 that made it look like a toy, but it still packed a punch. I used it whenever we made our escape or were scouting for prey in the jungle. Carrying two sets of ammo and the extra M-16 wasn't too difficult, but it added more weight to the equipment I had to carry. Fortunately, I was 6'5" in height and weighed 185 pounds, giving me the extra strength to haul all my heavy equipment around. In all, my load probably weighed around eighty-five to ninety-five pounds.

The Frog, who also was our radioman, determined the direction of our redeployment based on topo maps he had scrutinized during each of our setup positions. Once we had set up in our backup position, he would radio in our location by using some type of clicks on the mike to avoid speaking unless absolutely necessary. While out hunting the NVA, we always whispered so as to keep our voices from being heard from more than ten feet away. One unexpected result of whispering so much in 'Nam was that after arriving back in America I tended to be soft-spoken and didn't like raising my voice.

About two months after I had arrived in 'Nam, I received a penciled and poorly spelled one-sentence letter from my sister, Jill, telling me, "Pa done died and Ma is *goin'* downhill *fass*." I sent her some money for the funeral. Six weeks later, I received another one-line letter from my sister informing me, "Ma *dun gon. Tank yew* for *tha monee fer* Dad's funeral." I sent Jill what was left of my meager savings to help pay for Ma's funeral.

So, now, I was free. Didn't have to return to Kentucky after I left Vietnam unless, unfortunately, I managed to end up in a wooden box. Then I'd be shipped home to lie in that small Baptist Holy Roller church cemetery overgrown with weeds which was situated on the side of a mountain due to the fact there was little flat land in eastern Kentucky. Now knowing what I did about the world, a cemetery was the last place on earth I wanted to end up.

I, for sure, didn't want no bugler blowing "Taps" over my grave. Plus, as I will relate later in this story, I knew the Reverend Brother Amos would certainly exact his revenge on me by preaching that my KIA death was what happened to unholy sinners like me for defying him in church as I had previously done while I was a senior in high school.[11] But, fortunately or unfortunately, I would be dead and not have to listen to his misguided biblical ranting!

As a team, we three worked so well together that all three of us re-upped around the time I had spent my first ten months in 'Nam. After my first year I racked up thirty-one confirmed kills or hits and ten to eleven probable ones. We ran into trouble a few times and had a few close calls but managed to escape without getting into any shooting matches with Charlie.

---

11 KIA = Killed in Action

I elected not to take any leave during my second tour in Vietnam. By March 1971, I racked up another seventeen kills bringing my confirmed total to forty-eight kills and fourteen to fifteen maybes. Unfortunately, after kill number forty-nine, the sh-t rained down on top of us.

We had set up underneath a bamboo clump, probably not more than a half mile from the Cambodian border and extremely close to one of the several arteries of the Ho Chi Minh trail which led to Saigon. I lined up a 436-foot shot and put my target down. We immediately exited the rear of the bamboo clump and started out for our backup position when we ran straight into five gooks coming down a thin trotter, or path, which was hidden by three- to four-foot-high elephant grass some forty yards behind our bamboo clump. They opened up on us at the same time we opened up on them.

Eagle Eye took a bullet in his right thigh and went down while The Frog got one in his upper left arm but kept firing. One of the NVA, standing about seven or eight feet away, aimed at Eagle Eye and actually pulled the trigger missing the Indian by inches. I finished the NVA off with a head shot. But then, bad luck hit.

As the NVA was falling after being hit and killed, his trigger finger, now in a death grip, sprayed the area. Me—I wasn't so lucky. I got an AK round in my upper right shoulder, a round plowed by my lower left elbow. But the worst thing was I got solidly hit in my left knee. I went down. Boy, those bullets really stung like a motherf-cker! Fortunately, unlike our M-16 bullets, AK-47 bullets weren't designed to tumble once they made contact. Our M-16 bullets started to spin once they hit flesh, so their entry hole looked like a regular bullet hole while the exit wound was two to three inches round. AK bullets usually went straight through unless they hit bone; then it was a whole *'nother* story.

Eagle Eye and The Frog finished off the remaining gooks who made the mistake of charging us. The firefight had lasted fifteen to twenty seconds at most. Still, we knew we were in deep sh-t. We realized we had to quickly exfiltrate, or in civilian language—vamoose! The three of us wrapped our wounds as best, and as quickly as we could. The Frog and Eagle Eye were lucky; their wounds had entry and exit holes without any bones being hit or shattered. While The Frog radioed in our position and our intended escape route, Eagle Eye, after bandaging his thigh wound, hastily dressed my shoulder wound. It looked like the AK round had gone in right above my collarbone and exited cleanly. It still stung like hell.

Three minutes after our firefight we ditched all our equipment except our weapons, ammo, water, and our lightweight rescue radio. We stuffed small first-aid packets and compasses in our large jungle fatigue pockets. The Frog and Eagle Eye lifted me up so I could put my arms around their shoulders which slowed our flight exiting from the firefight area. We knew more gooks would be coming, and coming fast, as they would be able to easily track our redeployment route *'cause* we weren't covering our tracks as we hastily fled.

After some one hundred fifty to two hundred yards, The Frog found a small seven- to eight-foot-wide and twelve- to eighteen-inch-deep rivulet. As soon as we entered the stream, he turned left and we slowly marched, and, at times, stumbled upstream in the middle of the creek. The water was up to our calves, so walking was fairly easy but slow. Unfortunately for them, both my teammates had to half-drag me along. Plus, the longer we walked it really aggravated my knee. Due to my adrenaline, I hardly felt any pain from the shoulder or elbow wounds, but my left knee was really beginning to be a problem.

Wading some eight hundred to nine hundred yards, we came to a fork in the somewhat chilly stream. We took the left tributary which seemed to have a slower water flow. We waded another three hundred yards in ankle-deep water before we carefully exited the stream trying not to leave any trace as to our exit point. We knew we left a blood trail until we reached our original entry point into the creek during our hasty retreat. So, the NVA would find it and probably send men up and down stream looking for us.

We hoped and prayed we'd waded far past the point where they might stop and turn around. We intuitively knew Charlie would be flooding the area with men to hunt us down. We would have to keep moving, putting as much distance as we could between us and the NVA. They'd know from our blood trails at the site of the firefight until we reached the stream that one or more of us were hit so we needed to *didi mau* and get as far away as possible.[12]

Upon exiting the stream, we found ourselves in thick humid jungle. The rotting vegetation and no-see-ums assaulted both our nostrils and faces, forcing us to tie our camouflage bandanas over our nose and mouth. Since it was drawing close to darkness, we moved deeper into the jungle trying to leave as little trace of our passing as possible. After a long twenty-minute walk, we found a large, uprooted tree. We decided to halt there and hole up for the night.

It was now up to The Frog to figure out where we were and then find a location for the nearest pickup zone. All three of us were hurting. We knew we were in for trouble and might not make it out alive unless The Frog found a large enough clearing for a Medevac to land. We huddled together during the night in a two-foot-deep by six-foot-wide root hole created when the tree fell and pulled its large root ball out of the constantly damp jungle floor. Keeping the sound down, we continued to whisper as we discussed our precarious situation. There was no doubt among us—we were up sh-t's creek without a paddle.

Our wounds had almost stopped bleeding when we pulled off our hastily applied bandages and then re-wrapped them properly over the injured areas. My shoulder didn't hurt a lot from the clean in-and-out shot. My left elbow had taken a glancing blow from an AK round,

---

12 *Didi mau* is Vietnamese for "to run quickly."

so it was okay—just stung a lot. My knee was another thing as it was swollen and hurt something painful. Plus, the bullet hadn't exited, so every so often it was grinding against the kneecap or another bone, which was aggravating as hell.

Eagle Eye's thigh wound, he said, hurt like a bitch but didn't seem as serious as mine and he had little trouble walking. The Frog's arm wound stung but didn't appear to inhibit any movement. In my mind, it turned out to be a really sh-tty day.

It would be a long night. Our adrenaline high from the firefight and our flight had now worn off. We set up three-hour watches. Since I was hurting the most, The Frog and Eagle Eye insisted I take the first watch so I could get some rest afterwards. Tomorrow might be an easy day if we got picked up early, but it also might be a long day if we had to spend another night out in the fetid jungle. Infection, most likely, had already set in so we had to get out quickly otherwise all those nasty little microbes that existed in the Vietnamese jungles might cause us to lose a limb—or kill us!

We made it through the night. The pain in my left knee made for a restless and sleep-interrupted night and kept me in a sort of semi-sleep. Upon waking around 5:00 a.m., I debated about using one of the three morphine squeeze capsules which were contained in each of our rudimentary first-aid kits to alleviate pain. I decided not to as there was no guarantee we'd be rescued in the next few hours. Best to save it until it was really necessary to use in the next day or so. I just needed to ignore or endure the pain. Plus, with no food and our long escape route having sapped both our energy and strength, we hoped for an early rescue.

The next morning, Eagle Eye found a stout two-inch-thick tree limb about four feet long which he fashioned into a walking staff. Using his nine-inch-long Bowie knife that he'd brought from Montana before heading out to 'Nam, he carved and smoothed a rounded knob at the top of the cudgel so my hand wouldn't feel the jab of any wooden protrusion. He also hacked off the small branches and flattened out the remaining knobs. The makeshift walking staff would make it easier for us to travel and I wouldn't slow the other two men down as much as I had the previous day. Better to hobble than be dragged along holding onto their shoulders and further tiring them out.

Although he wasn't exactly sure of our location, The Frog had calculated we might have to travel another two to three hundred yards to find a pickup zone. So, at 5:30 a.m., we started out. We silently picked our way through the jungle pausing every five to ten minutes for me to rest. Around 8:00 a.m., after traveling several hundred more yards than The Frog had originally calculated, we finally arrived at the edge of a large two- to three-acre jungle clearing. Staying about four or five yards from the edge, we set up a firing position. Eagle Eye and The Frog decided to scout out the area on either side of our position for at least fifty to seventy-five yards to ensure we weren't close to any enemy positions or trotters. After fifteen to twenty minutes, each man returned and gave me a silent thumbs up.

The Frog set about using his radio to contact help. Using his clicking code, it took several minutes before he made contact and had his special ID number verified. To prove we weren't under duress—i.e., captured and forced to call—he had a special click progression of two rapid clicks, a two-second pause, and then one long two-second click. Due to our hurried and frenzied retreat, he wasn't exactly sure as to our actual position. Since we were operating so close to the Cambodian border when we made our last kill, we had no real idea as to our location.

Were we still in Vietnam, I wondered, or had we strayed into Cambodia? If we were in Cambodia, our asses were in a sh-tload of trouble.

At any rate, the Army sent up two Huey gunships and a Cobra to search for us. The Medevac would follow about a half mile behind them so when the Hueys, or the Cobra, located us, the Medevac could quickly swoop in and grab us while the other three helicopters circled the area looking for unfriendly individuals.

Now we played the waiting game. About forty-five minutes later we heard the gunships several miles off to the south of our position. The Frog radioed the information in and several minutes later the choppers moved closer to our position. The Frog made another adjustment, and Cavalry was soon hovering and circling overhead. As soon as The Frog was notified the Medevac was inbound, both men lifted me to a standing position and we then made our way to the jungle's edge. Eagle Eye used a small handheld mirror to bounce a signal off one of the gunships to confirm our actual position. The pilot did a wobble to acknowledge us.

The Medevac came in fast and landed with the two Hueys hovering about three feet off the ground on either side of it. The Cobra, circling above, laid down machine gun and rocket fire into the jungle on either side of our hiding place after we emerged. Grabbing me, both The Frog and Eagle Eye dragged me to the Medevac, which immediately rose as soon as all three of us hastily piled inside. We had made it!

During our Medevac flight to the hospital at Pleiku, the machine gunner told me that they picked us up in Cambodia. Arriving at the base hospital, The Frog and Eagle Eye had their wounds cleaned and bandaged up. Luckily, the AK bullets had passed through them without striking bone. The *médicos* told both of them that it didn't look like any infection had set in, but their wound areas needed to be cleaned daily and monitored every two to three weeks. So, they were lucky that they wouldn't be able to return to the jungle for a while until the Army okayed them for combat. On the flip side, they would be expected to do all the onerous camp-type duties until their wounds healed.

I, however, was headed for the operating table and then onto a hospital in Japan. We exchanged addresses as I knew this was going to be the last time I would see them in 'Nam—if ever again.

Eagle Eye, who knew from several of our conversations how much I despised living in eastern Kentucky, urged me to come visit him in Montana after he got out of the service. I told him I really would like to make a journey out to his area of Montana when the Army, or VA, finally cut me loose. He gave me his address. We shook hands and parted. Within fifteen minutes, the nurses arrived to wheel me into the ER.

After a preliminary operation in Pleiku and one night's rest, the Army flew me by chopper down to Bien Hoa, located just outside of Saigon.[13] There I was put on a hospital plane with twenty-five to thirty other WIA guys for our flight to Japan.[14] My knee was badly infected and the docs had to do two or three more operations over the next six weeks to save it and my leg. They told me I was going to be limping for the rest of my life and might need a crutch or a cane as I grew older. After recuperating in Japan, I was flown home to the States and stationed at a Veterans Hospital (VA) in Lexington, Kentucky, so as to be somewhat near my home. I just turned twenty-one when I arrived in Lexington in June 1971.

The folks at the VA told me I would be in rehab for about three to four months, not only to ensure my infection had disappeared but also because I needed physical therapy to strengthen and stabilize my left knee. Hopefully, when they finished, I would be able to put weight on it and awkwardly walk as best I could. They also told me the VA had rated me 100 percent disabled, so I would be receiving a nice tax free check every month for the rest of my life. While in the hospital, I was surprised one day when a full-bird colonel came to my bedside and pinned two Purple Hearts on my pajama top—one for the

---

13 Saigon is now known as Ho Chi Minh City after the North won the war in 1975.
14 WIA = Wounded in Action

shoulder and the other for the knee wound. I guess the bullet furrow on my elbow didn't count.

During the time I was in rehab I wrote and told Jill that I was at the Lexington VA. She came to visit once. Not only was Jill carrying a two-year-old boy who was somewhat underweight and which she still breastfed in front of me, but she was now also pregnant with twins. I tried to sound happy for her. Uneducated and dirt poor, I knew she was doomed to a life of poverty, something I was determined wouldn't happen to me. I told her I wasn't coming back to Shifflett's Hollow—because I was going to wander around the States and find a place to live, hopefully far away from Kentucky. I did tell her I would keep in touch and let her know where I was in case she ever needed to contact me.

Jill also brought a letter addressed to me from Eagle Eye. After his thigh wound healed, he was assigned to a rear echelon job in 'Nam as one of three waiters in the commanding general's private mess hall. So, he managed to survive Vietnam and had demobbed from the Army. Writing that he had returned to his home in Kalispell, Montana, which was located just north of Flathead Lake, Eagle Eye invited me to come out to visit. After Jill left, I immediately wrote to Eagle Eye and told him I would head his way for a visit whenever the VA finally kicked me loose. I gave him my VA's address for future mail delivery and informed him I would write when I was on my western hegira—another one of Miss Eula's fancy words!—to meet up with him.

THE LONER

Rehab took a bit longer than I or the VA expected. I needed another knee operation before more of the ubiquitous never-ending rehab. After ten physically tiring months of unending PT, they were ready to discharge me. Despite all the exercise I had to endure, I also forced myself to work out in the hospital's weight room. I wanted to ensure I would be in top physical shape when I left. A week before the VA cut me loose, I wrote Eagle Eye and informed him I would be on my way in a couple of days but would be hitchhiking out to Montana as I had no car. I also told him I had no idea how long it would take me to hitch across the country. It was mid-May of '72, so I guessed it would still be cold in the northern Montana mountains.

After my service as a sniper and what happened to me in Vietnam, I decided I needed to go it alone in life. I determined that I would visit Eagle Eye for a week or two, but then I would leave and gad about the country until I found a fairly isolated place to settle down. Little did I know at that time, but those idealized plans would really change once I arrived in Kalispell.

The PTSD nightmares still haunted me, and after what I heard from other vets, probably would never go away.[15] So, I figured it would be better for me to find a remote place—somewhere in the U.S. or Canada—where I could live and hole up. Of course, I realized every time I needed groceries I would have to visit a nearby town maybe on a four- to six-week basis. Hopefully, it would have a library so I could check out some books and learn more about the world Miss Eula introduced me to and which, most likely, I probably would never get to visit.

---

15 PTSD = Post-Traumatic Stress Disorder. After World War II, it was called "shell shock" before scientists changed the name with a more complicated nomenclature.

I wanted to be more educated, but I didn't want to go to no college or anything even though I had the G.I. bill which would pay for most of it. Still, I was damn tired of all the bullsh-t government paperwork I'd have to complete to get any college benefits. With the kind of reception most Vietnam vets received when they returned home, I knew with my bad leg I would stand out on a college campus. Plus, the word that I was a 'Nam vet would invariably somehow leak out and would draw unwanted attention to me which might not be too healthy. Not for me—but for some dumbass jerk of a college kid who might rag at me or try to get in my face and call me a baby killer. It would probably be the last time he ever mocked a Vietnam veteran after I finished realigning a few of his bones. The fact that I might end up in jail for doing so didn't phase me as the Army also taught me various ways to take someone out permanently.

As I didn't have any civilian clothes and really didn't want to buy some, I started out in my fatigue pants, a green T-shirt, and a thick Army jacket along with my old brownish Army-issued duffle bag, containing some extra olive drab Army T-shirts along with a couple of fatigue pants. I also had an olive green Army blanket I swiped from the VA hospital. The VA had given me a sterile, type of white plastic hospital cane. I quickly found an outdoor camping store in Lexington where I purchased a sturdy walking staff along with some camo shirts and pants. The store had a lightweight backpack which would be easier to use than my duffle bag, so I transferred what little I now owned from my duffle bag into the ruck. Keeping the heavy jacket and blanket, I disposed of the duffle bag, most of the army clothes, and the VA cane in a dumpster behind the store.

Although it was mid-May, it wouldn't be too cold so I could sleep rough along the way if I had to do so. I figured anyone seeing me in olive drab camo, especially if they were a veteran, might be inclined to give me a ride. Still, because of the unpopularity of the Vietnam War, a lot of people in the early 1970s viewed 'Nam vets not only with disgust and distaste but also a fear that we were all crazy killers of women and babies. That fact might definitely work against my ability to thumb a ride. Little did most Americans know, or even realize however, but many U.S. troops often patrolled in areas known as "free-fire zones" which meant that anyone—yes, anyone—we encountered in our operating area could be killed—men, women, and children. Fortunately, I never had to make that kind of decision. I operated strictly as a man killer.

My first ride, luckily, turned out to be a Korean War vet by the name of Angus Peete who drove me to St. Louis before heading off to Dallas. In St. Louis, after walking for an hour, I found a cheap motel named the Dew Drop Inn and stayed for two nights. I next managed to get a ride on the back seat of a Harley with a motorcycle gang called the Outlaws who were headed to Kansas City.

The gang, with their greasy beards and numerous tattoos, looked tough and forbidding. Yet every one of them had an American flag attached to the back of their black leather jackets along with their club patch of a skull and crossbones. One of their members told me they had admitted a lot of vets into their club—especially Marines who had fought in Vietnam. Not only did they all wear bandanas with a stars-and-stripes design, but every single one had an American Flag tattooed on their left arm and so did the numerous biker chicks who rode on the backseat behind them. Although I intuitively knew such gangs were into crime one way or the other, I still admired the tough guys for their display of patriotism.

From KC, I got a lift with a fiftyish-year-old Nebraska wheat farmer named Dan Dowdy, who turned out to be a World War II vet. He had some interesting tales about the war in Europe, so I gave him an abbreviated version of some of my more amusing Vietnam experiences, but I didn't mention my sniper exploits. We made our way north to Omaha where he dropped me just outside of the city. I spent the night in Omaha at a third-rate and seedy place called the

Cornfield Inn, with paper-thin walls and which, from all the comings and goings, I quickly learned was nothing more than a hot-sheet motel. No wonder the bed sheets were less than salubrious![16]

The next morning, after a somewhat sleepless and uneasy night, I got lucky and hitched a lift with an independent eighteen-wheeler driver named Tom Lincoln, who was headed all the way to Seattle with half a load of canned tomatoes he had picked up in Memphis.

Interstate 90 was not completed in 1972, so we ended up on a lot of two-lane highways through South Dakota and Wyoming which took a couple of days to drive. Finally, we reached the Montana state line. He stopped in Billings where he was able to pick up another half load of Alpo dog food going to Tacoma. Continuing west for a day, he dropped me off in Missoula where I found a small, cheap, twelve-unit motel named the Taj Mahal, which was operated by an older couple from India. Sleeping on the front seat of a semi for three or four days isn't exactly comfortable. I spent two days resting, catching up on my sleep, and working out the kinks I had acquired from sleeping in the eighteen-wheeler.

Route 93 out of Missoula was a two-lane road to Kalispell. Although the distance from Missoula to Kalispell was only 115 to 125 miles, it took me three days of walking (mostly hobbling along— thank goodness for my hiking stick!), as I hitched and slept rough before I finally arrived at my destination. I had Dave's address, so after walking with some hobbling between rest stops along the uneven streets around Kalispell for about two hours, I found his street and house on the western edge of town.

No sooner had I opened the gate to a small, neatly trimmed yard bordered by a white picket fence, than Dave burst out of his house onto the porch and gave me a huge bear hug as I limped toward him.

---

16 A hot-sheet motel rents out rooms by the hour either to its regular prostitutes' customers, or couples having illicit liaisons.

"Man! You're here! I don't f-cking believe it! *C'mon* inside!" he said as he put his arm around my shoulder. "I want you to meet my folks, my sister, and my lady friend! Wanna a beer? We got plenty!" Dave waved his arm and ushered me inside. "Hey, buddy, start out with this one," he said as he shoved the one he was drinking into my hand. I downed it in three large gulps and then crushed it in my palms.

Man, I thought, after all my days on the road heading west, *that really tasted good!*

With a greeting like that, who could resist? With his arm around my waist, we walked into his house. His parents were sitting together on a faded green couch that had a uniquely carved and decorative wooden base. The wooden design traveled up the arms. They quickly stood and greeted me with open arms, hugs, and asked me to call them by their names, Matilda and George, instead of "Mr." or "Mrs." As my Ma and Pa had taught me to be respectful to my elders, I had never called older folks anything other than "Mister" and "Missus," but George and Matilda's warm and friendly welcome made it a little easier for me to do so—although, at first, I was a bit uncomfortable doing so.

Across the room, sitting on another faded reddish sofa, were two young women. One, about twenty-five years old, raised an eyebrow and looked rather quizzically at me. She had warm and friendly hazel eyes which seemed to emit a mischievous sparkle as she looked up at me. The other woman, maybe about twenty years old, had beautiful black onyx eyes that seemed to bore right into my soul. Her raven-colored hair flowed down across her breasts almost to her waistline. She had a book in her lap and shyly glanced up at me. Dave grabbed my arm and led me across the room and introduced them.

"Jesse, this here's my sister, Nancy," he said as he pointed to the raven-haired girl and then to the redhead, "and my girlfriend, Alice."

I nodded to both of them and said, "Hello, nice to meet you," as I leaned over and shook their hands.

Nancy brushed aside her shiny and long pitch-black hair which cascaded over her rather smallish but pert breasts. She looked at me with something akin to awe, before she replied to my hellos, "You're the guy who kept my brother alive, aren't you?" She quickly stood, smoothing her multi-colored dress before walking toward me, whereupon Nancy gave me a totally unexpected quick hug of appreciation. I couldn't help but again notice her onyx-colored eyes which sparkled in the light and seemed to bore into and pierce my soul.

"Well," I sheepishly answered, trying to downplay my job in Vietnam, "it's more like he saved my life, especially when I took a bullet in my knee." I didn't mention I had most likely saved Dave's life during our fifteen- to twenty-second tête-à-tête (another Miss Eula word!) with Charlie.

She just nodded as Alice also stood, said hello, shook my hand, and put her arm around Dave's waist as she leaned over and kissed him. He just smiled and looked at her with adoration in his eyes.

After those introductions, the party began. More people—aunts, cousins, and friends—kept showing up. The Indian telegraph must have been working overtime! I couldn't keep any names straight. It wasn't long before we had twenty-five to thirty people crowded in the house drinking and all talking at once.

The din of so many people in a house as small as Dave's made me incredibly uneasy, causing me to experience some short flashbacks signaling me to avoid getting so bunched up. Whenever I felt really uptight during the party, I went out on the back porch. I did this several times. I looked at the white-capped peaks off to the northeast, which I later learned were called the Whitefish Mountains, while I gulped down the cool air and took a swig of my beer. After taking a five-minute break to calm down, I returned to the party. While on one of those breaks, Dave found me. He just nodded and threw his arm around my shoulder saying, "Yeah, bud, I know what you're *feelin'* so *jus'* try to relax." He patted me on the shoulder as I thanked him and we walked back together into the party.

After I was introduced to all the partygoers, most of them wanted to know what kind of duties Dave and I performed during the war that enabled us to make it back to the States in one piece. As I mingled and met more people, I gave each person a vague answer. I wasn't about to reveal that Dave and I were specialized snipers with an extremely risky job.

Probably for the best, I thought. *I shouldn't mention what we actually did during our jungle tour, or the fact most snipers never made it back to the States.*

So, I just told everyone Dave's Native American smarts kept all of us alive. Every so often I would bump into Nancy and we would chat for a few minutes before someone came over and interrupted us. Her onyx eyes mesmerized me every time we spoke, making me feel as if I was under some sort of voodoo spell that she had cast upon me. Yet, I didn't feel worried at such a nebulous intrusion into my mind. After each short conversation with Nancy, I sensed some sort of indefinable and vague connection with her. Strangely, I also felt her eyes were surreptitiously tracking me as I moved throughout Dave's house. I guess I should have felt somewhat uneasy at this unexplainable feeling but instead I felt at peace despite the party's noisy babble.

The impromptu party went on until midnight before everyone started to head home. Before each couple or single person left, they made a point to come over and thank me for taking care of Dave in 'Nam and also for being a veteran. Finally, it was just Dave and Alice, me, his parents, and Nancy. We ended up talking for a few more hours as John and Matilda, who appeared to be in their late forties, wanted to know a little bit more about what Dave and I had actually done during our multiple tours in Vietnam. I quickly gathered Dave hadn't told them much concerning what he did in 'Nam.

We both tried to whitewash our exploits. I'm pretty sure, at some point further down the line, Dave would tell John and Matilda and probably Alice too, what we really did in 'Nam's jungles. I figured that was a given. But for some vague and unknown reason, I hoped Dave wouldn't mention to Nancy what my real job had been during my extended Vietnam tour, especially concerning my forty-nine kills. I figured if there was a possibility she might learn that little factoid, it would quickly kill any friendship between us before it even began—if there ever was to be any kind of relationship!

It didn't take me long to figure out Nancy lived with Dave and Alice. Dave had an extra bedroom and told me I could stay as long as I wanted. I thanked him profusely because, as I later informed him, I had no plans whatsoever to return to Kentucky and really had nowhere else to go at that moment. I also informed Dave I didn't want to wear out my welcome and would shove off as quickly as I could. He just nodded, put his arm on my shoulder, patted me, and disabused me of staying only a short while. Instead, he told me I could stay a year or more if I liked.

"After all," he said, "we're survivors, Jess. Compatriots. We stick up for and help each other *'cause* only WE know what WE actually endured."

I humbly nodded in agreement as my eyes teared up at his kindness.

Kalispell had a library, so every five to seven days, using my walking staff, I hobbled about a mile down the road to it, checked out one or two books, trudged slowly uphill back to home, read them in a few days, then limped back to return them and take out a few more. Dave and Alice were gone for eight to ten hours a day as he had a job working for a construction company as a bulldozer operator. Alice, I quickly learned, was a registered nurse (RN) and had a job in the ICU at the local hospital. Nancy worked in the same hospital as an LPN. Every few days when she got home in the evening, she would make a sandwich for me or bake a pie for all four of us to eat later after dinner.

We'd talk while she worked in the kitchen. Nancy's deep black onyx eyes seemed to mesmerize me every time I found myself in her presence. I was fascinated by the apparent calming effect they seemed to have on me.

What is it? I wondered about those alluring eyes. *They seem to have some sort of a magical, mystical, hypnotizing effect on me.*

The months seemed to pass by quickly while I lived at Dave's house. It was now late April 1973. I decided I needed to find some vacant land out in the boonies where I could build a cabin. So, I started checking books out of the library on how to build one. From the detailed descriptions provided it looked easy, but I knew it wouldn't be. Plus, with my bad leg, constructing a cabin would be more than taxing and take far too long to accomplish without help. I knew that trying to hold a heavy wooden beam longer than fifteen feet and then trying to raise it into place would be impossible with no real lifting strength in my left knee.

Physically, I knew I would probably be able to take on such a construction project. But I quickly realized there was no way I could start to build any type of cabin starting in the spring and finish it by early October when winter started to march into northern Montana. Yet I continued to mention to Dave about locating some land.

As it turned out, Alice's father, Martin, had a couple of acres and a fifteen-by-fifteen-foot small tin-roofed cabin north of Kalispell. He said it was located on a five-mile-long dirt road off Route 93, just past the small town of Whitefish. Martin informed me that the property was sited on the south slope of the 6,587-foot Elk Mountain. In all, it was around thirty-five miles northwest of Kalispell. He used it for hunting, but now he was in his late fifties and rarely used it because he really didn't want to hunt so far away from Kalispell.

One day in late June just after my birthday, Martin took me up into the mountains in his black Ford-250 to show me his property. We headed north on Highway 93 until he turned off onto a national forest road just past Whitefish. Eventually we left the forestry road for a somewhat overgrown logging road which had various switchbacks as we slowly ascended some one thousand feet in elevation. Every so often I would glimpse far off and see beautiful vistas whenever an opening appeared through the foliage.

Finally, we arrived. About fifty feet in front of the cabin, down an eight- to nine-foot embankment, was a nice flowing creek about ten feet wide and two to three feet deep. The rustic cabin, which had a wood stove and one dust-encrusted window that after I rubbed the dust away with my elbow, had a magnificent view of Elk Mountain. I immediately fell in love with the weather-beaten shack.

Having spent about thirteen to fourteen months living at Dave's, I knew I needed to move along before I really outstayed my welcome, even though I carried my weight and paid for groceries and such. Plus, he and Alice decided to marry. I didn't want to be a third, or actually fourth, wheel in their house. It was time to go. I had saved up a lot of money from the time I was wounded until I was discharged from the Army and started to receive my monthly 100 percent disability check from the VA. I now had more than enough money to live on and would, by living alone, be able to save even more. After a quick five-minute negotiation with Martin, he sold the property to me at a very reasonable price. I paid him cash. We went down to the Flathead County records office and put the property in my name.

Another reason I needed to move was due to "The Terrors." I suffered deeply from PTSD. Every other night or so, I was subjected to vivid and nightmarish flashbacks in which I was involved in different firefights. At times, I would wake up screaming. When my screams were loud enough, I woke up Dave and Alice and sometimes Nancy. My flashbacks of Vietnam and what I had done during my term of service there really unsettled me. Dave would rush down the short hallway and into my room.

"Hey, hey, buddy, it's okay," he would say to me as he sat on my bed after he shook me awake. We'd talk a minute or so and I usually fell back to sleep quickly. I hated inconveniencing him, Alice, and Nancy. Plus, I knew it was time to go so my nightmares wouldn't disturb them any further. Sadly, the Vietnam War had indelibly imprinted me with its lasting effects. I hoped at times "The Terrors" would fade away, but in my heart, I knew they wouldn't. Yet, I am now convinced what occurred on Friday 13, 1976, had a direct effect of lessening their intensity and frequency. Now, forty-five years after the events described later on in this tale, "The Terrors" still visit me about once a month. Yet, unfortunately, sudden and unexpected loud noises still make me either jump or quickly start to lower my body to the floor and look for cover.

After purchasing George's property, I decided to move in within the next two to three weeks. As I didn't have a car, I needed to buy at least six months of supplies, especially since the snow up against Elk Mountain would isolate me. With Dave, Alice, and Nancy's help, I started purchasing enough canned food to last through the coming winter. I ordered a heavy fleece-lined work jacket along with some long underwear from an L. L. Bean catalog. I knew it would be incredibly cold and I didn't want to take any chances of freezing to death even though the cabin had a wood stove.

At a local camping store named Glacier Outfitters, I picked up a Coleman two-mantle lantern, plus six one-gallon cans of Coleman fuel. I'd need some type of light at nighttime and for reading. As a backup and to complement the Coleman lantern, I bought a large, foot-long black metallic flashlight that had three D-sized batteries, just in case the Coleman fuel ran out. Dave gave me a water purifier as a present for the snow I'd melt for sustenance when I couldn't get water from the creek.

Lastly, I knew I needed to buy some thicker-than-usual woolen blankets for the upcoming cold winters ahead. Fortunately, the store had them in stock, so I purchased three Pendleton blankets. Pendleton, I later learned, had been around since the 1860s. They had a long history of working with indigenous communities since the early 1900s. Their blankets celebrated Native American symbols and stories.

In my limited strolls about town, I had stumbled across a used bookstore aptly called Grizzly Used Books. Since I knew I'd be isolated in my forest hideaway for at least six months, I decided to buy as many books as I could on various and sundry subjects to keep me occupied during the cold wintertime when the snowdrifts would be high enough to prevent me from doing any outside chores (except using the outhouse!).

In all, I walked out of the bookshop with fifty to sixty used books with everything from mystery paperbacks to American, European, and Asian history tomes, along with a few books on art and some about the Vietnam War. They were too heavy for me to carry back to Dave's home, so I asked the bookseller if I could leave them there and come by later to pick them up. He agreed, and a few hours later Nancy helped me pick up the books.

A couple of days later Dave drove me to downtown Kalispell to Smokey's Handguns, Rifles, and Shotguns Shop where I purchased three used weapons—a Remington 12-gauge pump-action shotgun, a .225 Winchester, and a .357 Ruger Magnum pistol, plus several hundred rounds of ammo for all three weapons. With everyone's help over several days, I was able to move the food, clothing, books, and other supplies and equipment into the cabin.

On my last moving day, Dave and Alice, along with their respective fathers, plus Nancy, brought their chainsaws to the cabin. They cut up enough dead wood for my wood burning stove to have fuel for over a year. I ended up with a huge woodpile next to the cabin's front door. I was just blown away by their generosity and couldn't thank each of them enough. I just hoped the beer I had previously purchased for this occasion, which they all imbibed enthusiastically after their work was done, would be enough of a thanks for their efforts to see me settle in properly.

We returned to Dave's house where I spent my last night before moving to the cabin. I went to bed around ten o'clock. I was excited, but also dead tired. It was a Friday night and it had been a busy and emotional week. But then it happened! I had almost dozed off when I felt someone lift my bed covers and slide in beside me. I immediately woke up! It was Nancy and she was totally naked. In the dim light I could see her white bathrobe on the floor as she snuggled close to me.

"Shhh!" she whispered. "We don't want to wake my brother—or Alice." She then moved on top of me and gave me a long kiss to stop any protest I might have. I could feel the heat radiating out of her. After a few minutes, nature took over. We made love slowly and silently—kissing, fondling, and touching before I finally melted inside of her. At the end, just as I expended my essence, she moaned and held on to me rather tightly as she, too, climaxed. I collapsed beside her. We whispered for five to ten minutes before I fell asleep, holding her in my arms.

The next morning when I woke up around seven o'clock after an exceptionally (for me!) peaceful night's sleep, Nancy was gone. I wondered if I had imagined everything, but then I could smell both her perfume and her feminine sweat on my bed sheets. So, it had to be true. I rose, fixed breakfast, then tossed the sheets in the washer. No use letting anyone else know about our midnight tryst. A few hours later, I was set to go.

It was early August when Dave and Alice drove me to the cabin. Nancy had to work. We checked everything over, and, oddly, Alice double-checked to make sure I had enough toilet paper! We hugged and had a tearful goodbye. Dave promised he would check in on me every month or six weeks. I just nodded and thanked them both rather profusely. Dave and Alice told me they planned to marry in the spring of next year and I was invited. I wished them both luck and told them I would attend their ceremony unless, I jokingly told them, I ended up as a frozen-solid Iceman! They both smiled and laughed.

So, now, I was finally alone in my northern Montana cabin. I had turned twenty-three years old the previous June and now was a hermit. Living alone, I knew the horrors of Vietnam would, most likely, continue to visit me, but at least no one else would be close at hand and indirectly bothered by my PTSD and its ensuing dreams of the hell I had undergone.

After eating dinner on my first evening at my mountainside cabin, I took a chair, sat outside the cabin's door, and leaned against the rough-planked side of the wooden building. Although it was somewhat warm outside, a cool westerly breeze wafted through the trees and brushed gently across my face, signaling to me winter was coming soon. It felt good and I relaxed as nightfall descended.

My ears picked up the forest's night sounds and reminded me of my younger days in Kentucky. After several minutes I heard the solemn hoot of an owl which, after a few seconds, was answered by the solitary melody of another hooter further off in the distance. The back and forth of *"tu-whit, tu-whoo"* calls lasted for several minutes before both nighttime raptors fell silent. The forlorn calls of these birds of prey reminded me of the "Dueling Banjos" sequence in a movie called *Deliverance* that I, along with Dave, Alice, and Nancy, had attended in Kalispell last year. The film's violence had unsettled me. Yet, now, alone with my thoughts, deep in the Montana woods, I felt relaxed and peaceful. For once, I was truly alone! I slept well that night.

I hadn't been at the cabin for more than ten days when it happened. My ears, due to having been a sniper, instantly picked up the discordant sounds of someone or something outside of my shack. I immediately felt—no, sensed—an ominous presence nearby. Looking out the dust-covered windowpanes of the cabin's lone window, I discerned it was a grizzly. A HUGE grizzly! At least four hundred, maybe, five hundred pounds. He was a monster and was sniffing around the woodpile. I wondered if he was looking for grubs in the newly cut wood. Suddenly, he stood on his hind legs and looked directly at the window where I was standing terrified with my feet frozen to the floor.

The large, brown furry beast had to be at least seven to eight feet tall. I had no doubt the huge bear could not only smell me but also my fear! Sweat started to pour down my face and freely flowed from my now wet armpits. Intuitively, I knew he could see me through the dirty glass window. Dropping back down on all fours, the bear ambled over to the window, sniffed around the sill, looked up at me, and growled. My heart felt like it wanted to climb right out of my chest and flee! I could feel its increased beating as we both stared at each other from a three-foot distance.

If he decided to break in via the window, I wouldn't survive the onslaught trying to reach my Winchester. I stood with my feet frozen to the cabin's floor. I was incredibly afraid to go for my weapon! I figured if I suddenly moved, the beast might sense he was in danger and come through the window to get me. Then the beast snorted, gave a low growl, and then padded off into the woods. I knew he would probably return, so this animal's unexpected appearance was clearly a warning that I couldn't take any chances while I was outside.

Thus began one of the strangest relationships with a wild animal I had ever encountered during my entire lifetime. Every three or four days, Mr. Griz—my pet name for him—appeared. One time I was working outside. My Winchester was always within reach. I looked up and there he was about seventy-five feet away. Looking straight at me, he sniffed and then turned and nonchalantly ambled off, disappearing into the underbrush as silently as he had appeared.

But one thing puzzled me. After each week's encounter with Mr. Griz, "The Terrors" went into abatement and I slept better each night.

Was it coincidence, I wondered, or a sign my PTSD was healing? Or did the bear's mysterious appearances have some hither-known calming effect on my PTSD-torn mind?

A few times when I was inside the cabin, I sensed his presence but never saw him. One time he even came to the cabin's front door, growled, then scratched it several times with his long claws. I had barred the door with two four-by-fours, so I wasn't worried that he would be able to break in before I emptied my Winchester through the door. After he departed, I waited ten to fifteen minutes before I cautiously opened the door and saw his half-inch-deep and six- to seven-inch-long claw scratch marks in the planks of my wooden entry point.

After examining the claw marks, I turned toward my right to scan the wood line and was quickly brought up short. I was astounded to see a Golden Eagle feather stuck in the ground about three feet from the door. A thin, half-inch band of beads about two feet long was tied to it! I picked up the feather and beads and examined them more closely.

What in the heck, I pondered, did this talisman mean? Was it some sort of Native American amulet? And who would have put it there? *Maybe someone's sneaking around my cabin,* I thought to myself. I immediately slowly scanned the wood line of the surrounding forest before turning and walking back inside. I placed the objects on my one and only table. Thinking to myself, *I guess I'll have to keep an eye open for any strangers in the area. Plus, I'll definitely need to talk to Dave about this.*

After I walked inside, I found my hammer and a box of nails. I drove a nail into the wall next to my front door and then hung the feather and beads from it. Stepping back from my handiwork, I again scrutinized the mysterious present.

What did it mean? I wondered. *Who could have left it and why?*

Still, for the time being, Mr. Griz remained somewhat non-aggressive. I was the interloper and I guess he was just protecting his territory. My biggest fear came one day while I was using the latrine which was located on the side of the cabin some fifteen feet from the front (and only!) cabin door. I heard Mr. Griz approaching outside and could smell his pungent animal scent. He sniffed around the flimsy door—I could see him through the cracks—but he just snorted and moved off. Scared the pee willies—among other things—right out of me! I finished up, grabbed my Winchester, and inched open the thin door. Mr. Griz vanished so I quickly walked back into the cabin and barred the door.

By late August, the snow began to fall. I saw the grizzly a few more times, but by the end of the month, with eighteen inches of snow on the ground, Mr. Griz disappeared. I hoped he had holed up somewhere and gone into hibernation for the winter. But one thing still puzzled me. For some unexplainable reason, I didn't have "The Terrors" for about a week after I saw Mr. Griz and found the eagle's feather and beads. It was as if the bear—or was it the eagle's feather?—had temporarily healed or put my nightmares in abeyance. Yet, within six to seven days, "The Terrors" slowly seeped back into my life. When they did, the dreams seemed to lessen in intensity, and I didn't wake up screaming as often as I had in the past.

Now, what was that all about? I wondered one day. *Was the bear some sort of magical or mystical talisman?* Back in eastern Kentucky, many of the much older mountain folks looked on bears as a good luck omen. But, I continued to ruminate, *did that apply to grizzlies?*

I had no answer to my question.

Early one morning, sometime around mid-September—I failed to keep track of time as I had deliberately not purchased a calendar when stocking up on supplies—I heard a snowmobile far off in the distance coming in my direction. I stood by the front door and waited. About fifteen minutes later, a bundled-up figure appeared and pulled up in front of the cabin. It was Dave.

"Howdy, man!" he said as he dismounted from his snowmobile, giving me a big smile. "Thought I'd come up and check on you! Looks like you're still alive. No Iceman yet! Ha! Ha!" He pulled a six-pack of Budweiser off the back seat of the snowmobile along with a bakery box.

"Got you some beer and a little present from Nancy," he mentioned with a conspiratorial grin suggestively raising his left eyebrow and giving me a wink. He untied two bungee cords holding two packages firmly in place on the snowmobile's back steel rack and carried them into the cabin.

Gesturing with a highly exaggerated swing of my arm, I showed him inside. Placing Nancy's package on the kitchen table, he then quickly cracked open two Buds, handed one to me and took a long swig from his. The really cold beer was a welcome taste! We then sat down on the two sofas in front of the fireplace.

"What's been going on?" he asked. "No problems, I hope?"

"Well," I replied, "there seems to be a slight one." I then described my various encounters with the grizzly, along with the appearance of the feather and beads, which I drew his attention to on the wall. I mentioned how "The Terrors" seemed to lessen after each sighting of the mysterious bear. Dave listened in silence while I told my tale, but when I finished, he gave me a quizzical look and a serious expression descended over his face. He frowned, stroked his chin, and rocked back and forth on the sofa before he took a long sip of his beer.

"Jesse," he said with a serious tone in his voice, "you're going to think I'm absolutely motherf-cking, batsh-t crazy when I tell you something, but just listen." He continued, "I think you have encountered a mythical Spirit Bear. Otherwise, any normal *griz* would have made a quick meal of you—especially when you were in the can!" He chortled at his last remark. I laughed with him.

Continuing, Dave intoned, "My people have spoken of a sacred grizzly who has shown itself off and on for several hundreds of years, but *only* to our people. You're the first white man I know of who's actually seen it. As for the Golden Eagle's feather and beads, all I can say is that the eagle is a sacred bird to our people. But I'm baffled by what the beads mean. Why they both were left outside this cabin and by whom or what, I have absolutely no explanation."

I sat there across the sofa from Dave as disbelief spread across my face. "Dave," I said, "I find your story amazing and almost unbelievable. Why me?"

This makes no sense at all, I thought.

"I can't tell you why," he replied as he shook his head back and forth. "But," Dave continued, "I'm going to talk to some of our elders when I get back and see what they have to say. What's happened to you is incredibly strange, to say the least. Be careful when you have to go outside," he sternly warned. "Survey the area before you walk away from the cabin's door. Always, always," he deeply stressed, "carry your Winchester and double-check to make sure it's fully loaded with a round in the chamber! Around here, being in grizzly country, an unchambered round can be a death sentence."

We sat for a few more minutes and talked until we finished our second beers before Dave said he had to go. We stood. I walked over to the bakery box and opened it. Nancy baked me an apple pie!

Turning to Dave, I felt my face turning a bit reddish. "Dave, please thank Nancy so much for me! I know it'll be good, so I'll probably finish it off in two or three days."

Dave's mouth broke into a huge grin. He patted me on the back, gave me a sly wink, and promised he would relay my message to her. Then he walked out the cabin door, mounted on his snowmobile, waved, and quickly left.

Reentering the cabin, I closed and barred the door before I sat on my sofa and thought about what Dave said concerning Mr. Griz. I didn't really think much about his being some sort of an Indian Spirit Bear. I'd seen a lot of black bears back in the Kentucky woods, but they sure didn't act strange or anything like the one I had encountered in the Montana woods. Maybe, I thought, the Rocky Mountain grizzlies were different. While I hadn't seen a lot of unexplainable things during my short lifespan, I didn't discount the fact such things *might* occur.

Back in *Kentuc'* I had listened to several of my folks' friends talk about the "haints" they had seen. Apparently, it seemed those ghosts took the form of dead parents, siblings, or ancestors. I found it somewhat hard to believe such preposterous tales, but, as I will relate further along in this story, my mind was changed forever by what I experienced on August 13, 1976.

So began my first winter sojourn. The snow began to fall hard in late September and early October. Without a calendar, I just didn't care about keeping track of the days or months. After all I was living the way I wanted to live, so why should I care about knowing the day? It wasn't long before I had six to seven feet of the white stuff surrounding my cabin. Every day, despite the bitter cold and ever constant wind, I bundled up in my fleece jacket, went outside, and shoveled a pathway to the outhouse. Although I had not seen the Spirit Bear, I again realized "The Terrors" didn't appear as often as they had in the past.

One morning while I was out shoveling the snow, which had

accumulated during the night, I heard the far distant sound of a snowmobile. Just as I finished throwing the last shovelful of snow out of the "necessary" pathway, Dave pulled up with Nancy riding behind him.

"Well, isn't this a surprise!" I said. "Good to see you both! Welcome, Nancy!"

She smiled shyly and said, "When Dave told me he was coming up to see you, I asked if I could hitch a ride. And here we are!"

"Well, come in, come in!" I said as I motioned with my left hand. "This is certainly a nice surprise," I continued. "I'm really happy to see you both!"

A layer of newly fallen powdery snow lay over the more frozen snowpack which supported the snowmobile. After dismounting and sinking at least six inches into last evening's snowfall, they disengaged two saddlebags from the rear of the snowmobile. Carrying the black leather bags over their shoulders, Dave and Nancy walked over to the edge of the six-foot-high snowbank. Then holding on to each other, they semi-sidestepped and easily slid down the snowdrift and toted their saddlebags inside.

As we entered my humble abode, I immediately thanked Nancy for her baked apple pie that Dave had previously delivered. She just smiled and her onyx eyes seemed to mesmerize me. She doffed her knit hat and shook her raven hair. Despite the dimness of the cabin, her hair tresses appeared to sparkle and light it up.

I quickly stoked the fire and put more logs on. It would heat up the one-room cabin rather quickly.

"I brought you some Budweiser," Dave said as he pulled twelve beers out of his saddlebag. "Plus," he continued, "I have some information on the grizzly."

"And I," Nancy announced with some excitement, "baked you another pie!" She placed it on the cabin's lone and wobbly wooden table with an exaggerated flourish. "It's a peach cobbler," she said enthusiastically as her mouth turned into a large grin and her onyx eyes began their hypnotizing sparkle.

Oh, those incredible eyes, I thought to myself. *So beautiful and so mesmerizing!*

After profusely thanking them both, I guided them over to the two dilapidated sofas located in front of the fireplace and gestured for them to sit. Nancy sat next to me while Dave ensconced himself on the second sofa across from us. We chatted while sipping on our beers. They brought me up to date on what was happening back in "The World," an idiom Dave used before we both laughed. "The World" had been what we had called the United States while we were in Vietnam because we believed we were on some far distant planet out in the jungle.

"Hey, Jess," Dave said, "I've got some news about your *friend*, the grizzly."

"Well," I chuckled, "I wouldn't exactly call him my friend."

All three of us chuckled and took a swig of our beers.

"I spoke with the elders," Dave said, "and they all had a consensus Mr. Griz is most likely the Spirit Bear I previously mentioned to you. Two of the elders told me they had ancestors who saw a grizzly acting in a way which indicated it was guarding or protecting them from some danger. In one case it chased away a mountain lion which had crept up on their hunting party."

Dave continued, "In another instance, the ancestor crept too close to a bull buffalo he was stalking. The shaggy haired beast suddenly turned, charged, and tossed the hunter up into the air. He landed and was badly hurt. The bison started to lunge at the fallen man, perhaps to gore him, when the Spirit Bear appeared from out of nowhere, roared at the buffalo, and charged it. Even with the poor eyesight buffalo have, the bison quickly realized he was no match for the four to five hundred-pound grizzly barreling down on him, so he turned and fled."

Continuing, he told us, "The bear roared again, then came over and plopped down next to the badly injured man as if to protect or guard him. It even licked one of his leg wounds! As soon as the grizzly heard the rest of the hunting party approaching, he gave another roar and quickly fled to the edge of the nearby forest. The Spirit Bear's roars had guided the rest of the hunters to the injured man. After the hunting party bandaged him up, the badly battered tribesman described the beast and what it had done to protect him. The other hunting party members looked for its footprints and wondered why they had failed to find any trace of one. But, mysteriously, they too, found an eagle's feather attached to a band of beads stuck in the ground near the wood line."

I was intrigued by Dave's tale and asked him some further clarifying questions. I also told them my "Terrors" seemed to have lessened significantly after each of my encounters with Mr. Griz. For fifteen to twenty minutes, we discussed whether or not his appearances had anything to do with the change in the frequency of my nightmares. It was, indeed, an unfathomable mystery which puzzled me.

Dave told me the elders had some thoughts about the mysterious appearance of the feather and beads. The tribe's wise men told him they believed the objects might possibly have some sort of potent power and I shouldn't throw them away. The elders also believed the feather and beads might represent some kind of protection or mystical power. But they warned there might also be an ominous sign behind the amulet's appearance, so I should continue to be wary. Still, Dave continued, the tribe's seers had no explanation as to who, or what, might have left the amulet in front of my cabin.

"Well, Dave and Nancy," I said in reply to Dave's tale, "I guess I'd better hold onto the feather and beads. Maybe they'll indeed bring me good luck!"

Having wound down our thoughts concerning the Spirit Bear, the feather, and the beads, Nancy leaned over and placed her hand on my arm. As she looked at me, her onyx eyes again seemed to hypnotize me. She said, "Jess, I've got good news! I have been accepted into a two-year respiratory therapy program at Flathead Community College. I started in late September."

I was delighted, and leaned over and gave her a big shoulder hug, saying, "Wow!!! That's absolutely wonderful, Nancy! I know you'll be a great respiratory therapist and I'm really happy for you!"

She blushed as Dave and I spent some time discussing her future career. Nancy indicated she would continue to work as an LPN between her studies and classroom work until she received her degree in respiratory therapy.

After talking for several hours, Dave said they needed to get back. It would be a good hour-and-a-half trek out on their snowmobiles until they reached the area where they had parked their trucks and could load up the machines. I turned to Nancy and asked her if she would take some of the books I had finished reading and sell them back to the used bookstore. She readily agreed and said she would buy some more used books for me with the money she received for the batch of returned books. No mention was made as to when she might return with new books.

Dave rose and told Nancy to wait until he warmed up the snowmobile. So, she and I were alone. I reached for and held her hand. We both quickly embraced and held a long kiss as we entwined together.

As we parted I said, "I've missed you. Again, congratulations on your being accepted into the respiratory therapy program. I'm so happy and proud of you!"

She smiled as she rose from the sofa and thanked me.

We kissed again and had just parted when Dave yelled he was ready. I hastily grabbed ten or twelve books, dropped them into the saddlebags, and handed them to her. I also gave her another quick kiss before ushering her outside. I waited in the doorway until they quickly waved and were out of sight within, what seemed to me, to be seconds.

I was saddened to see them go. It had been a relaxing few hours. Now I was back into loner mode. I really enjoyed my time alone. I wasn't too outgoing around strangers. The war continually weighed heavily on my mind. Plus, I had forty to fifty books to read when I wasn't working outside the cabin. I usually retired around 8:oo p.m. and slept eight to ten hours, unless my sleep was interrupted by another Vietnam nightmare. Then I was usually up for the rest of the night as I couldn't get back to sleep. PTSD. I knew it would never go away, but I hoped in time, it and the nightmares would abate somewhat.

It took me only three days to finish off the peach cobbler Nancy brought me. As a rule, I didn't eat much. There was never a lot of food out in Vietnam's jungle, so we, and our stomachs, adjusted to less. It was a habit I carried back into civilian life. What small amount of energy I expended during the winter came from my daily clearing of the pathway to the privy from either new, or drifting, snow. Otherwise, I did little else and never got hungry enough to eat three square meals a day. One was usually enough along with the eight or nine glasses of water I normally drank to keep hydrated.

My weeks passed by peacefully. At night I heard either wolves howling off in the distance, or the owls hooting. During the day when it wasn't snowing, or the boreal wind had abated, I forced myself to get out and tramp around the cabin on top of the deepening powdery snow unless the wind had blown it away before it had time to harden. I used that tiresome chore for what stood for the little exercise I could accomplish.

On several occasions I spotted elk, or perhaps moose, tracks. I also saw numerous deer tracks, and one morning when I opened my cabin door, there were two deer about fifty feet away standing underneath a pine tree nibbling on its branches. Hearing me, they quickly turned and disappeared back into the woods kicking up snow as they took flight. Plus, there were always numerous small animal tracks that, except for birds, I was unable to identify.

Even though I was alone, I also realized the forest contained predators who might decide I'd make a good meal. One time, when I wandered toward the creek, I saw six or seven pairs of wolf tracks which came within twenty to twenty-five feet of the cabin. I hoped I would never have to kill an animal. After all, I was living in their territory and they had just as much a right to be there as I did. The PTSD constantly reminded me I'd killed more than enough people for several lifetimes during my stint in 'Nam. I didn't need to add killing any critters to my life—unless they were trying to kill me!

About three weeks after Dave and Nancy visited, I experienced four straight days of snow and bitingly cold wind which seemed to always find a crack in the exterior of my cabin and filter its cold breath inside. Outside it was dreary and overcast. The clouds seemed to lower themselves until they drifted through the trees with an eerie and ghostlike mist as the snow continued to pile up. After the snowfall stopped during the fourth night, I exited my premises in the early morning and attempted to circumnavigate my living quarters by foot. It was hard going because the powdery snow hadn't yet solidified. Thus, I found myself constantly sinking into the snow up to my knees. While I found the going a lot slower than I had imagined, I quickly realized I was creating a walkable pathway around the cabin—at least until the next snow!

I had trudged about three-quarters the way around my living quarters, when I heard a snowmobile off in the distance. It sounded like it was straining to push through the new powder.

Someone comin' my way, I thought as I watched my breath turn into mist. I picked up my pace as best I could. By the time I completed my circumnavigation of the cabin, about ten minutes had passed. The snowmobile's sound was much closer. I waited outside my door and within a short time, the machine appeared. I recognized Nancy right away.

She pulled to a stop, popped off her helmet, shook her glistening raven-colored hair and said, "Howdy, stranger!"

"Great to see you, Nancy," I enthusiastically replied as a wide grin crossed my face. "*C'mon* in."

She waded through the snow and slid down the eight-foot snowbank right into my arms.

We had a rather long lingering kiss before I led her inside and shut the door.

"What brings you all the way out here at this time of the winter?" I curiously asked.

"Well, I'm bringing an invitation from Dave, Alice, and myself," she replied before quickly continuing. "It's three days before Christmas, and we all want you to come in and spend it with us."

"Wow! For real?" I queried. "I don't want to be in anyone's way," I weakly protested.

"Yep! Sure is. We all want you to spend Christmas and New Year's with us," she replied as she bounced over to me, grabbed both sides of my now open jacket, drew close and planted a nice warm kiss on me. Afterwards, we seemed to lose our clothes rather quickly and ended up under the three Pendleton blankets I kept on my bed.

An hour later, we emerged from our blanket-like cocoon and hastily dressed in the chilly room.

"With your extra weight," Nancy commented, "it's going to take us a lot longer to reach my truck. I had to park another four miles further down the road, where the county stops plowing. The snow is too high for my truck from there to the trailhead which we normally use." She glanced at her watch. "It's almost noon now. If we're lucky, we might make it home around six."

After pouring water on the almost dead fireplace ashes, I gathered up some dirty clothes and shoved them into a bag. I quickly closed the cabin, mounted the snowmobile behind Nancy, held lightly onto her waist, and we took off. Since she'd broken trail coming out to my place, the return trip was a little bit easier but still took us almost three hours to travel eight to nine miles to reach her fire engine red Chevy 1971 C/K10 truck.

So began a rhythm in my life of spending Christmas and New Year's with Dave, Alice, Nancy, and their families. Plus, there were other holidays, like Easter, Veterans Day, or Memorial Day when they came and picked me up for short three- to four-day visits for which I was gratefully appreciative. After all, it was nice to take a hot shower instead of a quick dip and scrub in the icy cold creek! Plus, I did get to do my meager laundry which was becoming rather threadbare. When Nancy noticed any threadbare pieces, she threw them away and took me shopping for more.

I slowly began to feel as if, for once, I had a real family who cared for me. My time with them was quite different from the way I had been raised. Growing up in backwoods Kentucky, I always felt isolated except when I attended elementary and high school. Since Shifflett's Hollow was so far off the beaten track, I didn't often get to see many of my high school acquaintances. Only a few of my high school friends would drive six to seven miles on the twisty, curvy gravel and dirt road to pick me up and take me to town to attend football or basketball games. Hell, due to the narrowness of the road, even the school bus turned around about two miles from my house leaving me to trudge the last stretch of road in good, bad, rainy, and snowy weather. Not a lot of nice memories. I was glad I hadn't returned to my Kentucky home in the sticks after my wartime tour of duty.

At the conclusion of my quick sojourns with Dave and his family, I always felt refreshed when I returned to my mountain hideaway. Plus, my "Terrors" seemed to abate during those Christmas interludes. Still, in some mystical way, I began to miss being with Nancy more and more. The longer I stayed in my cabin, the more I seemed not only to pine for her, but also, I began to think of her daily. Our trysts were far and few between and usually late at night so as not to wake Dave or Alice who slept two rooms down the hall. We both learned to whisper in hushed tones! Yet, subconsciously, I believed Dave and Alice probably knew that Nancy and I were spending the night together. But neither one of them ever gave me a raised eyebrow, a knowing smile, or a subtle nod to indicate either one of them knew we were sleeping together. If they did indeed know, they were certainly incredibly discreet about that knowledge.

Of course, whenever Nancy rode up to my cabin for a day to bring me books or supplies, we had a little more time alone together. After the winter snow melted in the spring, we explored the area around my cabin site, sometimes walking a half mile or a little bit more in one direction or the other. Our explorations of the forest depended on how much my leg could take before the pain started to set in causing us to turn back and head for the cabin. Although the creek was always cold, we enjoyed crossing it to where we usually sat on the large flat rock and ate our picnic lunch. During our hikes, we never encountered Mr. Griz but I remained constantly vigilant and armed in case something untoward was to occur. At various times during our excursions, I always felt somewhat uneasy, as if someone—or something—was silently stalking us, but, although I sensed it, I never saw anything.

Early January 1974, Dave and Alice scheduled their wedding for mid-May. Nancy, who had just finished her first year studying respiratory therapy and passed with sterling colors, picked me up and brought me back to Kalispell for the festivities. No sooner had we walked into Dave and Alice's abode when Nancy, holding her nose and teasingly sniffing in the air, grabbed my arm and told me to get a quick shower because we were going shopping for some new clothes for me. I chuckled, then put up a small and useless protest (about the clothes—not the shower!) which obviously didn't work. So, I quickly hopped into the shower. No sooner had I stepped underneath the hot water when Nancy suddenly appeared and joined me. I guess we were lucky no one else was at home!

Driving into town, Nancy parked in a small lot behind some of the stores facing Main Street. First stop was Dusty's, a jeans emporium, where after Nancy's seal of approval, I purchased three Levi's. She then led me across the street from Dusty's into the Bar-H, a clothing store. With Nancy's approval as to size, design, and fit, I ended up with four brightly colored western shirts each with pearl-colored snap buttons. Of course, Nancy insisted one of the shirts had to be white for the upcoming nuptials. I chose one, after Nancy's nod, that had raised embroidered western jacquard (another Miss Eula word!) designs in white. A few doors down from the Bar-H, we dropped into Jack's Men's Shop where I purchased two packs of Hanes underwear with six briefs in each package.

Since Kalispell was the gateway to the western entrance of Glacier Park, a lot of tourists stopped there to stay overnight in one of the many hotels which dotted the Montana landscape around the town. Those same tourists also dropped a lot of money on dining, shopping, T-shirts, and souvenirs.

Exiting Jack's, Nancy grabbed my purchases, told me to wait while she took them back to her car, then hurried down the street. Quickly returning five minutes later, she grabbed my hand and we ambled down Main Street until we reached Glacier T-shirts which had many colorful tees displayed in its front window. I definitely needed some new T-shirts, and with her approval as to the design on each shirt, Nancy let me pick out five with various colorful Montana and Glacier Park scenes. Just as we were about to leave the shop, I espied another tee I just had to have. On the front was a picture of a huge grizzly bear swiping its paw into water with a trout flying upwards into the air. I bought it.

Leaving Glacier T-shirts, I thought we were, at last, finished shopping. But, NO! My onyx-eyed beauty grabbed my arm tightly and led me across the street to the town's barber's establishment. I tried to stop dead in my tracks on the sidewalk, but she quickly and firmly admonished me.

"Look, buster, you're getting your hair nicely trimmed for the wedding and your beard also needs tidying up!"

"But—" I started to protest as I scratched my rather long beard which had begun to turn grey in spots.

"Jesse," she quickly interrupted and shook her finger, "there are no 'buts.' You WILL get your hair taken care of for my brother's wedding. End of discussion."

So, I complied and meekly followed her into the barber's shop where she proceeded to instruct the barber exactly what my hair and beard needed to look like by the time we departed. Forty-five minutes later I emerged with my hair significantly shorter and my Grizzly Adams beard nicely trimmed into a two-inch length. Looking at myself in the barber's mirror, I realized Nancy had been right. Yet, I noticed that some grey hair had also crept into the sides of my head.

Geez! I thought. *I'm too frigging young to have grey hair. I'm only twenty-three! Hell, almost twenty-four.* But, I sadly remembered, the 'Nam had really done a job on me.

On our way home, Nancy swung by the Salish Trading Post, a store devoted solely to Native American goods and crafts. The owner, who looked like he was a centenarian, greeted us as we stepped inside. Nancy greeted him in the Salish language, and as I later learned, continued with her proper tribal identification. I glanced around the tidy store and enjoyed viewing all the Indian art hanging on the walls while she talked to the owner. Then, holding my hand rather firmly, she marched me over to a jewelry case containing thirty to forty turquoise pendants for bolo ties. We examined a few before the shop's wizened owner handed me a pendant in the form of a bear set in silver.

Had he heard, I wondered, from the Indian telegraph about my encounter with Mr. Griz?

Then, I stupidly realized, of course, the entire Salish nation has probably heard about the crazy White Man, who had purchased George's cabin up in the middle of bumf-ck nowhere and who also had encountered the Spirit Bear.

At any rate, the deal was sealed and I quickly purchased the pendant. It set me back some $200 but it looked absolutely beautiful when I held it up to the ceiling light. The weathered shop owner also threw in a leather bolo string tie with silver-tipped ends. I slid the decorative clasp upwards and quickly realized the purchase was well worth it after seeing the smile on Nancy's face.

The store also had some beautiful Navajo-made earrings, pendants, and rings. Despite her half-hearted protests, I insisted on buying her a piece of jewelry for the wedding. After looking at a few sets of earrings and trying them on, she settled on a multi-colored pair which were rectangular in shape and dangled underneath her earlobes. She wore them out of the store after I purchased them.

As we left the store, Nancy held my hand and said, "Now you've got a very nice tie to wear to the wedding with the white western shirt you just bought."

Aha! I smiled. So there was a method to her madness!

Two days later, Dave and Alice were wedded in a ceremony attended by seventy to eighty family members and friends. Afterwards, their reception was held at a local golf club and the happy couple climbed into Dave's truck and headed out on their honeymoon. They would spend the night in Missoula and then fly to the Hawaiian island of Kauai for their vacation. I was happy for them both. Good people. And they had done so much for me.

Nancy and I had the house to ourselves! We had a wonderful time being together for three days. While sleeping beside her, I didn't have one episode of "The Terrors"! After our short and delightful hiatus together, Nancy drove me back to the cabin. She was attending a summer school session which started on June 1 and involved on-the-job training in the hospital for her continued respiratory training program. The summer session would last for three months. Knowing she would be incredibly busy, I doubted I'd see much of her over the summer.

About a week later I turned twenty-four years old and realized I'd seen and done a lot in my short lifespan. Life had thrown me a lot of curve balls, and somehow, I had managed to overcome them and push onward. Despite Vietnam and all the death I had seen, I was content with my life even though I still suffered from the effects of my knee wound and PTSD. I had my cabin and, of course, a good woman in Nancy.

Still, I was amazed that we had become lovers. Our affair was not something I had ever expected to happen. Since we did not often see each other, I think the distance helped bring us closer when we were together. We hardly talked about our relationship—or where it was headed. We seemed happy just to let things evolve without either one of us putting pressure on the other. She appeared to be both excited and cheerful when we were together, which made me a lot happier.

I spent the summer of 1974 ranging around the forest every day, hiking as far as my knee would allow me before signaling it was time to head back. At times on those short hikes, I sensed a wraith-like presence which seemed to shadow me. I knew it probably had to be Mr. Griz but I never laid eyes on him. During these hikes, when my mind sensed an unknown presence, I felt somewhat uneasy. Instead of being the hunter, as if I was back in Vietnam, I now felt the tables had turned, and I was the one being stalked.

It was, I thought, an interesting conundrum. If it was Mr. Griz, why was he silently tracking me? Yet, at the same time, my intuition told me I still needed to be constantly alert because, out there in the woods, the beast could easily make a quick lunch of me if he so desired.

I also spent a lot of my free time chopping wood for use during the wintertime. One day, as I rested on a chair outside my cabin door basking in the warm sunlight and reading a book by Daphne DuMaurier, titled *Rebecca*, I heard strange crashing noises coming from the woods off to my left. It wasn't long before Mr. Griz appeared at the wood line, about a hundred feet away. He stared at me, and I at him. Knowing my .225 Winchester was fully loaded and leaning against the cabin's wall two feet away, I decided to sit tight and see what Mr. Griz would do, so I set my book aside. For several minutes he stood on all fours while he sniffed the air around him. As he swung his head back and forth, he emitted a low growl every few seconds as the wind brought a myriad of new scents to his sensitive nose. I'm sure my sweat and aroma was included in those smells. I had absolutely no doubt in my mind that he could see and smell me. After a few minutes, he lay down as if to send me some sort of subliminal signal he wasn't as dangerous as I might have believed.

The grizzly knew I was there, but he made no move to approach any closer. Little did I know at the time, but two years hence, the Spirit Bear would play a significant and incredible—no, almost unbelievable—role in my life. It would be a life-altering event which no one would find credible—especially you, my reader. Most likely, as we used to say back home, they would think I was just a little "tetched" in the head. But I know it was all true because I was there and experienced it first-hand. And what happened changed my life forever.

Mr. Griz and I stared at each other for about fifteen minutes. Every so often he swatted at the flies swarming around his face. Since the wind was blowing toward me, I could smell his scent even from a distance of one hundred feet. The odor was somewhat musty mixed with a woodsy and earthy smell as it wafted over to me. Then, with no warning, he suddenly stood and shook his fur coat, sending leaves, twigs, and pine needles flying everywhere. Taking a last look at me, he gave a loud growl, turned, and ambled nonchalantly back into the woods disappearing from sight in seconds.

To me it seemed Mr. Griz and I were developing some kind of incomprehensible and unfathomable strange symbiotic relationship. Every seven to eight days, usually while I was always relaxing and reading outside with my chair tilted against the cabin's wall, he would make an unexpected appearance. Sometimes he just magically materialized from the wood line without a sound, which I found most unsettling. It was as if he was a ghost who had suddenly materialized out of nowhere. On other occasions, I could hear him tramping through the underbrush and huffing and grunting along with a low growl. Yet, he always exited the wood line at the exact same place and kept the one hundred-foot distance between us.

At times during these somewhat regular weekly visits, after Mr. Griz had emerged in his entirety, within a minute or so, a filmy-like mist began to materialize behind his head. It slowly surrounded the rest of his body making his torso invisible. I felt as if I was looking straight through him because I thought—or imagined—I could see the wooded background behind where his large body should have blocked it out.

Am I hallucinating? I wondered. Whenever this mysterious invisibility manifested itself, I just shook my head in total disbelief. *Such invisibility, inevitably,* I marveled in awe, *is causing me to conclude I might be going crazy! Is living in this wilderness really such a good thing for me?* I was astounded as to why these occurrences were happening to me.

Oddly, on the morning of the next day after his first misty and ghostlike appearance, I found a second talisman stuck in the ground outside of my cabin's door, except this time, it consisted of two Golden Eagle feathers and another band of beads! I gathered them up, walked back inside my cabin, and hung them on a nail next to the one I'd already placed there.

What was this all about? I asked myself. *What was the purpose behind these eagle feathers and the bands around them?* I wondered, *were they some sort of charm to protect me?*

Perhaps I would never know.

Dave and Alice, back from their honeymoon, visited in early July. I could hear Dave's blue 1970 Chevy C/K10 slowly chugging its way along the steep forest road. As they stepped out of the truck, I greeted them both with a big hug and invited them inside. Dave grabbed a case of Dos Equis out of the truck bed and Alice picked up a bakery box. I intuitively knew who had made me something delicious. After Alice placed the box on my table, I took a quick peek. Nancy baked me a blueberry pie!

We sat on the sofas in front of the fireplace, its embers dead, and drank the Mexican beer. I asked them to tell me about their visit to Kauai, which they jovially described in great detail while they showed me numerous photos of the beautiful Hawaiian island and themselves. They mentioned a yacht cruise they'd taken around the southwest part of the island to view Kauai's Nāpali coast which was inaccessible by car. In all, I gathered, they experienced an unforgettable and wonderful time on their honeymoon. I was happy for both of them.

Alice casually mentioned Nancy by telling me she had been exceptionally busy with her summer internship. I asked her to pass on not only my best wishes to Nancy, but also thanks for the pie. Dave and Alice never asked me any type of probing questions or made any indirect comments in hopes of eliciting my thoughts concerning my relationship with Nancy. Yet, I got the distinct impression they already surmised, or knew, we were lovers. Dave told me Nancy had a three-day break coming up in a week or so. Alice added that she might try to come up to visit me for a day. I just nodded and nonchalantly smiled.

Our discussion soon turned to my numerous encounters with Mr. Griz. When I mentioned the invisible phenomenon, they were stunned and sat with their mouths agape. Dave just shook his head. They were even more astounded when I mentioned I found a second set of feathers. I pointed to the cabin's wall where I'd hung the charms.

"Jess," Dave said, "you really need to be extremely careful with the Spirit Bear. Don't be lulled to sleep by his sudden non-threatening appearances. I have no idea what's happening, but it certainly defies logic and is incredibly eerie."

I assured them both I was being as careful as possible because I, too, had no idea what was happening or what Mr. Griz's random appearances meant.

"Well," Dave said, "I'll mention this new information to the elders and see what their thoughts and opinions might be. The next time I'm up here, I'll pass on their comments." Then, half-jokingly, he asked, "Are you sure you're not part Indian?"

His unexpected question got a laugh out of each of us.

I scratched my head, shrugged, and said, "Well, my Ma always *tolt* us we might be descended from a Cherokee or a Shawnee tribe but she weren't too sure about it. It was just some sort of family myth handed down through generations. So, what you said *jus'* might be true."

I suddenly realized, as I talked to Dave, almost every time I mentioned my Kentucky background, I tended to revert to my hillbilly argot which I tried so hard to lose. I made a mental note again to try and stop doing it. Where I lived in Kentucky, no one kept any type of family tree or records, except maybe in their Bibles. Most people in Appalachia were poorly educated and could only remember as far back as their grandparents, then the ancestry line mysteriously dimmed or faded into nonexistence. Most likely their failure to accurately recall their progenitors was due to the fact there had probably been some inbreeding or mixing of races in the distant past which needed to be covered up.

Dave nodded and said, "Well, perhaps that explains why the Spirit Bear has chosen to reveal himself to you, because, as I told you previously, Jesse, he's only revealed himself to Native Americans. I'll mention to the elders you may have some Cherokee or Shawnee blood."

We talked for another half hour until Dave said they had to leave because they needed to get home and dress up for a couple's party they were attending in a few hours. We rose. I walked them out to the truck and bid them a sad goodbye.

A few weeks later, Nancy came for a four-hour visit but it was the last time I saw her until the end of her summer study. About a month after Dave and Alice's visit, Dave showed up early one morning. Exiting his truck, he greeted me.

"Hey, Jesse, it's Saturday and for once, I don't have to work over the weekend for the construction company."

Dave brought some beer—Budweiser this time—so we popped tops and relaxed, taking sips as we sat outside on pine needles, our backs resting against two pine trees. The day was warm with only wisps of clouds peeking through the pine treetops. After some small talk about Alice and Nancy, he took a long swig of beer and then set the half-empty can down beside him and looked seriously at me.

"Jess," Dave said in a more serious tone, "I spoke with the elders as I promised. They agreed the Spirit Bear's invisibility is definitely significant. Not one of them however, had any idea as to what it means or foretells. The wise men did tell me the appearance of the second set of feathers and beads is indeed an important omen. They all now believe those items stand for some sort of good luck and protection. But"—he emphasized, pointing his finger up and down at the rug—"they emphatically warned me you shouldn't get complacent over the protective part. Mr. Griz may be a spirit, but he might turn on you in a second. I did tell them you might have some Cherokee or Shawnee blood in you and they all agreed that's why you can probably see the Spirit Bear." He looked at me with a smile as he patted me on the back and knowingly said, "So, I guess your family myth might be a little bit true."

I shrugged my shoulders and just nodded my head a few times. "Dave, you said 'probably' see the Spirit Bear. Are you suggesting I might only be imagining him?"

"No, no," Dave replied. "I'm sure he's real, but you still need to take precautions. Bears, especially grizzlies, as you know, are unpredictable. They have three-inch long teeth and a bite that exerts 1,100 psi which will easily crush your head like an egg."

Dave continued, "Since it's likely you might have some Indian blood, the elders emphasized to me the bear's prior encounters with our ancestors always had to do with some type of *nebulous* protection. They have no idea why you might need protecting but they warned me to tell you to be on guard or extremely careful while you're outside."

"Wow!" I said. "Your information just boggles my mind. Protection? Humph! I wonder what the beast's purpose can be vis-à-vis with me? You know I go for short hikes in the woods here, and at times, I have sensed the presence of something—perhaps Mr. Griz—when I'm out wandering around. I wonder if the Spirit Bear is looking out for me, or is he some sort of warning to stay closer to the cabin?"

"Sorry, Jess, I can't tell you anything more. I'd say don't alter your routine around the cabin, or while you hike, but *be aware*, and carry your rifle fully loaded—that includes *always* keeping a round chambered when you're outside. That one round may save your life."

I nodded and thanked him for the sage advice.

We popped open two more beers and talked for another twenty or so minutes. As we finished off our second Buds, Dave said, "I *gotta* get back to Kalispell, Jess, because Alice has planned a dinner at our home with two other couples."

"Welcome to married life!" I joked giving him a great big grin as I patted him on the shoulder.

He just smiled as we both stood, and said, "You ought to try it—it's not so bad!" He gave me an enigmatic smile, raised his eyebrows, and gave me a thumbs up.

Now, what does he mean? I thought as I smiled at his comment. Did he really think, or hope, or was he surreptitiously hinting that Nancy and I should get married? Did he even approve of our relationship? I didn't have a clue as to where my relationship was headed with Nancy as I had never had any type of serious discussion about it with her. As I thought about what Dave had just said, I pondered, *Has she said something to Dave or Alice?*

Dave had given me much to ruminate over. But I now knew he had to know we were lovers.

I walked him over to his truck. We shook hands and patted each other on the shoulder. We said our goodbyes, gave each other a brief manly hug, and then he was off in his blue C/K10. Just before he passed out of sight, he gave me a wave out of his window and then raised his arm and gave me the peace sign with his two of fingers. I waved back with the peace sign.

A week later, Mr. Griz dropped by as I was sitting outside in my chair tilted against the cabin's wall. I had been idly whittling on a piece of wood with no thought as to carving it into any kind of shape. This time, without any approaching signs, the bear ambled out of the woods a bit closer than on previous occasions—perhaps fifty to sixty feet away. My alert senses banished my idle torpor and musing. Quickly checking my Remington's location, I looked at him with some awe, a bit of wariness, but also curiosity.

Then I realized, *If he charges me, fat chance I'll have of stopping him with a bullet before he's on me. That'll just piss him off. I'd be better off running inside the cabin, closing the door, and hoping I can get the bars in place.*

I just couldn't imagine a grizzly bear protecting me. I thought, *This defies nature's law. What does it all mean?* I just didn't know if I could believe Dave's, or the elders', information. *Was something ominous and deadly inexorably headed my direction at some future time? And would the bear be part of it as some form of protection?* Swinging his head for four or five minutes and sniffing in the air, Mr. Griz stood on his hind legs and roared. No sooner had the roar died down than he turned and vanished back into the wood line. I couldn't even hear him moving through the woods.

Once early on after one of Mr. Griz's unexpected appearances and departures, I cautiously edged over to the wood line where he had emerged and exited. I hoped to examine his tracks leading back into the forest. I was amazed and surprised to find no visible trace of his footprints or any trace of his claw marks in the pine-needled forest floor. There was no indication whatsoever of the heavy bear's passing. Shaking my head with skepticism, I stared into the woody void. The forest had suddenly swallowed him up without a sound, perhaps, into some other dimension. He had simply vanished into thin air as soon as he turned and entered the wood line. Something beyond my keen sense was happening and I had absolutely no idea what it was or how I was supposed to mentally accept Mr. Griz's sudden and mysterious appearances.

I vaguely remembered an episode on the TV program *Star Trek* that I watched a few times after entering the army, but prior to being sent to 'Nam. In each installment, as I recalled, people were materializing back on the *Starship Enterprise* or on some new and weird alien world. I did find that concept just a little bit unbelievable but, here and now, the same things "appeared" to be happening to me.

I marveled, *was Mr. Griz a ghost? Or a figment of my imagination? Or, worse, was I hallucinating? Or really going mad? What kind of bear leaves no tracks or claw marks in the spongy wood soil?* I pondered about this turn of events and shook my head in disbelief. I was both puzzled, mystified, and intrigued all at the same time. I went through the exercise of looking for his tracks a few more times, but the result was always the same. Nothing. So, I gave up on looking for his prints.

It would be the last time I saw Mr. Griz that autumn as he probably went into hibernation. Fall was now in full swing and the air smelled of snow. My nose was correct. The next morning, after his apparent vanishing act, I woke to a dusting of snow, and when I looked out the cabin door, my eyes caught the wind moving what turned out to be a third set of feathers and beads. This time there were three Golden Eagle feathers, and the beaded band was twice as long as the previous ones I had found. I leaned over and picked them up.

Hmmm, I thought. *There has to be some sort of hidden message from whoever, or whatever, is leaving these. What the hell does it mean?* Then, for the first time, I realized there were no human footprints where the feathers had been stuck into the soil. I scratched my head. These trinkets made me feel uneasy as I placed the third set on the cabin wall next to the others.

Were they some sort of good luck charms—harbingers of luck to befall me? Or did their mysterious appearance foreshadow some malevolence in my future should I choose to remain living in my cabin up here in the middle of bumf-ck nowhere? Or were these charms some sort of messenger sent to keep me unsettled? Or were they a warning for me to leave and never return?

I thought about Nancy. I realized she'd be in full swing of her second year of studies by now. I was extremely happy for her because she was continuing her higher education. I knew I couldn't accomplish such a feat. Although I had confidence in my ability to meet most of life's challenges, I knew my eastern Kentucky education was far less than that needed for me to be accepted into any college or university. After all, college meant sitting in a classroom with twenty-five to thirty other people which would make me incredibly uneasy. After my experience in 'Nam, I hated being bunched up in crowds and tried assiduously to avoid them with a passion. Bad things happened in crowds, none for the good.

Seated around and among young naive college kids just scared the hell out of me. Worldly-wise, I knew far too much about the fate awaiting them at the end of their studies. They certainly had no clue as to the rough and tumble of what the real world would throw at them after college. Plus, I knew we'd be bunched up in a small classroom, maybe with no windows, with nowhere to go, hide, or take cover, should something untoward occur. I knew I couldn't carry a concealed pistol into a classroom, but I sure could hide my hunting knife in a shoulder sheath inside my tightly closed jacket.

The war's hidden effects continued to haunt me. I'd be trapped. Another Vietnam flashback played in my mind—*Don't mull around. You're a prime target for a grenade, an NVA ambush, or a mortar round.* Plus, as I previously mentioned, I didn't want my veteran's status revealed. It was no small wonder why I had become a loner. You can't live a settled life after killing people without being in constant fear of some unexpected live-or-die situation.

Another week elapsed and about mid-September winter hit with a chilling blast and dumped a foot of snow overnight. To my mind, it was an ominous sign. I quickly intuited I'd be in for a rough and extremely cold winter. The Siberian Express winds blasted down from the Arctic, picked up speed as they crossed Canada with a fury, and insured, by my reckoning, even though I didn't have any type of temperature gauge, that the temperature had plummeted far below zero.

I hoped that I'd be ready and prepared for winter's onslaught. During the summer I'd managed to chop up a lot of dead wood. I calculated I had over ten cords stacked up against the cabin's outer wall. I also checked for any chinks in my cabin's walls and filled them in with mud which hardened as it tightly filled each crack. I knew the thinness of the wooden walls wouldn't stop the cold from turning the cabin's inside into a chilly living area. But I had the fireplace to partially stop whatever cold seeped inside.

A few days later, Dave came up on his snowmobile and brought me back down to Kalispell because I needed to do some shopping. On the way down to town I mentioned the arrival of a third set of feathers. He shrugged, shook his head, and warned I needed to be more alert than ever.

Returning to Grizzly Used Books, I made sure to stock up on sixty-plus tomes from swashbuckling adventure stories by F. Van Wyck Mason, along with Westerns by Louis L'Amour and Luke Short. I even picked up some espionage novels by Helen McInness along with five to seven of the Travis McGee detective series by John D. MacDonald. In keeping up with my self-education, I also purchased histories of the Greeks, Romans, and a few on America's Revolutionary War period.

After loading up on books, Dave drove me to Glacier Outfitters where I purchased a few more personal comfort items like a thin rubber mat for my bed, two additional heavy Pendleton blankets, more body underwear, and ten pairs of woolen socks. Spotting some snowshoes, I surprised myself by purchasing a pair. With a walking stick for my bad leg and using the snowshoes, I had much more mobility. Now I could wander out and explore or just take short hikes several hundred yards away from the cabin. Finally, I picked up some small plastic containers about two inches long, each with a compass on their top, which were unscrewed. They fit easily into my jacket pockets and contained about fifty wooden matches each. I knew they might come in handy.

Dave came to visit using his snowmobile in October and November. He always brought some Dos Equis or Budweiser. I really appreciated his checking in with me every so often. Yet, I often wondered if he visited me more as an obligation for my saving his life back in the 'Nam, which neither one of us ever mentioned, or if he just enjoyed our brief visits and man-to-man discussions.

After all, unless they had been there, no one could really understand how the war affected us, what it was like, and what it did mentally to those of us who participated in it and survived, only to return to an America that thought we all were baby killers.

When Dave and I were alone we occasionally talked about Vietnam. We had a deep bond and tended to recall the more amusing incidents rather than having any deep conversations as to what we actually did as snipers, or which kills were more memorable than others. In all, we tacitly understood that the subject was *verboten*. The war we knew would never entirely really leave us. The darkness of our shared wartime experiences enabled us to have a *simpatico* relationship, which others, who had never experienced war, would never truly understand. Yet, our lives had been tremendously and psychologically altered by what happened to us during our Vietnam service. We intuitively knew we would never have the same type of life we led as younger men prior to being dropped into the middle of a jungle firefight for the first time.

It appeared to me that Dave came across as if, magically, he had somehow worked past the war and its horrifying side effects. In sum, he definitely appeared to be much more at ease with life in general even when we discussed 'Nam. Perhaps his calmness was due to his being my spotter and not a licensed executioner like me; although, while we were out in the jungle, he had also racked up seven or eight kills—confirmed by me! Whereas, I was still haunted by my Vietnam combat experiences. The PTSD was there, sitting on my shoulder— never leaving me alone, nagging at me. Perhaps, it was the forty-nine kills buried somewhere in my subconscious that unexpectedly came to the forefront of my mind. I just didn't know. Anyhow, I had to get past it even if only partially, but right now I enjoyed living alone and not having to deal with being around lots of people.

In early December, not two weeks after his last visit, Dave suddenly appeared early one morning.

I welcomed and ushered him into the cabin.

"What's up?" I asked. "This visit's somewhat unusual."

"Got something for you, Jess, and thought I'd better bring it up pronto." He reached into his jacket and handed me a letter. "It came to the house yesterday. It's from Jill. I knew you'd want to read it right away." On the outside upper left-hand corner was Jill's address in her uneven and barely legible scrawl. I opened it and started to read her almost indecipherable spelling written with a pencil in overly large, third grade-type of block letters.

Deer Jessy, Robert done got kilt in a cole mine cave inn. They ain't foun his body cuz it be burred unner a lot of roks. Dey say it mite bee ah yer befo they done fine him. I gots three kids. No monee and nothin'. Rob's parents done tolt me I cain still liv wif dem. But I gotta git a job now down at the cittee restaurant. Mr. Tate, he dun own it and tolt me I can bee a waittruss. If u got any monee u cain spare, pleese sen me sumpthin. Tanks. Hope u r OK. Yore sistah, Jill.

I just shook my head and handed the letter to Dave. He quickly scanned it. On several occasions I described my family situation to him so this development was no surprise to either of us.

"Well, this sure is a damn bad turn of events for Jill," I commented. "Let me get my checkbook. I'll send her a $3,000 check and hope it helps. Would you please take it with you and mail it? I sure would appreciate it."

Dave gave me a shoulder hug, smiled, patted me on the shoulder and said he would. I got my checkbook and wrote Jill a $3,000 check hoping it would help her a little bit. I handed it to Dave and he promised he'd mail it tomorrow. I thanked him profusely, told him to say hello to Alice and Nancy, and then he was quickly off.

After Dave departed, I sat in my chair in front of the fireplace and thought about my sister. I realized there wasn't a thing I could do except to send her some money every so often. I hoped she hadn't lost her good looks in the six years she'd been married. But as I well know, in the backwoods coal country mountains of eastern Kentucky, people tended not to eat properly, much less see the closest dentist who was located in Huntington some sixty-plus miles away. Thus, by their late twenties or early thirties, most backwoods people had already lost two or three teeth, or more.

I prayed Jill hadn't lost any teeth. Even though I was living alone, I always made sure to brush my teeth daily and use toothpicks. Maybe, I finally mused, another coal miner will marry her. With three kids, I sadly realized it was probably a forlorn hope. Otherwise, with no education, she was doomed. She was trapped in an unforgiving world with no way out. It saddened me.

Winter piled more snow up against my cabin. Still, I was getting some exercise by shoveling snow every day and throwing it up over an eight-foot-high snow embankment, but the ever-constant wind was always bitingly cold. It quietly and viciously crept inside of you, silently freezing your entire body. I always made sure my ears were tightly wrapped in a scarf, and I never stayed outside long for fear I might wind up with frostbite. Yet, it took more and more time for me to clear the pathway to the outhouse. After a while my left knee started to ache. I found myself taking longer breaks inside to warm it up before I went back outside to continue my shoveling. And this physical errand became my daily job!

About ten or twelve days after Dave's departure—I never kept the days or weeks straight in my head—while I was out shoveling snow, I heard the sound of a snowmobile. It was Nancy. She hopped off the machine and slid down the snow embankment and gave me a long lingering kiss before we walked back inside the cabin.

"It's Christmas time, Jesse," she said as she entered. "Time for you to come down from your cave and spend the holidays with us!"

I readily agreed, kissed her again, quickly gathered up my stuff along with a bag of books I'd finished, and we were off to spend Christmas and New Year's together. Once we returned to Dave's place, the first thing on my agenda was a nice hot shower. Oh, boy! Did it feel good! Borrowing Nancy's C/K10 while she was at work, I did a little shopping and purchased presents for Dave, Alice, and Nancy, plus I bought a box of Whitman's Assorted Milk Chocolates for Dave's parents. The holidays flew by quickly before Dave took me back to the cabin several days after New Year's. It was now 1975 and I was fast approaching my destiny.

Winter passed quickly by and before I knew it, a springlike warmth was now in the air. The snowmelt had increased the creek's flow and it rose some four to five feet in height during the last weeks of March and early April. Then April breezed in with warmer weather bringing with it many varieties of wildflowers blooming on either side of the creek. I always enjoyed viewing the plethora of colors as they emerged and blossomed. I reveled in smelling the various scents as they wafted through the air outside my cabin. Their redolent fragrances brought me a feeling of inner peace and joy. I made it through my second winter and was truly enjoying my life living alone although it was nice seeing Nancy and Dave every so often.

In June, just after I turned twenty-five, Nancy drove up and brought me back to Dave and Alice's for her graduation. A few days later, I watched her walk across the stage and receive her hard-earned diploma. She was now fully licensed as a respiratory therapist and the hospital had offered her a position at $20,000 a year! She took the job!

Nancy had a few days before she began her new job. The day after she graduated, she asked if I'd like to go to Missoula with her for two days. I hesitated, but Nancy quickly added, "I told Dave and Alice a year or so ago we were lovers. They approve, so there's nothing for you to worry about." I grinned, readily nodded my head, and quickly agreed to go with her.

So, off we went in her red C/K10. We shopped and wandered around Missoula holding hands as we explored and purchased more items in various stores. I felt so at peace while I was in her presence. Nancy found more than a few shops where she bought several dresses along with some most alluring lingerie. In each shop after she tried on a particular dress, she asked my opinion as to whether or not I liked her choice. In my short lifespan of twenty-five years, having never shopped with a member of the female species for women's clothing (or underwear!), I was somewhat embarrassed at expressing my opinion on any type of women's wear. I tried not to turn red when Nancy asked for my opinion, especially when she held up the tantalizing undergarments, most of which were black, red, or translucent, and seductively lacy.

So, I simply nodded my head and said, "That really would look nice on you!" Or, trying to be somewhat neutral in my reply when I didn't particularly care for an item, I opined, "Maybe that's not quite right for you." At which point, Nancy simply smiled and nodded, put the garment back on the dress rack and looked for another piece of apparel. At night we dined out and fully enjoyed our brief time together. It seemed we never stopped talking to each other.

On our second day, we stumbled across an Indian store named The Dream Catcher that sold many different pieces of handmade Native American jewelry. Nancy found a pair of beautiful rectangular earrings about a half inch wide and two inches long depicting a tree with red blooms and two ravens sitting on its branches. She also found a turquoise and sterling silver Squash Blossom necklace that really made her onyx eyes stand out when she donned it. Both pieces looked absolutely stunning on her and I had no hesitation in purchasing them. She wore them out of the store.

Alas, our brief sojourn came to an end and we reluctantly returned to Kalispell. Both of us, it seemed to me, thoroughly enjoyed our time alone together. On our drive back to Kalispell, Nancy and I briefly discussed our future. We agreed we enjoyed our love affair as it was and were not in any rush to make future plans as to where our relationship was headed. Nancy informed me that she wanted to work for a year or two before we made our liaison more permanent. I told her I would take my cues from her and we agreed it was probably best for us to take things on a day-by-day basis. Inwardly, the more I spent time with Nancy, the fonder I became of her.

I wondered what it was about me that attracted her. *After all, she was really attractive and could have lots of fellas. Why pick me? I was nothing more than an uneducated hick from the sticks.* And, I continued to muse, *I sure didn't think I was all that attractive in looks. I inwardly knew I would continue to puzzle over just what it was that she saw in me.*

On our arrival, Dave and Alice greeted us as if we had just returned from a honeymoon, giving each of us a brief hug with Dave enthusiastically patting me on my back. We sat around the house and enjoyed a few beers. With a little prodding from Alice, Nancy quickly displayed her new clothes (except the lingerie!) and jewelry which they both admired. Alice commented upon each item as Nancy exhibited it. As our eyes glazed over, Dave and I ended up with a thousand-yard stare—or a deer in the headlights look—during Nancy and Alice's mini fashion show.

When the clothes show ended, Dave gave me a wink and then said with some joviality in his voice and a deadpan mischievous look as he patted me on the shoulder, "Well, Jess, you sure gave my little sister some real nice stuff." He paused several seconds as he extended and turned both of his hands upward and teased, "But where's the engagement ring?" He scowled at me before heartedly laughing.

My mouth dropped a mile and I'm sure my face must have turned beet red as all three of them broke out in a hearty laughter. But Nancy's onyx eyes lit up in a sparkle. She gave me a wink and a quick loving smile before leaning over and kissing me. She then gave Dave a gentle swipe on the shoulder, smiled, and mockingly shook her finger at him before saying, "Brother, that's none of your business! We're just fine with things the way they are!"

Both Dave and Alice grinned like Cheshire cats as they each gave the other a brief look, winked, and silently nodded with a knowing smile on both of their faces.

And so, the summer of 1975 quickly passed. My "Terrors" came less often. I enjoyed my days of solitude at the cabin. Almost every week, without fail, Mr. Griz made his mysterious and conspicuous presence known but he never approached closer than sixty to seventy-five feet. During those brief encounters, I began to feel a kind of kinship with him. I was deeply puzzled and pondered on the significance behind my fleeting meetings with the grizzly.

As in times past whenever he appeared (or should I say mysteriously materialized?), the body below Mr. Griz's head seemed to disappear into a transparent mist on every third or fourth visit when he deigned to make himself known. Every so often I thought I caught sight of a nanosecond flash enabling me to see the pine trees on the other side of the enigmatic animal. Or was this ethereal bear something else? On other occasions I thought I glimpsed an ephemeral yet indistinct manlike figure in the mist behind Mr. Griz's head. The indistinct figure gave me the impression that it must be riding the bear! I was puzzled by the bear's purpose in making himself known to me. Still, I remained cautious and always had my Winchester close at hand.

Although Nancy's work schedule enabled her to spend two days with me every three to four weeks, strangely, Mr. Griz never made an appearance while she was visiting. When she came to stay, we often took short hikes throughout the woods and found different places to stop and picnic. During one of our picnics around mid-August, an eerie and unsettling event occurred.

We waded across the creek in front of my cabin and set up our picnic on the same flat rock overlooking the cool flowing water. As we unpacked the small picnic basket and laid out our lunch, we exchanged pleasantries. Nancy had just picked up her sandwich to eat when she abruptly turned her head back and forth and then swiveled her body so as to look into the depths of the forest behind us.

"Jesse, do you feel it?" Nancy said as she unexpectedly gave a slight shiver. "There's something, or someone, out there watching us!"

The hairs on the back of my neck immediately began to prickle. I quickly grabbed my Winchester, stood, and surveyed the forest making a quick 270-degree turn as my back was to the water.

"It's got to be Mr. Griz," I replied as I spoke in hurried staccato sentences. "He's nearby. I think I smell him. We better get back to the cabin. Quickly!"

Nancy quickly gathered up our lunch and hastily returned each item to the wicker basket which she had brought to the cabin on one of her numerous trips to see me.

At warp speed I reverted to my sniper days in Vietnam. I automatically chambered a round, and then, with some chagrin, watched the previously chambered bullet fly past my head as I instantly placed the Winchester into my shoulder pocket. I became fully ready for a kill. The thick underbrush made it somewhat difficult to discern anything more than fifteen to twenty feet away. As I continued to look around, I tried to peer into the forest's dark depths, as I slowly swept my rifle back and forth awaiting an attack that I sensed was near. My subconscious had automatically blocked out insignificant sounds like the subtle noise clothing makes against a person's body when they move an arm or leg. The gurgling creek also faded into the background.

Having gathered up the picnic items and placing them into the osier-woven basket, Nancy rose and moved behind me. She stood on the creek's brink and I immediately worried about accidentally bumping into her if I suddenly had to move backwards. Going back into my flashback mode, I realized for us to retreat as we edged down the creek's six- to seven-foot-high embankment was both foolhardy and an exercise in futility. Our awkward and unstable descent would leave us wide open to attack.

I whispered over my shoulder to Nancy, "Go ahead and go down the embankment. Cross the creek. Hurry to the cabin. Bring both my loaded shotgun and Ruger .357. Come back to a spot about halfway between the cabin and the creek and wait."

"Love you and take care," Nancy whispered as she turned to go but then abruptly halted and hissed. "Jesse—" she said in an undertone. I glanced back at her for about two seconds before returning my eyes to the woods and the unseen danger that apparently lurked there. Pointing to her left, Nancy said *sotto voce*, "There's something back upstream."

Upstream, there was a small clearing some twenty-five to thirty feet off to our left. I sensed something was tramping through the woods toward the small forest glade. By now both of us could hear branches cracking. Yet, neither one of us could discern any movement. Whatever it was seemed to be totally invisible.

And then the noise stopped. We both could feel the gentle wind blowing through the pine trees. But an ominous and deathly silence permeated the woods. I continued to sweep the area in a 270-degree arc.

"I think we ought to move as slowly as we can back to the cabin," I whispered.

Nancy silently nodded, stooped to pick up my hiking stick, and held it as she had already looped the picnic basket around her arm. By holding the Winchester, there was no way I could use my cane. She turned in the direction of the cabin and took one step to go down the creek's embankment.

And then it happened!

In less than a nanosecond, from out of nothingness, with no sound whatsoever, Mr. Griz materialized in the middle of the small clearing off to our left and let out a gigantic roar which not only startled both of us but caused us to jump an inch or two off the ground. Nancy even gave out a small cry. The bear was standing at his full seven- to eight-foot height which was most worrisome to each of us. If he dropped and charged, we were toast. There was no way we could flee and not be caught while we stood on the edge of the embankment with the creek below us. Trying to get down the slope and then wading across the creek, if we were lucky enough to get into and wade across the two-foot-high water level, would certainly be futile with a four to five hundred-pound grizzly charging us at a full speed of thirty-five to forty miles per hour.

Hell, I thought, *he can take one large leap off the embankment and land right on top of both of us.*

Mr. Griz stood there for over a minute as we stood mesmerized by his awesome appearance. Swaying back and forth, he started sniffing as if he was picking up some other scent. Nancy and I remained frozen in our tracks. Although I had my Winchester, I knew by the time I raised it and shot, Mr. Griz would be upon us. I would have to be one hell of a good marksman to bring down such a large fast-moving and massive animal with one shot. We both found ourselves in a no-win situation. I began to feel like Custer, who must have realized he and his two hundred-plus men were doomed when three thousand-plus Indians surrounded and then charged him.

Suddenly, with no warning, Mr. Griz dropped to all fours, roared, and charged off into the forest. We heard a yowl as a 175- to 220-pound cougar suddenly crashed out of the underbrush not ten feet away! It looked at us with panic in its eyes, then paused at the creek embankment, peered quickly down at the flowing water, then skedaddled from us and tore off through the forest. Mr. Griz's roars reached a crescendo. We both heard another catlike yowl from a rather pissed-off mountain lion. Mr. Griz was definitely chasing it as his roars faded in the distance. In some magical and unexplainable way, both Nancy and I realized Mr. Griz had come to our rescue from the mountain lion which had been stealthily creeping up on us.

We both expeditiously descended the creek's bank, gave a quick glance up and behind us at the bottom, then entered the chilly stream. Wading across the stream as quickly as possible, we took care not to slip in the still cold mountain water as we traversed the creek and ascended the opposite embankment. At the top we took another look back in the direction of the now quiet woods and walked slowly over to my cabin. As we trod back to my shack, we discussed in whispers what we had seen and heard. Despite the chilly water, both of us were bathed in beads of sweat that reflected in the sunlight so as to give each other a semi-golden glow. It had been a close encounter, but the gods of luck in the form of Mr. Griz had smiled upon us that day.

"We have seen the Spirit Bear," Nancy commented as we entered my ramshackle home. "And, as the legend says," she continued, "it was definitely protecting us from the mountain lion."

"Well," I replied, "my doubts are slowly disappearing, but I'm still not sure I'm all in as to Mr. Griz's purpose in my or your life, Nancy."

"I guess we should just be thankful he appeared when he did. The cougar must have been stealthily sneaking up on us," she pointed out as she leaned over and kissed me. I kissed her back with some energy, and we soon left our wet clothes on the floor. An hour later Nancy said she needed to get home. We dressed and walked out to her truck holding hands.

"I will tell the elders," she said, hopping into her C/K10. "I'm sure they will have an opinion as to what happened to us today."

I gave her another quick kiss through the truck's window and then she was off. I watched as she and her truck disappeared down the forest road. We had experienced something momentous and magical during our interrupted picnic. I sat outside my front door with my chair tilted against the cabin's wall, cracked a beer, and took a couple of sips. Contemplating the incident as I sipped, I just couldn't come to any decision as to the significance of the event. Little did I know at the time, it was just the prelude to what would happen to me in a year that would make a true believer out of me as to the Spirit Bear's power and mysterious purpose.

The next morning, another set of Golden Eagle feathers mysteriously appeared at my front door. This time the bundle contained four quills plus a band of beads at least two feet long. I looked around for human or bear prints but discovered nothing. The pine-needled forest floor was undisturbed. I hung the fourth set with the rest of the charms and pondered as to the purpose or meaning of these multiple sets of eagle feathers.

I couldn't help but wonder again, *was I going to be in some future trouble and needed as much luck or protection as these talismans seemed to be indicating? Was Mr. Griz actually delivering these amulets to me? If not, who?* I had no answer.

This entire incident with the Spirit Bear caused me to think about God and what plans He might have in store for me. I couldn't help but reminisce about my so-called "religious" upbringing.

Because of my initial experience with religion both in my childhood and teens, combined with fire and brimstone preaching, I still wasn't sure I believed in God and His message of salvation and redemption, especially after I had killed some NVA in Vietnam. I'd been raised a Southern Baptist, but only went to church when my parents decided to attend. I think Ma actually made Pa attend as I often heard her scolding him about going to church, which I'm sure was designed to lay some sort of a guilt trip on him. Yet they only attended somewhat sporadically and always dragged me and Jill along.

After listening to an illiterate, hellfire, Bible-thumping so-called preacher by the name of Brother Amos Lecter, who called us sinners and said we were all going to the netherworld if we didn't repent, I didn't have much of a belief in God, or religion of any kind. There was nothing good about Jesus or God in the backwoods preacher's message every Sunday. Nothing except how guilty and evil we all were in God's eyes. "REPENT! REPENT!" he would yell, hammering on the flimsy wooden pulpit every five or ten minutes, causing more than a few parishioners to jump. One could easily see the spittle from his mouth arc out and fall on the floor in front of his makeshift wooden lectern. So, his droning sermons almost put me to sleep. Maybe, I thought surreptitiously, his fist pounding was meant to keep us awake while he babbled on and on?

Yet, after reading parts of our worn and decades-old family Bible (especially the New Testament!), I realized God and Jesus were more about love of mankind and not sin or hell. So, when I was forced to accompany my parents to church, I just shut down internally, tuned out, and went through the motions like an automaton. In a lot of ways, I thought all this religious stuff was nothing more than backcountry hogwash, or merely mumbo jumbo.

But the worst part of attending church was having to atone for your sins by confessing out loud to the entire thirty-five- to forty-five-member congregation. Brother Amos pointed at you, called out your name, commanded you to stand up, voice your sins, and REPENT. This foolishness happened twice to me. The first time I was only thirteen years old and was so incredibly terrified and embarrassed—mainly because I couldn't think of any sins I'd committed—so I made some up. The congregation just nodded and said amen when I finished. I vowed then and there no such mortifying thing would ever happen to me again.

Thanks to Miss Eula's loaning me various books on religion, I knew a lot about the world's major religions—Taoism, Hindu, animalism, Islam, Catholicism, Methodism, and Episcopalian, to name just a few. Thus, I knew the preacher man was totally off base. Beyond scaring everyone each Sunday, he was obviously in it for the money generated by fellow Appalachians who were poor, just like my parents.

The second time occurred during my senior year in high school. Determined that I was never going to be that embarrassed ever again, I waited for this opportunity for a long time and had mentally rehearsed over and over what I was going to say. It was not pretty, to say the least. I remained furious that the preacher would treat members of his congregation with, I firmly believed, such disdain and disrespect.

The night before my parents dragged Jill and I off to church set the stage for the preacher's denouement in my mind. Brother Amos saw me with four or five friends in town the previous night. We were loitering on the steps of a closed and boarded-up store with paint peeling off every outside wall. There were a lot of closed stores throughout Appalachia. Each one of us was holding a glass jar from which we were obviously imbibing hooch. We had easily obtained the firewater from our local moonshiner, Mr. Pervis, who also was a member of our church. We just stared at the sky pilot as he shuffled along and passed us. Momentarily pausing, Brother Amos looked toward us as if to say something, thought better of it, and scurried off like a dog with its tail between its legs.

In church the next day, after fifteen to twenty minutes of boring "fire and brimstone" spouting from his flaccid lips, the preacher man pointed directly at me saying in a thunderous voice, "Stand up, Jesse Holder, and admit your sins before Almighty God and this congregation of redeemed sinners!"

What happened, I wondered as I began to stand, *to Jesus's love for us?*

There was no way I was going to let myself be humiliated again. So, I slowly stood, drew up and stiffened my 6'5" frame, turned, and silently looked at the entire congregation for about twenty seconds, which appeared to savor the fact I was now in the spotlight and about to confess my horrible salacious teenage sins. Yet, with my prolonged silence and apparent calmness, I could see some unease begin to creep into their eyes as many of them began to shift uncomfortably in their wooden pews and turned their eyes away from me.

Brother Amos impatiently drummed his fingers on top of the open and spittle-stained pages of his Bible as I turned back and faced him. For about ten seconds I stared fiercely and directly into his eyes which startled him as if I was a mountain lion mesmerizing him before jumping on top of his intended kill. The preacher was not used to being silently challenged by one of his flock and nervously shifted his feet. This time everyone was going to be shocked.

"Well, boy," he said with some angst, as his voice started to tremble a bit. "What do you have to say for yourself? Confess!!!" He impatiently continued to tap his fingers on the pulpit but now with an irregular discordant rhythm.

Is he getting nervous? I thought. *Great!* I smiled smugly at him. *Now he's going to get a taste of his own medicine!*

I stared at him for about ten more seconds, savoring what I was about to say. Then, in a soft but firm and deliberate voice, which could probably be heard throughout the sitting congregation, I spoke.

"You, Brother Amos, are a FALSE prophet! What happened to Jesus and God symbolizing love? You NEVER talk about that aspect of the Bible! Every Sunday you pound your fist on your rickety homemade lectern and say we all are sinners who must REPENT!" I raised my voice with each sentence and jabbing my finger directly at him, said, "You ought to be ashamed of yourself and your misguided beliefs!"

His mouth began to quiver and Brother Amos, not looking directly at me, appeared as if he was going to cower behind his rostrum.

I continued increasing the volume of my voice even more so no one could claim they didn't hear what I said. It appeared from the ever-increasing loudness of my intonations that everyone in the sanctuary was now awake. I shook my finger at the sermonizer as I continued, "You NEVER preach about GOOD! To you, we must continuously atone for our sins, but you, preacher man," I said scathingly, "are the DEVIL." I screamed the last sentence as I pointed and continued to jab my index finger at him. With much satisfaction I could see the false prophet start to cringe and hide behind his unsteady and makeshift wooden pulpit. His mouth dropped as he nervously shuffled his feet back and forth.

You could hear a pin drop in the church. Everyone sat stunned in their pews and the preacher's mouth continued to drop almost down to his flabby waist. Sweat suddenly materialized underneath his armpits, staining the un-ironed white shirt he was wearing as he cowered behind the pulpit as if it would somehow protect him.

I turned, looked at my parents, and said loudly, "I'm sick and tired of this F-CKING BULLSH-T and I'm NEVER coming back into this den of iniquity again!" I emphasized my words even louder and pointed at each of them as they sat there like deer caught in a car's headlights at what I had just thundered out so boldly. Next, I swept my arm in a wide circle as if to include all those in attendance, and continued, "GOD is good and you, preacher—YOU ARE A GODLESS MAN!"

My Ma looked as if she was in total shock, but Pa just sat there stunned. Both looked so embarrassed by my unexpected condemnation of the preacher. I turned, ordered people in my pew to get the F-CK out of my way, stomped loudly out of the sanctuary, slammed the door, and walked the five miles home. When my parents and Jill returned home several hours later, I could see my Pa was steamed. He started to say something but I marched right up to him, looked down, grabbed his shirt, put my face six inches from his, and firmly said, "Don't." He looked up at me and realized he wasn't about to win any argument, especially since he had been weakened by the black lung disease. He knew I could easily overpower him. I was an angry young man.

After my church oration, whenever I met people from the congregation, they either lowered their eyes, or walked across the street to avoid me. I was sure they ALL thought I was THE DEVIL.

My teenage friends gave me a wink, a thumbs up, or a high five as the news of my speech spread.

Enough about religion! I returned to my thoughts as to my participation in the Vietnam War, which really made me wonder. I had killed at least forty-nine people—if not more. I speculated, was there a God? Why would He allow all this maiming and killing? If He was all about love and forgiveness, how could He permit me to kill other people and then allow me and many others to be wounded, maimed, or killed? Plus, why would God stick me with "The Terrors"? It all made no sense.

Vietnam had definitely turned me into a non-believer. I wanted to accept that there was a God, but all the war's death and destruction, along with my PTSD, gave me pause. And now I had just experienced an inexplicable encounter with a four to five hundred-pound grizzly. The unexpected confrontation was most unsettling to me as it seemed, instead of devouring us, he was throwing some sort of invisible net, or shield over us. I often thought about Mr. Griz over the next few days.

Was he really protecting me or Nancy, or us both? Or, was I going to end up as his lunch one day? I tried to get back into my normal routine, but memories of our spoilt picnic haunted my dreams for a few days and "The Terrors" returned with a vengeance.

Maybe, I finally thought one day, a prayer or two wouldn't hurt. But I didn't really know how to start, so, mentally, I shoved that idea aside after several days.

A week or so later while I was chopping wood, Dave drove up, parked, and sauntered over to where I had paused next to the woodpile.

"Hey, Jess, how *ya doin'*, my friend? Nancy told me about what happened while she was up here," Dave said with a worrisome look on his face. "She went to the elders and spoke to them about Mr. Griz."

"Yeah," I replied, "it pretty well scared the piss right out of me! I'm sure Nancy was scared out of her wits!"

"The elders," Dave paused, "are deeply concerned about what is happening between you and the grizzly." He continued with wariness in his voice, "They think these encounters with the Spirit Bear are most unusual and disturbing—perhaps even ominous. They told her—which Nancy immediately related to me—you really need to be incredibly careful. They believe you are in some sort of unknown danger, and you should leave here and consider coming back down to live in Kalispell."

I nodded and then spoke, "Dave, you know, after what you and I went through in 'Nam, I've been more than cautious. I'm really most appreciative of your, Nancy's, and the elders' concern. While I cannot explain these *incidents* with the bear, I realize what I'm about to say must sound a little nutty to you, but something deep inside of me is telling me to stay. There's something odd going on here. I need to see it through to whatever ending is planned for me, whether it be good—or fatal."

We went back to the cabin, popped a few Dos Equis, and drank them as we further discussed the unusual events concerning Mr. Griz and the cougar. During our discussion, I suddenly realized that Nancy and I were the only people who had actually seen Mr. Griz. I wondered why the bear hadn't appeared to Dave. After an hour or so of talking he clapped me on the back and said he had to go.

"I'll tell Nancy," he said as he got into his blue C/K10. "But she's not going to be happy. She's really worried about you. And, well, you know, Alice and I are also concerned about you. Oh," he paused, a grin spreading across his face, "just in case you didn't know it, my sister likes—no, loves—you a hell of a lot, Jesse. I'd hate it if *something* happened to you. It might destroy her."

"Please reassure her for me, Dave," I replied. "I won't let anything happen to me. I promise not to take any unnecessary risks, but this has to play out, my friend. And when it does, I know in my heart I'll be the last one standing."

He gave me an enigmatic smile, waved, and was off in his truck.

Dave had given me much to contemplate.

My third winter soon set in with two huge snowfalls over the next month. By early December I had a snowbank some five or six feet high outside the cabin. Dave or Nancy came up to check on me a couple of times between September and December. Then around Christmastime, Nancy appeared on her snowmobile to pick me up for my regular stay during Christmas and New Year's. Because Dave and Alice knew Nancy and I were, so to speak, an item, Nancy told me when we got to the house we no longer needed to sneak around. She continued and told me she was going to sleep with me in my room. I just grinned and said, "Okay!"

For some particular reason, those days between Christmas and New Year's seemed to zip past Nancy and me much more quickly than in previous years. Our short Yuletide interlude was soon over. By the end of my sojourn, I knew I was definitely in love with Nancy. Trying to reconcile my feelings for her versus my life as a loner, which I had lived for the past four-plus years, presented me with a conundrum I couldn't quite grasp, or resolve, in my mind. I was faced with, as Winston Churchill opined, "A riddle, wrapped in a mystery, inside an enigma."[17]

I knew a reckoning was headed straight at me and I would soon be arriving at one of life's forks in the road. Would it be an agonizing choice? I just didn't know except I realized life was about to force me into making a pivotal decision. Was I, to paraphrase Robert Frost, taking the road less traveled, and if so, where was it leading me?

With the passing of New Year's Eve, it was now a new year—1976.

Little did I know or realize at the time, that the year of 1976 would put an indelible stamp on my life and imbue me with a new and healthy respect for the Spirit World. Curiously, I wondered, *could a person believe in God and also accept that there are creatures from the beyond? Was that even possible?* I had no answer to my questions. Plus, the circumstances surrounding my life and how I had lived it since arriving in Kalispell would radically transform me after the coming events in the month of August. Indeed, what a momentous year it would turn out to be and I had no inkling as to how my future was about to be upended and forever changed.

So, early New Year's morning Nancy returned me to my forest lair. The first few months of the year moved slowly along, but by mid-May, the snow had melted and the wildflowers along the creek's embankments had returned to all their splendorous glory. I reveled in their plethora of colors—blues, yellows, whites, and lilac. In the mornings I would rise and open the cabin's door to let the scent of the flowers and spring waft inside.

17　This quote is from a BBC radio broadcast delivered by Winston Churchill on October 1, 1939, to describe the interests and intentions of Russia upon the signing of the Nazi–Soviet Pact about a month after the outbreak of World War II.

Nancy dropped by in early June for a two-day stay. It was my twenty-sixth birthday. She brought a cake that she had baked. When I opened the box, there was a lovely chocolate cake with one candle! Upon seeing it, I thanked her profusely and then said, "Well, I guess you're going to have to treat me like a baby and spoon feed me with this cake!"

Nancy just laughed, then kissed and gave me a ferocious hug. Her beguiling onyx eyes drilled deep into my heart and soul. Gosh, I really loved her!

Maybe, I thought, *I'm finally coming out of my shell and accepting more of the external world out there besides just living and hiding in my cabin. Is my isolation drawing to a close?* Mentally I started preparing myself for a huge change to my life and the way I lived.

During those two days, we hiked a few hundred yards from the cabin alongside the creek's downstream and took time to explore the forest. On the afternoon of her second day, while we were sitting outside the cabin and talking, we heard a crash in the woods and Mr. Griz lumbered out of the forest's underbrush about forty-five to fifty feet away. Except for our interrupted picnic encounter when he had materialized about twenty-five feet away from us and went after the cougar, he had never appeared this close and the hairs on the back of my neck stood up. I was on full alert. Taking a quick glance to my left side, I knew my Winchester was within reach. But Mr. Griz just stood there nonchalantly as he sniffed the air. Satisfied all was well, the grizzly gave a grunt, walked down the yard, crossed the creek, and disappeared into the underbrush on the other side.

Nancy and I discussed what we had just seen but came to no conclusions. Intuitively, we both realized that we were part of something inexplicably unique. Both of us agreed we were playing a part with no idea as to where the next act would lead us. We just sensed that both of us were going to experience something beyond our comprehension.

I later thought, *was the Spirit Bear protecting us from some unseen danger, or unknown threat? Could he be some sort of guardian angel? Or, was he just making an appearance to let us know he was always nearby?* Although I became instantly alert during his visits, I continued to have this inexplicable feeling he didn't pose a danger to me—or Nancy. When I mentioned this thought to her, she agreed, but cautioned we still needed to be extremely careful.

The next morning when we awoke and went out to use the latrine, there was a fifth set of Golden Eagle feathers and a two-foot-long band of beads stuck in the ground in front of the door. I picked them up and we both examined them before I hung them up inside the cabin. Nancy and I discussed this occurrence as this was the first time the mysterious appearance had happened while she was visiting me.

Nancy's two days whipped past, and she returned to home and work. It would be mid-July before I saw her again for another two-day visit.

PART III

THE SPIRIT BEAR

The summer of 1976 slowly inched its way into early August. I spent my days chopping wood for the coming winter and reading. Sometimes, with my Winchester in hand, I walked down to the creek and took a quick two-minute bath in the chilly stream. Late on the afternoon of Thursday, August 12, Nancy unexpectedly showed up. I was surprised by her visit as I had seen her a few weeks earlier and didn't expect to see her for at least another month or more. But here she was, and I was exceedingly glad to see her. Nancy explained she had an unexpected two-day break from her hospital job and decided to surprise me.

She brought a couple of steaks, two potatoes, some orange peppers, a case of Dos Equis, and a bottle of white wine for herself. We grilled the meat, peppers, and potatoes outside and then sat next to the grill as night crept silently down upon us. A light boreal breeze blew through the woods and with it came the smell of the pines and the gentle sounds of the nighttime forest. Soon our ears picked up a musical blending of various discordant sounds which I had come to love while living in my cabin. We listened as two owls, who were at least a quarter of a mile apart, exchanged greetings in the woods. Or were they mating calls? We even heard some wolf howls in the distance as the frogs in the creek broke out in their own unmelodic orchestral cacophony. Nancy and I sat silently at peace holding hands and enjoyed the woodland concert before retiring early.

Friday, August 13, 1976. An ominous day. We cracker boys (some people called us hicks or rednecks instead) from backwoods Kentucky were raised by our parents and their friends to call Friday the Thirteenth the "haints" day, which meant, *if'n* you didn't look out, you might likely get into real trouble during that unlucky day. Bad things might happen to you on what was also known as "Ghosts" day. Backwoods poorly educated people tended to be incredibly superstitious when Friday the Thirteenth rolled around. I believed it was nothing more than unsubstantiated folklore—a mere fairytale. I usually ignored all the hogwash surrounding the supposedly "evil" day. To me it was just another twenty-four hours.

But this particular Friday the Thirteenth was to be the most significant day of our lives which would forever be changed with far-reaching circumstances. Waking, I didn't think about the day's date or its supposed inauspicious meaning. In truth, since I didn't have a calendar in the cabin, I had absolutely no idea it was a Friday, much less the thirteenth. Only after what happened to both of us would I learn the propitious date and remember it with nostalgia. Plus, I would indeed, NEVER forget it!

Had I but known, I later wondered, would I have been a little bit suspicious or more cautious? I doubt it.

Nancy was sleeping next to me. Our lovemaking was everything I could have dreamed of it being. I was content. I had a wonderful woman in my life, and all was well. Little did I know or sense but, in just a few hours, my unknown and misguided feeling of blissfulness and security was about to go haywire.

I quietly slipped out of bed and walked outside wearing only my boxer shorts. After exiting the latrine, I could see there were no clouds wafting across the clear blue sky. A faint wind blew gently through the pines and assailed my nostrils with its sweet forestry scent. I was surrounded by peacefulness and beauty. No bad malodorous smells assaulted my olfactory nerves. I breathed in nature's fragrance and smiled. It was too bad that I wasn't a clairvoyant; otherwise, I probably would have wished we slept in all day.

Hmm, I thought rubbing my chin, *it's going to be a great day! Maybe Nancy and I should have a picnic on the flat rock across the stream.* Continuing my train of thought, I wondered, *What could happen to us? Hopefully nothing untoward or upsetting will happen this time we have lunch on the rock. After all,* I mused, *would nature strike twice in the same place? I doubt it.*

But a little birdie in my mind nagged at me—were we tempting fate? But then I quickly dismissed such an ominous thought. Little did I know, I would soon discover my optimistic morning musings were nothing more than a pipe dream.

I went back inside the cabin to wake Nancy. As I leaned over to give her a kiss, she grabbed my arms and pulled me onto the bed.

"Gotcha!" she said as she kissed me.

An hour later we left our bed completely naked and had a light breakfast of Rice Krispies in our birthday suits! During our meal I described to her how beautiful it was outside and suggested we have a nice big picnic lunch on top of the flat rock across the stream where we had been so rudely interrupted during our last excursion. She readily agreed but suggested we ought to take a morning hike so we'd definitely be hungry around lunchtime. I quickly agreed to her proposal.

Nancy suggested a quick bath in the creek to wash off our lovemaking. I grabbed my Winchester and two towels. We ran down to the stream in our birthday suits and took a quick and chilly dip in the brook, soaping each other down, laughing, and then dunking underwater to wash off the soap. We coupled again. Dropping underneath the water, I noticed the creek seemed not only to be running a little faster and a bit colder than usual but also its water level appeared to be three to four inches higher than normal.

Probably the result of the two to three days of heavy rains around the area of Elk Mountain during the past week, I thought. *Nothing to be greatly concerned about.* I inwardly chuckled. It was an omen that I had totally ignored. And, oh brother, was I ever so wrong and would find out so in just a few fateful hours. Our joyous morning was about to take an unexpected turn.

After quickly bathing and drying off with the towels we had brought with us, I picked up my Winchester which I had toted down to the stream and carefully laid against a fallen log within arm's reach. We then made a quick dash back to the cabin where we dressed in the dim light for our morning hike.

We decided to head into the woods behind the cabin. Previously, we had hiked in the area once but hadn't ventured more than a couple hundred yards. I grabbed a small backpack containing useful items like a plastic bottle of water, matches, some first-aid stuff, and a flashlight that I might need on a short hike. Nancy and I took our time walking through the trees and stepping over the felled moss-covered logs. I carried my Winchester on my shoulder. Every so often the sun's warm rays beamed down on us as we walked across a small glade with a tiny opening in the pine canopy over our heads. Wildflowers bloomed around the edge of the surrounding forest.

We could hear birds chirping in the woodland as if to urge us onward. Some forty-five minutes into our trek and crossing another such glen we discovered a well-used animal trail heading in a northwesterly direction. The beaten path was so well used it appeared to have a curious appearance and similarity to the NVA trotters I encountered in Vietnam. We opted to follow the track to see where it might lead. Plus, sticking to a footpath would certainly be easier on my left leg and knee.

I silently intuited that some unknown force was guiding and pushing us onward, albeit, in a somewhat involuntary manner. Although we had been hiking far longer than usual, my knee, mysteriously, seemed to improve the farther I walked. This should have been a sign to me that something was not quite right, but I ignored my inner feelings.

After another ten minutes on the well-defined trail, we rounded a small hill and espied six to seven huge, twenty-foot-long by ten-foot-high-sized boulders leaning helter-skelter up against each other. It was as if the granite megaliths had just been mysteriously plopped there in the middle of the woods from the above heavens. They almost looked like Indian teepees from a distance. The animal trail led us directly toward the colossal-sized boulders. Approaching the tumbled rocks, we quickly found a large standing stonelike triangular opening between two of the largest monoliths. The trail led right into the darkened opening. We warily peeked in and discovered we had found a cave that was seven to eight feet wide and ten to twelve feet deep.

The outside light filtering through the pine trees was bright enough to creep partway into the half-lit cave so we decided to enter and explore. I pulled my flashlight out of the day pack to illuminate the interior of the darkened area. The smallish cavern was about eight to ten feet tall and had a musty scent. On the floor we discovered several tufts of what appeared to be bear hair. Realizing we were most likely standing in Mr. Griz's lair, and he might at any moment decide to make an appearance, we both agreed to make a hasty exit before the Spirit Bear returned.

As we turned to leave and walked three or four steps back toward the entrance, Nancy suddenly stopped in her tracks, grabbed my arm, and pointed upward. Taking my flashlight, she pointed the yellowish beam toward the ceiling. On either side of the tilted granite entrance were some faded pictographs painted in red which we did not see upon entering the lair. The ancient images were incredibly old because several were incomplete, but a trace of the original colored figures remained. Time and erosion had caused the images to fade or disappear altogether. We stood frozen in our tracks and stared upward in awe.

What an exciting find, I thought. *Wow!*

Despite our need to immediately vacate what we believed to be the Spirit Bear's den, we continued to stare in awe at the prehistoric finger paintings for a minute or so.

Realizing time was slipping by far too quickly, with some urgency in my voice, I said, "Nancy, we need to get out of here as fast as we can! I don't want Mr. Griz showing up and trapping us inside this cave. Plus, I'm also worried that due to the presence of these ancient pictographs, we may have unwittingly entered a spot that might be sacred to your ancestors. I'm anxious we might inadvertently be violating this cave by our presence."

"I know, Jess," she replied. "But please give me another minute. This is important. I want to see if I can interpret what the drawings say, or at least memorize them to the best of my ability. I'm praying I can accurately describe these pictographs to the elders. These markings are so old and were probably made centuries ago by my ancestors."

As we stood holding hands and looking upward, we both almost gasped at the same time. A greyish shimmering mist began to materialize before our eyes. On the left slab right above our heads, six Golden Eagle feathers tied together with a beaded leather band magically appeared and floated down into Nancy's hands. We were both shocked by this sudden occurrence.

Nancy," I asked with amazement, "what in the world is happening?"

"I don't know, Jess, but whatever it is, it's a sign. I don't know whether it's good or bad. I feel we need to leave *now!*" she stated with some urgency in her voice. She grabbed my hand and quickly walked toward the miniature-sized grotto's entrance, pulling me along. As she did so, the feathers and leather band that she was holding vanished as we stepped out of the cave. Strangely, neither one of us seemed surprised by their disappearance.

After we had departed from what might have been either Mr. Griz's den or a sacred spot of long-ago Native Americans, my knee began to ache several minutes later. I told Nancy so we slowed our pace. When we arrived at the glen where we first found what we believed to be the animal trail, miraculously, the trail continued on the other side, vanishing off into the woods toward my cabin. This unexplainable and mysterious appearance of the hitherto non-existent path jolted me. I could feel the hair on the back of my neck standing up.

This, I thought, *is not a good omen. Something unseen is guiding us home or into a trap.*

"Nancy, are we in some sort of a dream?" I asked. "I know the trail wasn't on that side when we first approached and entered this glade."

"I can't explain it, Jess," Nancy replied as she shook her head back and forth. "All I can surmise is there is something happening that's beyond our ability to accept or even understand," she continued. "Yet, oddly, I don't sense any type of evil lurking nearby. I feel the spirits of my ancestors are guarding us, so let's push onward." She paused before resuming her thoughts. "After all, it looks like smooth sailing, and less trouble for your knee, as we head back to the cabin."

I agreed by silently nodding my head, but my senses were wary. Something just didn't sit well with me.

The track was indeed smooth. By now my knee was really beginning to nag at me. Finally, about an hour later, we arrived at my cabin. Nancy pointed out it was half past noon as we emerged from the forest.

"Well, we made it!" I excitedly said to Nancy as I breathed a sigh of relief. We were home. We were safe—or so I thought. As Nancy agreed with me, she turned to look back at the track we had just travailed.

"Jess!" Nancy grabbed my arm. "Look!"

I turned around. The forest trail had vanished! Both of us just stared into the forest wondering what just happened.

"What the f-ck," I said, "is going on? Is this a dream?"

Nancy just shook her head in disbelief.

"I sense this entire forest area is filled with spirits," she opined as she held up and swept her arms in a 360-degree circle. "It must have been a sacred spot for my ancestors," she continued.

She and I then agreed we, indeed, had experienced some sort of supernatural phenomenon.

"No one will believe us," I commented.

"I think it best for us not to say anything to anyone. Except I *will* speak to the elders again and listen to their advice."

After several more minutes of discussing this unfathomable occurrence, we decided to rest a while before we had our picnic. An inexplicable miracle (if indeed it was a miracle) just happened to us. While I rested on the bed, Nancy took a small bucket which I used to carry various items, along with my Winchester, and walked down to the stream where she filled it with the stream's cold water. Returning with the pail, she soaked a linen cloth in the chilly water which she then took and wrapped around my now throbbing knee.

She joined me on the bed and we both quickly fell asleep after our mysterious exploit in the woods. Waking about an hour later, we started to prepare for our mid-afternoon lunch. Nancy grabbed the wicker basket which she left behind on one of her visits. After fixing some sandwiches, she placed them and a couple of sodas in the basket, and we were off for our picnic.

Stepping outside the cabin with my Winchester, I saw that the day continued to be a beautiful cloud-free afternoon. I turned and said to Nancy, "We're going to have a really nice afternoon for a picnic!"

She gave me a cute smile, nodded her head, and then grabbed my hand. Her onyx eyes sparkled with delight.

Well, as it turned out, it was going to be an afternoon we both would NEVER forget.

We approached the creek without a care in the world. I was happy. Nancy was happy. We just seemed to bask in each other's presence.

It's the simple things in life which you do with ordinary regularity that can suddenly and unexpectedly go so horribly wrong in just a matter of nanoseconds. We were about to find out the hard way the devastating effect of taking those little things for granted. It almost became a fatal decision.

As we descended the embankment, I noticed the creek's flowing water seemed a bit higher than when we had previously bathed in it a few hours ago. Nancy entered the water carrying the picnic basket. I was several feet behind her. Suddenly, with no warning, Nancy slipped.

"Oops!" she said, and the picnic basket flew out of her arms as if she was a quarterback lobbing a Hail Mary pass. As the wobbling wickerwork traveled downstream it arced upwards about three feet in the air, seemed to waffle, then crash landed upside down in the now swift flowing waters of the creek.

Now on her back, Nancy slid a couple of feet before coming to an abrupt halt in the two-foot-high chilly mountain stream.

"Jess, my right foot is jammed!" she said with a little bit of panic. "I can't free it!"

"I'm coming, Nancy!" I hastily turned, waded back two feet, and placed my Winchester against the creek's embankment. I quickly rotated my body about ninety degrees and hurriedly sloshed over to her.

Reaching her, I grabbed Nancy under her armpits, got a firm stance on the creek's bottom, and tried to pull her backwards. I was unable to get her to budge. I tried again. And a third time. And then a fourth. Nothing. I was flummoxed. The strain on my knee caused sharp pains to run up my leg. Nancy's foot appeared to be solidly jammed underneath and between two rather large rocks and the increased flow of icy cold current (or was that my panicked imagination?) kept it wedged there.

I waded a few feet downstream of the rock and felt around where her foot was lodged. I tried to grip and pull it upward and away from her foot. It was heavier than I had anticipated and wouldn't budge since the increased water flow was pushing against it. Although it had only been two or three minutes since Nancy had slipped into the water, I could see her teeth begin to chatter. My hands were getting cold from the water. I knew I had to do something, or hypothermia would really begin to set in. I felt as if I was running out of time.

As I turned to wade back upstream to try and pull her loose again, my left foot hit a slick stone, jamming my heel into a triangular niche between two underwater rocks. The onrushing current twisted me to the left and I was consumed by an incredibly sharp pain.

"Oh, SH-T!!!" I screamed as I fell into the water. My left knee felt as if someone had stuck a red-hot poker into it. My war wound had now come back to haunt me big time when I least expected it. I certainly didn't want, or need, the ensuing pain that now agonized me.

Sh-t! I said to myself. *I'm in a f-cking sh-tload of trouble now! Damn! Damn! Damn!*

I stood back and the agonizing pain hit me like a railroad train. I scrambled back to Nancy with my left knee on fire. I gritted my teeth and silently prayed that she would not see my desperation. Next, I braced my right foot against a rock and again tried to pull Nancy free. Nothing. My left leg was practically useless. The water was damn cold and I knew we both were only minutes, if not seconds, away from hypothermia. What to do? I decided I needed to use the Winchester as a lever. I might ruin the rifle, but at least Nancy would be free.

"Nancy, I'm going to crawl over and get my Winchester and try to use it as a lever," I told her.

"I'm getting really cold, Jess! Please hurry!" she pleaded as she visibly shivered.

I turned and started to crawl across the creek to where I laid my Winchester. But, a sudden flash of movement above the embankment immediately caught my eye.

I looked up.

"SH-T!!" I screamed.

Staring down at me from the top of the embankment, not seven or eight feet away, was Mr. Griz!

"F-CK! F-CK! F-CK!" I howled. I knew with my now almost useless left leg there was no way I could scramble another three to four feet through the freezing cold water to reach my rifle. I inched my way back to and behind Nancy, and held her upper torso up, keeping her head above the water. I could see she was beginning to fail.

Damn! The water is frigging cold! And now we're about to die!

Sh-t! Sh-t! Sh-t! I thought as we both stared upward at the furry beast now inexorably looming over us.

Mr. Griz swayed his body back and forth while gazing at us with his deep, almost hypnotic eyes as if he was trying to mysteriously ascertain what we were doing in the creek—or which one of us to eat first! But there was something odd about his appearance. As he swayed back and forth, an aura magically appeared and surrounded his entire body. It seemed to both of us as if his fur had partially turned into a soft golden-yellow color. His hair seemed to be brightly glowing thin spikes about two inches long, which emanated from his body.

Is he surveying his next lunch? I wondered as my teeth began to chatter from the cold and fear. *This is the f-cking end*, I thought. *After all the sh-t I endured in Vietnam, this is how my life ends. Damn!!! Sh-t!!! F-CK!!! F-CK!!! F-CK!!!* I wordlessly and silently screamed.

As I held her, Nancy looked up at the bear and with chattering teeth loudly chanted something in Salish for about thirty seconds. Mr. Griz stopped his swaying, looked down at us, and stared. Then, he rose up on his rear feet and seemed to look twice as big as he towered over us.

Feeling the end was near, I gripped Nancy and whispered in her ear, "I love you!"

"I love you, too, Jesse," she replied and grabbed my shirt as I kept her head above the water.

We both thought that we were going to die in the next few seconds.

Our fate was now in Mr. Griz's hands—or paws! There was no way for us to escape. Better for us to die in this freezing creek before he decided to devour us.

At least, I thought, *dead from hypothermia, we won't feel anything when he comes to feed.*

But then something so incredibly bizarre began to happen as both Nancy and I stared upward at the looming ursine danger with his three-inch long teeth. The Spirit Bear started to dematerialize right before our eyes! A greyish cloud seemed to envelop the standing beast until he completely vanished within its mist. He had become invisible just as he had every so often on the other occasions when he visited me at the cabin. But after the mystical shadow disappeared, what happened next stunned us.

As the cloud faded, a tall muscular Indian warrior emerged. He was dressed in deerskin with Golden Eagle feathers in his hair held there by a beaded bandana which had the exact same design as all the rest of the charms previously left at the cabin! The beaded bandana wrapped around the Indian's head and held his raven black hair in place.

I figured we were both already dead and all this was now a dream as we transitioned to the other side.

But the warrior was soon to disabuse me of my death thoughts. He hurried down the embankment and waded into the water. Placing himself in front of Nancy, he reached underwater, grabbed the rock, and with a huge heave he brought the boulder up to a ninety-degree angle. Nancy wiggled free! She pushed away from the stone with her left foot. When she tried to use her formerly trapped right foot, she gave a slight groan as I pulled her backward away from the rock trap.

"Jesse, my right foot is on fire!" she said. "I think I may have broken something!"

The Indian, without saying a word, waded to Nancy, stooped, and picked her up. He waded over to the creek's edge, climbed the embankment, and set her down. As this scenario was playing out, I used the hanging branches of a nearby tree and awkwardly managed to pull myself to the creek's side. I wanted to climb out, but I was just too cold and exhausted to do so. Plus, by now my knee was killing me.

I held on as best I could to the creek's small side embankment as the icy current pulled at me. The warrior swiftly moved back down the embankment, stepped into the water, scooped me up with apparent ease, and carried me up the slope. He set me down next to Nancy who was shivering as her teeth chattered nonstop.

The warrior then picked Nancy up and walked up the gentle slope to the cabin and disappeared inside. He quickly returned and carried me into the cabin, setting me down on the bed where he had previously placed Nancy.

During this entire unbelievable episode, the warrior did not speak a word.

And neither did we! We were too awestruck to utter a sound.

After the silent warrior settled me on the bed, he turned, walked to the door, swung back around, and looked directly at us. Standing in the center of the doorway, he nodded his head and placed his right fist on his chest.

Nancy again intoned what I thought to be a prayer in Salish. In an instant his entire body was cloaked in a golden aura. There was a bright flash of light and he was gone. Now, in his place, stood the Spirit Bear who was also bathed in a similar golden light! Mr. Griz had a beaded eagle feather in his mouth. Giving a low growl, he turned and bounded across the clearing, vanishing into the forest.

Even though both Nancy and I were absolutely stunned by this startling chain of unexplainable events, we quickly stripped off all our wet clothes. Using some of my towels, with our teeth chattering, we dried ourselves off as best we could and climbed under the three blankets resting on top of my bed. We held on to each other for warmth and talked about what had just happened to us. We kissed and our ensuing lovemaking was incredibly tender and sweet before we each fell into a heavy and uninterrupted sleep.

An hour or so later, I woke, rose, hobbled over to my clothes rack, sat on the sofa, and with much difficulty, put on some dry clothes. On previous visits Nancy left some of her clothes. Pulling them off the rack, I limped, mostly hopping on my right leg, over to the bed and gave them to her. In a minute or so, she was dressed.

"What do we do now, Jesse?" she asked. "As you can see my ankle is really swollen. I can't drive the truck as my right foot won't allow me to use the accelerator. And your left leg is practically useless."

"Yes," I replied, "but with my right foot I can use both the accelerator and brake. I think—no, I pray—I can get us home."

Holding on to each other, we exited the cabin and slowly managed to hobble over to Nancy's truck. Thank goodness the 1971 model was an automatic; otherwise I don't know how we would have made it out of the woods and down the bumpy timber road to Kalispell. Somehow, we made it to Alice and Dave's home where we called Alice at the hospital who then called Dave. He rushed over to the house, arriving at almost the same time as Nancy and I.

Together they put both of us in their individual trucks and drove to the hospital. By then my knee had swollen to the size of a small cantaloupe and my entire left leg burnt up with an unbelievable throbbing pain. Nancy's ankle seemed to be swollen but she didn't have a lot of pain. We had made it to safety, but boy, would we have a story to tell Dave and Alice!

I wondered, would they really believe what befell us?

THE BEYOND

RESOLUTION

As it turned out, Nancy only had a badly sprained ankle which the docs wrapped with a plaster of Paris cast almost up to her knee. It was, the docs told her, a "walking cast." Within a week she was able to return to work using a cane. I wasn't so lucky.

Due to my previous VA operations, my knee now had a massive injury. I worried about losing part of my leg. In addition to the initial operation after I arrived at the hospital, over the next five months, I would have to endure two more operations including knee replacement surgery. I lost about one inch of my femur, leaving me with a much more conspicuous limp. In addition to a higher heel on my left shoe, I would also need the support of a sturdy cane or walking stick for the rest of my life. I figured it was a small price to pay for not losing my leg from the knee downward.

The day after our rescue by the mythical Indian, Dave was kind enough to return to the cabin and lock it up. Hospital-bound, I wouldn't be living there any time soon. Upon returning late Saturday afternoon, he walked into my hospital room to tell me he had secured the cabin. I thanked him profusely from my hospital bed, when he brought out a bag he'd been carrying.

"Jess, I've got a surprise for you," Dave said as he reached into the paper bag. "I think you will find it somewhat interesting."

Whereupon he pulled out a dozen Golden Eagle feathers bound together with a leather-beaded band.

My mouth fell open. Both Nancy and I had given Dave and Alice an abbreviated version about what happened to us as they took us to the hospital. And now, Dave displayed another set of Golden Eagle feathers.

"Where in the world did you find this, Dave?" I asked as I examined the now, I believed, sacred amulet.

"It was hanging on a nail on your front door," he replied.

"But," I hesitated at this new revelation, "I don't have a nail in the front door!"

"Well, you do now!" Dave grinned as he replied. "Plus, when I first saw them hanging on the door, they had some sort of mystical and shimmering aura, almost like an indistinct halo, encircling them. As soon as I touched them, the glow disappeared. Just vanished into thin air!"

I just shook my head in amazement. *Another mystery I'll never be able to solve,* I thought.

"Did you see the other feathers I had hanging up inside the cabin next to the door?" I inquired.

Dave shook his head. "No, they weren't there, just the nails," he replied.

We discussed this enigma before he took his leave, as I was feeling sleepy. So, we bid each other goodbye. I asked Dave to take the latest Golden Eagle feathers with him, saying I'd keep them after I managed to leave the hospital.

Nancy dropped by the next day. She now had a sturdy hospital cane to help her walk with the plaster cast on. As she sat on the bed next to me, we discussed the entire incident but couldn't come to any conclusion as to what it all meant. We speculated as to the meaning of our mysterious rescue. All we could do was guess as there really was no earthly or cogent explanation for what had happened to us.

Nancy also told me what she had chanted to Mr. Griz as he loomed over us and we prepared to die in the creek. She intoned the following

Salish prayer, "Great and Mighty Spirit Bear, we honor you! We are your children and mean you no harm. We are in deep trouble and about to die! We beseech you—please help us! Grant us this favor and we will honor you all our lives." She then related what she had said to the warrior after he had settled us in the cabin's bed. She repeated the Salish prayer and then translated it for me as to what had passed her lips: "O great warrior, we thank you for this wonderful deed you have done for us. We will be eternally grateful and worship you and the Bear for the rest of our lives." We both agreed that Mr. Griz and the Indian warrior had saved our lives, and we would honor both entities for doing so. Nancy then left my hospital room after giving me a nice long kiss.

Two days later at about 2:00 p.m., there was a knock on my hospital room's door.

"Please enter!" I replied, wondering if the person was going to be a nurse with a needle or a doctor checking on me. I much preferred the latter and definitely not the former.

Instead, I was surprised to see an elderly American Indian, perhaps in his eighties or nineties, dressed in full regalia, jauntily enter the room and stand at the end of my bed.

"Please come in, sir, and have a seat." I gestured to a chair next to the left side of my bed. I had a remote suspicion as to the purpose of his visit.

He nodded, walked over to the chair, and sat. His presence seemed to fill the room and take command of it. Amazingly, I immediately felt like a small mouse coming face to face with a sidewinder rattlesnake in the desert. There was no way to escape.

"Mr. Holder, my name is Two Elks," he began in a gravelly but distinctly clear voice. "I am the shaman for our Salish tribe. It has come to my attention that you and Miss Nancy Ironman had an interesting encounter on Elk Mountain a few days ago."

As I lay propped up against the pillows piled between my back and the bedstead, I nodded as he firmly continued. I continued to be mesmerized by his voice.

"I would like, if you don't mind," he opined, "for you to relate to me everything that has occurred to you and Miss Nancy at your cabin since your occupancy of the land that you purchased from Mr. Martin."

"I would be pleased to do so, Mr. Two Elks," I replied. "But it is indeed a long tale."

"Please continue, Mr. Holder," Two Elks replied in a stern but friendly and fatherly tone. "I have all the time you may need."

It took over two full hours for me to narrate what had happened not only to Nancy and I at the cabin but also my individual experiences with the Spirit Bear and the unexplained appearances of the eagle feathers and bands. Occasionally he stopped me to clarify a point or two before nodding at me to continue. At the end I laid back, totally mentally exhausted.

Two Elks rose, thanked me, and as he readied to leave the room, said, "Mr. Holder, you and Miss Ironman have encountered something no other living members of our tribe have ever experienced. I believe your encounter with the Spirit Bear and Indian is truthful but"—he admonished in a fatherly tone—"a majority of the people will not. I caution you as to whom you might tell this story. You will be met with skepticism, disbelief, and scorn. If I may be so bold as to advise you, it is probably best for both of you to keep this between yourself and the Ironman family."

I believed him. No one would believe this incredibly unbelievable story concerning Nancy and me.

"Thank you, Two Elks," I answered. "I deeply appreciate your advice and will be most circumspect in keeping this tale between myself, Nancy and Dave, and their extended families."

He stood and asked, "May I offer you a Salish blessing?"

I silently nodded and Two Elks reached over the bed and placed both of his hands on my left knee area. In a low voice he chanted something in Salish for about thirty seconds before he raised both arms and extended them palms upturned, toward the hospital room's ceiling. Then, lowering his arms and turning, he silently departed.

I wondered what Two Elks would do with the information I had willingly imparted to him. I thought it might become Salish lore. Overall, his visit puzzled me.

The hospital let me go after a week's stay to recuperate from my knee operation. The orthopedic doctor told me I was in for at least one, if not two, more operations. He also informed me I would need both a raised heel and a cane for the rest of my life as I wouldn't be able to walk without one. I just nodded.

At least, I thought, *I'm alive and I can live with the disability as best I can.*

Dave and Alice insisted I stay with them, so I moved back into their home once again. But this time Nancy slept with me in what had once been my former room.

Several weeks later while Nancy and I were discussing the Spirit Bear incident, I had an epiphany.

"Nance," I wondered as I had just had a mind-blowing revelation, "I know the Spirit Bear plays a part in your folklore, but there's nothing about the Indian associated with the bear, is there?"

"No," she replied. "I have no knowledge about the warrior we both saw."

"Well, listen to this! You may think I'm crazy, but hear me out," I posited. "What if there is some kind of association between the Christianity I was raised to believe in and your Salish beliefs? Suppose, just suppose, the Spirit Bear represents both my God and your great spirit God, and the Indian warrior is Christ? After all, the warrior seemed to emerge from the bear as if he was its son just as our Christ immaculately emerged from Mary as God's Son."

She found my question to be somewhat contra to her Salish beliefs but opined we should discuss this with Dave and Alice before approaching the elders.

After Dave and Alice arrived from work, Nancy and I discussed my thesis with them. They both demurred saying we definitely needed to consult with the elders and obtain their thoughts about the whole episode. So, word was sent to the elders. We waited.

Two days later we were summoned to the home of one of the five elders. Two Elks was not present. The remaining four were all men in their seventies and eighties who I sensed had a feeling of wisdom and peacefulness about them. Alternating, Nancy and I both described what happened. Every so often one of the five men interrupted us to clarify a point or two. When we ended our tale, the elders agreed they needed to discuss this episode among themselves and would get back to us in a day or so.

Three days later we were summoned to a different elder's home. This time Two Elks was present. Upon entering we greeted each of the wise men. After the introductions, Nancy spoke in Salish to the tribe's leaders. She told me later that she had given the elders a Salish greeting of respect. The wise men then moved to a circle of chairs in the living room. As they took their seats, Two Elks gestured to us to sit in the two empty chairs at the bottom of the circle.

We sat and Two Elks gave a blessing in Salish. The wise men looked at us with some ancient understanding in their eyes. Starting at my right and taking turns around the circle, each leader proceeded to impart his opinion as to what had befallen us. They each believed Nancy and I had indeed encountered the Spirit Bear of their folklore. Then one of the wise men, the oldest in the group—an octogenarian at least—looked directly at us and firmly stated they all had absolutely no idea as to what or whom the warrior represented. They had never heard in all their lives about the Spirit Bear turning into a warrior.

Another elder spoke up, "As to your theory about the Spirit Bear being your God and the warrior being your Christ, we really have no ancient lore to guide us." He paused as if gathering his thoughts. "However, because most of your blood is white man's blood, it may be possible your Christian beliefs may have had an influence on the Spirit Bear and warrior. There may be some connection because we have never heard of any warrior being surrounded by a halo, such as is believed your Christ may have had from time to time."

He nodded to us as if to say the meeting had concluded.

We thanked the elders for their valuable time and thoughts. Standing, we bade them farewell and took our departure. Nancy and I pondered this information and let it sink in as we hobbled out of the house and found Dave waiting for us. When we arrived home all four of us discussed what the venerable leaders said but neither one of us could come up with a suitable explanation as to what actually happened to Nancy or myself.

Seven months later in early April, after two more knee operations, I was able to walk with some lingering pain which the docs told me would, most likely, be with and plague me for the rest of my life. Nancy and I decided to visit the cabin for the first time since the incident. I wanted to clean out the premises because I knew I could no longer live there alone. My exacerbated disability would certainly prevent me from doing normal everyday chores outside.

Upon our early morning arrival, we found that everything seemed to be in place. Entering the cabin, we saw it was just as we had left it, except this time there was one Golden Eagle feather with a beaded band lying on the table! Picking it up to examine, I saw the feathers appeared to be quite new. I mentioned this observation to Nancy as I handed it to her.

She just looked at it in awe and pointed out something I had missed.

"Jess," she said with wonder and awe in her voice, "look at this band of beads—it has a small design of a cross in it!"

Taking the band from her, I examined it and said, "Wow!" I was stunned. Then I immediately had a thought and as I held the beads and feather, raising them upward toward the cabin's ceiling. "Nancy," I said, "perhaps we shouldn't say anything to Dave and Alice, or the elders, about this cross."

Nodding her head, Nancy replied, "I think you're right, Jesse. This should be our secret."

I silently nodded back.

We decided to clear out my remaining personal stuff which took us an hour. After loading it all in the truck bed, Nancy turned to me, saying, "Jess, if you're up to it, why don't we take one last walk up to the rocks where we found the cave?"

I somewhat reluctantly agreed to do so, realizing my knee might prevent us from completing our walk, but I was willing to try. Hoisting the Winchester over my shoulder, we set out. As I took each step on our hike, my knee, mysteriously, began to experience less and less pain. By the time we reached the glade, where we discovered the animal trail leading to the rocks, an hour had passed. To our amazement, there was no longer a path on the other side. It seemed to have totally vanished.

As I stared around the clearing, I turned to Nancy and said,

"Nance, you're not going to believe this, but with every step I took as we approached this clearing, I began to feel less pain in my knee."

"Jess, that's wonderful! Do you think the pain has gone for good, or is this occurrence temporary?"

"I don't know, honey. We'll just have to wait and see."

After a few minutes' discussion, we decided to continue through the woods to see if we could find the monster boulders. I wondered, were they also another figment of our imagination?

Winding through the forest, it took us another hour to find the rocks. By the time we reached the gigantic cairn of boulders, there was little to no pain in my knee.

I silently wondered, had our *hegira* to the monoliths been akin to Mohammed's trip to Mecca? Had I been mysteriously healed? Or would my pain return? I just shook my head in disbelief.

We cautiously approached the cave's entrance. It was deadly quiet. Nothing stirred from inside. We entered the partially dim chamber. Shining the flashlight on the floor, I saw there wasn't a piece of bear hair anywhere. In fact, except for a few dead leaves which had blown in, the lair looked as if it had been entirely swept clean!

"Look, Nance," I pointed out. "There's nothing on the floor!"

Nancy nodded as she took my flashlight and swept the light up to the ceiling over the grotto's entrance. We both gasped. The pictographs had vanished! We walked over to the entrance and looked up as we examined the ceiling. Nothing! Now, indeed, we were faced with another conundrum. Both of us just silently shook our heads in amazement.

We agreed to leave and head back to the cabin. It took us about three hours to wend our way back through the woods to my lodging as I had to pause several times to rest my leg and knee. Strangely and unexplainably, the closer we neared the cabin, the more my knee began to hurt. I mentioned the pain's return to Nancy.

It was midafternoon when we arrived back at the edge of the clearing in front of the cabin. The pain in my knee, oddly enough, was only about half of what it had been before our journey into the forest. I silently prayed for it not to get worse.

Had we entered and left some kind of sacred healing ground? Or, had we mysteriously entered some sort of otherworldly dimension? Or was I imagining all of this? I wondered as the cabin came into sight. It just made no sense to me.

As we stepped out of the woods, the clouds above turned dark and ominous while the wind blew through the pines causing them to sway back and forth. Thunder sounded off to the west. I saw a flash of lightning.

We both looked upward and were shocked to see a figure materialize within the quickly rising thunderhead. Nancy saw it first.

"Jess, look!" She pointed upward at the dark approaching cloud.

In the middle of the inky darkness of ominous storm clouds was an outline of the Spirit Bear. It turned toward us, stood up on its hind legs, and gave a tremendous roar—or was it only the thunder we heard?

As we watched the standing form of the Spirit Bear, it started to fade into nothingness. Instead, in its place was the same Indian warrior, surrounded by a bright halo, except this time his arms were extended out at a ninety-degree angle from his body as if assuming a figure on a cross. His head nodded to us and in a nanosecond, he vanished!

"I think, Nance, this is an omen of some sort, but I'm not sure what. I think we ought to head home, especially before the storm hits."

Driving home, we discussed both the cave and the mysterious appearance of the Spirit Bear and the Indian in the clouds but couldn't come to any firm decision as to what had happened both on the ground or above in the murky clouds. It, along with the mysterious abatement of pain in my knee, was an unsolvable enigma. We both knew what we had seen but other than Dave and Alice, or the elders, we told no one else of the strange occurrences in the forests near Elk Mountain. It would be our secret.

The next week I proposed to Nancy, and she accepted. Since I had not spent much of my VA disability money after moving into the cabin in August 1973, I now had a large nest egg in my savings account. Nancy and I decided to search for a small house. It took us about ten days before we found a nice three-bedroom home with a barn on eight acres just outside of Kalispell. We purchased it and moved in a few weeks later.

Because August 13, 1976, was such a propitious and life-altering day, we decided that such an auspicious date should also serve as our wedding day the next year. The ceremony was conducted by the elders, mostly in Salish, which I didn't understand, except when Two Elks, after a long blessing in Salish, spoke English and told me I could kiss the bride! I gave Nancy a long and passionate kiss which had all our guests clapping and laughing. As I looked up from our kiss, I saw off to the west that the clouds had formed into the outline of a bear. I whispered in Nancy's ear to look up and she saw the cloudy figure. Then, the atmospheric winds quickly tore it into different shapes. Later, we decided it was a sign telling us our marriage would be long and happy.

AFTERWARD

It has been forty-five years since the joyful day when Nancy and I married. We had three children—a boy and two girls. And now, we are grandparents. Our two girls, Martha and Karen, graduated from college and each, after further studies, later acquired a PhD. They met their husbands while in graduate school and are now teaching at universities in Las Cruces, New Mexico, and Flagstaff, Arizona. Our son, Dan, attended the Virginia Military Institute (VMI) in Lexington, Virginia, and entered the Army as a second lieutenant. After twenty years and two wars, he's now a one-star general with several Purple Hearts, among other things. I suspect he will earn a few more stars before retirement.

Dave and Alice had two kids—a boy and a girl, named Nathan and Donna—both of whom attended college and also received higher degrees. Nathan, like his father, volunteered for the Army and is now considered a "lifer," having put twenty-three years in and going for thirty. Donna married a history professor who teaches Asian history at the University of Richmond in Richmond, Virginia, and who also writes both history and short storybooks.

Once a year or so, I receive a letter from my sister, Jill. About eighteen months after Robert's death, she married a guy named Drew who also worked in dead-end jobs in the coal mines and had three more kids by him. All her kids are now grown and have either married or work in the coal mines.

Several years after Nancy and I wed, Jill wrote and told me that Robert's body had never been recovered because it was far too dangerous to enter the mine shaft where he had died due to the continued fragility and instability of the mine's ceiling. Other smaller cave-ins occurred in the same area after Robert's death, so the mining company closed the shaft.

I haven't seen Jill since early 1972 when she visited me while I was recuperating at the VA hospital in Lexington. She's a widow now, as Drew, like our father, came down with black lung disease and died several years ago. Around Christmas each year, I usually send her a check for $1,000. I hope she finds it useful.

As for me, several months after we married, and at Nancy's urging, I applied to the University of Montana in Missoula. Being a veteran and Purple Heart recipient really helped me in obtaining entrance to the school. Plus, I received twenty-four hours of life credits. So, two or three times a week, plus summer school, I commuted from Kalispell to the university for my studies and was able to graduate in three years with majors in history and creative writing.

Sitting in a classroom with so many young and naive students bothered me somewhat, especially when the classroom had no windows. Despite that the Vietnam War was over, I still couldn't get over the feeling of being trapped and tensed up more often than not. I almost managed to allay and banish my fears by always arriving fifteen minutes early to class whereupon I commandeered a chair in a corner where I could sit with no one behind me. I discouraged any student from sitting next to me by giving them a hard stare along with a head shake. That way I would be able to constantly survey the room and exit door as I silently steeled myself for anything untoward. Because of the way I carried myself, none of the students ever dared to take any classroom corner chairs which I had so confidently claimed.

Being older, I asked more pertinent and pointed questions of the professors. Sometimes, I even startled them with an observation that I guess they hadn't considered. I was happily surprised when the younger students started to approach me after class and asked me to clarify something I said in the discussion that day. I was always glad to answer and converse with each of them as to my take on specific aspects of our studies that particular day. I watched as they intently and hastily scrawled my responses in their notebooks.

Before I realized it, our hallway discussions slowly flowed into the university's cafeteria. There I began to hold sway at a long lunch table (always the same one near a corner!) as eight to ten of the "kids" fired questions at me, or we debated the various subjects in our studies. Only once during our lunchroom "semi-seminars" did someone ask me about my leg. I paused and rubbed my chin for about fifteen seconds as six or seven of them looked warily at me and I, in turn, surveyed each of their faces.

Putting on my best smile, I replied, "Well, guys, simply put, I had an accident." This seemed to satisfy the small group, and no one asked any further questions. It was as if they all tacitly agreed never to ask me again. Of course, I knew my answer would spread to the other students who regularly attended our lunch table discussions but weren't present that day.

After graduation, I used what I learned in my creative writing classes and started to write short stories. Many of them were about a young man growing up in eastern Kentucky, or about Vietnam vets and their experiences during and after the war. At Nancy's urging I sent them off to magazines that featured short stories, and to my surprise, the editors started publishing my work! My best one, with embellishments, was a tale about a "Brother Arnold" and his encounter and comeuppance at the hands of a young man in church one Sunday!

My dear beloved Nancy pestered me for several years to write this story so our kids and grandchildren will know how we met and experienced the mystical episode up on the mountain which finally brought us together for life. My creative writing major enabled me to write this tale. Since our last day at the cabin (which I sold to another Salish), neither one of us has ever returned to that location. Nor has either of us had any inclination to do so.

I thank God for bringing Nancy and I together. I vaguely remember some lines from a hymn I learned so long ago in that Holy Roller Southern Baptist church way back in eastern Kentucky where I grew up—the one with overgrown weeds in the cemetery situated on the side of some nameless godforsaken mountain. They seemed to ring true in my life:

Your Name is Power,

Your Name is Healing,

Your Name is Life![18]

God gave me the strength and power to survive such a horrible and wasted war. By sending Nancy to me, he healed 90 percent of my PTSD from my Vietnam tour and all the killing I had done there. Finally, through the Spirit Bear who saved both Nancy and I, God had given us both a further life to live and be as one in our marriage.

We never saw another Spirit Bear or Indian warrior except the one in the clouds at our wedding, but I still believe he is out there in the wilderness waiting to give aid to someone else in the far distant future.

Yet, I wonder all the time—did all these occurrences actually happen?

---

18 Songwriters: Jesse Reeves / Dustin Smith / Raina Patt / Kristen Dutton / Carlene Prince / Abigail Benton / *Speak Jesus* lyrics © Integrity's Praise! Music, Here Be Lions Publishing.

The Time Traveler: A Conversation with Longinus and an Alternative Account for the Resurrection

THE BEGINNING

Earth date 3516. My name is Sydney Winestein. I'm a Time Traveler (TT). I live in Israel, which survived the Great War III of 2025 when half of Earth's countries were annihilated by nuclear bombs and the planet's population dropped by 95 percent.

Russia, fed up with its failure to conquer Ukraine, threatened to unleash its nuclear weapons against the North Atlantic Treaty Organization (NATO) countries who had blockaded and embargoed it. When Russia launched its Intercontinental Ballistic Missiles (ICBM), NATO responded in kind by destroying the Soviet country west of the Urals. Moscow was obliterated. The NATO block took a few hits from the outmoded, poorly maintained, and defective Russian missiles, which were manufactured in Pakistan. Many of those missiles, due to poor upkeep, blew up on their launch pads while others simply missed their targets entirely or strayed off course into other countries.

China, afraid it would be next, fired its missiles not only at the NATO countries in Europe but also at the continental United States. Unfortunately, one of the Chinese missiles malfunctioned, went off course, and struck the city of Hyderabad, India. The sub-continent, fearing the attack came from either Pakistan or China, retaliated by decimating both Pakistan and sending its missiles over the Himalayas into China at the same time that U.S. missiles also rained down on the Red Communist regime, killing 90 percent of the Chinese population.

Israel, in turn, fearing that the Iranians would take advantage of the chaos and try to wipe it off the face of the world, practically flattened every major city in Iran with its nuclear weapons. That done, the Israelis, fed up with the Palestinians, wiped Gaza off the world map with non-nuclear weapons, leaving hardly a living soul left in that area next to the Mediterranean. The Israelis then marched into the pseudo-Palestinian country and killed everyone else, thus ridding themselves of a festering problem that had been plaguing and pestering the Jewish nation since the 1940s.

It was Armageddon to the entire planet and God's apocalypse all rolled into one massive catastrophe for the earth and those who lived innocently on it.

What was left of the world after this horrific exchange of nuclear weaponry? The earth, specifically the northern hemisphere, experienced a nuclear winter, and lost 95 percent of its remaining population within three to four months as most of the earth's residents died from either starvation or the toxic fallout. It took about six months for the radioactive dust storms to filter south across the equator and affect all the countries in the Southern Hemisphere that had been untouched by the nuclear holocaust. Most of the animal and human life in the Southern Hemisphere perished within a year (except for the rats and roaches!).

So, what happened to those humans who survived? My home country of Israel went underground. Unbeknownst to the rest of the world, the Israeli government had, for years, anticipated the above narrated scenario. They built massive concrete and steel reinforced tunnels two hundred-plus feet underground.

Our ancestors learned how to grow food hydroponically. Meat vanished entirely from our diet. Over the next three hundred years, we became vegans and we slowly realized that our lifespans started creeping up rather dramatically. Before the war, the average lifespan of an Israeli was around eighty years, but after the nuclear holocaust and a three hundred-year timespan, we were living 100 to 125 years. My father and mother died at 106 and 117 years, respectively. I am now seventy-five and feel as if I am only forty years old. Plus, I don't look even close to my age! Although our scholars had discussed this increased lifespan *ad nauseam*, the only conclusion they came up with is that our longevity was somehow linked to the radioactive dust that had settled over the earth and over time had slowly seeped into our underground water supply due to the porous desert rock above our heads.

Even more strangely, after another four hundred years, a few of us discovered we had a unique gift and could time travel (TT). Our first TT was a man by the name of Joseph Baumgartner, a nuclear scientist. One day, as he was walking into his laboratory where he studied radioactivity, he started to think about Socrates in ancient Athens. His three lab assistants saw him walking down the lab aisle toward them scratching an itch on his head over a baffling algorithm he wanted to solve when he simply evaporated before his aide's eyes.

Baumgartner later detailed in his written account that he felt as if he was inside of a dark black whirlwind for several seconds before he was deposited on a street in Athens. He was shocked to realize that he was also dressed in Greek clothing! As he wandered down the street, a passerby greeted him in Greek and he in turn, surprisingly, replied in Greek! He was totally flummoxed and taken aback by this unexplainable turn of events. As he walked, he felt some coins jangling in a pouch attached to the cord around his waist. Reaching into the leather bag, he withdrew one and realized it was a drachma.

I must be dead, Baumgartner thought. *Yet, somehow, this all seems so real.*

As he wandered about, he soon discovered an agora, where many people were shopping or bartering for various foods and goods. Finding a vacant bench, he sat down and observed the marketplace. It didn't take him long to learn that people were discussing the trial of Socrates, which had taken place a few days earlier. Having read the classics as a teenager, Baumgartner realized it must be 399 BC.

How in the hell have I returned to 399 BC? he wondered with some uneasiness.

An elderly man, with a limp and using a walking staff, approached and sat down on the bench. They started to talk. Baumgartner quickly ascertained that Socrates had been put on trial for impiety and corrupting the youth. Found guilty, Socrates was sentenced to death and had been forced to drink a cup of hemlock that morning. The crowds were informed of his death a few hours later.

He and the elderly man discussed Socrates for a while. Baumgartner, who knew about Socrates and how he died, kept his cards close to his chest while talking to the oldster. He decided not to let on that he knew anything about the Greek philosopher. Fearing that either the old man or someone else might report him to the authorities, Baumgartner didn't want to draw attention to himself. After fifteen to twenty minutes, the old man said he had to go. He stood and bade Baumgartner goodbye. The scientist was stunned by this turn of events.

Have I really traveled back in time to 399 BC? he wondered to himself in amazement. *And what in the world did I do to end up this far back in history? Will I ever be able to return to my world? Or am I dead?*

He decided to use one of his coins to get a drink. Across the bench, on the other side of the street, a vendor was selling wine. Baumgartner stood and started to walk toward the wine booth. He reached into his leather pouch and withdrew a drachma. He realized he had no idea as to the worth of such a coin and wondered if he would receive any change.

No one will ever believe me if I'm fortunate enough to return to my own time, he thought as he shook his head ever so slightly. *Unless I'm really dead and this is what happens to some people as they transition over.*

As he approached the vendor he started to think about Socrates and his laboratory and scratched another itch on his head. With no warning, he immediately found himself within the inky black whirlwind cloud slowly spinning around. The blackness lasted only a few seconds and Baumgartner found himself back in his laboratory with his three lab assistants staring at him in horror.

"Sir," they all said, "what happened to you? You vanished right before our eyes not two minutes ago."

Baumgartner was stunned. *Was I really only gone two minutes ago? What happened to me? Was I really in Athens in 399?* He tried to explain the unexplainable to his assistants, but was sure they didn't believe him. Unsure of the phenomenon, he called a meeting of his fellow scientists to discuss this mysterious occurrence.

Several days before the meeting, he decided he would try to return to ancient Greece at the time of the battle of Thermopylae in 480 BC. Try as he might, he could not duplicate his previous time travel until one of his brilliant and most observant assistants with an eidetic memory reminded him that just before he previously disappeared, he had been scratching his head.

So, thinking about the ancient Greek battle of Thermopylae against the Persians, he scratched his head and suddenly found himself among Persian warriors who were climbing a secret path leading to the rear of the Greek army. A traitor named Ephialtes revealed the existence of a trail that would enable the Persians not only to block the Greek leader, Leonidas I, but also prevent the Greeks from escaping. Baumgartner then watched as the Persians destroyed the entire Greek army led by Leonidas I. Scratching his head as this tragedy unfolded and thinking of home, Baumgartner found himself back in his lab.

A week later, over one hundred fifty people attended the meeting in a huge, underground one thousand-seat auditorium. Not only did some seventy-five to eighty of his fellow academics attend, but the word spread, and others outside the scientific community filtered in, too. Most of the men and women were incredulous by his otherworldly tale. Many shook their heads in disbelief. Baumgartner knew they were thinking he had gone crazy.

After some more discussion, along with questions and answers, he clapped his hands for silence and said, "Let's do an experiment. As I told you, I was thinking of Socrates and scratching my head when I disappeared. Wondering how to 'come back,' so to speak, I again thought of Socrates and scratched my head again, instantly finding myself back in my lab. All of you sitting here imagine someone in the past, or an era in time, to think about and if you do transition, remember to think of the same person or time era again to return here to the present. Do not forget the head scratches."

More than a few members of the crowd verbally showed their disbelief and incredulity by muttering under their breaths. Many of them silently thought Baumgartner had lost it. Others tentatively reached for their scalps, but then quickly dropped their hands back in their laps. Still others tried scratching their scalps while looking at him rather quizzically.

The nuclear scientist stared up at the now silent audience from his podium. Suddenly, it began to happen. One by one people in the different parts of the auditorium started to disappear. In all, within a minute there were seven empty seats.

Those who remained gasped and twisted around in their seats to look at the vacant ones. Those sitting next to the now empty seats just gaped in disbelief. They reached over and patted the now empty seats. Everyone seemed to be awestruck. The crowd's voices, murmuring at first, started to rise until the auditorium was a cacophony of unintelligibleness—a Tower of Babel.

But then, the miracle happened. Those who vanished started to materialize in the seats they had previously occupied. A deathlike hush stole over the assembled group as one after another the missing began to reappear. After several minutes all seven of those who had mysteriously disappeared materialized right before their eyes. The auditorium was in an uproar as everyone started speaking at once. The babble quickly turned into a discordance of unintelligible noise as the members of the audience started to question the returnees. Baumgartner pounded his rostrum with a gavel calling for silence.

"Would each of you please stand and tell us what happened to you?" the scientist asked after the room quieted. The tales he and the assemblage heard were astonishing. As each one of the three women and four men related their stories to the assemblage, one could almost hear a pin drop in the huge, cavernous room.

One of the women went back to the early 1970s and met Israeli Prime Minister Golda Meir. One of the scientists traveled to Great Britain in the late 1600s and met with Isaac Newton. Another man, whose ancestors moved to Israel in the 1980s, found himself in the Vietnam War in the middle of an August 1969 attack by the North Vietnamese Army (NVA). He related that he materialized on a jungle landing zone called LZ Becky, a small American artillery base in the tropical jungle rainforest near the Cambodian border. He saw and met one of his ancestors, a young American G. I. whom he talked to and then saw killed by a North Vietnamese rocket. One of the women ended up in Italy during the Renaissance where, during the early 1500s, she watched Michelangelo paint the ceiling of the Sistine Chapel.

The members of the audience were stunned. Hardly a word was spoken as each of the seven related their time trip. When the last of the seven finished their story, Baumgartner stood behind the podium and spoke.

"Ladies and gentlemen," Baumgartner suggested, "as strange as these tales are, I believe what happened to me and these others is due to some unexplainable gift some of us have been given. There must be something in our DNA that allows this to happen. Perhaps, it is a result of being exposed over the last fifteen hundred years to minute, or infinitesimal atoms of radioactivity that may have filtered into our water or our present underground living area. If I, or the other seven individuals can repeat our strange journeys into the past, then I think we should call ourselves 'Time Travelers.'"

In the following weeks, several of the original seven along with Baumgartner repeated time trips to various eras of the past world. One even went back to the Jurassic Age and viewed dinosaurs. More people, not present at the meeting that day, who lived in the underground world that was modern-day Israel, discovered they, too, could time travel into the fathomless past. Oddly, it was soon discovered that only about 5 to 8 percent of the inhabitants of this underground city could time travel.

All the TTs explored various former worlds and passed on their rare gift to only one of their children who, in turn, passed it on to their scions.

So, I, Sydney Winestein, being a direct descendant of Baumgartner, inherited the ability to TT. I had taken several trips into the past and successfully returned to the great relief of my wife, Leah. During one of those trips, I discovered that I also had the ability to shapeshift and change both my body image and clothing along with somehow, mysteriously, speeding up time. With my return from each trip, I started to contemplate the one trip I wanted to take but kept putting it off in my mind. I often discussed the pros and cons of such a penultimate trip with Leah, who was not only most supportive of the adventure, but also urged me to attempt it.

I wanted to go back and witness both the crucifixion and resurrection of Christ. Little did I realize at the time, but this proposed trip may have changed history along with the advent and spread of Christianity. I needed further information as to what had taken place that day and weekend. Sadly, there was only one document that I could use to do so—the Christian Bible.

So, off I went to our massive 57 million-plus volume library. I met with the head librarian, an ancient-looking and garrulous crone named Marilou Myerwicx, who was, despite her loquaciousness, especially helpful since she had an encyclopedic memory. Also, as everyone who used the library knew, you crossed her at your peril; otherwise, you wouldn't be able to locate much of anything pertaining to your quest.

She suggested I look at several of the various Christian Bibles that were on the shelves. That way, she intoned, I would have various versions to compare. Using her modern Genesis 57 laptop, which was designed by our Israeli scientists, she pulled up the pertinent passages on both the crucifixion and the resurrection in the New Testament—Mark 15:52–16:20; Matthew 27:57–28:20; Luke 23:50–24:53; and John 19:38–21:25. She then informed me that Matthew, Luke, and John not only provided more information but that Luke and John in particular were more extensive in their details. Mark, she informed me, was brief and the ending to his version had been under debate by biblical scholars down through the ages. I thanked her most profusely after she directed me to the pertinent library section.

Our cavernous library was approximately three miles long, with a twelve-foot-high arched ceiling and about fifty feet wide. Two sections of ten-foot-high bookshelves, each separated by four feet, lined both sides of the walls. Every bookcase—each about twenty-five feet long—also had a ladder on rails enabling one to climb and slide past the rows of books in order to locate any one in particular book.

In front of the shelves were working tables and chairs along with a computer to access even more sources. In the middle of the tunnel was a set of two railroad tracks each about three feet wide, upon which ran an almost noiseless electric conveyance seating ten people. When you arrived at the section where you wanted to do research, you simply pushed a button on the armrest and the tram slid silently to a stop. You exited, found the books you needed, took them to an empty table, and began to work. When you wanted to leave, you simply crossed the tracks at the designated spots, pushed a button on a post next to the tracks, and a tram soon arrived to return you to the library's entrance.

I was particularly interested in a nebulous figure, known as Longinus, whose name popped up every so often in relation to the crucifixion. He was purported not only to be a Roman Centurion under the command of Pontius Pilate but also the person who made sure orders from the top were followed by the eighty to ninety men under his command. According to legend, he pierced Jesus's side with a lance, now referred to in Christianity as the "Holy Lance." I wanted to see if there was any historical information concerning this elusive witness to the crucifixion and the rumor that, after piercing Christ's side, he became an instant convert to Christianity.

I first delved into Matthew, Mark, Luke, and John to get some basic information concerning the crucifixion. I quickly learned that by the end of the Great War III in 2025, most scholars agreed that the four gospels were the work of unknown, but relatively well-educated, Greek-speaking Christians and were composed from c. 66-110 AD—Mark was the first (66-75 AD), followed by Matthew (65-85 AD), then

Luke (65-95 AD), and finally John (75-100 AD).[19]

My research led me to discover that the modern names of the "Four Evangelists" were added in the second century (101-200 AD). Scholars were certain that none of the four gospels were written by eyewitnesses, and all were end products of long oral and written transmission.[20] This information confirmed to me my original thesis concerning the gospels of Mark, Matthew, Luke, and John. I now had no doubt that errors had occurred with each succeeding oral history or transcription due to embellishments and deletions. After all, as the trite saying goes, history is written by the winners who, of course, can put their particular positive spin on what is written.

Ascertaining this information, I decided to find out the age of the first extant fragments of the four gospels—Mark was written in Greek on parchment (150-250 AD), Matthew was written in Greek on papyrus (150-300 AD), Luke was written in Greek on a papyrus known as Fragment 4 (175-250 AD), and John was the oldest, written in Greek on papyrus (75-100 AD).

From my earliest university religious studies, I knew about the Jewish-Roman historian Flavius Josephus (c. 37-100 AD) whose following description of Jesus was well known in Jewish circles:

(63) Now, there was about this time Jesus, a wise man, if it be lawful to call him a man, for he was a doer of wonderful works—a teacher of such men as receive the truth with pleasure. He drew over to him both many of the Jews, and many of the Gentiles. He was [the] Christ; (64) and when Pilate, at the suggestion of the principal men amongst us, had condemned him to the cross, those that loved him at the first did not forsake him, for he appeared to them alive again the third day, as the divine prophets had foretold these and ten thousand other wonderful things concerning him; and the tribe of Christians,

19 "Evidence for an Early Dating of the Four Gospels." Accessed June 19, 2024.
https://www.evidenceunseen.com/theology/scripture/historicityofthent/evidenceforanearlydatingofthefourgospels/
20 https://en.wikipedia.org/wiki/Gospel. Accessed June 19, 2024.

so named from him, are not extinct at this day.[21]

The problem with the extant manuscripts of Josephus's books is that none have been dated before the eleventh century (1001-1100 AD). As I soon discovered, at some point they were edited by the inclusion of Christian phraseology which strongly suggested the presence of some interpolations thus calling the authenticity of certain passages into question.[22]

After several days of extensive research and learning the basic facts surrounding Jesus, his pastorship, the crucifixion, and the resurrection, I was finally ready to tackle the legend surrounding Longinus. By this time, I knew I was delving into some murky truths, half-truths, outright lies, and mythology. Yet, I wanted to be as prepared as possible for my future trip into the past.

Longinus's name first appeared in the apocryphal Gospel of Nicodemus (a.k.a. the Acts of Pilate), which is of unknown and dubious authenticity although it was widely circulated as being true. Nicodemus appears in the Gospel of John as an associate of Jesus.[23] In Nicodemus's Gospel, certain biblical figures—names not found in the canonical texts—are identified as Longinus, who received credit for spearing Jesus on the cross. The two criminals crucified with Jesus were named Dismas (a.k.a. the "Good Thief") and Gestes (a.k.a. the "Impenitent Thief").

Longinus, supposedly after piercing Christ's side, is reported to have said that Jesus was the Son of God and thus is treated as one of the first Christians and Roman converts. Still, as I further learned, the name Longinus did not appear to have been known to the Greeks until his name appeared in an illuminated gospel manuscript dated

---

21 https://www.pbs.org/wgbh/pages/frontline/shows/religion/maps/primary/josephusjesus. html#::text=Jospehus'%20Description%20of%20Jesus&text=(63)%20Now%2C%20there%20was,and%20 many%20of%20the%20Gentiles. Accessed June 19, 2024. "The Antiquities of the Jews" (93–94 AD), Book 18, Chapter 3." *The Works of Josephus*, trans. William Whiston. Peabody [MA]: Hendrickson Publishers, 1987. Sadly, scholars question the validity of this quotation.
22 https://en.wikipedia.org/wiki/Josephus_on_Jesus.
23 Nicodemus was a Pharisee and a member of the Sanhedrin, the Jewish governing body. See the Gospel of John 3:1–9.

586 AD. Another legend says that Longinus had an eye affliction and after he thrust his lance into Jesus's side, supposedly some of Christ's blood fell upon the Roman Centurion's eyes and he was healed, thus bringing about his conversion. This tale defies logic as a blind or even partially blind Centurion would never have been allowed to continue as a Roman soldier. So, I quickly dismissed that story.

According to some biblical scholars and historians, Christ was crucified on April 3, either in 30 or 33 AD. The debate as to the correct year has never been settled. It was a Friday and also known as the Day of Preparation. The next day was the Jewish Sabbath. Since there were no extant records to confirm that date, I had to take the writings with the proverbial grain of salt. Then, according to Christian tradition, the resurrection took place three days later, on Passover, more commonly known as Easter Sunday.

I knew if I intended to return to the day of the crucifixion, I would need to be a rank higher than a Centurion. After some quick research, I thought it would be best for me to assume the rank of a Roman Tribune who was sent on a fact-finding mission to the Promised Land by order of the Emperor Tiberius. That way, if indeed I did locate Longinus, or someone else who was responsible for stabbing Jesus, having a higher rank would ensure a certain amount of respect and, hopefully, honesty. To that end, I studied several different books on the uniforms that both the Centurions and Tribunes wore around the time of Jesus to learn what I needed to wear when impersonating a Roman Tribune.

One of the final tasks I set for myself while working on the research was to memorize maps of what Jerusalem looked like during the time of Jesus. I located more than a few maps of the city in that period of time. I placed them in my memory, hoping all the while that I would at least remember most of the salient details.

After several weeks of research, I learned as much as I could and would be somewhat prepared for my trip back in time to the crucifixion. I was tired from all the research. When I arrived home that day after winding things down at the library, I sat down with Leah and described in detail what I had learned over the last ten to fifteen days. She listened attentively and then urged me to spend a few days relaxing and unwinding before undergoing what might be an exhausting trip into a past where, when I returned, I might end up dispelling any myths surrounding the Christian beliefs concerning both the crucifixion and the resurrection.

Leah mentioned that the knowledge I learned might change the Christian religious world if I decided to share it. I told her that when I returned, I would share what I saw and observed with her and we would then determine whether to keep the information to ourselves or share it at some later date with our two children, Rebekkah and Michael. We even might choose to share it with the world even though there probably weren't all that many Christians left in various parts of our radioactive earth. The only existing Christians we knew of were living in a former missile silo near the ghost town of Minot, North Dakota; also an Australian group who also occupied a silo in the Outback near the Aborigines' sacred place known as Uluru, which was once named Ayers Rock; and some Mormons living far deep in a desert cave system near St. George, Utah. All these small groups lived totally underground.

So, for a week or so, I rested and contemplated my trip into the murky past surrounding Jesus, his crucifixion, and resurrection. Over the next few days, I experimented with taking trips back to ancient Rome where I observed the military dress of various Tribunes. I wanted to be sure that when I arrived in 33 AD Jerusalem I was dressed as accurately as possible so as to pass any inspection leveled at me by any Roman soldiers I might encounter. On these trips I also discovered I could speak Latin fluently.

Back in my home, I relaxed a few more days, mentally preparing for time travel back to the most significant three days in Christian theology and belief. Yom Kippur, also known as the Day of Atonement, was the holiest day in the Jewish calendar. It was fast approaching. Thus, my journey would occur during the most memorable days of our two religions. As tradition called for, I would spend the ten days prior to Yom Kippur by fasting and in fervent prayer.

I decided to leave the day after Yom Kippur, hoping that some luck would follow me on my journey. Of course, I was reminded of the brief Yom Kippur War of October 1973, which Israel won some fourteen centuries ago. The war was still emblazoned on every Israeli's mind as to the perfidy of enemies and was still taught to every Israeli schoolchild. It reminded me that I needed to be as careful as I could so as not to antagonize anyone I met during my return to the past and to keep my eyes open and alert to any pitfalls I might encounter.

The Crucifixion

The day after Yom Kippur ended, Leah and I rose early. I was eager to leave on my fact-finding exploration of the past, but Leah sat me down and made me a large breakfast. Who knows when I might eat again or how long this time travel might last, she pointed out. So, I ate. When finished, I stood and walked away from the table into the middle of our living room. Leah, who followed, kissed me and wished me godspeed. I thought about a Tribune's uniform and the day of the crucifixion, pressed my fingers to my head, and scratched.

The ink black whirlwind immediately engulfed me. It seemed that for some unknown reason the blackness lasted a bit longer than previous trips. When the wind ceased, and the inky black mist faded away, I found myself just outside Jerusalem's Second Wall near the Gennath Gate dressed as a Roman Tribune. I looked up at the hill in front of me. It was Golgotha and I could see three men on crosses at its top along with a large crowd surrounding the execution ground. I decided to climb the hill and observe the brutal proceedings. On my way to the top, I passed several Roman soldiers on their way downhill. Each one made a gesture of respect by raising their right fist over their heart. I returned the gestures, nodded at each man, and continued upward.

After a not-so-arduous climb, I arrived at the cleared and flattened top of the hill known as Golgotha. The crowd, recognizing my rank, quickly parted to let me through. There was a Roman soldier standing in front of each cross keeping the crowd at a distance of fifteen feet. Christ was hanging from the middle cross. The two men on either side appeared to be dead with their dried blood splattering onto their hands and feet. Christ, I observed, appeared to be in the throes of his last moments with his now milky deathlike eyes watching the crowd. Blood dripped from his scalp where the crown of thorns was placed on his head. It also dripped profusely from both his hands and ankles, pooling at the bottom of the cross.

The soldier in front of his cross appeared to be the highest in rank so I strode toward him. We saluted each other.

"I am the Tribune Gaius Cassius Falcidus," I said in a very stern commanding voice. "I'm here to observe these proceedings."

"Ave, your honor!" the man replied. "I am called Septimus Maximus, at your service. I'm in charge of this execution."[24] He bowed his head an inch or so and then rubbed his right eye which was teary with a slight greyish film over it. A scar running from his forehead crossed over the eye and down his face to the chin.

---

24 "Septimus Maximus" means the greatest seventh son. Perhaps his parents believed he would achieve more than their first six sons.

I nodded, thinking, *Well, his name is definitely not Longinus, but, according to legend, his eye looks damaged.*

"Where do you hail from, Maximus?" I asked.

"I was born in Rome, your honor. I am a proud Roman! People born outside of Rome are only Italians, but I am a true Roman!"

"As well you should be," I replied with a smile. "I, too, am a true Roman!" I said with pride.

As I finished my last sentence, Jesus groaned and spoke.

"I thirst!" he said.

Maximus said, "Excuse me, Tribune. I need to do this."

I stood by watching as Maximus turned, picked up a hyssop branch, stuck a sponge on the end of it, dipped it into a bottle of sour-smelling wine, and held it to Christ's mouth.

After Jesus sipped on the sour wine, he looked down at us, then moved his deadened eyes over the crowd and said, "It is finished." With a loud exhalation of breath, he died and sagged on the cross.

I stood there in awe. I had just witnessed the horrific and excruciatingly painful death of the man who became the God for all Christians.

Maximus gave a loud whistle and within minutes more Roman soldiers appeared. As I stood by, Maximus directed his men to take down the bodies and break the legs of the two criminals. Seeing that Jesus was already dead, Maximus ordered his men not to break his legs. Instead, Maximus took his spear and pierced Jesus's side. Suddenly he stepped backward as if in much surprise as both blood and water flowed out of Jesus's side.

As if in awe, Maximus knelt and touched both the flowing blood and water. Withdrawing his hand, he shook it to get rid of the liquid. I saw a tiny globule fly off his hand and hit his right eye. He quickly reached up with his left hand and wiped his eye as he stood. He turned to me, stunned. Felt his eye again. His jaw dropped and I knew from my research what had just happened to him.

"Tribune," Maximus said, "it's a miracle! The vision in my eye is completely restored! That man truly is the Son of God." He shook his head in wonder as his troops took the three bodies away. "It's a miracle! It's a miracle!" he kept uttering under his breath.

Although I read about this miracle in my research, I was still in awe and amazement. A miracle just happened before my eyes. So, at least that part of the legend was true.

THE SPY MISSION

I patted the soldier on his shoulder and said, "Why don't we repair to a tavern, and I'll buy you a drink or two?"

Septimus Maximus just nodded as if in shock and continued to mutter, "I can see! I can see!" He repeated it over and over as we walked down Golgotha and entered Jerusalem by the Gennath Gate.

"I know a good tavern," Maximus said. He took the lead, and I followed. We soon found ourselves ensconced in a tavern where I saw and nodded at other Roman officers as we sat down. Sitting at a small square table, which abutted the outside wall of the dingy barroom, we ordered two cups of wine from the slovenly looking waitress. I wanted to pry more information out of him, so by drinking at a local barroom, I hoped that would put him at ease.

Sipping on our red wine, which didn't taste too bad, I casually asked Maximus, "In my observations around Jerusalem, I've heard the name Longinus mentioned. Do you know of such a Roman and who he might be?"

"Oh, yes, sir, I have," he replied. "He is my commander. He's in charge of our maniple and assigns smaller groups like mine to tasks like this crucifixion.[25] He likes to take credit for all our accomplishments. When he hears about my eye, he'll probably enhance the story and claim it was he who had an eye restored."

"Well, that certainly sounds typical of the commanders in every legion," I commented as I smiled and gave him a conspiratorial wink and nod. Continuing, I asked him, "Well, what's next for you, Maximus?"

"Well, Tribune," he said as he lowered his voice almost to a whisper, "I have a rather serious job to accomplish this night." He downed the rest of his cup of wine.

"Oh," I said, feigning some mild (but definitely not too eager!) interest as I raised my eyebrows. "Sounds as if you have had a long day already! You must not be getting a lot of sleep?"

I signaled to the tavern's owner for another round of wine. I wanted to make sure that Maximus would continue to talk and tell me more as the wine might relax his thoughts and mouth.

"For sure, Tribune! But not tonight," he replied.

Maximus nodded, then lowered his voice again to a whisper after the tavern owner brought us two more cups of wine, set them on the table, and left. "Well, since all the rumors have said that this Jew Jesus will rise on the third day, Pontius Pilate has ordered Longinus to find out where the Christ's body is buried and steal it. I'm to find

---

25 A maniple in the Roman army consisted of a unit of one hundred twenty men with more flexibility on the battlefield.

out the location and pass on the information to Longinus, who has told us that he will lead a party of six to eight men to find and whisk the body away."

"Won't that body snatching only confirm that this man Christ has risen from the dead and give more impetus to the new Christian religion?"

"It might," he thoughtfully replied. "But at least we will have the body and will display it on the fourth day to prove the man was a fake—just an ordinary religious charlatan who died and didn't rise from the dead. It certainly will quash all the rumors about the fact that a man can be resurrected from the dead. That fact alone will be the end to this new religious movement."

"What about your eye and what happened to it when you touched his blood?" I asked.

He put his fingers up to his right eye and lightly rubbed it. "I think I have experienced a miracle, Tribune. But how and why it happened to me, I cannot tell," he replied.

"Perhaps," he continued, "there may be something to this new religion, which some are now calling Christianity. Yet, I don't believe that it poses any threat to Rome, or the Roman Empire. Miracles are miracles, aren't they?"

I gave Maximus just a slight nod.

He added, "If this Christ was indeed so powerful as to bring about the miracles we have heard about and what happened to me, then he may be the Son of a God more omnipotent than our god, Jupiter."

He continued, "If after a week or so my eye stays healed, then I might have to give this new religion some serious thought."

"Well," I said, "this gives us a lot of food for thought, doesn't it?

My job in coming to Jerusalem was to gather facts about this new movement, its leader, and his followers and transmit the information to our emperor. What he then does with it, heaven and the gods only know. But I certainly see no threat to Rome. After all, I think this body of Jews known as the Sanhedrin was extremely jealous of this man Jesus and felt he posed a threat to their authority. That's why they were so insistent on having him put to death. After all, whenever anyone poses any kind of threat to authority, those in power do what they can to eradicate that individual."

Maximus nodded, then said, "Tribune, I must leave and report to Longinus and tell him that the crucifixion has been accomplished and that I'll continue to work on locating where this man Jesus has been buried. I'll also inform him as to why my eye appears to be healed."

I stood and clapped him on the back. "Best of luck to you, Maximus. I need to go and gather more information. It has been most helpful to learn about your perspective concerning the events that have occurred here in Jerusalem."

We stepped out of the tavern and gave each other the Roman salute before turning away. I had to find a quiet place and figure out my next move. I already knew from my research that Joseph of Arimathea took Christ's body. To that end he placed the body in a newly hewn stone tomb surrounded by a garden that lay below the summit of Golgotha about halfway between it and the Gennath Gate.

I exited the city by that gate and walked to the garden. It was growing late, and the day was drawing to a close. A small group of people consisting of ten to thirteen men and a sole woman were standing around what must have been Christ's tomb. I saw one of the men gesture toward the city and say, "We must leave before sundown. Who knows what the Romans or the Sanhedrin might do if they catch us here? Let us go and find the other disciples. But first, let all of us roll this stone in front of the tomb's opening."

I watched as all the men grabbed a four-and-a-half-foot diameter stone and rolled it into place. As they worked, I wondered if five or six Roman soldiers had the strength to roll the stone back when they came to steal Christ's body. I knew I had to do something to prevent the Romans obtaining possession of Jesus's body.

The men stood after finishing their onerous task. I heard one of the men say as he wiped the sweat off his brow, "Let us all go to Yosef's house, where the others are waiting, take dinner, and mourn our loss." Some of the men and the woman nodded, so they set off for the Gennath Gate and soon disappeared into the city.

What to do? I asked myself. *I have to find the disciples and alert them to the upcoming danger. Plus, I need a believable story to convince them that the Romans, led by Longinus, are, for nefarious reasons, bent on stealing Christ's body.*

I approached the Gennath Gate and found the soldier in charge of that entrance into the city. After saluting him, he appeared shocked by the appearance of a Tribune in front of him. I could tell he was worried about talking to such a high-ranking Roman soldier as myself.

"Relax, soldier, I'm not here to inspect you and the other two guards. My name is Tribune Gaius Falcidas, and you are?"

"Tribune, my name is Lucius. I am in command of this gate," he quickly replied. He seemed to relax only a bit but appeared to still be nervous that he was talking to a Tribune.

"I'm here on a fact-finding mission for the Emperor Tiberius. I need to know if you, or either of your two guards, are familiar with the location of a home occupied by a man known as Yosef. Don't worry if you don't know, but perhaps you can send one of your men to find out."

Nodding, he replied, "I don't know, Tribune, but I will send one of these men to a few local taverns and he might be able to learn the information you need." He turned and pointed at one of the guards, whose name I subsequently learned was Titus, and instructed the underling to go into the city and find out where Yosef lived.

I turned to the man and instructed him, "Be careful when you locate the house. Just act as if you are passing along the street on other business." I stressed, "And do not, under any circumstances, look directly at the home except sideways out of one of your eyes." I continued by sternly admonishing him, "And return here by another route. I don't want to arouse anyone's suspicions that the area is being scouted or observed. Just act normal. Do you understand?"

Titus nodded, saluted both Lucius and I, and turned and hurried off. Making small talk, I chatted with Lucius. About ten minutes into our discussion, I casually asked him where Roman officers go to drink and be entertained. He pointed to a street to the left of the small plaza located behind the gate.

"Tribune, it's about one hundred yards down that street and it is called Avram's. It has a lantern outside the front door. They serve good red wine and beer, plus they have the cleanest whores in the city. In fact," he continued, "they just got a girl in from Syria last week who's named Dvora and whom, I understand, is most adept at keeping your interest. But I'm told she's incredibly expensive."

I shrugged nonchalantly, thanked him, and patted him on the back giving him a wink and knowing look. We continued chatting until about twenty minutes later his minion returned with the information I needed. Titus related to Lucius what he had learned as I listened to the conversation. When he stopped, and fearing I might get lost even after receiving the directions, I turned to Lucius and said, "Commander, would you take me to a block within distance to Yosef's home?"

Lucius replied, "Gladly, Tribune!" He then turned and spoke to both guards, instructing them to close the gate and await his return.

Lucius and I marched off. After a brisk fifteen-minute walk, as the dusk of the approaching darkness threw a pall over the city, we arrived at a point about seventy-five yards from Yosef's home. Lucius pointed it out in the fading light. I nodded as I leaned against a corner of a house located catty-cornered from Yosef's home.

"Now, Lucius," I instructed him in a whisper, "leave me now and return to the Gennath Gate." I pulled five or six silver coins of various denominations from an opening in my leather belt and placed them into his hand. "Do not speak of this encounter to anyone and give both of your men a coin to be quiet. This incident never occurred, and you have no idea who I am. Are we clear about that?"

"Yes, Tribune," Lucius replied as he saluted me, turned, and strode off in the direction of the Gennath Gate.

I faded back into a small niche on the side of the house and quickly shapeshifted into the clothes of a poor Jerusalem trader. I also took on a different appearance with my face, making it wrinkled and pockmarked, along with white hair. I made my nose twice as large with a wart growing hair out of the end of it. I decided to shadow Lucius back to the gate. I cautiously trundled along so as to throw the gatekeeper off the scent should he turn around and double back to spy on me.

I quietly followed the Roman gatekeeper, catching sight of him some thirty yards ahead of me. Keeping to the shadows on the opposite side of the narrow street, I trailed Lucius until he arrived back at the Gennath Gate. I watched as he gave some coins to each of his men. Still, I waited another five minutes to assure myself he and his two underlings would remain at the gate.

Then, I shapeshifted back into my Tribune persona and stepped into the street. Since I had some time and the evening was young, I decided to check out Avram's. I needed verifiable information before meeting with the disciples. I would have to make myself a more believable individual so they could save Christ's body from being stolen by the Romans in the coming morning hours.

I strode purposely down the unlit street with my hand on my sword in case I was accosted by some robbers. I quickly found Avram's. I could easily hear a raucous din from outside as I approached the tavern's open door and saw the lantern Lucius mentioned hanging on its right side. Entering, I saw a roomful of Roman soldiers drinking either beer or wine. A hush quickly descended throughout the room and I saw each soldier stiffen a bit and stand a little straighter as the conversation seemed to fade away. I doubted they had ever seen a Tribune in this foul nest of drunks and debauchery.

I pulled out a gold coin and flipped it across the room to the bartender who caught it in mid-air. "Drinks for everyone!" I shouted. The soldiers immediately relaxed, raised their cups my way, and said almost in unison, "Hooray for the Tribune!" They all downed whatever was left in their cups as the bartender and several of his fully bosomed serving maids began refilling their cups.

A Roman soldier stood from a table in front of what appeared to be a curtained stage and approached me. He saluted me and I returned his salute.

"Tribune, my name is Longinus, and I am a Centurion with a local maniple. Would you like to come to my table and drink with me and some of my men?"

"Why, thank you, Longinus, I will!" I patted him on the back. "My name is Tribune Gaius Cassius Falcidus. I'm here on a fact-finding mission for the Emperor Tiberius," I told him as we approached his table. As we began to sit, I clicked my fingers at a nearby serving girl to get her attention, then held up two fingers and pantomimed drinking. She nodded and hurried off.

We sat and Longinus introduced me to his two drinking mates

whose names I quickly forgot as I wanted to concentrate on what Longinus had to say.

"Can you tell me anything else about your mission?" he asked.

"I can only say that I am here to observe conditions in Jerusalem," I replied. "It appears that this Christ fellow was something of an irritant or threat to the power of various Jewish officials who wanted Pilate to execute him."

"Yes, that is true," he admitted. "I had a team of soldiers, led by Septimus Maximus, whom I charged with crucifying this man who claimed to be the Son of God, along with two other criminals. Strangely, Maximus has claimed to have been cured of his eye affliction from the man's blood when they took him down from the cross. I ordered him to never tell that story to anyone or he would end up in prison." Interestingly, as Longinus related this information, he rubbed his right eye.

Was that a strange coincidence? I thought before asking, "Was this Jesus a real threat?"

"No," he replied, "but I think I'm going to appropriate the healing eye story as happening to me, which ought to give the Jewish officials pause about wanting to uselessly kill any further upstarts they might want Pontius to execute. Should there be another Christlike figure claiming to be able to accomplish miracles, I can say such a person is a copycat of sorts because their Jesus healed my eye. No one would dare contradict me and that should calm down the so-called believers of another fake Messiah as they refer to this Christ fellow."

The serving wench reappeared with our cups of wine. I noted that the ties to the front of her blouse were so loose as to leave nothing to a lascivious man's imagination, especially when she bent over the table and placed the wine cups in front of us. Her blouse was so thin that even the blindest person could eye and appraise her bosoms.

I nodded at Longinus's last comment. "Sounds like a good story to me. Surely history will remember your name!" I now knew how the legend surrounding Longinus and his so-called "miracle eye" would pass down through the ages.

Poor Septimus Maximus, I thought. *He'll never get the credit he is due.* But then, as throughout the world's history of military conflicts, it was the officers who always claimed credit for the heroism of those under them.

"Tribune," Longinus stated as he lowered his voice, "Pilate has assigned an interesting task to me and my two men here along with a few more soldiers."

I gave him a questioning look and raised my eyebrows.

"Two hours before the cock crows, I'm to take my hand-picked soldiers and go to the tomb of Jesus which Maximus located and passed on to me. There we will whisk the body away to a secret place and keep it for four days. These followers of Christ have predicted he will rise from the dead on the third day after crucifixion. But, since we have the body, nothing will happen on the third day, and they will be discredited and quickly lose their false hope. Their religion will disappear as fast as it was started!" he gleefully contended.

Longinus smiled as he related the story before continuing, "Then, on the fourth or fifth day, we will bring his body to the main plaza, not only to display it but also behead the corpse and show these people he hasn't risen, thus proving he was nothing more than a fake or fraud."

If I knew anything about the Romans, once they were in possession of Christ's body, they would immediately behead it. An act such as that would most likely put a quick end to Christianity. Longinus rubbed his hands together and grinned as he described that the Romans intended to wipe out all belief in Christianity.

I immediately knew I needed to quickly divert his attention so as not to arouse his suspicions that I was in any way interested in the information he had just relayed to me. I didn't want to take any chance whatsoever that I was interested in his orders to steal Jesus's body. So, I abruptly changed tact and asked Longinus, "What about this Dvora whore who plies her trade here? Is she any good, or just another prostitute?"

"Oh, no not at all, Longinus. She's the real thing and, if I do say so myself, incredibly adept in bed! Being my rank, the tavern owner has let me use her for free, but he charges lesser soldiers almost a month's wages to bed with her." That said, Longinus raised his hand and motioned for the tavern owner to come to our table.

"What can I do for you, Longinus?" the man asked when he arrived at our table. He nodded to me to acknowledge my rank.

"The Tribune wants to examine this Dvora," Longinus replied. "Bring her out so that we might get a closer look."

The man merely nodded, walked behind our table, parted the curtains, and disappeared behind them. Within a minute, he was back gripping the poor girl's wrist. A lot of catcalls and whistles arose from the other Romans in the tavern at Dvora's sudden appearance. Indeed, this Dvora was everything both the gatekeeper Lucius and Longinus had described. She was scantily clad in translucent material with nothing else to cover her figure underneath it, which left nothing (and everything!) to the imagination. I stood and took a minute or so to examine Dvora as I circled around her. She had shaved her entire body and her prominent areolas were dark and high pointed. An unknown musk-like scent exuded from her skin.

"Thank you," I said to the tavernkeeper. "She is indeed what everyone has said she is, yet I will pass on her." The man's face dropped. No doubt he thought that as a Tribune I would pay good gold for bedding the newest addition to his stable. Sadly, Dvora looked no more than fifteen or sixteen years old. To lift up the barkeep's spirits I handed him a small gold coin for bringing his newest whore out for display.

Looking down at Longinus, I said, "Well, I wish you good luck in your morning task. I must go now, as I still have a few errands to fulfill this evening." Patting Longinus on the shoulder, I nodded to him and the other two men sitting with him as I turned and ambled out the tavern's door.

MEETING WITH THE DISCIPLES

I hurried back to the street where Yosef lived, found the previous niche I had used, and quickly shapeshifted back into the poor Jerusalem shoe trader. My cover story, in case anyone was to stop me and ask, was that I was a man who often frequented Avram's every week or so spending coin I didn't have for such folly and was now on my way home. I added a stout walking stick to my shabby ensemble so that I could lean over as if I had a stooped back. I prayed the disciples would find my story believable.

Now for the difficult part of my journey back into time. I was about to alter history, or at least the Bible narrative. I needed to gain entry into Yosef's home, meet with the disciples, and convince them that they needed to move Christ's body before it was stolen by the Romans in the coming early morning hours. I hoped my story would be plausible enough for them to believe me. If not, I had another trick that would convince them. With that in mind, I crossed the street and knocked firmly on Yosef's door.

About thirty seconds later I heard a stout bolt unlocking the door. It was opened by an old, wizened man with deep dark eye sockets that seemed to bore right through your body. He only opened the door a few inches, hiding the rest of his body behind the stout wooden entrance.

"Are you Yosef?" I asked.

Nodding somewhat reluctantly, he replied, "Who wants to know?"

I introduced myself, saying, "My name is Abram. I'm a poor shoe trader traveling through Jerusalem. I have come upon some valuable information that concerns this Christ figure who was just crucified today. I need to speak to his disciples whom, I have learned, are present in your home."

"Wait here. I'll be back shortly," he said as he quietly shut the door and threw the lock bolts back into place.

I leaned nonchalantly against the doorframe for several minutes. *Well*, I thought, *either he'll come back and tell me they're not there, or perhaps one of the disciples will come out to speak with me further.*

About five minutes later, the lock bolts alerted me as the door creaked open a few inches. This time it wasn't Yosef, but an older individual with long white hair and a full greying beard.

"Who are you?" the man asked rather gruffly.

I introduced myself again telling him that I had vital information concerning Jesus.

"Why should we believe you?" he asked with an abrupt and quizzical tone in his voice.

"Please, sir," I replied as I stretched my arms out from my sides, still holding my walking staff. "As you can see, I'm a poor man, my hair is white, and I am old and wrinkled. Search me if you like. I bring only news for you and your group and nothing more. You can choose to believe me or not, but I have something of great import for you all."

The man let the door open wider revealing another younger man holding a short sword. The older man stepped forward and quickly frisked me while the swordsman alertly watched. I had no doubt the younger man had been instructed to plunge the weapon through my chest if I made any sort of false move.

"Please, sirs," I pleaded. "I do have important information for all of you. Just give me time and hear me out. Time is of the essence and cannot be wasted."

The older man reluctantly nodded and then motioned me forward with his arm as he stepped past me into the house. I followed, noticing that the younger man quietly closed and locked the door before following behind me with his blade at the ready. I hobbled slowly forward as we seemed to be heading toward the rear of the house.

We entered a large room. The disciples were all sitting on the floor around a large roundish and short-legged table having a meal. There were also two women seated among them. With my unexpected entrance into the room, they all looked up at me with fear, mistrust, and a deep sadness in their eyes. The younger man behind me with the unsheathed sword casually leaned against the door frame as I stepped into the candlelit room.

The older man spoke, "Friends, this man's name is Abram. He purports to bring us vital news about our slain Christ."

The men murmured among themselves with much doubt showing on their faces. A silence stole across the room as everyone's eyes turned toward me. I took a few seconds to scan each of their faces as they looked anticipatingly at me.

"Friends," I started out by introducing myself before continuing,

"I have grave news for all of you." I decided to be as blunt as possible. "The Romans are planning to steal your Christ's body from the tomb two hours before the cock crows tomorrow morning."

Several of the men stared at me in disbelief while others just shook their heads as a few gaped and frowned at me.

"What is their purpose?" asked one of the men at the table.

"The Romans, and the Sanhedrin," I replied, "do not believe that your Christ will rise from the dead in three days. They intend to steal the body, hold it somewhere for four days, and if he does rise in their captivity, they will cut off his head, and then display it on a long pike before the crowds to prove he didn't rise from the dead."

A hubbub from the table arose as they all looked at me as if I was telling them one huge, fantastical lie.

I raised my hand and asked for silence. More than a few men continued to stare suspiciously at me. Some appeared to finger their knives strapped to their robes. Before anyone could interrupt me, I continued with my story telling them about my encounters with Septimus Maximus at Golgotha and Longinus at Avram's.

When I finished, everyone in the room looked at me with doubt in their eyes while their body language was tense. Most just shook their heads and looked at me as if I was nothing more than a mad man who came to tell them an audacious and unbelievable tale. I remembered Shakespeare's play *Macbeth*, as it seemed to appear that my tale was "full of sound and fury, signifying nothing" to the assembled group.

I stood there gazing across the room for a few seconds before speaking again. It was time to use the ace up my sleeve.

"Friends, I know that most—or all—of you doubt what I have told you, but please believe me that time is ruthlessly ticking by. You cannot wait. It is incumbent upon you now to move your Christ's body to a secret place until he will rise again on the third day."

One of the men stood and faced me. "My name is Thomas," the man spoke up boldly. "Why should we trust or even believe you?" This was the only person in the entire group who had actually introduced himself. I wondered, if during the delay in bringing me back to speak with the disciples, they all had decided to remain anonymous. Thus, that was why no one would say his or her name, just in case I was deemed a Roman spy. Yet, had I indeed been a supposed foe, I grimly doubted if I would be allowed to leave the room alive.

I slowly looked at everyone in the room. A hush fell upon them all as they stared at me eagerly anticipating my answer.

"You all may not believe me, but I can prove to you that what I say is true. I come from far, far away. In fact, I have traveled here from several thousand years in the future."

I snapped my fingers and shapeshifted into my real self, Sydney Weinstein. Nothing about my dress or clothes looked like anything they had ever seen before. I watched as most of the room reared back in fright.

"This figure you see before you is the real me. But wait," I said, holding up my index finger. "I need to show you more!"

Again, snapping my fingers, I shapeshifted into the Roman Tribune's regalia. "I am now the Tribune Gaius Cassius Falcidus." Everyone in the room reeled back. Several men started to stand, their hands firmly grasping their daggers.

I again held up my hands and spoke to everyone. "Before you do anything rash, my friends, I have one more persona to put before you."

I shapeshifted back to Abram, the poor shoe trader. The room was dead silent as everybody stared at me.

I put them at ease. "Friends," I said holding my arms out as I continued, "as I said previously to you, I come from far away. The world needs your new Christian religion. It will spread far around the world in the coming centuries. It is up to you to save your Christ's body so that he will rise on the third day."

As silence descended upon the room, Thomas again asked, "Can you take the form of Jesus to prove once and for all you are who you say you are?"

"No," I replied. "I cannot do so. That is beyond my ability. Either you have faith and believe or my journey here to warn you is all for nothing. You all must decide on your own as to what needs to be done." As I finished my sentence, I decided to shapeshift into Thomas. Within seconds, everyone stood and pointed at both the real Thomas and me, the fake one. A loud babble broke out. I quickly returned to the Abram's personage.

"I thought one more demonstration might help you all," I said loudly to the confused crowd. So, I raised my voice and said, "Now, hear this! I will accompany you to Joseph of Arimathea's tomb and watch over you as you remove Christ's body. But together you must decide where to take and hide it until the forthcoming third day. That must be your secret. I do not want to know. It is up to you now to prove to the world that your Christ really is the Son of God. Please escort me to some other room of this house so that I cannot hear your deliberations."

I turned to the young man who was still behind me with his sword at the ready. "Please take me to another part of this house, so the disciples may secretly discuss where to convey Jesus's body." He silently nodded and then beckoned with his head to follow. We walked down the hallway I originally traversed until we arrived at the front door. The swordsman turned to his left and continued down another hall before opening a door and ushering me inside.

HEADING TO THE TOMB

I waited another fifteen to twenty minutes before the door opened. It was the older white-haired individual who had originally escorted me to meet the disciples.

"My name is Peter," he said introducing himself. "For now, I will trust you, but should you make any false move, one of my men will not hesitate to kill you. Understood?"

I nodded my head as Peter continued. "We are going to split up into small groups of three or four," he said. "You will come with us as we have many ways to get past the city walls."

I followed him. We left the house with two other disciples, one of whom walked behind me. We walked several blocks toward the Gennath Gate. It was dark and late. Clouds covered the moon which decreased visibility quite a lot. Nothing stirred although there was a slight breeze that blew leaves across the pavement. About fifty yards from Jerusalem's wall, Peter turned into a small alley filled with garbage and castoff items. We wended our way past the debris in the darkened alley for about thirty feet before he stopped at a small three-foot-wide alcove and knocked on a door with four staccato raps and then two firm knocks.

The door was immediately opened by a fortyish-year-old man who merely nodded as if expecting us but said nothing as we entered what appeared to be a storage room. "This is the owner," Peter whispered. The owner moved over to a side wall and beckoned to the other two younger disciples who accompanied us. All three men lifted several large wooden crates and a wine cask away from the wall. Underneath was a three-by-three-foot metal plate lying on the floor. Although it appeared the metal plate was securely fastened with four rounded overlarge screw-type bolts, all three men easily slid it across the storage room's wooden floor. Underneath the plate was what appeared to be a metal trap door. The home's owner bent over and lifted it up. As I edged closer, I saw a black hole and could smell the stench of dead air as it rose into and permeated the room.

One of the younger disciples moved over to the edge, sat down, and holding on to the hole's side rim, lowered himself into the blackness until he was standing at the bottom with his head about a foot below the hole's rim. Meanwhile, the owner of the home lit two torches. He handed one to the man in the hole and the other to the younger disciple. Peter gestured to me to enter which I did with ease. He followed me and was then followed by the disciple with the torch.

I found myself standing in a five-foot-high tunnel about four feet wide. A trickle of water—or was it sewage?—ran down the middle of the tunnel flowing off into the darkness that awaited us.

"This tunnel will take us underneath the city wall," Peter whispered. Signaling the first disciple to lead the way, we started off. Since I was still disguised as an old man with a walking staff, it was easy for me to bend over so as not to hit my head on the low-hanging ceiling even though, when I forgot about the rough stone vault, I took a few unexpected bumps as we trudged slowly along.

We soon came to an area that appeared to have been chiseled out of heavy stone blocks. In the dim light I could see thick, curved pieces of metal supporting the ceiling every one or two feet.

"This is the outer wall," Peter whispered. To my eyes, the foundation of Jerusalem's Second Wall was not only impressive but also appeared to be solidly built. "Our ancestors," he continued in a low voice, "constructed this tunnel hundreds of years ago."

We continued forward. The wall's foundation appeared to be approximately twenty-five to thirty feet thick at its base. I wondered how much deeper the base of the wall was but decided to keep quiet. After another one hundred feet or so, the tunnel angled slightly upward. In another minute or so we came to a halt. Before us was what appeared to be a solid rock wall. It looked impenetrable. Peter reached up, feeling along the upper edge of the rock before pulling out a finger-sized rounded piece of metal adroitly hidden in small, nondescript indentation above the door. Grasping it, he pulled. We immediately heard a click as the sound of what I surmised were hidden bolts slid back into the tunnel's walls. Peter pushed on the slab which pivoted slowly inward on the right side until it was at a ninety-degree angle in the small passageway. The first torch-bearer stepped past the stone slab and each of us followed in a single file.

We now found ourselves in a small room approximately twelve to fifteen feet wide by fifteen feet long. A stone bench had been chiseled out of both sides of the room. Upon each side shelf were several ossuaries. I intuitively realized we were in a tomb that probably belonged to an important Jerusalem family. I stared all around it in amazement and noted inscribed figures on the four walls. Peter motioned us forward as we passed through a two-foot-wide opening into a much larger room.

I noticed that there were *loculi*, or burial niches, lining the pentagonal side walls of this mausoleum. The niches were stacked in three rows. Further glancing around, I observed that on one side wall it contained eleven or twelve *arcosolia*, or arched niches, where ossuaries were placed. There were several stone benches below the niches. I counted three wrapped bodies in linen grave clothes lying in repose on them. A sickly smell of death permeated the room.

I knew from my research before I underwent this journey that once the soft tissue had decomposed, the family would reenter the mausoleum and remove the cloth wrapping before taking the bones and placing them in an ossuary.

To have such an extensive tomb, I thought, *this family must be well connected and wealthy.*

In the meantime, as I looked around the burial chamber, both of the younger disciples were pushing, or sliding, a large square rock backwards from one of the walls at what I surmised was the front of this tomb. After several minutes of straining, the rock rested about three feet outside the wall. Fresh air flowed into the tomb.

Peter turned to us and whispered, "We're in a garden where our Lord's body rests. Follow me." The four of us squeezed around the rock and stood. The now partially obscured moon allowed me to see that we were, indeed, in a well-kept garden. "Come," Peter said motioning with his hand. "Our Lord's tomb is over this way."

We started out and I noticed three separate groups of disciples who seemed to mysteriously materialize in the semi-darkness. In all, excluding myself, I counted eleven men. We silently arrived before Christ's tomb. Five or six of the younger men approached the rock that sealed the tomb and worked for several minutes to roll the heavy boulder four or five feet away from the entrance.

The men stood at the entrance without speaking. Peter strode forward and faced us all. Bowing his head, he prayed in a low voice, "O great Lord and God, we are surrounded by enemies and have come to take your Son's body to a safer place so that no one may desecrate it. Please guide us while we await his resurrection on the third day. Amen." Each person followed with an amen.

Peter then pointed to five of the disciples and instructed them to enter the tomb and remove Christ's body.

AFTERMATH

I turned to Peter and said, "Peter, it is time for me to go. My journey is almost over, and I must return to my home. I will move a distance from his tomb and stand watch until the Romans arrive to see their reaction when they open the tomb."

Peter placed his hand on my shoulder and spoke, "Go with God, my friend. Thank you for the help you have given us. Surely you will meet God and our Lord when you ascend to heaven. I hope it will be alright if I leave one of my men with you so that he can also observe the Roman's reaction when they arrive to do their evil job and report back to me."

"Thank you, Peter. I don't mind if one of your disciples stays with me. I intend to hide and observe their reactions. I will change my persona back into the Roman Tribune. That way I can keep your man from anything untoward should we be discovered, as I'll outrank any Roman here."

Peter nodded, then turned to one of the younger disciples and spoke, "John, follow this man and stay with him until he bids you to leave and do not be frightened when he changes into someone else."

John, who looked about twenty-one or twenty-two years old, simply nodded. I motioned for him to follow, and we strode off through the well-kept garden and climbed uphill about fifty yards until we reached a large bush about five feet tall and ten to twelve feet round. Once I reached our observation point, I turned to see in the half-moonlight the remaining disciples rolling the boulder back into the entrance of Joseph of Arimathea's tomb. In the dimming light, as moonbeams danced in and out of the clouds lighting up the area where Jesus's body rested, I could see five of the disciples carrying his body off into the darkness.

I turned to John and said, "Do not be frightened, as I am about to turn into a Roman Tribune."

John just nodded and stared at me. I shapeshifted back into the guise of the Tribune Gaius Cassius Falcidus. As I materialized, John took two steps backward and gaped at me with awe as if he still couldn't believe, despite seeing my previous transformations in Yosef's home, that I was the same person.

"Please don't worry, John. Despite what you have seen, I am still the same person," I told him in a fatherly voice. He just nodded. "Now, we wait and observe. You may sleep a while if you want," I said to the tired young man. John laid down and stretched out. Within minutes he was asleep.

Somewhat unsure of the correct time, I guessed that it must have been around two in the morning. Standing behind the bush, I shifted my feet to stay on the alert. About an hour later, with no clouds obscuring the moon, I detected a quick flash of light from the Gennath Gate as it opened. I counted seven or eight men slip through its small opening before the gate's doors were quickly shut and the light disappeared.

"Here they come!" I hissed. I nudged John with my boot. He awakened and stood next to me.

Off in the distance I could hear the Romans approaching. Although they must have been trying to keep their noise down, they weren't doing a good job of it, as every so often I could hear the clank of their armor. John and I watched from our vantage point as eight soldiers slowly materialized in the spotty moonlight. They kept their voices to a murmur until one voice stood out; I recognized Longinus's voice as he gave orders to several of the soldiers to move the boulder away from the entrance to what had been Jesus's tomb.

Both John and I watched as five or six soldiers rolled the boulder away from the tomb. One of the men lit a torch. We both watched as Longinus bade the torch man to step into the tomb to confirm that Christ's body was there. The soldier entered but immediately backed out.

As the wind was blowing in our direction, I could distinctly hear what the soldier had to say in an excited voice, "Centurion, there is no body!"

"What!" said Longinus loudly. "Give me that torch!" He motioned to the man holding the torch who lost no time in handing it over to his irate leader. We watched as Longinus entered the tomb. The wind died down as he exited.

"Damn it! Someone's taken the body!" Longinus screamed as he reemerged. "Spread out and look for any clues!" he ordered. The soldiers dispersed in different directions. I hoped we wouldn't be discovered, but one soldier appeared to be headed our way.

"John," I whispered, "move these branches back and we'll try to shield ourselves as best as possible." We moved into the bush, but I was worried we might still be exposed if the approaching soldier walked behind the bush. I had quietly drawn my sword but hoped I wouldn't be forced to use it.

We could hear the Roman soldier nearing our position. He stopped in front of our bush. We heard a jingle of clothing and armor. Then, much to my surprise, the soldier relieved himself into the bush, giving off a great sigh as he did so. Giving a grunt as he finished, we heard the rustle of cloth as the man walked away. I breathed a sigh of relief. John and I avoided being discovered. We both scooted out of the bush and stood behind it.

The moon came out from beneath the clouds and shined down on the assembled soldiers. I could hear Longinus frustratingly say to his troops, "Just leave the damn boulder where it is. No need to roll it back now that someone else has probably stolen the man's body." He continued, "Well, men, back to the city!" They marched off. Several minutes later I saw a glint of light as the Gennath Gate was opened and then quickly closed. That was my last view of Longinus who, by stealing the thunder from Septimus Maximus, a nondescript Roman soldier who had been cured by Christ's blood, would eventually go down in history as the Roman who stabbed Christ on the cross and would later claim that Christ's blood cured his eye, thus becoming the first Christian convert.

I knew from my research and reading the Christian New Testament that the third day after the crucifixion was also the first day Christ rose. That day, Mary Magdalene approached the tomb in the early morning hours while it was still dark. She discovered that the stone had been rolled away from the entrance. She turned and hastily left to find Peter and tell him of her discovery. Whether this part of the Bible story is accurate, or her act of finding the tomb open was all part of the disciples' plan to deceive and mislead any of the Romans or Sanhedrin who might have been surreptitiously spying on the tomb, is best left to history.

Once the Romans were back inside Jerusalem, I turned to John and said, "I think it's alright now for you to leave me and return to the city. I don't intend to remain here much longer."

"Thank you, sir, whomever you may be," the young man replied. "Peter bade me to tell you safe travels back to wherever you came from." With those words, he slipped away into the darkness. I followed his shadow with my eyes until he disappeared into the night.

THE RESURRECTION

I had one last chore before I returned back to my own era. I needed my extra powers to shift forward in time.

From my research, especially John 20:19, I recalled that the eleven disciples had gathered together in a home on the night of the Sabbath after Mary Magdalene encountered Jesus that morning when she approached his tomb and found it empty. The disciples were now in dire fear that other Jews, along with leaders of the Sanhedrin, might find and either imprison or kill them all. This extermination would quash all hopes for the burgeoning Christian movement to spread and bloom.

To that end, I needed time to shift forward about thirty-six hours in this realm. I could see wispy traces of sunlight peeking through the clouds off to the east. As I watched the coming sunrise, I heard the distant creak of the unoiled hinges of the Gennath Gate. I turned toward the gate and watched the doors slowly open. People would soon be rising and coming out to the garden or to the area where I was standing, which was, as I could see in the coming light, about halfway up the hill to Golgotha. I sent up a silent prayer asking if the disciples were still meeting at Yosef's home; otherwise, I knew it might be difficult trying to find them.

Without letting any further time lapse, I shifted into my former persona of Abram, the poor shoe trader. In that disguise, I knew I would attract far less attention than a Roman Tribune. Having accomplished that task, I time-shifted forward to the late afternoon of the Sabbath and then slowly wound my way down hill and soon entered the Gennath Gate. I decided to try Yosef's house first, so I set off hobbling down the road, while using my walking staff to support me.

About fifteen minutes later, I approached Yosef's front door. I knocked loudly. After a minute or so, I heard the bolts being pulled back followed by the door being opened only a few inches by Yosef.

"Yosef, it's me, Abram." Continuing in a low voice, I asked him, "Are the disciples here? I need to speak with them one more time."

The old codger just grunted before tersely saying, "Wait!"

He closed the door and threw the bolts.

He sure is a suspicious old man, I thought to myself. *And with good reason. These are dangerous times to live in. No wonder everyone seems to be afraid.*

After several minutes, I again heard the door bolts being withdrawn and Yosef's face appeared.

"They are not here. Come in and wait. I have sent someone to pass on your request," he said rather tersely.

He opened the door further and I slipped by him. Josef escorted me to the back room, and pointing at the table, said, "Sit!"

So, I sat and waited. About forty-five minutes later, I heard someone coming down the hallway. It was John!

"John!" I said as I stood. "It's good to see you again after telling you in the garden that it was time for me to depart. I have something further to tell you and the rest of the disciples. Can you take me to them?"

"Yes," he replied. "Follow me." He motioned with his left arm for me to rise and accompany him.

Instead of turning left to go back down the entrance hall, he turned right and walked down a short hallway until he stopped at a sturdy wooden door. After throwing the heavy bolts, John eased it open and carefully looked out both ways before turning and putting his finger to his lips for me to be silent as he motioned me forward. We emerged into a thin, three-foot-wide alleyway that seemed to wind around the backs of several homes. We slowly moved down the alley, doing our best not to make any noise while trying to avoid stepping on the trash and throwaways in the dim light.

I followed him for about a hundred yards until we reached a wider alley. John put his hand out to stop. He poked his head around the corner. Next, he waved me forward and we quickly crossed over to the larger alley. This was a routine we would both follow in the coming minutes. By now the sun had begun to sink in the west, leaving the alleyways with dim lighting. We continued to traipse behind another row of homes until we started to wind back and forth in various and sundry alleyways and homes for another fifteen minutes until John stopped at a small, nondescript alcove and knocked on its door. This time the code of knocks was much longer and different, but I didn't bother to memorize it.

Several seconds later, the door opened and a young girl, motioning silently with her right arm, ushered us inside. We walked down a short hallway before turning left into a large room. All the disciples were there. They all turned and viewed me with silence and some distrust.

I bowed before speaking, "Thank you all for agreeing to see me again. I have learned some new information which will certainly be of great importance and relief to you."

The group looked uneasily at me. I held up my hands, "No! No! No! Hopefully I bring good news. You all will be happy to hear what I say—"

My sentence was abruptly cut short when the entire room was bathed in a sudden flash of light and Jesus stood in the middle of the room among his disciples. As one, they all moved back in shock.

Jesus said, "Peace be with you." Then he showed them his hands and opened his tunic to one side to display his spear wound. As one, they all moved to him, feeling his arms and viewing his horribly scarred hands. From my position in the front of the room I could easily see his stigmata and that his flesh was solid when each man touched him in awe. There was nothing ghostly about him. He was, indeed, a real living man.

I tried to keep my astonishment to myself. I had achieved my mission.

It was definitely time for me to leave. I unobtrusively sidled out of the room and walked down a long hallway until I came to an open room. I entered and shut the door quietly behind me.

I smiled at what I had learned, saw, and accomplished on this trip. It had, indeed, been eye-opening.

THE RETURN

I knew it would take me only seconds to return to my world. To that end, I morphed back into my regular clothes. Gazing up at the moon, I scratched my head and thought of Leah and our living room. A dark whirlwind immediately surrounded me, generating a sound of wind blowing down a tunnel.

Suddenly, out of the darkness and wind, I heard a voice which startled me.

The stern and stentorian voice said, "Thank you, Sydney Winestein, for all you have done to insure My Son's purpose here on earth. Mankind will be much better for it!"

The whirlwind engulfed me for a few seconds more before I found myself in my own living room with my beautiful wife, Leah, sitting on our sofa staring at me in wonder and awe. She quickly rose, grabbed, and kissed me.

"You're back," she said as she stroked my head and gave me another kiss.

"How long have I been gone?" I queried.

"You left three days ago," she replied. "No one," she continued, "has ever taken time-travel trips for such an extended period of time. Please tell me what happened."

We moved over to the sofa and sat. It took me about two hours to relate to Leah what had happened and what I had done. Finally, I told her about the "voice" in the whirlwind.

"Who do you believe it was? Or did you imagine it?" she asked.

"I know, Leah, no matter how strange it may sound as to whose voice it was, the voice was real, not in my head," I replied.

We discussed my trip a few more times over the next three or four days and wondered whether or not we should reveal anything about my journey to others. We finally decided that to tell anyone about my journey back into time would serve no purpose. Leah suggested that I write everything down for posterity while the details were still fresh in my mind. We would keep the paper and pass it along at some appropriate date in the far distant future to our children. After a week or so, I completed writing a thirty-three page essay on my excursion into the past. Both Leah and I sealed it in a waterproof packet which I then left on the bottom shelf of our family safe.

I breathed a sigh of relief. Did I, I wondered, really make any difference in mankind's history or not?

But, as many of us that know, there is one immutable fact—Christ rose on the third day.

Author's Note: This story turned out to be the most difficult short story I have ever written. Taking more than two years, this involved—as you, the reader, can tell from the footnotes—a lot of research to try and adhere as closely to the Bible's New Testament narrative as possible. Yet, I took some liberties with the Bible's accounts to interject other possibilities to the crucifixion and resurrection story. After all, that's what fiction is all about, isn't it? Biblical history during the time period of Jesus tends to be incredibly murky, thus allowing alternate interpretations as to what exactly happened in Jerusalem around Easter in 30 or 33 AD. After all, the first extant pieces of the New Testament only date back to around 125-200 AD, giving various unknown Christian writers time to modify and improve upon the canonical gospels presented by the four disciples—unnamed until the third century—Matthew, Mark, Luke, and John.

THE PLUNGE

Threechopper beat its wings as it banked to the
right over the lush green jungle canopy below
as it started its descent towards LZ Ike, located
a mile away.[26] We men of Bravo Company, 2-8 1st Air
Cav, had just been picked up from some vine-infested
jungle glade and were being shuttled in for LZ duty
after three hard weeks in the bush.[27] We were involved
in several firefights and lost seven to eight men due to
wounds and untimely battle deaths.

I was sitting in the doorway of the Huey, legs balanced on the skids,
loosely holding onto the webbing behind the pilot's seat. We were
descending rapidly toward Ike as a monsoon shower, about two to
three miles in the distance, slowly moved toward the LZ, like a window
curtain blowing in the gentle afternoon breeze. The dark grey sheet
of rain descended upon the jungle. In a way, emulating Mussorgsky's
"Night on Bald Mountain" in the movie *Fantasia*, it resembled red
hot molten lava being emptied from a gigantic cauldron.

With any luck we would be safe, sound, and in a hooch on the

---

26 LZ Ike: the army named its Fire Support Bases (FSBs) names of Presidents (Ike), girls (Becky), animals (Mustang),
  etc. Ike was the actual name of an LZ in the Vietnamese jungle where the author spent some time during his tour of
  duty.
27 LZ (Landing Zone): any place in the jungle where a helicopter could land troops or supplies; also a small fort (known
  as an FSB) in the jungle with artillery pieces surrounded by an earthen berm with bunkers and artillery.

LZ before the slow-moving downpour struck.[28] I certainly hoped so, because I wanted to be dry at least for a little while. The ever-present monsoon rains kept us in a state of constant wetness—our clothes literally rotted off our backs, sometimes in only three or four days—so that we often looked like a band of homeless tramps.

Flying low to avoid being a target high in the sky from either an enemy's M-51 machine gun or a B-40 rocket with a range of approximately 475 to 500 feet, we were about fifty feet over the treetops and about a half mile from the LZ when it happened.[29] The chopper hit an unexpected cross current of wind, probably generated by the approaching rain, which flung it sideways to the left and plunged it into a sudden deep dive. The jolt was so sudden I had no time to think.

Suddenly I was all alone—falling through the cool Vietnamese air with my eighty-five-pound rucksack of food, medical supplies, and ammunition still attached to my back. My helmet was gone, spiraling as if in slow motion before it disappeared into the jungle canopy beneath me. I remember seeing it as I fell sideways toward the fast-approaching trees that would certainly impale me on their uplifted arms.

Sh–t! I remember thinking. *I'm a dead motherf-cker! No, I'm not gonna die! Jesus f-cking Christ, this can't be happening to me! Not after all the crap I've been through! I'm due to go home in three weeks!*

In microseconds these thoughts rushed through my mind as the green canopy opened to receive me.

No way, Lord, I thought. *It can't be my time yet!* Although, I grimly realized, it probably was. I vaguely remembered twisting in midair—or had the wind turned me over so that my heavy rucksack was underneath me? I prayed that somehow, it would miraculously

---

28 A "hooch" is made from a poncho and can be a temporary or permanent dwelling.
29 B–40: a shoulder–fired anti–tank grenade launcher carried by the North Vietnamese Army (NVA) & Viet Cong (VC, short for Vietnamese Communist).

absorb the shock of the fast-approaching limbs. *Maybe, just maybe*, I hoped, *if it does, I'll stand a chance of living.* As I hurtled downward, all these thoughts rushed through my brain in the span of the three to four seconds it took before I hit the trees.

The treetops met me with a crash. I blindly grabbed out, grasping for anything I could hold onto. I had to slow my descent! Limbs ripped through my hands—a thick vine tore through my right hand, stabbing me with a lightning-like pain that was immediately transmitted to my brain. A couple of vines grabbed me, slowing my descent before they broke under my weight. I cried out in agonizing torment. I bounced off several tiers of thin moss laden limbs. Another large vine reached out, held me temporarily, then broke under the strain, sending me spinning to the ground.

I hit the ground on my left side with a hard bone-rattling thud.

The shock of landing on *terra firma* was somewhat diminished by the shock that I was still alive—albeit for now. Lying on my left side, the rucksack, miraculously, had taken most of the punishment from my unexpected exit from the chopper. I lay still as my entire body ached in pain. Unfortunately—or fortunately—my left arm and shoulder had taken the brunt of the impact, and my left knee ached.

Lying there on the ground, I was stunned for several seconds.

"My God, I'm still alive!" I whispered softly to myself. I really wanted to shout, but immediately thought better of it. Charlie might be nearby, and if he found me, I'd surely have my throat cut or a bayonet to my heart.[30] The gooks only took prisoners who could walk and were officers; otherwise, as an enlisted man, I was of absolutely no use to the enemy. Plus, I was in no condition to walk.[31]

Gingerly I tried to move. I brought my right arm up. The palm, as

---

30 Charlie = NVA or VC
31 "Gooks" is Korean slang for person carried over from the Korean War; generic term for enemy.

expected, was a mass of torn skin—shredded from trying to grip limbs and vines to slow my descent. I moved my fingers and as I did so, a searing pain shot up my arm. I knew nothing was broken. Next, I tried my right leg. It was intact but sore and stiff. I lifted it up and down several times and bent it at the knee multiple times. No hip injury. I noticed that my pants legs were torn to shreds. I slipped my right arm out of the ruck's harness and turned to my left. I was instantly struck by an agonizing pain. A white flash seemed to explode between my eyes. Then blackness descended.

I came to several seconds (or was it minutes?) later. I lay there on my back.

What just happened? I asked myself.

I tried to move the fingers on my left hand. I was able to curl them, but something else was wrong. I tried to lift my left arm again, but a searing pain, starting at the shoulder, shot down the entire arm. Gritting my teeth, I cautiously moved my head to the left. My shoulder ached beyond belief and my neck was stiff. Looking down at my injured left arm and using my right hand, I pulled the torn and partially shredded left arm sleeve of my multi-pocketed green camouflaged jungle shirt up the arm. By the misshaped appearance of my forearm, I could tell either the ulna or radius bones were broken below the elbow. I laboriously shoved the shirt back down my arm.

Good! I thought to myself. *No bones through the skin, so I'm okay, although my left arm appears to be broken,* I commented silently. My left kneecap ached—it felt as if it was dislocated. Cautiously, I tried to move my left leg. It wouldn't budge due to the pain emanating from my knee which seemed to nail my leg to the jungle floor. *Think! Damn it! Think about what to do next. How am I going to get out of here? No one is going to search for me until maybe tomorrow—if ever! They may just not do anything and list me as an MIA. So, what do I do?*[32]

---

32 MIA = Missing in Action

Having been a combat medic, I knew I had to take care of my external injuries first. Then I needed to crawl somewhere, find shelter, and hide.

Using my right arm and leg, after struggling for a minute or two to drag my left arm through the harness of my ruck, I managed to sit up. I slowly pivoted around and looked at the flattened rucksack. It and several vines had slowed my descent and saved my life. My medic's bag was strapped on the ruck's aluminum frame down behind the nape of my neck. It, and my five-pint canvas canteen on top of it, cushioned the impact around my head when I hit. I quickly unzipped the bag with my good hand. Plastic and glass containers lay in fragments throughout the bag. Digging further past the few pill bottles that survived the impact, I found an intact morphine capsule! Plus, my rolls of gauze bandages and pads along with some salve for cuts and scratches hadn't ripped open.

The tube of salve was half full. I placed it in my left hand. My fingers could still work somewhat awkwardly even if I couldn't lift my left arm! I squeezed the remaining salve into the palm of my right hand. The blood had started to clot. The cream stung and was extremely painful as I spread the salve over the torn flesh. The stabbing pain was too intense to complete the job all at once but after a while I finished. I accomplished my mission. The pain of my endeavor made me weak and a little dizzy. I located a gauze roller and gripping it in my left hand, managed after what felt like an eternity to somehow wrap it around my right hand, leaving the fingertips exposed. I would need them for later use. I had my P-38 can opener on a thin chain around my neck.[33] Thank goodness I had kept it tucked underneath my green T-shirt; otherwise, during my precipitous descent through the canopy, it might have gotten snagged on a limb or vine and that would probably be "all she wrote" for me! Finally, using my P-38, which we normally used to open our

---

33 P-38: a small one-and-a-half-inch-long, collapsible metal can opener to open C-Rations; C-Rats, or C's which were standard canned meals eaten in the jungle.

C-Rats, I cut and secured the gauze wrapping with tape.

Then, like a lightning flash, it hit me. I didn't have a weapon to protect myself. Not as if that would help if five or six gooks found me. I'd be dead meat! I looked around, hoping against hope to see my M16. It was, however, nowhere to be seen in the ever-darkening gloom of the dense jungle floor.

Oh well, I thought, *it's probably hanging from some tree limb or embedded in the rotting humus of the jungle floor.* Instinctively I looked up, hoping to see it hanging from an overhead vine. *What a wasted effort!* I thought grimly to myself.

I went back to my first aid. I took a gauze pad and wiped all the scratches and small tears on my arms and legs that I could reach. I further examined my body for other injuries, only to find none.

How I survived is a miracle, I thought.

The shoulder injury, fractured arm, and dislocated kneecap precluded my walking out of the jungle. Well, I was stuck and that was that—I had no choice but to abandon my ruck. It was just too heavy to drag. I would need to hide it. My medicine bag, however, weighing about thirty pounds, could be dragged. I went through the medic's bag and cleaned out the broken glass and other stuff I wouldn't need. Scooping out some earth, I buried the items under the wet spongy jungle floor. I kept my water purification tablets and found an undamaged bottle of Benadryl in a side pocket. Although we used Benadryl for insect stings, I knew it would be somewhat good for the agony of pain and stiffness to follow my unexpected plunge to the jungle floor. Working with one hand was slow and somewhat agonizing. Once, forgetting my left arm was injured, I shifted my weight onto it. The pain was instant and so was the nirvana that followed it.

I came to—maybe seconds later? In the distance I could hear the drumming of the rain as it pitter-patted its way across the thick jungle canopy. I had to hurry. Had to hide my ruck. Had to find shelter.

I delved into my ruck and found four or five C-Rats undamaged. After being in the jungle for seven days, I had a few C's left. I stuffed them into my jungle shirt's side pockets. They'd have to last if I was going to spend any time out here. I also found another rolled-up green T-shirt, which I placed in my almost empty medic's bag. It would help to keep me warm. Both my poncho and poncho liner were intact, so I rolled them up and crammed them into my medic's bag, as well.

The drumming grew louder. It wouldn't be long now before the rain reached and enveloped me. The trees swayed in the air as the approaching monsoon shower pushed the air in front of it. Along with the advancing downpour, I began to smell—really smell—the damp, musty, decomposing jungle floor for the first time. The putrid decay, like rotting fruit or a dead animal, now wafted over me. When we were out patrolling in the jungle as we hunted Charlie, we rarely paid attention to the ever-present stench around us because our bodies and clothes reeked from sweat and dirt and fear. Our nostrils seemed to filter out the jungle's rancidness. But now, lying on the jungle floor, my nose began to pick up the fetid stink of the foliage and the rotting leaves underneath me. It was more malodorous, if not extremely putrescent. I wanted to gag but knew I dare not for fear of giving my untenable position away.

Three of the four one-pint plastic canteens that I normally carried were broken along with the five-pint canvas canteen, which had cushioned my head at impact. My one-pint canteen, half full, survived unscathed. That wouldn't last long. I would need water. I detached the canteen from the C-ring which held it to the ruck's frame as raindrops began to splash through the leaves.

The drumming was coming closer.

I had to hide my ruck and get away from the area of impact. There was a small bamboo clump about ten feet away. I grabbed the ruck and, although in great pain, crawled on my right side and dragged it over to the bamboo. I lifted the thin leafy bamboo limbs and shoved the ruck underneath them as far as I could. Brushing away my drag marks so as to wipe out any trail that Charlie might spot, I slowly inched back to my medic's bag just as the rain descended in torrents and engulfed me.

Coming down in sheets, the moisture made visibility beyond ten feet virtually impossible. Trying to orient myself—not great when you're lying flat on the ground—I began my crawl to LZ Ike, praying I was headed in the right direction. At least I was crawling in the opposite direction from where I had stashed the ruck. The wet jungle floor made it somewhat easier to move and I tried using my right leg to brush over my trail as I inched along. I tried to keep next to the multitude of bushes that inhabited the jungle floor, leaving as little trace as possible of my passing.

I have to find another large bamboo clump, I thought to myself. I would be reasonably safe and partially dry under the branches. Then I could use one of the morphine capsules and get some much-needed rest.

The rain beat down on my back and head. Several times, as I crawled toward an unseen goal, I tilted my head to the sky to swallow some rainwater as it dripped off the overhead trees. The sound of the rain was so deafening that one couldn't hear a thing except the drops hitting the leaves and pounding the sodden earth. A person could walk within five or six feet of me, whistling, and I wouldn't be able to hear him so loud was the sound of water hammering both the trees and the ground.

After fifteen to twenty minutes or so, the torrential sheets of rain began to abate. I espied a large green bamboo clump about twenty-five away. I dragged myself toward it. My journey seemed to take forever. After what seemed to be an eon, I finally reached it, crawled under the branches, and got as close to the base as possible. Having made it this far, I collapsed.

When I woke up, it was dark outside. The cloud burst had left me wet and cold as it moved onward. All I could hear was the dripping raindrops all around me.

I lay still and listened. God! I was really stiff and sore all over. My left arm ached. I felt for my medic's bag, found, and unzipped it. Feeling around inside, I found Benadryl and morphine. I took two Benadryl pills out, popped them into my mouth dry, and swallowed. I had absolutely no idea if they would help with the pain. At that point I could not have cared less. Along with a morphine capsule I knew I would obtain some relief. I blindly felt for a morphine syrette. Tearing the paper and plastic wrapping away, I took the needle and jabbed it through my clothes into my left leg before squeezing out the pain killer. Perhaps psychologically, I prayed, both would lower the pain level.

Within minutes I drifted off again.

I don't know what woke me, but almost instantaneously I was fully awake. My subconscious must have alerted me that something, or someone, was out there and heading my way. I didn't move! I didn't want to breathe! My ears strained in the darkness to hear what I hoped I wouldn't hear. There it was again! Movement. Something, or someone, was moving out there. I still couldn't distinguish whether it was man or beast.

I silently prayed that it wasn't a tiger. If so, I would never have a chance. It would make a quick end to me. Yet, if the sound was human, it would be the NVA. If discovered I would still meet a quick end, which might be somewhat better (and less painful!) than being eaten alive by a tiger!

My right ear was next to the ground. I imagined all kinds of things, but I knew—I knew—it was Charlie! No way Colonel what's-his-name would authorize or even send out a night patrol for one G.I. who was after all, probably dead.[34] The U.S. Army would, on extremely rare occasions, send out night patrols, which were extremely dangerous. After all, as an infantryman—the lowest of the low—I was expendable. I wondered if they'd even bother to send out a patrol in the morning to look for me—or my body. I doubted they would. It was then that I realized I was truly f–cked big time.

I could hear footsteps now. Closer! I guessed there were two to three gooks from the noise they were making as they brushed through the jungle's undergrowth. I froze in place and didn't move a muscle—not an inch. If they found me, I was a dead duck.

I prayed they wouldn't accidentally trip over or find my rucksack.

Had I shoved it as far as possible underneath the bamboo? I wondered.

Where was my rucksack anyway? Ten feet away? Twenty? I couldn't remember. My head was still aching. Sweat trickled down my face. I desperately wanted to wipe it away, but dared not move. I knew I was also running a bit of a fever.

Sh-t! I realized. *That's all I need—get a fever, go delirious, and blow my position.*

No! I thought vehemently. *I won't let it happen!*

The moon had come out as the raindrops dripped from one leaf to another before they reached the jungle carpet and were silently absorbed into it.

There were two of them. They were whispering in low tones. I could hear them murmuring back and forth as they set down their loads.

____
34 G. I. or Government Issue: a term applied to an American soldier, carried over from World War II.

Are they setting up for the night? I wondered. *If so, I'm f-cked! I'm really hurting and I'm so damn tired. I know I'm* gonna *fall asleep and give myself away when I fall asleep.*

Through a few bamboo branches, I could barely make out two men as the moonlight filtered down through the misty trees.

One of the men had a machete—probably U.S. Army issue, which he found or took off a body; or, more than likely, that he'd bought on the black market that operated out of Saigon. Many of the NVA, or VC, used M-16s, which they'd stolen off the docks of Saigon, or picked up from a dead American after a firefight.

The moonlight reflected off the blade. I prayed that he wasn't going to start hacking away at my bamboo hiding place. I dared not even move an inch!

Damn! I realized. *He's walking toward my hidden position.* Surely, they hadn't spotted me, or perhaps the trail I had made across the jungle's floor leading to where I was hiding. I knew I hadn't moved or done anything to give away my position. *Maybe they smell me—or my blood!* I thought. A cold sweat trickled down my brow. I held my breath, only to hear my heart pounding like a gong, deep within my chest cavity.

With no weapon, I realized, *and my inability to move quickly, I am truly F–KED!!!*

He grabbed a thick bamboo limb and whacked it off. He chopped through two more bamboo shoots. Each time I imagined the machete coming down on my neck like a guillotine. The thought sent shivers through my body.

The cutter dragged the bamboo limbs over to where his buddy stood. By now that man was also brandishing a machete. Both men used their machetes to strip down the limbs, which they cut into five-foot lengths. Using some type of rope or twine, they bound the bamboo into a tripod-like apparatus.

I suddenly realized what they were doing. They weren't setting up a tent to sleep under; they were constructing a primitive rocket launcher! It would have a time-delay fuse enabling them to exit the launch area before the LZ artillery could respond. During my tour, I saw a few of the same type of primitively constructed launchers along the edges of jungle clearings near to LZs.

The gooks would mount their rocket in a sling under the tripod's binding. Next, they would take two short pieces of bamboo and prop up the front of the rocket at an angle so that, upon ignition, it would arc up and land somewhere inside the LZ's perimeter. After setting up their deadly weapon, both men worked on what had to be a time-delay fuse. Once installed, they would then *didi mau* from the launch site and be long gone when the rocket ignited and fired off. This would result in a quick reply by the LZ's artillery to the gauntlet the NVA had thrown down.[35]

It was then that I suddenly realized, *Oh, damn! Artillery! I might soon be a dead man! It can't be!! Sh-t, sh-t, sh-t!!*

Within minutes of the rocket's launch, if anyone on Ike had a sharp eye, Ike's artillery would zero in on this area. I had to either stop the rocket launch or crawl out of here.

Wait a minute, you fool! I thought. *You don't know a thing about defusing rockets! You'll probably blow yourself up, you idiot!* Even if I was able to take it off the tripod, it might be the last thing I ever did in my life. Did I really want to take that risk?

I have to get out of here! I decided not to touch, or tamper, with the rocket. Too dangerous. *I'll wait and try to crawl away.*

---

35 *Didi, dee–dee,* or *didi mau.* Vietnamese for "to run quickly," "go, go quickly," or "get the hell out of here."

The two NVA had completed their operation. There it was—a large, long, and round projectile, probably a 122 mm communist rocket, mounted on the bamboo tripod launching pad waiting to rain death and destruction down on LZ Ike.[36] The two men squatted down beside the weapon.

Damn, I thought. *Are they going to be here all night? I sure hope not.* I knew I wouldn't be able to stay awake all night. For the last two nights I'd had a total of four hours of sleep. I was now running on pure adrenaline. I was dead tired, sore, hurt, and stiff. The Benadryl and the morphine were really beginning to work on me. I felt so drowsy. To top it off, I could feel an insect crawling up my chest. It inched its way across my cheek. The itching drove me crazy! I wanted to squash it. But one move might give me away. I prayed for the bug to depart. Instead, it started to wander down my chest!

I felt myself going down Alice in Wonderland's rabbit hole. Nepenthe was beginning to swallow me. Through my haze, I realized a pungent odor was drifting my way. They were smoking some grass! I hadn't seen them lighting up, but from my angle I could see them passing a joint back and forth, cupping the lighted tip in their hands. My mouth watered. I almost let out a groan but suppressed it. With my sores and stiffness, a joint would certainly relax me now, and it would take my mind off the dull pain permeating my body.

I have to stay awake, I realized. *Otherwise, I'm in deep sh-t!*

The two men squatted there for another fifteen minutes or so before one stood up. He fiddled with the rocket for a few moments, then turned and beckoned to his companion who rose and followed him. They walked within three feet of me. I hoped my stink didn't give me away.

The bug on my chest had been joined by a companion who was now walking up my leg. I waited—the wait was maddening. The bugs

---

36 122 mm: a communist rocket capable of traveling, with a booster, twenty-two kilometers.

were drinking my sweat—and maybe dried blood. I wanted to give the gooks plenty of time before I moved, so I slowly counted to three hundred. Finishing my count, I quickly squashed both bugs. There would be more, I was sure, but for now, I had to get out of there.

Knowing I had to get as far away as possible, I would crawl. My mind said move, but my body flat-out refused. The effect of the Benadryl and morphine finally kicked in and everything started to become fuzzy. The pain seemed so far away. So . . . far away.

Move! I vaguely thought. *You've got to move!! To . . . move. . .* Then, nothingness.

Later—I didn't know how long—I remembered hearing a hiss like fireworks make on the Fourth of July. Then Morpheus stole me away, again.

The night erupted into Dante's *Inferno*, with a blinding flash that immediately roused me from my pain-induced stupor. The fuzziness instantly disappeared. The artillery on LZ Ike was being fired in response to the rocket. After all, the red legs were showing Charlie that they were good and pissed off.[37]

The thundering crash and shaking of the earth underneath me immediately told me that I would soon face my own special kind of hell—if not oblivion.

The whistling of a 105 mm artillery shell passed overhead and erupted at least fifty yards behind the bamboo clump in a dazzling display of reddish white light.[38] The fragments of shrapnel hummed through the jungle, striking leaves and vines on their way to mete out retribution. I flattened my body onto the ground and prayed an artillery or mortar shell, or the ensuing shrapnel, wouldn't land on top of me. Fortunately for me, there were only five or six more artillery

---

37 "Redlegs" is slang for artillerymen. During the Civil War, Union artillerymen wore red stripes on their trousers.
38 "105 mm" is short for U.S.–fired 105–mm howitzer with a range of 11,500 meters.

rounds, and they were wide in relation to where I was hiding.

"Please, Lord, let me live!" I mumbled aloud to myself. *Please*, I silently prayed about the incoming, *don't land on top of me!*

Yet there was more hell to come. Off in the distance I heard sounds of *Whump! Whump!* Ike's mortar pits started chiming in and firing screaming death.

The sharp crack of incoming mortar shells exploding off to my right chilled me. I recalled one night in the boonies, while we stayed in the middle of a gook position we'd found earlier in the day, Charlie walked mortars right smack dab across our position.[39] I vividly remembered that night. At the time, I'd been trying to dry out my poncho liner for the past three days. Finally, it was dry. I slept warmly underneath the poncho I'd erected to keep the monsoon rain out. Suddenly the night erupted with incoming mortars! We jumped into our foxholes in the pouring rain as fifteen to twenty rounds walked directly across our position. I inadvertently dragged most of my poncho liner outside as I hurried into my foxhole. The incoming missed everyone, but now my poncho liner was soaking wet again and that really pissed me off.

Now, lying helplessly underneath the bamboo clump, I heard Ike's mortars as they started to land ever closer to my position. One exploded about fifteen yards away and its shrapnel whistled by and bounced into my rattan-like shelter. Using my arms as best I could, despite the injury on my right hand, I cradled my head. I just knew the next one would be right on top of me. I wanted to scream. I wanted to yell for them to stop—they were going to blow me away!

But, I thought sanguinely, it really wouldn't make any difference. I was almost surely dead as far as they were concerned. *Hell, they probably won't even send out a patrol in the morning to find me. I'm just another MIA.*

---

39 "Boonies" is the jungle, short for boondocks, or "out in the sticks."

The next incoming round whistled down ten yards to my left. Again, the thick bamboo clump absorbed the force of the exploding shell. I knew the mortar men would traverse the area. I prayed I would survive the swing back.

The noise of the exploding incoming marched off to my left and then, inexorably, started back, getting closer and closer. I could tell the detonations were behind me, so I guessed I was safe. Another round crashed thirty or forty feet behind me and then the mortars ceased. I heaved a big sigh of relief. For now, I hoped I was safe. And then an ominous silence descended upon the jungle. You could hear a pin drop. After a minute or so, the insects struck up their incessant and unceasing cacophony.

I was alive. Somehow, miraculously, I survived the artillery onslaught. My body was drenched in sweat. My clothes, first soaked by the rain, now stunk with my perspiration.

Well, I optimistically thought, *at least I'll be out of here tomorrow*. Or was it today already? At any rate, a search party would surely be sent out to search for my body, or at least locate the rocket's launch sight.

So, I'd wait here, give them a shout when they came near, and be taken to the LZ. It was all going to be so simple—or so I ambitiously thought at the time. My hopes would soon be dashed.

I dozed off.

I have no idea how long I slept. Suffice to say, the sun was far up in the sky when its piercing light filtered down through the greenery of the jungle's canopy, striking the bamboo leaves and awakening me with a start.

Where was I? Then I remembered—my nightmare was actually real. I brushed an ant from my face and scratched my crotch. We didn't wear underwear in Vietnam. It was too confining. Made you sweat all the more in your groin area. I had to piss.

I wasn't going to "foul my own nest," so to speak. After checking for gooks, I crawled out from underneath my clump and crawled over to where the launcher had been set up. The power of the takeoff caused the limbs to fall down and splay out in three directions. My injured arm and shoulder felt better, although they were both stiff. One of the launcher's bamboo poles would make a good walking stick, so I untied the fallen tripod. Grabbing the thickest one, I propped it upright, and using my good arm and leg, climbed up hand by hand. I tested my damaged left leg and put a little weight on it. Thankfully, it didn't fold out from under me. Yet the kneecap was swollen.

I decided the best thing to do would be to take my piss next to the remaining tripod poles. That way, if any other gooks came along, they might smell it and believe that one of the men who set up the rocket had done his business at some point before leaving the area. I also checked my groin for leeches and other bugs. Satisfied that all was well, I hobbled slowly back to my temporary bamboo home.

The sun was now overhead. I could hear choppers coming and going from Ike, which was only about a half mile away. Sadly, none flew overhead. Even if one did, no one aboard would be able to see me underneath the thick green jungle canopy.

Surely, I thought, *a patrol had to be headed this way by now!*

I looked wistfully in the direction of the LZ which lay unseen somewhere to the east of my position. Being on the edge of the jungle, I gazed toward Ike. The savannah-like terrain interspersed with bamboo clumps rising above it was filled with dense elephant grass some five to six feet tall. Also, there were small strands of trees between me and my destination.

Sitting down, I dragged myself back under the bamboo. Using my staff, I reached out and tried to erase any markings of my passage that it might have left. My shoulder still ached, but I could move it. The pain seemed to have lessened.

Or was that my imagination? Maybe, I hoped, it wasn't broken or dislocated. Perhaps it was just bruised and extremely sore from my fall.

I hoped I wasn't deluding myself. Yet, I had to do something about my left arm, so I decided to place a splint on it. Several of the bamboo's myriads of arms were the size of my little finger. I tried to break a four-foot piece off. It was green, and after working it back and forth for a minute, it splintered. Slowly, and as quietly as possible, I continued to bend it in two directions. Finally, after ten minutes or so, it broke into a four-foot-long piece. Working with one arm turned out to be exhausting. I decided to rest.

Without trying, Morpheus stole over me. When I woke up, the sun was at two o'clock. I was thirsty and just a little bit hungry. I took a swig of water from my canteen. Then another sip. It was hot, stale water, but it tasted delicious. Using my P-28 in my right hand, I held the tin steady with my right foot. After much work, I managed to open both a tin of crackers and a cheese tin. Using the fingers of my right hand to spread the cheese on the crackers, I scarfed down my meager meal. There was some cheese left in the tin, so I licked the metal insides being exceedingly careful not to cut my tongue on the sharp edges. Next, I scraped out a five- to six-inch hole in the rotting jungle floor, put the cans in it, and then buried them.

Now, I realized I had to get some sort of splint on my left arm. I knew I would have to break the severed four-foot branch into three pieces, tape them together, and then tie or tape them to my arm. I had no idea how long it took me to make two more breaks, but somehow I accomplished the task with sweat dripping down my face. I found my tape, and using my teeth to rip the adhesive, I taped the pieces together. I tried to get rid of the splinters at both ends but was unable to do so with any success. Using my right hand, I managed to rip off my left pants leg below my swollen and badly bruised knee. The cloth ripped away easily as the moisture and dampness of the past two weeks had rotted it. Plus, there were also tears in the cloth from my unexpected descent that made the cloth easier to rip. Wrapping the bamboo splint in the torn cloth, I taped it and placed the improvised splint on my right thigh. Gingerly, I picked up my left arm and placed it on the splint. Then, taking the tape, I wrapped it around my arm and the splint just above my wrist and past the elbow.

By the time I finished, I was sweating profusely. Sweat trickled down my forehead and into my eyes and dripped off my nose. I could also feel the moisture running down my back. I wiped my face with my torn, olive-green T-shirt that stank of sweat, dirt, grime, and the ever-present smells of the jungle.

Sitting back against the bamboo, I figured it was around four o'clock—and still no patrol!

What the hell is going on? I wondered. *Where are those guys? Isn't anyone going to come looking for me—or the launch site?* Then, like a lightning bolt that struck my feeble brain, it dawned on me. *They've probably given me up for dead,* I thought. *Colonel what's-his-name wasn't about to authorize a search for some dumb G.I. who had the misfortune of falling out of a chopper. He'd most likely ordered his Command Sergeant Major to write me off as an MIA.*

After all, despite being a medic, I was, in the U.S. Army's eyes, a nobody. Just another body. Furthermore, I realized, if they hadn't sent a patrol out by now to look for the rocket site, they probably weren't going to do so—ever! *Sh-t!* I mumbled to myself. *I am truly and royally screwed!*

This meant I was on my own. I was going to have to crawl or hobble my way to the LZ and pray when I emerged from the elephant grass that some trigger-happy doofus on the LZ wouldn't start shooting at me. Suddenly, the LZ seemed to be a thousand miles away. Between it and me were both NVA and U.S. OPs, trip wires, barb wire, not to mention booby traps followed by G.I. Claymores located inside the perimeter of the LZ's three- or four-strand concertina wire.[40]

Well, I thought, *I'm going to have to do this on my own.* My wounds were surely infected by now and I felt a bit lightheaded. Perhaps I was running a fever. Time, too, was against me as I was running out of water and strength. I had a pit a mile deep in my stomach. I had no choice but to wait until darkness. I'd be safer moving then. Less chance of being seen and therefore less chance of my own side blowing me away. Just one major problem—I just might stumble into a friendly or unfriendly L.P. In truth, I was more apprehensive of my own people wasting me than I was of Charlie zapping me.

Having made the decision to head toward the LZ, I lay down underneath the bamboo and soon dozed off. After a while I woke up. The afternoon sun stretched its last rays across the jungle canopy as the sun and its fading light quickly disappeared around me. An evening breeze came up and cooled me off. No cloudbursts today—thank God. I self-consciously crossed my left hand's fingers. Sometimes I hated the rain. So far, the monsoon rain had held off.

Maybe, I prayed, *it'll be a dry night.*

Somewhere off to my left a "F-ck You" lizard started to shriek. I'd heard about the "F-ck You" lizards when I arrived in 'Nam—but just thought someone was pulling my leg and that they really didn't exist. When I heard my first one, I was dumbfounded. The lizard would crank up its screech and then begin its taunting cry, "F-ck You! F-ck

---

40 OPs were observation posts manned during daylight hours (called LPs [listening posts] at night) by a two- to three-man fire team located one hundred to two hundred yards outside an LZ to detect enemy movement or activity so as to give advanced warning of any probe or attack; it was considered a suicide duty. "Claymore" was an antipersonnel mine with a one-pound change of C-4 (dynamite) behind six hundred to seven hundred steel mini-balls which blasted out in a fan-shaped pattern with a lethal range of around fifty meters. Concertina wire was barbed wire with one-inch-long razor blades every six inches; it was strung out along the ground to impede enemy troops.

You! F-ck You!" Each call was a little less in volume, until it faded off and ceased. I used to count how many times the lizard would say "F-ck You"—seven to nine times was about average. The lizard off to my left was really vocal. Soon it was answered by another and then another. Their cacophony seemed to make the jungle come alive with a myriad of sounds, which was a good indication that Charlie wasn't in the vicinity, but I knew I couldn't count on it.[41] Even the songs of the night birds were somewhat muted.

I took one or two sips of water and held it in my mouth, counting off thirty seconds before I swallowed. A small breeze came up and brushed against my cheek. Thinking a "F-ck You" lizard had dropped on me, I nearly jumped a mile into the air before I realized what it was. Scared the pee-willies out of me!

With the sun now down, darkness descended quickly upon my jungle lair. From the top of the canopy to the musty floor, an indefinable murkiness permeated the air. Feeling woozy, I fell asleep again. When I awoke, I immediately intuited it was late—perhaps nine or ten? I didn't know for sure. Unfortunately, my flimsy $25 Seiko watch strap had been torn off my wrist during my precipitous descent. The sounds of the lizards had all but ceased, but the sound of the ever-present bugs still broke through the night air. The mosquitoes, which swarmed around my face, buzzed like a Cobra gunship making a run on Charlie's positions.[42] Night was Charlie's time. We feared the night in 'Nam. Charlie moved and attacked at night. G.I.s died at night. It was an ominous time. My morbid thoughts made me shiver.

The moon rose and beamed down on the savannah in front of my hideaway. I knew that the LPs for LZ Ike would be in place by now, and except for one man staying awake as a guard, the other two men were most likely asleep. Whenever it had been my turn to go on a

---

41 The "F-ck You" lizard is a Tokay gecko. The "F-ck" sound is fairly clear and short; it is then followed by a half–second delay before being a stretched–out "You."

42 Cobra gunship: an assault helicopter carrying rockets, M–79 grenade rounds, along with an electric type of Gatling gun capable of firing six thousand rounds per minute.

night LP with two or three other guys, while one man stayed up, we took turns sleeping. We'd split the night into shifts so that one person would only have a three- to four-hour watch; it was the only way one could catch up on his sleep in 'Nam. If the guard fell asleep while on watch, then the team stood a better-than-even chance of never returning (except in body bags) to the LZ.

I could hear the LZ's mortar crews firing—probably zeroing in on the LPs. Once a fire team reached their previously assigned position and set up, they would call in mortars to bracket their position. If you somehow managed to blow your position to Charlie, then the LZ could ring you with mortar fire and, hopefully, scare Charlie off, provided he hadn't blown you away by the time the mortars arrived. Sometimes guys never returned from an LP. They fell asleep once too often.

The mortars seemed to be bracketing on what was probably an LP a hundred yards or so off to my left. I crawled out from my hiding place. It took several minutes for me to pull myself up my walking stick before I could stand erect, albeit I was still somewhat unsteady on my legs. I figured that if I could get between where the LP was located and the LZ, I might stand a good chance of being picked up in the morning.

Clouds brushed against the moon and slowly drifted across its bright countenance. Darkness descended even more over the savannah as the moon appeared to be racing from cloud cover to cloud cover.

With a sigh of relief, I slowly lowered myself to the ground. Feeling around for some dirt, I grabbed a handful and smudged it over my face. It sure wouldn't do for the sporadic moonshine to brighten my face and be seen by Charlie, or someone on the LZ with a Starlight Scope.[43] I'd get blown away in a "New York minute."

---

43 A Starlight Scope was an image intensifier which used the reflected light from the stars and moon to identify targets at night. The ones we had in Vietnam in 1969 had not been totally developed and perfected and as such made seeing a target at night somewhat difficult.

It took several minutes for me to stand again. I hobbled over to the bamboo clump, leaned over, and dragged out my medical kit. Although I planned on making it to LZ Ike by tomorrow for sure, I still might need it. It had a strap, which I draped over my shoulder. Then I slowly edged out from underneath the jungle's thick cover into the five- or six-foot-tall elephant grass.

Walking was both painful due to the pain in my left knee and difficult as my makeshift walking stick seemed to get caught on every blade of elephant grass. After fifteen to twenty minutes, I stopped for a breather and turned to look back at the jungle's edge. It seemed to me I had only walked seventy-five to one hundred feet. There was a slight wind, and every rustle of the grass caused me to freeze for a few seconds. Just about the time I got used to the sound of the grass swaying back and forth as I pushed through it, the clouds began to break away from the moon. Their shadow swept across the savannah, bathing me in moonlight. My shadow was silhouetted against the grass. I decided to take a break as I was already bathed in sweat. I felt tired and was extremely tempted to go back to sleep as I sat back down.

Somewhere off to my left wafted the faint smell of pot. It had to be the LP. Those fools! If Charlie came along, it would be all over for them—unless that was Charlie smoking the weed. Then I might be in a lot of trouble. After several minutes, even though the temptation to lie down was strong, I knew I had to keep moving.

It seemed to take much more time for me to stand. I was weak and most likely a bit dehydrated. Looking across the moonlit sea of elephant grass I could see seven- to eight-foot-high conic mounds of dirt. They were the ubiquitous termite mounds that we saw all the time while patrolling in the jungle and its adjacent fields. Usually, they were about seven to eight feet round at their base and about six feet high. To me, every time I saw these mud-hardened taper piles of dirt, they reminded me of the 1563 painting by Pieter Paul Bruegel titled *The Tower of Babel*, that I saw and admired in an art book while I was in college. There was a small clump of trees about fifty feet off to my right. Determined to head toward it and take a rest under them, I hoped I could make it that far as my left leg and knee were beginning to ache.

Some fifteen minutes later, I managed to arrive at the strand of five or six trees. I sat down, using a tree trunk as support for my back. My face was bathed in sweat. I wanted a drink so badly. I took a piece of my tattered T-shirt and ripped it off. I dipped it into my canteen, which was now less than a quarter full. I pulled the rag slowly out of the canteen between two fingers squeezing the water out of the rag's fibers back into the canteen before I took the damp (and probably dirty!) cloth and put it into my mouth.

Mmm! God, that tasted so good! I continued to suck on it until there was no more liquid in the cloth. I repeated the same process two more times. I had to conserve my water just in case I didn't make it to LZ during the upcoming day. My self-enforced rationing was becoming more and more difficult as my body strength was ebbing away by the hour.

Off to the north I could see a dark cloud inching its way toward the LZ. The trees began to sway slightly. Intuitively I knew another cloudburst was on its way. I needed to take cover. I crawled further into the small copse of trees hoping they would protect me from the full onslaught of the oncoming rain.

As I did so, I fervently prayed I wouldn't disturb a three- or five-stepper, a deadly venomous snake in the krait family. Rumor was that upon being bitten by this snake—I didn't know for sure—that one could only walk another three or five steps before one died from their highly toxic venom. Fortunately, I didn't encounter either one while crawling into the center of the trees.

By the time I crawled the four to five feet into the trees, I suddenly realized I would need more water. I pulled the poncho out of my medical bag and tied the four corners to the tree limbs about two feet off the ground. I could hear the rain approaching from far off. When the rainwater dropped on it and pooled in the center of the poncho, I could lie somewhat safely under it and collect the water after the rain petered out.

I was exhausted. I dozed off.

The rain struck with a fury. Buckets and buckets poured down. The accompanying wind blew under my poncho, as the pelting windblown rain awakened me from my sleep. I wondered how long I had been asleep. Fifteen minutes? Twenty? It didn't matter. I was soaked. There was never any rest whatsoever for the weary in 'Nam. I began to shiver.

I grabbed the poncho liner from the medical bag and wrapped it around me as best I could. My fever had returned, and my injured knee ached. I reached down and felt it. There was a miniature inferno perched on my leg and the swelling around the knee seemed to have grown. I fumbled around for the Benadryl bottle, took two out, and shoved them down my throat. Sticking my head out from underneath the poncho, I tipped its edge toward my mouth and gulped down some cool rainwater. God, it tasted good! I drank until I was full. I was still chilly from the rain and wet clothes. Lying on my right side, I curled up and pulled the poncho liner over my trembling body and instantly fell asleep, again.

Hours later the rain abated. I dozed off and on during the monsoon rainfall. The silence and dripping rain awakened me. We didn't get much sleep in 'Nam and certainly never over two or three uninterrupted hours, so I was used to being awakened during the night. Due to our lack of sleep in Vietnam, we were at times walking around like zombies. We were mere shells of ourselves. My poncho sagged and dipped in the middle and almost touched the ground with its reservoir of water.

Hunger gnawed at my stomach. I had to make it to the LZ that day or else I would starve—or, at least, I thought I'd starve! I knew my energy was slowly being zapped from me. I opened my last tin of crackers and wolfed them down. Tipping the edge of the poncho, again I drank my fill of water. God knows what kind of unhealthy microscopic organisms were probably in the water, but I could not have cared less. Although, I thought glumly, they would really make me sick down the road!

An unnatural swish in the elephant grass drew my attention toward the sound. Someone, or something, was moving out there. I wondered if my poncho reflected any moonlight. Peering out through the leaves and palm-like fronds, I could see movement off to my left. The moon suddenly broke its cover from behind the clouds and revealed four men walking slowly through the elephant grass about twenty yards away. They were walking single file, about five yards apart.

Gooks!!!

Holy shit! I thought. *What am I gonna do now?*

The moon was suddenly obscured by another cloud except for a lone moonbeam which peeped through and revealed the four men were marching off toward the general area where I believed our LP was located. I fervently prayed our guys weren't still smoking grass. If they were, Charlie was about to lay some numbers on their ass.

The four men vanished into the darkness. Maybe they were a gook sapper squad.[44] A minute or two later, gunshots and tracer rounds broke the night's stillness. There were several explosions. I couldn't tell if they were Chinese-manufactured *chicoms*—the NVA's equivalent to a grenade which were supplied by the Chinese Communists (hence, *chicoms*). I immediately heard the *Whump! Whump!* of the LZ's mortars.

---

44 "Sappers" were enemy demolition or assault teams who were adept at deftly crawling through many strands of concertina wire or mine fields, enabling them to penetrate defenses. They were usually armed with explosive satchel charges which they would activate and then throw into bunkers.

The incoming mortar rounds lit the sky with their phosphorescent flashes. Whistling artillery shells screaming overhead and exploding with great ferocity broke the night's stillness. I hated to hear the spinning whine of shrapnel in the air. The sound always brought death or a nasty injury. I watched and prayed the incoming shells wouldn't land close by. Fortunately, not one did.

Suddenly, I saw two dark figures half-running, half-walking, and stumbling past me. Gooks! The other two were probably dead or dying. I didn't care. The dull pain returned with a vengeance and I knew my fever wasn't going to fade away. Probably some infection. I blanked out.

I awoke to the hot sun streaming down on me. Condensation from the underside of my poncho dripped onto my face. The fever was still with me—I felt like a G.I. who had been on a two-day drunk. My head ached and I felt incredibly dizzy. I had to move. I had to keep going even if at a crawl. I tipped my poncho and drank as much water as I could. It was warm and beginning to taste stale already.

Only God knows what I'm swallowing. I had to stay alive and maintain some strength to make it to the LZ—if that was possible!

I must have slept late as the sun was directly overhead and waning toward afternoon. Having drunk my fill from the poncho, I dipped the water toward its edge and filled my canteen. I then drank from the poncho's edge again. Having filled up, I pushed the rest of the water off by raising my arm against the underside of the poncho. It was do-or-die time. I would have to take the poncho down, roll it up, and leave it and its liner in the copse of trees. I would still drag my zipped-up medical bag, hope for the best, and pray my staff would somehow help.

A cool breeze was blowing as I crawled out from underneath the trees that had been my refuge. Lacking food and water, I was just too tired, or weakened, to stand. I paused a moment to get my bearings and started crawling on my right side through the high elephant grass. Every so often I tried to sit up and raise my head above the top of the grass, hoping that there might be a G.I. patrol out that I could attract. But none appeared.

How long I crawled is beyond me. Every fifteen minutes or so (or was it only five or ten?), I paused to catch my breath, wipe the ubiquitous sweat from my forehead and eyes, and tried to mentally block out the now ever-constant and worsening pain in my arms and knee. It was slow going. If any gooks or G.I.s came along, they would probably have no trouble in following my trail in the tall, cool green grass. If the former did, I was a dead duck, but hopefully, if the latter, they might out of curiosity follow it and find me. I fervently prayed for the latter scenario.

Slowly, inch by inch, I laboriously crawled toward the LZ. My right arm and leg were doing most of the work while I used the staff to push me forward six to eight inches at a time. My arms and legs were becoming sorer with each push forward. At one point, I paused and took about five minutes to partially stand and peek over the top of the elephant grass. It seemed like it was almost an impossible task for me to accomplish.

I could see the LZ's concertina wire was only about two hundred feet away. I wanted to fully stand and wave for attention, but I realized some trigger-happy lookout might see me and decide discretion was the better part of valor and blow me away. I thought about yelling, but even with the water I had gulped down, my throat was dry and parched. I had to keep plodding along and save my water.

I was becoming frustrated at my slow arduous progress toward safety. My fever made it hard to concentrate. All I wanted to do was to lie down and go to sleep. My pain level was high and pulsating throughout my body, urging me to stop, quit, give up. Yet I knew I had to continue. It was my only chance to stay alive and help was six to eight inches closer with each push through the grass.

A black cloud suddenly obscured the sun. Within minutes the wind picked up and the sheets of the monsoon rain descended. I was caught in the open with no shelter. The downpour drenched me to the bone. I lay on my back and drank in the pelting pellets of rain.

At least, I thought rather grimly, that was one way to conserve the water in my canteen!

I started to shiver and the fever pounded my head. I passed out, shaking and a bit delirious. Darkness. When I came to, I could feel the cold trying to permanently seep into my body. I vaguely realized I was still alive. The cool nightly breeze whipped at my rain-soaked body. I could see the stars in the heavens above me. I had to move. Get to the LZ.

Even though it was now nighttime, I had to keep going. To stop was death. The drive to stay alive took all my concentration. My crawling took on an automatic motion like a robot. I inched forward with a shooting pain in my left knee every time I propelled myself forward. Every five to six feet, I was forced to rest before moving onward. I was fast becoming unable to clearly and intelligently think. I kept repeating to myself, "The LZ's at point X and I have to make it." Several times the pain and fever forced me to pass out.

Finally, I remembered I still had some pain meds in my medic's bag. I felt around for my medic's bag. It was gone! For several minutes I just lay there groggily trying to figure out why my medicine bag had disappeared. I guess I had left it behind somewhere during my crawl through the elephant grass.

I thought stupidly, *How could I have done that? How could I have left it behind and not miss it?*

My mind was becoming hazier the further I traversed through the tall grass. I determinedly realized the need to forge onward. I don't remember stopping but I probably passed out from lack of food, pain, and physical exhaustion.

It was near dawn. I could see sunlight beginning to bring forth a new morning off to the east. The birds were chirping as the pale grey morning light filtered its way over the jungle and descended gently upon the savannah. I had to start out on my journey immediately.

This was it! This HAD to be my last day! It was do or die now. I was near the end of my rope. If I didn't make it out of the elephant grass, it would be game over for me. I was going to make it to the perimeter or else some gunner on a chopper was bound to see me as the morning helicopters came into the area to drop off supplies for the LZ. I realized that being exposed in the elephant grass might also bring down machine gun fire from the chopper. I wiped my face off with my incredibly dirty green T-shirt to ensure that if someone spotted me, that they would see my white face.

With gritty determination, I started crawling ever so slowly toward the LZ. Exhausted, I was in really dire straits as I paused every three or four feet to rest. I knew the perimeter was only a couple of hundred feet away. Yet the fever was taking over and I found it more and more difficult to think clearly. Not only that, but agonizing pain was also sweeping over my entire body.

I have to make it! I told myself. I knew I had little time left.

Suddenly, as I dragged myself forward there was a mad rush. Something slimy with scales dashed past me. My heart stopped beating and my Adam's apple nearly swallowed itself as two iguanas ran past me, spitting with their long tongues and piercing me with daggers in their yellow eyes as they disappeared into the elephant grass. I began to shake all over. After all, they were harmless, but they sure scared the sh-t out of me. I must have rudely awakened them from their morning slumber.

Thank God, I thought, they were only lizards and not a snake! The thought of snakes sent shivers down my spine. I hoped I wouldn't encounter any before I made it to the edge of the grass.

Finally! About ten feet further on and thirty minutes later, I broke out of the elephant grass. I could see the multiple strands of concertina wire surrounding the LZ. It was only fifty yards away. The morning mist rose above the LZ's bunkers and dew sparkled off strands of the concertina wire that lay about twenty-five feet away. The sun began to break through the clouds off to the east. I could hear people moving about on the LZ and could smell fresh-cooked eggs. My stomach churned and gurgled out loud as if it was asking me to feed it. My mouth was dry. I knew I was not going to be able to yell and attract attention.

Inexorably, I crawled toward the concertina wire. Finally, I made it! Fortunately, no one on the LZ had detected my movement and tried to blow me away. Moving alongside the wire for a couple of feet, I found a trip wire for a flare. In my delirious state, hazy with fatigue, I reached out and pulled it—praying the pop and flash would attract attention and not bullets.

Days later I came out of a haze in a clean, white-sheeted hospital bed. A nurse told me I was in the Philippines awaiting transfer to the States.

My ordeal was over.

✗✗✗

Author's Note: This short story was written in the late 1970s, some seven to eight years after I returned from Vietnam. In looking through a box of my many completed and uncompleted short stories dating from the early 1960s-1970s, I found it. Although it was completed, after some editing, I was able to include it in this book.

THE
BODY

It had been a bitter, long, hard winter—much colder than in the last ten to fifteen years. The plethora of the winter's never-ending snowfall increased the Rockies snowpack's height to record levels all over the mountain ranges from New Mexico to Montana and into Canada. The thicker-than-usual snow buildup meant far away reservoirs at Lake Mead and Lake Powell would begin to refill from their all-time lows. Come the spring runoff, a lot more of the lifesaving water would flow out from underneath Colorado's high glacial masses.

At first, the glacier fed water trickled out in the form of hundreds of small rivulets which flowed lazily downhill. Then, as the days warmed up in May, the water began to gush out from underneath the thousands-of-years-old ice packs throughout the Rockies region to form multiple brooks and rills. With each hour the driblets became faster, flowing until they met somewhere downhill and formed into larger creeks and rivers.

But this year's snowpack had much more liquid to spew out. What had been multiple four- to five-foot-wide brooks now became roaring creeks ten to fifteen feet wide, destroying everything in their paths.

It would be a good year for the farmers in the valley below as the mountain silt would partially cover their fields. Their crops would benefit from all the extra water which the ground had absorbed, giving hope to some of the tillers of the soil that they might even be able to harvest two crops this year. What a bounty!

But with everything good that mother nature gave out, there were, in some cases, unexpected results. One of the wider flows, named Shalako Creek, after a millennium of erosion, dug away at the thin layer of soil and rubble lying over the granite base that lay a few short feet underneath the fast-moving stream. The volume of water forced its moss-covered banks to erode another two to three feet on each side.

The gushing stream ended its downhill trip in a stretch of hundred-yard-long rapids as the milky white water reached the flat lands. The now semi-river was confined between the previously deep and age-old channels that contained the flow within much higher banks. The stream, with its thousands of cubic feet of water per second, began to slow as it wandered and temporarily spread itself out into the pastures depositing new dirt. But the flow, which receded rather slowly, had uncovered something unexpected.

On one downhill bank just at the end of the rapids, the bones of a partial leg with a strange-looking foot lay exposed and sticking out of the embankment.

The wheels of fate began to inexorably turn.

As summer progressed and the crops grew and ripened, the local farmers used previously created three-foot-wide by five-foot-deep channels to funnel the life-giving water of Shalako Creek to their various fields. Most of the pastures were 250 to 350 acres and this year they thrived on the abundance of water that belched forth from the glacier high up on Trappers Peak.

George Taylor's three-hundred-acre pastureland lay next to the mountain's slope from which Shalako Creek flowed. The stream had a good flow. At first, he checked on it every week or so, as it supplied water year-round to Dead Horse Valley, as the surrounding area was known. With the spring runoff this year, the mountain had deposited a lot of fertile debris that came from higher up on its slopes.

Taylor's, and the adjacent fields located below his, thrived this year. Although it was somewhat difficult to access his field, George began to check his crops weekly. He lived on the western downslope of the Rockies just outside of Phippsburg, Colorado, a settlement of only two-hundred-plus souls located twenty to twenty-five miles southwest of Steamboat Springs, the county seat of Routt County.

To access his property, George had to drive southeast on Highway 131 on a paved, narrow, two-lane road for about ten miles before turning right about a mile north of the little 399-person town of Yampa. Here, he exited onto a dirt road which snaked around the northern edge of Dead Horse Valley. The unkempt road wandered its way southwest and followed a medium-sized stream coming from the 11,978-foot-high Trappers Peak Mountain which was within the Flat Top Wilderness. After a few more miles, he turned left off the dirt road onto a faint but well-used track.

To survey his acreage, he always brought his horse trailer occupied by his trusty black coal steed, Midnight. The twelve-mile-long dirt track that passed for a road was rutted with a lot of potholes and bumps. Due to the weight of the horse box, it usually took him about seventy-five minutes to travel to his pasture along the winding and rutted road. After topping a medium high ridge, he could see the layout of the farms ahead of him. Straight ahead lay a seven-mile-long valley with a two- to three-mile width that spread out from a few hundred yards against the flanks of Trappers Peak into a five- to six-mile length as it sprawled out into the flat lands to the southwest.

Seven to eight farmers owned the valley's lands and cooperated in the spring planting by using two rental tractors from a local John Deere merchant in Steamboat Springs. All these tillers of the soil knew each other well. Around late April to early May, they usually gathered together in an encampment situated in a small glen-like area carved out eons ago on the northeastern side of Dead Horse Valley. There, they spent over a week taking turns operating the tractors, planting seeds, and spending some guy time together. Only one of them was married, as this western area of the state was a forlorn, lonely, and harsh place to live—much less raise a family—so wives usually didn't last long in the hostile environment of western Colorado before they left their spouses and moved on to more populated towns and cities. As the women dubbed it, they needed to move on to "real civilization."

Today, for some reason, George decided that instead of circling his pasture which abutted Trappers Peak, he would ride alongside the southern edge of Shalako Creek where it emerged at the downslope of the mountain. His decision to do so would entail much consternation on his part.

By early June, after the spring spate of water, Shalako Creek returned to its normal flow. The water level had dropped significantly, exposing a myriad of small and large granite boulders where the former snowmelt rapids wreaked havoc. The hot June sun whitened the leg and foot bones protruding from the southern side of the creek. The unusual looking bones had been washed clean by the spring flow and now lay exposed some two to three feet below the top of the creek's embankment.

Despite the heavy rainfall the previous day, Taylor took his time riding alongside the southern rim of Shalako Creek, making sure that

Midnight didn't step into any holes from the spring floods that had disrupted the topography bordering the creek. Also, due to the recent rain, the ground near the creek's edge was still somewhat soft. During spring planting, he and the other farmers cleared the trees, stumps, and tree limbs that had washed down the mountain before being deposited on the flat area of the adjacent fields which bordered both sides of the stream. Any large rocks they encountered were pushed or shoved back into the creek with the hope that in the future they would impede erosion.

As Taylor rode leisurely along the creek side, Midnight suddenly neighed and came to an abrupt halt.

"What's going on, *ol' boy?*" George asked his nervous steed as he patted the stallion's neck. His mount pawed the dirt next to the creek bank. It was as if the horse sensed or smelled something untoward. George slid off the horse's back, continuing to stroke the spooked animal's neck as he looked around. Wary of rattlesnakes that might have been washed down the mountain, he looked around but didn't see anything. So, he sidled carefully over to the side of the stream, testing the firmness of the ground beneath him and then looked down.

He gasped, "Holy sh-t!" Below him, half-hidden by the overhanging bank, he saw the leg bone of a skeleton. But this didn't look like the leg and foot of just any old skeleton he had ever seen! While the leg looked normal, the foot had, instead of toes, five- to six-inch-long curved, claw-like talons. George stood there gaping at the strange bones beneath him.

What the hell is this? he wondered. *And what kind of dinosaur might this thing be?*

Although he had a cell phone, there was no coverage in the valley. He would have to drive out to Yampa to find a cell tower. Retreating from the bank, he kneeled down and picked up ten to fifteen three- to four-inch rocks and made a small cairn to mark where the bones rested.

✗✗✗

The wheels of fate began to inexorably turn.

✗✗✗

After riding Midnight back to his horse trailer and securing the horse inside, George started his drive out of the valley and back to civilization. Two hours later, as he neared Route 131, he saw that he had enough bars to make a call. He personally knew the sheriff, Jefferson "Jeff" Monroe, as they had grown up together and attended the same schools in Routt County. As he left home that morning around six, he looked down at his watch and realized it was almost noon.

His childhood buddy ought to be in his office and finished with his daily paperwork that, according to Jeff, never eased in its inexorable flow. The vast majority of it would either be from the State of Colorado's law enforcement agencies or, even worse, federal government asshole bureaucrats who knew nothing about law enforcement west of the Rockies and could not have cared less—just as long as they continued to send out more and more idiotic paperwork to justify their empty, superfluous, and inane jobs.

Jeff, who hated the feds with a passion, once described them to George, saying, "They are not only dimwits who are dumb as a rock but jackasses with their heads up their butts."

Parking on the side of the road, he dialed the county sheriff's office, identifying himself to Brenda Butler, Jeff's receptionist. She was another elementary school chum, who was single, and as George remembered, carried around 250 to 275 pounds of flab. Everyone knew she loved to snack on Little Debbie cupcakes as she was always brushing crumbs off the front of her blouse. Behind her back, Brenda was known as "The Blob" or "Momma Grizzly," but no one in the sheriff's office—at least those who valued their lives—dared calling her by either of those pejorative monikers! George told her he had an urgent matter to discuss with Jeff that needed the sheriff's immediate attention.

Brenda turned and shouted in her nasally voice and twangy Western accent, "Jeff, *yer* buddy George's on the phone. He says it's urgent!"

Jeff picked up his phone and said, "Howdy, George, long time no hear." George just chuckled as they had eaten lunch together only a few days ago. "How *ya* been?" Both men exchanged pleasantries for about a minute before Jeff asked, "Okay, George, what's up that's so urgent?"

As George described what he had discovered, Jeff's mouth gaped open. "Are you sh--ting me?" he asked in disbelief. "Are you absolutely sure it's a human type of leg?"

"No doubt, Jeff," George replied as he continued. "I seen it with my own eyes. It's the weirdest thing I've ever seen in my life."

"Well, George, I'm way *outta* my depth on this. I think I'd better call the archeology department at the University of Colorado in Boulder and see if they can help us in any way. *Gimme* your number in case someone wants to contact you immediately for further information. Also, let's meet tomorrow in the morning at the Yampa turnoff, say, around nine-ish? I *wanna* see this leg!"

"Sure thing, Jeff, *an'* thanks for taking my call."

Both men hung up. The sheriff leaned back in his chair, wondering, *What the hell has George stumbled upon?*

"Brenda," Jeff yelled, "can you get someone on the phone at the anthropology or archeology department of the University of Colorado in Boulder? I need to talk to someone high up—like, maybe, the head of the department. Tell them it's important with a capital 'I.'"

"Sure thing, Jeffy!" she replied with a smirk on her face as she licked the latest cupcake crumbs from her fingers and then brushed them off her ample bosom.

God! He hated it when she called him by that name! But he knew better than to cross her, or she could really f-ck up his incessantly flowing paperwork. *Sh-t!*

Five minutes later, Jeff was talking to Dr. Jackson "Jack" Massey, the Chair of University of Colorado's (UC) anthropology department. He quickly described what his friend George had discovered.

"This seems most unusual, Sheriff," Massey commented. "Today is Wednesday," he continued. "Since it's summertime, I think I can swiftly put together a three- or four-man team and be out there late Saturday afternoon. Now, Sheriff, let's be discreet and extremely cautious about this find, if you will"—he cautioned Jeff—"just in case this isn't what it appears to be. Let's keep this 'discovery' as secret as possible, until we understand what this site has in store for us."

"I totally agree, Doctor," Jeff replied as he swiveled his chair away from facing the office door and lowered his voice so that Brenda couldn't hear him. "I won't tell anyone in my department. I do have a deputy who lives in Yampa and is responsible for that southern portion of our 2,300-plus-square-mile county. I'll inform him that I'll be in that area and can't comment on why, just in case this all turns out to be a false front."

The two men further discussed details and planned as to where they would meet up and what kind of vehicles would be needed. They also exchanged private cell numbers so that they could stay off any type of official air waves.

The next morning Jeff met George at the turnoff on the dirt road just north of Yampa. Since Jeff's county sheriff's truck had a much higher jacked-up clearance, he suggested that George leave his truck, and they ride together to the site. Along the way, Jeff related his conversation with Massey and the need to keep everything on the Q.T. With his three-foot clearance, the drive took only thirty minutes as George directed his lifelong friend to the location of his unusual discovery. When he sighted the small cairn, George pointed and told Jeff where to pull up.

Both men dropped down to *terra firma* and walked over to the now slow-flowing Shalako Creek and looked over the edge of its seven- to eight-foot-high embankment. George and the sheriff squatted down while Jeff took several minutes and stared at the exposed leg with its talons. Neither man spoke.

Unbeknownst to both men, their appearance on the creek's edge was detected. Lying high up on a ponderosa tree limb a hundred yards away, a small, round, six-inch object began to whirr as it transmitted an invisible ultrasound-type beam into the sky above the men.

$$\times\times\times$$

Jeff stood, saying, "I want to get a better view, George. I've got a rope in my truck, so I'll attach it to my push bumper, slide down, and get a real up-close look." The sheriff walked over to his truck, pulled a rope out of a side compartment, and attached it to the bumper. After putting on some heavy gloves and holding onto the rope, he dropped off the edge and walked himself down the embankment until he touched bottom where he was at eyelevel with the protruding bones.

Jeff took off one glove and slowly extended his hand until he touched the exposed foot. With his fingers he explored the foot and slid his hand up what appeared to be a tibia. As he did so, he suddenly felt a tiny vibration and an unexplainable warm electrical charge go through his fingertips and to his ears, which experienced some sort of ultrasonic soundwaves with a high-pitched, almost undetectable buzzing. He jerked his hand away.

Looking up at George, Jeff said, "Sure feels like real bones to me. But the weird thing is, George, I could feel some sort of infinitesimal vibration. And, there's this weird sound along with some electric static."

"Well," George opined, "that's really strange! It's too early in the morning for the sun to warm anything up. Plus, that side of the bank is in the shade!"

Jeff put his glove back on and climbed back out of the creek bed. After untying and stowing his rope, he said, "George, let's head out. There's no use wondering about these bones and what I felt. Maybe, subconsciously, I wanted to feel something. Hell, I just don't know. We'll wait for Massey and his crew to unearth it and see what we've actually got. *Somethin'* tells me this *ain't* human."

George nodded his head in silent agreement.

The wheels of fate began to inexorably turn.

The two friends left the scene and drove back to the main road. Along the way, they made small talk, catching up on each other's life. Before separating, they both agreed to meet on Saturday after they had heard from Massey and his crew as to when the archeologists might arrive.

When George woke around 5:00 a.m. on Saturday morning, he decided to head out early and wait for the UC crew at the Yampa turnoff. Having nothing else to do and knowing he would be biding his time—it might be six hours or more—George decided to take along *Don Quixote,* a book by Cervantes, which he had wanted to read for some time. After a quick breakfast of oatmeal with raisins and orange juice, he packed a lunch along with several flavored bottles of ICE water which he stuffed into his Yeti cooler. He then left for the rendezvous point and arrived around 7:30 a.m.

He parked in the small parking area at the Highway 131 cutoff to Dead Horse Valley. Off to the east, some fifteen-plus miles in the distance, rose the west slope of the high and mighty Rockies in all their glorious and magnificent granite splendor. He noted the blood red sun as it continued its rise over the Rockies and made its daily journey across the sky. George settled in to read. Several hours later, his cell rang. It was Jeff.

"I'm on my way, George. Just left Steamboat. Hope to be there in an hour. Heard from Massey. In addition to himself, he's got a crew of four—two archeology profs and two graduate students, one of whom is a young girl. They left at 6:00 a.m. and will be there around two-ish."

"Sounds good, Jeff," George replied. "I'm already parked on the dirt road just off the 131, outside of Yampa. Saw your deputy drive by a while back. I waved and he waved back but didn't stop."

"That's great," Jeff replied. "I told him I'm meeting you and others and not to worry about seeing anyone strange at the Yampa cutoff."

"I'll be here when you arrive," George replied. They talked for a few minutes more before hanging up. George took a drink of his flavored ICE water and continued reading *Don Quixote.*

About forty-five minutes later, Jeff arrived in his personal truck, which looked like one of those humongous monster trucks one sees at a demolition derby. He parked it in front of George. The huge truck, with five-foot-high tires, had at least a four-foot clearance with attached foldout-type aluminum ladders on either side, enabling the driver or passenger to climb up or down. George climbed up into the passenger side of the brightly painted truck which was detailed with flames flowing from the center of the front grill alongside both of the sides, ending in the middle of the tailgate. On each side of the truck's flames, Jeff had the custom-painted word "Flamethrower."

"Nice truck, Jeff," George commented once he took a seat.

"Yeah, I got into demolition derby stuff about ten years ago. A friend of mine over in Glenwood Springs built it for me. I haul this baby all over Colorado, Wyoming, and up to Montana. I've won a few trophies at big truck meets, but I'm not in it for the prizes. Just the thrill of driving one of these monsters and the incredible adrenaline surge is enough to satisfy me."

There was a beep on Jeff's cell. He looked down at the message and said, "Doc Massey and his crew are at McCoy about twenty miles south of here, so they'll be here in twenty to twenty-five minutes."

George nodded. Both men started reminiscing while they waited.

About twenty-five minutes later, a caravan of three trucks appeared from the south and pulled in parallel to both the Flamethrower and George's truck. Everyone exited their vehicles, stretched, and introduced themselves. Massey, who looked to be in his late sixties, brought along two assistant professors, Henry "Hank" Washington, an expert in dinosaur bones, and Sergeant "Sarge" Garfield, who was well known in his field as an expert in the Native American culture of Colorado and adjoining states. The two grad students looked to be in their mid to late twenties and introduced themselves as Jackson Turner and Jennifer Whitebird. Whitebird told Jeff and George she specialized in both the indigenous cultures of the Colorado Plateau and the Anasazi culture, which both men subsequently learned had flourished in the Four Corners region until around 1350 AD before suddenly and mysteriously disappearing into the mists of time.

Jeff told the assembled group that he would lead the way into the site. Massey said that they would take a quick look at the bones and then set up both their tents and an excavation area. Everyone returned to their trucks and set out for George's pasture. Although it was easy driving for Jeff in the Flamethrower, he drove at a slow speed so that the four-truck convoy could stick together. After a forty-minute drive, they arrived at the site. All four vehicles pulled up in a straight line about fifty feet from the southern edge of Shalako Creek.

After exiting their trucks, and an exhortation from George to beware of soft soil on the creek's bank, the group cautiously approached the cairn next to the creek's rim. The UC crew looked down at the white leg and foot with its curved talons.

"This is, indeed, incredibly strange," Massey commented with a large amount of puzzlement in his voice. His crew nodded silently. "Okay," Massey continued, "let's get our tents set up and then outline the excavation area above whatever this strange thing is."

An hour later, three sleeping tents were set up about fifty feet back from the southern edge of Shalako Creek. They also dug a slit-trench latrine about twelve inches wide, four feet long, and two feet deep, which they located fifty feet further south from the nearest tent. George and Jeff couldn't help but notice that Whitebird and Garfield were sharing the same tent.

Their chores having been accomplished, Massey and his group started to mark out the area to be excavated. They decided that they would start by digging a four-foot-wide trench some ten feet long above the bones. Next, they erected one canopy over the excavation site and another adjoining it that was used for dining or studying whatever they unearthed.

Massey decided he wanted to view the bones up close. Jeff then told him what he had observed, felt, and heard. The white-bearded man nodded and stroked his chin as Jeff related his findings before telling him he had a rope and would attach it to his truck's push bumper.

"Okay," Massey said. "Hank, get the Geiger counter and rope it down to me after I'm standing on the creek bed."

Jeff secured the rope and handed the end of it to Massey, who was donning his work gloves. The rest of the group stood on the edge as Massey edged himself slowly over the creek's rim. Standing in front of the bones, he asked Hank to slowly lower the Geiger down to him. After activating the Geiger, Massey slowly worked it back and forth from the end of the foot to the dirt bank.

"There's a very minute amount of radiation," Massey commented as he indicated to Hank to pull up the Geiger counter. "But it is so infinitesimal as not to be a worry about exposure," he continued. "I'll now run my hand across the bones to get an idea as to their composition."

As soon as Massey's hand touched the tibia, he quickly looked up at Jeff. "Sheriff, it's like you said. I can feel a transient vibration and some sort of ultrasonic sound when I touch it. But, as soon as I take my hand away, they cease. I haven't any idea what this all means, but when we get whatever is buried uncovered, perhaps we'll know more."

The wheels of fate began to inexorably turn.

Massey then roped himself back up the embankment and stood erect when he was on firm land again. Turning to his crew, he told them to unpack all their digging gear and have it ready to go by six the next morning.

Jeff turned to Massey and told him that he and George would depart but would return the following day. George warned the entire crew to beware of wolves and bears that occupied the area and instructed them to tightly cover up their food and put it back in their trucks for safekeeping. Everyone nodded and thanked both men as they climbed into the Flamethrower and departed.

"Well, George, tighten your seatbelt," Jeff laughed. "I'm *gonna* let this baby roll and see how fast we can get back to your car!" George simply nodded as the Flamethrower lurched forward. Fifteen minutes later, after what George thought was the most hair-raising ride he had ever experienced, they arrived back at the intersection of the Yampa cutoff and Route 131.

Bidding each other goodbye, both men agreed to meet at seven the next morning at George's home in Phippsburg where Jeff would pick up George.

✗✗✗

As the sun started to settle down behind Trappers Peak, Massey and his crew set up a charcoal grill. Using their kitchen utensils, they fixed up a meal of hamburgers, rice, and beans. After dinner, they washed the kitchenware and secured the food inside one of the trucks. With the chores done, they sat in their chairs around the table and discussed tomorrow's dig. Each archeologist voiced their thoughts about the remains that George had discovered. Hank, who also had a paleontology background, was of the opinion that the bones belonged to some sort of undiscovered dinosaur.

It grew dark with the sun setting behind Trappers Peak. As they sipped on their various brands of beer, night began to descend. At first, it seemed like any other night. Even though it was summer, a slight chill began to fill the air. Suddenly, with no warning whatsoever, a glowing object with a streak of light behind it sped through the encampment about ten feet over their heads. It traveled so fast that everyone immediately stopped talking and searched the darkening skies.

"Was that a meteorite?" one of them inquired.

Whatever it was, the object suddenly reappeared above their

heads, where it hovered and emitted a reverberating sound that seemed to pierce their eardrums but without the expected pain that comes from hearing such a high-pitched sound. It emitted a burst of light similar to an old-fashioned photography flash, then vanished in a nanosecond.

The university crew sat stunned in their chairs unable to speak before everyone started to speak at once. Three of the five commented that they just saw something unbelievable. It couldn't be true. Were they hallucinating?

As they discussed the unexpected visitor, or whatever it was, they looked up into the dark night sky which was strangely void of any visible stars, although it was a cloudless night. What they saw next stunned the archeologists as they continued to gaze upward into the pitch-black sky. Above their heads, about twenty-five feet in the air, were seven or eight glowing objects about the size of a duckpin bowling ball. A hum, almost indistinct, seemed to be emitting from each one as they circled overhead. This display continued for about a minute and each of the campers felt a vibration, or pulsation, pass through their bodies. Then, without any warning, the objects streaked off to the north at incomprehensible speeds and vanished in less than a second. The nighttime stars magically appeared.

The group sat there in astonishment. No one spoke.

What had they just seen or experienced? Did they just see a UFO? If not, what in the world was it?

Massey decided he would call Jeff and report the eerie occurrence, but he quickly found out that he had no cell service as they were camping in such a remote area. He shrugged his shoulders and nodded his head back and forth. *Damn!* he thought. *I should have brought my sat/nav phone. Now, we're cut off! Guess I'll just have to wait until morning to discuss this eerie occurrence with Jeff and George,* he thought with some resignation.

No one could come up with an opinion as to what they had seen. Was it a UFO? They sat and discussed the otherworldly experience for over an hour before retiring to their blowup mattresses and sleeping bags. Although each one of the archeologists was deeply disturbed by what they had seen, they all mystically fell into a deep sleep until each one amazingly awoke at exactly six the next morning. After a hasty breakfast, they commenced excavating the site.

The wheels of fate began to inexorably turn.

By seven the next morning, Jeff was in George's driveway. He picked up four small burritos and two large sodas at Jose's, the only eatery in Phippsburg, which both men ate as they made their way in the Flamethrower to the dig site. Since crime was at a low in the county, Jeff informed George that he had taken up to a week off to see this unexplained situation to an end.

They arrived at the Shalako Creek site about 8:00 a.m. As they stepped down from the Flamethrower, Massey rushed over to the two men and quickly related the strange events of last evening.

Jeff told him, "I've got a sat/nav. I'll call my office and ask my assistant deputy to put some feelers out to a friend of mine at Denver's Weather Channel to see if they picked up any type of blip on their radar or satellites for the western slope of the Rockies in Routt County. I'll tell him to keep everything vague. Just say I had an unsubstantiated report of something in the sky and wondered if they spotted anything on their radar."

Jeff walked back to his truck, took the sat/nav out of the glove compartment, and called his deputy. He explained to his assistant sheriff that he was just north of McCoy, which was in Eagle County.

Jeff didn't want to give away his actual location in Dead Horse Valley to his deputy, so he deliberately misled him as to his whereabouts. As a cover story, he told the assistant sheriff that he had encountered a hog farmer who lived north of McCoy in Routt County who "thought" he saw something strange in the sky last night. The hog man, Jeff informed his deputy, asked him if he might have seen some sort of UFO. George told the farmer that he would see what he could learn and get back to him.

Jeff instructed his deputy to call a friend of his at the Weather Channel in Denver and ask him if any unexplained blips, or weather phenomena, had showed up on his radar or satellite last evening. He cautioned his sheriff to keep the conversation casual and vague.

"You know how people monitor our police channels, so we don't want to freak out anybody in case this a false sighting," he told his employee.

About fifteen minutes later, the deputy called Jeff back and told him that his Denver friend had checked and no one in his office saw or detected anything. Jeff thanked his deputy and hung up.

Well, Jeff thought with relief, *nothing to be concerned about.*

✗✗✗

Double double, toil and trouble,

Fire burn and cauldron bubble . . .

Something wicked this way comes.[45]

✗✗✗

Unfortunately for Jeff, George, and Massey's crew at the excavation site, Jeff's innocuous inquiry had an unintended consequence that later would not be appreciated by anyone in the group. As a precaution, the NSA monitors every sat/nav system in the U.S., especially those owned

---

45 Hudson, Rev. H. N., A.M. The Works of Shakespeare – Vol. 4. Cambridge (Great Britain): John Wilson and Son, 1881, 307.

by law enforcement. Its computers not only picked up and recorded Jeff's call to his office, but also intercepted both his deputy's call to Denver and his return call to Jeff. All three calls were immediately flagged because the abbreviation "UFO" was used in each conversation. The computer generated a "must listen" alarm to NSA's terrorist team, which, after listening to the calls, immediately took steps to set up a deep search into the subject of the calls.

Within minutes, members of NSA's terrorist team were able to pinpoint the actual location of Jeff's sat/nav phone. It definitely wasn't anywhere near McCoy, Colorado. The situation now became a "Red Flag Event" that had to be immediately investigated.

What was the Routt County sheriff involved in at Dead Horse Valley? NSA's investigators wondered. *And why had he misled his chief deputy as to his actual location? Was he involved in something illegal? What was really happening in Dead Horse Valley? Could it be a potential terrorist training site? Something nefarious, they surmised, must be taking place in such an isolated area. They knew that they had to ascertain exactly what was going on in Dead Horse Valley.*

The terrorist team at NSA immediately labeled this state of affairs as a "Priority One" case and sent out an encrypted memorandum to other governmental agencies within and outside the secret Fort Meade complex, informing them this was now an "all hands on deck" situation. In turn, those agencies contacted certain no-name government agencies that had the extra manpower NSA deemed necessary and useful for their purposes.

The wheels of fate began to inexorably turn.

After his sat/nav calls, both friends saw that the archeological team was busy after getting an early start that morning. Approximately one foot of the soft dirt from the outlined trench had already been removed. The two graduate students, Jackson and Jennifer, were busy scraping away the soil using their small, pointed, five- to six-inch-long spades. Next to the trench stood a portable sifter with a dirt mound underneath it. Jackson was in the process of shoveling it away as Jennifer carefully dumped more loads of dirt on it for screening.

Jeff and George quickly noticed that the two assistant professors weren't getting their hands dirty compared to the grad students who, it appeared, were doing most of the grunt work. Both Hank and Sarge were sitting under the canopy at a portable table set up next to the trench and were using a thin brush-like instrument on small samples of dirt that had already been shifted. Massey was standing on the streambed carefully scraping away at the embankment surrounding the protruding bones.

As Jeff and George approached, they greeted each person before standing on the embankment looking down at Massey.

"Found anything yet?" George asked.

Massey looked up before replying, "Not much, but both the radius and fibula *seem* to be a bit thicker than a normal leg. Still, I have no idea what this thing is, but I don't believe it's human!"

"Have you touched the leg or foot again and felt anything?" George asked.

"Yes," the older man replied. "I've brushed against the bone several times, and it's like receiving a small electric shock which causes my fingers to mysteriously vibrate."

"You have any idea as to what might be causing those symptoms?" Jeff asked.

Massey shook his head and opined, "Not a damn thing. This

is just too weird. I feel like I'm in some sort of sci-fi movie on a strange planet. I think by late this afternoon, with luck, both Turner and Whitebird will be down within a foot from the main part of the skeleton. By tomorrow afternoon we should have fully uncovered it. I hate rushing an excavation like this." The white-haired prof continued, "But, in this instance, a little bird is telling me that time is of the essence."

The three of them chatted a while before George and Taylor headed back to the Flamethrower. After climbing up into their seats and closing the monster truck's doors, the two men chatted about the new developments.

"*Whaddaya* think, George?" Jeff asked. "I know *ya* got a bit more education than me as you went off to that agricultural college in Texas after we graduated from high school."

"I just don't have a clue, Jeff. I only took one anthropology course as an elective for my degree, but I sure don't remember much about it," George answered.

Jeff tapped his fingers on the giant steering wheel. "Do you think we should tell someone in the government about this, depending on what Massey's crew finds tomorrow?"

"I don't think so," George replied. "I think Massey should be the one to contact the appropriate authorities; although, this is my land, and I own everything in or on it. If this gets out, the f-cking feds, or those namby-pamby bureaucrats in Denver just might come in and f-ck everything up."

George continued, "You know, Jeff, if word of this discovery gets out and it is as strange as we think it is, every F-CKING Tom, Dick, and Harry is going to descend upon my land looking for more of the same. *An'* don't get me going about the damn news media. Except for Fox, or the BBC, you can't trust *'em* as far as you can throw *'em*! TV cameras, drones. Sh-t! I'll be swamped with all kinds of fruit nuts. *An'* some of my crops will get damaged by uninvited idiots not only driving over and tramping my land but also the fields of the other farmers out here. I *jus'* think that if I give Massey the right to take what he's uncovered, the 'discovery'—if indeed there is one—ought to be kept secret."

"I certainly agree with you," Jeff sanguinely replied. "Plus, as you know, I'm down seven to eight deputies and the f-cking supervisors won't give me any more funds to hire the necessary manpower. Some of my guys are working double shifts and The Blob complains all the time about her hours, even though she's *pullin'* in $50k to $60k a year. Our county tax base is shot to SH-T. Hell, George, Routt County is so big that sometimes it takes one of my deputies two or three hours to drive to a remote area to follow up with a rancher. He's forced to use any of the hundreds of unpaved back country roads, many so rutted that he's forced to drive ten miles an hour, to reach his destination and look into any type of complaint."

He continued exasperatingly, "And Sheriff Clarkson over in Moffe County next door has the same problem and his county is over two times our size! There's a manpower shortage in almost all of Colorado's rural counties. Damn! I'm just so f-cking limited in personnel resources!"

"Jeff, I'm sorry about that," George replied before continuing. "I know your hands have been tied. But don't worry. I DO NOT"—he emphasized, pointing his forefinger in the direction of Dead Horse Valley—"expect you to station, or have any of your men check on my or anyone else's property out here. I'll have to get together with the other farmers, if necessary, and figure out what we can do."

"A .30-6 Winchester might do the trick!" Jeff grinned widely, giving both men a laugh.

The two friends continued to sit contemplating the consequences of this so-called discovery. They sat silently in the Flamethrower for a few more minutes watching the archeologists go about their business. A few minutes later, they observed Massey walking over to Jennifer, who was excavating the southern end of the trench. He squatted as he talked to her and motioned with his finger, pointing down at the area in front of him where the trench ended. She nodded and started to work there as Massey stood up and then walked away.

Curious as to what Massey said to Whitebird, both men climbed out of the high clearance vehicle and slowly ambled over to see what Jennifer was now doing. She had started to dig deeper into the south end of the trench.

George asked what Massey had said to her.

Jennifer replied, "He wants me to start at this end, dig down to the two- or three-foot level to ascertain how deep the skeleton is buried. And hopefully, if its head appears, we'll have an idea as to the height of whatever is buried here."

Both George and Jeff silently nodded. They watched her for a few more minutes before walking over to Massey who was sitting on a chair drinking from a bottle of water. Glancing at his watch, Jeff saw that it was 10:15 a.m. He asked the department head, "What do you think, Doctor Massey? How's the excavation going?"

"I'm hopeful that by late this afternoon we'll be down to the top part of the skeleton," the white-bearded prof replied. "Jennifer, hopefully, will have located the head and started to uncover it. We're not finding anything in the dirt. We're sifting through the screen, which is a good thing as that means there's probably nothing of interest buried on top or on the sides of the creature. That'll enable us to dig a bit quicker."

Both Jeff and George nodded before George told the archeologist that they were headed home and would return late that afternoon to see what the team had uncovered. Massey nodded and told them he'd see them later. Both men walked back to the truck, climbed up, belted themselves in, and departed. On the drive back to George's home, they decided that Jeff would pick up George at his house in Phippsburg around 4:00 p.m. that afternoon.

After dropping George at his house, Jeff drove back home, thinking about the strange events of the past few days. He prayed that this "find" didn't totally uproot his life. All he wanted to do was live a nondescript life where only a few people knew him. He decided to take a nap.

He would be totally unprepared for the coming events.

Late in the afternoon, George, who also took a nap, awoke to his cell phone ringing. It was Jeff saying he'd be outside in five minutes. George checked his watch. It was 4:30 p.m. He slept a bit more than he wanted but felt refreshed. Stepping out of his house, he saw Jeff in the Flamethrower driving helter-skelter down his half-mile long driveway and leaving a cloud of dust swirling behind his truck as he neared. George scrambled into the truck, and they took off for Dead Horse Valley not knowing what awaited them.

As usual, the drive in Jeff's monster truck didn't take long and they pulled into the archeologists' encampment about forty-five minutes later. They quickly noticed that the entire crew was staring down into the trench at the spot where Jennifer Whitebird had been excavating. As they alit from the truck, Hank Washington rushed over to the two men.

"Hey, guys, you won't f-cking believe what we've found! You know I have a paleontology background, but I'm just so blown away at this that I can't even describe what this creature is!" All three walked over to the trench and stared down aghast at what lay beneath them.

Massey turned to both George and Jeff, saying, "Gents, I have absolutely no explanation whatsoever as to what this is. I'm just dumbfounded!"

Jennifer had fully uncovered the skull. The dead and empty eye sockets blankly stared up at the group. The skull was what George thought, as he stared at it, an abomination. The group stood silently in a semi-circle around the far end of the trench looking downward.

"George," Jeff said as he stood there shaking his head, "this is just too f-cking weird. I've NEVER seen anything like this in my entire life."

"What is it, Massey?" George asked. "Is this real or is it some kind of fake?"

"Honestly, George, I just don't have a clue. Yesterday, when I examined the leg and foot sticking out of the embankment, I could have sworn on a thousand Bibles that it was some type of birdlike bone! Now, I'm stunned and just a tad bit uneasy. I NEVER expected anything like this." He shook his head in disbelief.

"What do you guys intend to do?" Jeff asked.

"Well," Massey sanguinely replied, "it's late. We'll stop for the day, then get up early tomorrow and uncover the rest of this dinosaur-like beast."

Jeff and George continued to stare down into the trench at the exposed skull. It was a skull, but not like any human's head. Instead of a normal mortal's skull, this one was not anything one could ever imagine belonging to any earthly lifeform.

"Jennifer," Jeff queried, "did you experience any type of vibration or ultrasonic sound when you touched it as you moved the dirt aside?"

"Yes," she replied, "but it was very faint. I can't explain anything more. I just felt more and more terrified as I uncovered it."

"Okay, group," Jeff spoke, using his take-charge voice, "as of right now, this needs to be top secret. No one"—he shook his finger at each of them—"is to say anything about this, whatever the hell it is. Nor will you make any attempt to contact the outside world." He stressed his words forcefully. "I'm afraid I'm going to have to ask each of you to turn your cell phones over to me, even though there's no service out here. I'll keep them locked up in my truck for the time being. Does anyone here have a sat/nav?" Jeff turned his head and looked directly into the eyes of each person in the university group, all of whom stared at him in dumb silence.

"Let's not forget," Jeff continued, "that this 'thing' or 'creature,' or whatever the hell it is, could still be dangerous or harmful in some unknown way. We have no idea what this being is, but from now on, we need to be extremely careful around it. Especially since no one has discovered what the electric-like vibrations and sounds originating from it could do. They might change into something that's unexpectedly dangerous. George and I will stay here tonight, and we'll all get up tomorrow at 5:00 a.m. Then you guys can start uncovering the rest of this creature."

Everyone in the group nodded their heads in agreement. They all seemed eager, yet somewhat uneasy at the further uncovering of the mysterious "thing" that lay in the ground beneath them.

George continued to look down on the uncovered head and shook his head in disbelief.

God, help us! the old cattleman thought. *What in God's earth have I discovered? Can it harm us?* He shuddered, thinking about the potential trouble that was sure to come out of this unfortunate find. *I wonder,* he continued to muse, *is the world even ready for this? Or will they panic like America did in 1938, when Orson Welles broadcast H. G. Wells's novel,* The War of the Worlds, *the night before Halloween, which practically scared the entire nation into believing that we had actually been invaded by aliens?*

George continued to stare downwards into the excavated pit. The skull of this supposed "being," if it really was a living and breathing creature at one time, was horrendous. It would scare the sh-t and piss out of anyone due to its unexplainable origin.

Could it be an alien? If so, how, or when, did it arrive here? he wondered. *No one would be able to accept the inevitable fact that it likely arrived from a civilization so technologically advanced that no nation on earth would be able to militarily counter such beings. It would scare the hell out of everyone. What had God wrought?* George just shook his head in disbelief.

The hideous head of the being beneath his feet with its empty square eye sockets stared eerily at him. The whitened skull was as square as a dice cube. No rounded bones. There seemed to be no decomposition to the entire facial structure. Just sharp ninety-degree angles. It had no mandible, just a perfectly two-by-three-inch square opening for a mouth. The nose, if one could call it a nose, was cylindrical in shape and rose about four to five inches above the face but had no obvious openings. Two rounded four-inch holes on either side of the skull must have been for hearing, George silently observed. But even stranger were the two five- to six-inch-long horns, just above the ear holes, that curved inward over what might have been the creature's forehead.

Jennifer walked over to the canopy-covered excavation site and covered the body with another tarp—to keep the moisture out, she told Jeff, who had just wandered over and stood next to his friend as they both looked silently upon the monstrosity lying below their feet.

God only knows, Jeff thought, *what else the UC team will uncover tomorrow.*

✗✗✗

The wheels of fate began to inexorably turn.

✗✗✗

Meanwhile, back at Fort Meade, NSA's headquarters in Maryland, various clandestine entities assembled for planning conferences. The meetings were to decide on how to use a secret military team to neutralize the supposed threat. Also under discussion was what equipment was necessary for the Colorado take-down commandos. They were still in the dark, not knowing exactly what or whom they might encounter. There were still too many unanswered questions. Was it a real threat, or not? If a threat, what kind of a threat? Sheriff Monroe's sat/nav had been silent for most of the day. What did that mean? Why wasn't he back in his office in Steamboat Springs? A simple call to the sheriff's office might answer that question, but they didn't want to tip their hand in any way, because someone, or a government agency, was suddenly interested in what was happening in Dead Horse Valley. Their myriads of super-secret satellites circling the earth and observing every square yard of land and sea on the planet transmitted pictures of Dead Horse Valley from the previous night, plus something unexplainable to the satellites' high-definition cameras. The photo analysts identified the archeologists' encampment at the far end of the valley. Was it a terrorist training camp? What were their intentions? What lay beneath the two blue canopies? And, observing the dirt mound that lay next to the smaller canopy, they wondered why, or what, were these people digging up next to Shalako Creek?

Could it be the entrance to a subterranean bunker? Or an artillery or a rocket launch site? But even more disturbing, not only to the photo analysts but also to the various NSA team leaders, was the image that the satellites spotted the night prior. They picked up the movement of unidentified objects circling above the camp that seemed to have unmeasurable speeds and mysteriously disappeared in a split second. Were they a new type of drone? Or were they something even more sinister and ominous like a new type of supersonic guided missile?

The NSA head honcho, Elvin Whitmaker, decided that something had to be done and done quickly. Better to act and err than be caught in the outhouse with their pants down while a timber-back rattlesnake bit their ass. To that end, he set up a conference with all the heads of his various teams along with the unnamed heads of several black ops teams. Orders would soon be issued.

The wheels of fate began to inexorably turn.

Back at the expedition's dig, everyone started to fix dinner under the canopy. Jeff brought steaks and potatoes for everyone, so he started the crew's grill and took care of the cooking as the rest sat around the table and chatted. The weather had been warm the entire time the university crew was there. The archeologist team enjoyed the food and the cold beer. Massey, who didn't like beer, nursed a bottle of Ketel One Vodka, which he told Jeff he kept on ice in his ancient Igloo cooler. Both George and Jeff silently observed that the prof seemed not only to savor the liqueur but also imbibed it slowly with some moodiness in his demeanor.

The two lifelong friends, being older than the younger members of the crew, abstained from the alcohol. Jeff made it a point to say that, even though he was off duty, he couldn't drink as he might find himself needed in an emergency. George, who had had bouts with the demon drink in his teens and early twenties, also refrained from sipping anything alcoholic.

After dinner, everyone sat back on their chairs and randomly talked about different experiences in their lives. Some were funny while others were informative. Yet, strangely, the subject of what lay in the trench beside them wasn't mentioned. It was as if referring to the creature had suddenly become taboo. Perhaps the archeologists were uneasy with what they had uncovered, or what else might lie beneath the dirt, and were inwardly trying to steel themselves for what they might uncover tomorrow.

One member of the group mentioned music, which started a lively conversation as to who was everyone's favorite musician, or musical group, and why. Massey started. His favorite was Ahmad Jamal, a jazz pianist, because overall, he enjoyed jazz. Hank chimed in and said, "The Stones." Need he say anything more? Sarge added that he liked Latin music and Gloria Estefan. Jennifer piped up and said she liked Jack Gladstone, a Native American from Flathead Lake, Montana, whose music told wonderful stories about her Native American heritage. Jackson, it appeared, was the odd man out. He told the group that he loved heavy metal like Black Sabbath and Iron Maiden. That revelation brought a dead silence to the group.

Sarge interjected, "What about you, Jeff, or George? Who are your favorites?"

George said, "*Aw*, really," while Jeff snorted.

"*C'mon,* guys!" Sarge urged.

"Okay, okay," George replied. "I like Willie." Jeff then followed saying he preferred Hank Williams.

It was a relaxing, enjoyable, and animated conversation. The group seemed to be at ease.

But the night was still young and something unexpected and unsettling was about to startle everyone at the campsite. As they sat in postprandial relaxation, no one noticed the appearance of a round Golden Orb that had somehow materialized underneath the canopy and now hovered in the air above their heads until it made a high-pitched, almost ultrasonic sound, forcing everyone to look upwards.

The entire assemblage pushed back on their chairs and stood as one body. The Golden Orb slowly rotated in a counterclockwise direction before shooting a beam into each person's face for no more than two seconds before it moved to the next person, stopping only after it had aimed its golden laser-like light on everyone's face.

"What's it doing?" asked Sarge. "Is it taking our picture?"

Massey, who seemed stunned by the appearance of the otherworldly Orb, spoke up. "Everyone, DO NOT," he strongly emphasized, "make any sudden moves. We don't have a clue about this, but it has to be related to the creature we've uncovered."

At that point, the rotating Orb emitted a high-pitched shrieking sound, forcing each individual to cover his or her ears. Yet, just as abruptly as the sound pierced each person's head, it stopped. Then, as they looked at the Orb in stunned silence, it flew slowly out from underneath the canopy and hovered outside as if silently beckoning them to follow. Some unknown urge, or force, not only drew everyone outside but also forced them to look up into the darkening night.

The Golden Orb rose until it hovered about ten feet above their heads. Then it started a whining high-pitched sound that, this time, had no effect on their ears. Like when a magician says, "Presto!" the sky filled with ten to twelve Golden Orbs circling ominously overhead. Each one had a golden glow as it moved through the sky. The stunned group looked upwards at this incredible, if not unbelievable, array of Orbs. Each person found himself wondering, *Are these things going to harm or kill us?*

The round Orbs continued to circle clockwise over their astounded heads for about thirty seconds. No one spoke. They all just gaped at this entirely unexpected occurrence. Then, each person heard an audible hum. The mysterious objects formed into a straight line and zoomed off to the north before completely disappearing within seconds. Everyone continued to look at the dark sky with amazement on their faces.

George broke the ice, saying, "Okay, lady and gents, we've just seen the unexplainable. It means something, but what, I don't know. Whatever, or whoever, these things are, it doesn't appear they wish us harm, at least at the moment. I think, however, we need to be exceptionally careful, especially you two in the excavation crew, lest we make a misstep in exposing the creature."

"I totally agree with George," Jeff added. "You guys need to be extra careful tomorrow. Treat those bones with extreme reverence as you uncover them."

That said, everyone went back to the table and sat down to discuss and theorize what had just taken place and wondered out loud as to what it all meant. Hank, the bone specialist, and Jackson, his undergraduate PhD student, both posited that they ought to just cover the thing back up and break camp. Massey stepped forward and told everyone that they needed to forge ahead and decide what to do once the monster was totally uncovered. To that end, he said all five of the UC crowd would be involved in tomorrow's dig so that they might uncover the creature as quickly as possible. Jeff told the group that he had several weapons in the Flamethrower and that both he and George would be carrying them tomorrow as a precaution against anything untoward.

After another ten- to fifteen-minute exchange of thoughts and ideas, everyone decided to go to bed so that they could wake up early and continue the excavation. George and Jeff told the archeologists that since they were older and needed less sleep than everyone else, they would take two-hour shifts throughout the night to guard against anything unexpected. After the archeologists departed for their tents, both men privately agreed they were up against a power that neither one of them, or their weapons, could stop. They agreed not to mention their thoughts to the UC group for fear of alarming them. Still, neither Jeff nor George could possibly have envisioned, or even imagined, what lay in store for them tomorrow.

It would be a long night (and an even longer night for the people at NSA!).

✗✗✗

The wheels of fate continued to inexorably turn.

✗✗✗

At NSA, their satellites picked up the objects circling overhead the archeologists' camp. Using one of their most advanced top-secret satellites, they were able to zero in so close to the location that they could pick out and identify the facial features of everyone present in the bivouac area. As they continued to minutely identify and photograph every feature of the camp, the NSA people noted that every two hours Jeff and George exchanged places outside of the monster truck and that they were armed.

Whitmaker, having reviewed each of his secret group's plans, called all the team leaders to his spacious office at 11:00 p.m. and gave the "GO" order, reminding each team leader sternly that this was a TOP-SECRET mission.

"My orders to you," Whitmaker told the group, "are verbal. After your mission has been completed, each of you will write after-action reports, which I will vet before they are submitted to the higherups" (meaning his boss, the president).

Earlier in the day, one of the no-name agencies involved in the operation had secured the use of three unmarked Blackhawk helicopters from the Navy Seals' headquarters stationed in San Diego. After fueling up on the Navy aircraft carrier named *Ronald Reagan*, which was in port, the three choppers departed at dawn from San Diego and flew northeast towards Area 51, the U.S. government's incredibly Top-Top-Top, Super-Secret installation far out in the Nevada desert north of Las Vegas. They would refuel at Area 51 before heading to

Colorado Springs and landing in a restricted area belonging to the U.S. Air Force Academy.

After refueling at the Air Force Academy, they took onboard eighteen anonymous military-type personnel, dressed in camo and who had no identifying unit or name patches. They had been delivered overnight from an unspecified location in the southern U.S. Along with the secret military force, there were two nondescript civilians who had been hastily flown in on a private government jet from Washington, D.C. From Colorado Springs, the three Blackhawks flew west over the Rockies, hugging the terrain while they slipped through various mountain passes until they touched down in another restricted area at the small Eagle Colorado Airport.

Again, after refueling, the three choppers set off to a secret location some ten miles northeast of McCoy. Tightly hugging the terrain, and only flying ten to fifteen yards off the ground, they landed on a grass-covered area several hundred yards from the Colorado River. About the size of two acres, this was one of the few hundred unmapped and active black ops sites in the U.S. It was surrounded by Douglas Firs, tall Ponderosa, along with lumber pines.

There appeared to be no usable road within miles of the secret base. Hidden along the edge of the tree-line was a low-level bunkhouse, half of which was underground. Its walls and roof were disguised by painted camouflage-like colors to match the trees overhead. The teams were greeted by two similarly clad men who had no identifiable military patches or rank on their wood-like and greenish Army-issued clothes. The small building had bathrooms which the chopper crews and passengers immediately used. Even though it had been a long day, the eighteen members of the military-type personnel set up sleeping areas in the woods, while the two civilians used the bunkhouse.

Now, as usual in any and all military-style operations, it was time to wait while the bigwigs, probably located in some secret and bombproof location in Washington, D.C., made up their minds what to do next. Of the eighteen men, one appeared to be their commander when he ordered them to stand around him. He told everyone that the scheduled operation was set for tomorrow. Yet, he still did not mention the operation's purpose, but instructed the group to clean and double-check their weaponry.

The leader, who probably had the rank of a full-bird colonel due to the secretive nature of the operation, also instructed his personnel to set up four-man listening posts around the perimeter of the three Blackhawks, even though the copters' pilots and crews would be sleeping in them. They were, he warned his soldiers, now in Indian territory and had to stay alert in case anyone stumbled upon the base or tried to infiltrate it for nefarious purposes.

What the commander didn't tell his men was that inside the bunkhouse there was a small room where the two caretakers manned radios and a perimeter system with three outer rings of buried cables—which, if they were either stepped on or walked over, would sound an alarm inside the soundproof control room. The concentric rings stretched out a quarter of a mile from the bunkhouse. In addition to the rings, there were also seventy-five to one hundred mini-cams and motion detectors overlooking the rings, covering every square inch of land, should anyone approach the clandestine base.

The warmish June darkness settled down on the black ops base.

✗✗✗

The wheels of fate continued to inexorably turn.

✗✗✗

Jeff woke up around five and climbed out of the truck. George was leaning against the front side tire of the Flamethrower as he watched the sun rise and the camp come alive.

285

"Hey, *how ya doin'?*" Jeff asked as he passed some beef jerky to his friend.

"Thanks, *ol'* boy, and I'm doing fine," his friend replied as he chewed on the jerky.

"See or hear anything else *las'* night?" Jeff queried.

"Not a damn thing!" his old friend answered.

"Me, too! Although it just seemed too damned quiet out there," Jeff commented.

"Yeah, almost too f-cking quiet!" George replied. "I didn't even hear any critters stirring *'round, an'* I know there are tons of white tails out here that *shoulda* been grazing in the field. And I didn't spot one single coyote, which almost never happens."

"Well," Jeff opined, "we'll just have to keep an eagle eye out! *Somethin' jus' ain't* right."

George simply nodded before saying, "I think we had better keep our sidearms handy . . . *jus'* in case, *ya* know?"

"Yeah," Jeff replied as he adjusted the .357 on his hip.

What a momentous day it would turn out to be, although neither man had any idea what was going to happen to them. For now, the area was calm as the UC crowd set about eating breakfast. The rancher and the sheriff silently chewed on their jerky while taking sips of soda which they had just taken out from Jeff's cooler. The camp appeared somewhat subdued as the archeologists started setting up their equipment for the day. It was 6:45 a.m. and the bright sun hammered down upon the entire campsite.

Both George and Jeff noted and commented that the sun's yellow beams seemed to be unusually bright and more intense than usual. There were no clouds in the sky.

Little did anyone know, and much less realize . . . it was the calm before the storm.

Unbeknownst to all parties concerned, or involved in the events of that day, another observer was watching their endeavors. Matters appeared to be approaching a "Triple-A" alert.

✗✗✗

By 10:30 a.m., George and Jeff, while trying to continuously survey in all directions, walked over to the pit and stared down at the work below them. Several minutes later, both men resumed their patrol throughout the camp.

Slowly and meticulously the archeologists had uncovered the creature. The *oohs* and *ahhs* as each of the team members uncovered another part of the intact skeleton shifted to an excited murmur along with patches of silence and grunts of disbelief. At first, every time one of the excavators touched any part of a bone, they jerked their hand away after feeling a vibration and electric warmth run down their fingers, hands, and arms. But, after a while, each of the diggers acclimated to the mysterious feeling and were able to touch the skeleton for longer and longer periods of time.

This was especially helpful when they needed to move the bones from one side or the other so that they could remove the earth sticking to the underside of the body. Whenever they were forced to gently move the bones, they quickly discovered—unlike most skeletal remains they had unearthed during previous digs—this creature's bones did not crack or separate. Instead, the entire skeleton seemed to be eerily connected at every joint—another mystery the archeologists would have to unravel once they transported the being to a lab.

In gently lifting the head to brush away the dirt, Jennifer found a gold strip embedded on the back of the skull with the following letters and numbers: X-365-43. She called Massey over and showed him the engraved plate.

"What does it mean?" she asked the white-haired department head.

He just shook his head and instructed his crew to continue unearthing the skeleton, which by noon was entirely free of the earth that had encased it for eons.

Staring down at what they had uncovered, the crew stood silently as they observed this strange and monstrous creature. Everyone could now clearly see that the being's arms were crossed, and it had seven long, claw-like fingers on each hand. The talons, for lack of a better description, were ten to twelve inches in length. And, stunning the entire assemblage, as Massey pointed out, whatever this creature was, it had a long, ten- to twelve-inch solid-boned tail. There were no spinal disks that one might discern in a human being. The creature they observed was also approximately eight feet and four inches tall. The other leg, the one not sticking out of the creek bank, crossed over the creature's knee area.

What have we found? everyone wondered. Could this be some sort of undiscovered species? Or was it some sort of alien from outer space? Everyone seemed baffled and taken aback as the implications of such a find sank in—what might this mean to humankind?

They decided to take a lunch break and discuss the creature's origin and purpose.

No sooner had everyone seated themselves under the dining canopy when Jeff and George, who served two tours in Iraq as a sniper, detected the *WHUMP! WHUMP! WHUMP!* of beating helicopter rotors several miles off in the distance. Both he and George quickly rose and stepped out from underneath the canopy and looked eastward.

"Somethin' ain't right, George," Jeff said with some alarm and suspicion in his voice. "Those rotors sound like Blackhawks. Plus, since we can't see *'em* yet, they're flying low, hugging the terrain. The military NEVER flies training ops out here, and when they do, I usually get a heads up from the DOD four to five days ahead of time. I don't like this development one damn bit!"

George, who experienced a lot of combat, agreed with his friend. "Sure sounds ominous to me. Plus, I think they're *huntin'* someone and we are probably the bait!"

The sounds of the rotors drew nearer when about a mile off to the east, three Blackhawks rose up ominously from behind a far ridge. By approaching from the east, the helicopters had the sun behind them, so the individuals in Dead Horse Valley would be staring directly into the sun's rays, causing them to squint and be somewhat blinded. The menacing birds were now headed toward the encampment at top speed.

"Better get everyone together, Jeff," George said hastily. "This don't look good one f-cking bit! The SH-T'S about to hit the fan!!!"

Jeff walked over to the UC crew, who upon hearing the Blackhawks, had emerged from underneath the dining area canopy, putting their hands on their foreheads, squinting off in the distance toward the approaching helicopters.

"Everybody, stay together, stay calm, and remain cool!! Right now!" Jeff instructed the group. Continuing, he said to his pal, "George, grab my .357 and take your .30-6 to the Flamethrower right away. And here"—he tossed George the keys to the truck—"lock it up after you put *'em* inside."

George, fielding the keys, grabbed Jeff's pistol as instructed and hastened over to the monster truck. Pulling the ladder down, he opened the driver's side door and placed the weapons on the front seat. Then he locked the door and climbed back down.

As he walked back to Jeff, George noticed the three helicopters were approaching at a faster rate of speed. They were now about a quarter of a mile out. He continued to look upwards at the ominously approaching birds, when they suddenly began to split up. Both men noticed and commented upon the fact that these Blackhawks had no identifying marks. One started downward and set down on the north side of Shalako Creek directly across from the dig. A second circled and landed to the west between the camp and forest line. The third descended to the ground about fifty yards to the southeast of the encampment.

The prop backwash from the third helicopter's rotors blew down all the tents, the two canopies, and scattered the chairs. The large canopy over the dining table was blown into the excavation site and entirely covered the creature's now exposed body. As soon as each Blackhawk landed, six military commando-type figures all dressed in camouflage rapidly jumped to the ground where they spread out and took up positions about five yards apart, facing the encampment. Each commando was wearing dark sunglasses and carried some sort of military-style rifle with an extra-large scope attached to it. The camouflaged men had now effectively surrounded the archeological dig, blocking every means of escape.

The wheels of fate continued to inexorably turn.

"Okay, gang," Jeff shouted above the subsiding noise of the rotors as the military-type figures took up positions with their weapons at the ready. "No one make any sudden moves! Keep your hands where they can be seen at all times! DO NOT make any sudden move unless you have a death wish! These people probably have orders to shoot to kill if any of you make any suspicious movement." Again, he emphasized, "They won't think twice about killing you! Is that understood?" He continued to shout, "Also, don't say a damn word unless someone comes up and asks you a direct question. Then, EVERYBODY, keep your answers short! DON'T, DON'T elaborate. Got it?" Each member of the archeological team nodded their heads rather reluctantly. They all looked scared to death.

George, who was standing next to Jeff, said, "What the F-CK, Jeff?"

"I don't know, buddy, but this doesn't look good. I hope we all live and don't end up as prisoners in Guantanamo or some other sh-thole in the world!" he said. At this point, two nondescript civilians appeared at the open door of the southernmost Blackhawk and then descended to the ground.

Jeff spoke rather exasperatedly, "George, look! Oh SH-T, we got civilians! F-CKING U.S. government!!! SH-T! SH-T! SH-T! They're F-CKING SPOOKS! What the hell kind of sh-t have we inadvertently stepped into? The damn government has sent two nameless top-secret idiots!"

The two men were both dressed in plain black pants, white shirts, one in a black pinstriped jacket and the other in a brownish tweed coat, along with thin black ties. After alighting from the chopper, both started to walk toward the dig area. Each of them wore extremely large dark sunglasses. The man in the black suit carried a thin leather briefcase. All three rotors on the Blackhawks wound down and ceased rotating as the two men walked steadily toward the seven shocked individuals.

"With the choppers shut down, Jeff, I think we're going to be here a while," George murmured under his breath.

Both men stepped forward to meet the civilians.

The two spooks stopped about five feet away. No one moved to shake a hand.

"Ah, Sheriff Monroe and Mr. Taylor, for our purposes today, I'm Mr. Smith and this is my colleague, Mr. Jones." Smith held up his right forefinger and each of the armed soldiers surrounding the group snapped their weapons off their shoulders taking multiple aims at George, Jeff, and the archeological crew.

"Do any of you have any sort of weapons?" Smith asked.

Jeff quickly replied, "George's and my pistols and rifles are locked in my truck." He pointed at the Flamethrower.

Jones nodded his head to the right and one soldier from their chopper detached himself and hustled over to the Flamethrower, placing himself in position between the truck and the encampment. The remaining five members of his unit then spread out to fill the missing man's spot.

"Well, Mr. Smith and Mr. Jones, as owner of this property, I'd sure like to know why you, or someone in our fine U.S. government," George said with a sneer in his voice, "has the audacity to launch this obviously secret military operation on my land?"

"We're not here to discuss that aspect of our visit," Jones abruptly replied. "We want to know what you're doing out here."

Without replying, George turned, pointed his finger, and motioned for Massey to join them. The white-haired professor ambled somewhat hesitatingly over to where George and Jeff were standing.

"Professor, would you introduce yourself and mind explaining to these two individuals, Mr. Smith, the man in the tweed coat, and Mr. Jones, who's in the navy blue jacket, why we are out here?" George asked.

"Gentlemen," Massey started out, "this may take some time. Why don't we sit down at the table and draw up some of the overturned chairs." He gestured with his hand toward the dining area.

Smith and Jones looked at each other before Jones gave his companion a slight nod. The four remaining archeologists started to walk toward the table as Massey instructed his team to gather the upturned chairs and place them around the table. He then instructed them to stand together in a group about ten yards away.

Jeff edged up closely behind the professor while they stood waiting for the chairs to be put in place, and quietly whispered to Massey, "Don't mention the Orbs until last."

Massey simply gave a slight nod to acknowledge he understood Jeff.

Massey sat at the head of the table, while Smith and Jones sat on one side across from Jeff and George.

It took Massey twenty to twenty-five minutes to explain to the government agents what was taking place at the encampment before he stopped, paused, took a sip of water, and continued with his final bombshell.

"Gentlemen, am I to presume you are here because your satellites picked up some type of unidentified objects flying over our camp during the last two days?" Massey asked.

Smith, after receiving a nod from Jones, replied, "It has come to our attention that some unusual objects were detected flying around your camp."

"Well, gents," Massey said, looking directly into the sunglasses covering each spook's invisible eyes, "here's what I have to tell you. I apologize in advance if you find my explanation somewhat incredulous, and most likely, unbelievable. As we say in Pennsylvania where I grew up, this is filled with a bunch of hooey! All I can say is what I, and the others here, have observed. I might also add that there is absolutely no reasonable, much less credible, explanation as to these occurrences." Massey went on to explain the mysterious interactions the group had encountered with the Golden Orbs and their light beams.

When Massey concluded his explanation, Jones stared at him for a moment or two and then asked, "Is the creature you have described lying over in that trench covered by the canopy?" The bureaucrat pointed in the direction of the now obscured pit that now held the monster's uncovered body.

Massey nodded, then looking over at his crew, instructed them to uncover the creature. As soon as the canopy had been removed, both Smith and Jones rose from the table while Jeff and George remained seated. The two government spooks walked over to the pit and looked down. George and Jeff both tried to see if the two spooks had any reaction, but their dark sunglasses, if indeed they did have an effect, made it undetectable.

Smith turned and said to Massey, "Professor, please wait over there with the rest of your team while we speak with Monroe and Taylor." Massey just shrugged, nodded, then stood and walked over to his fellow archeologists.

Smith and Jones returned to the table and sat down. Jones leaned down, picked up his briefcase on the ground, placed it on the table, and opened it. He drew out a significant number of papers, which he began to flip through. After several minutes, he looked up and stared at George.

"Mr. Taylor"—he spoke in a typical government-ese singsong voice as if repeating by rote or verbatim from some arcane, obscure, and long-forgotten Congressional rule, regulation, or law—"it is my opinion that by allowing these UC folks to dig up this 'thing' you have found, that both you and they have violated about four or five federal laws, including one act that prevents any person from disturbing native American bones, trinkets, etc. These laws carry sentences of fifteen to twenty years each, plus fines of up to $100,000. In addition, once you discovered these remains, you were required to notify the appropriate state and federal governmental authorities within twenty-four hours, which you failed to do. That's another five years and a $25,000 fine."

George just stared at Jones before speaking. "This is my DAMN F-CKING land and I'm entitled to uncover whatever I find on it!" Then, unexpectedly, he pounded the table.

Jones quickly replied, "I'm afraid not." He shook his head ever so slightly. "You see, this creature resides on federal land."

"How the F-CK is that possible?" George asked with incredulity. "I've got a deed and a plat showing the metes and bounds of my property which clearly ends at the tree-line over there," he said, pointing to the woods. "And this creature is definitely located on it!"

Jones shifted through some more papers before withdrawing a U.S. Forestry Service map delineating that its land now extended further east from the forest-line onto George's farmland and ending some twenty yards past where the creature now lay.

George sat there stunned, thinking, *The slimy USG is F-CKing me over! How much worse is it going to get?*

As an answer to his unasked question, Jones then produced a certified copy of deed showing the metes and bounds of George's farmland with his signature on the deed. "Mr. Taylor, this is now your original deed." Jones shoved it across the table. George picked it up, glanced at it, and threw it down.

"BULL-F-CKING-SH-T! Just what are you MOTHERF-CKERS

trying to do to me?" George roared and again pounded his fist on the table.

Unperturbed, Jones looked at him and spoke, "It appears that you are now in a vast amount of legal trouble, Mr. Taylor. It's going to take you years and years of litigation before you end up losing everything you own and start serving time, and at your age, will surely be a life sentence with no hope of parole."

George continued to stare angrily at Jones. "You MOTHERF-CKING pieces of government SH-T!!!!" he said angrily. "Go crawl back into whatever foul latrine you just emerged from! Oh, and while you are doing that, go F-CK yourselves after kissing my ASS!"

Fearing that his friend was about to attack the two men, Jeff grabbed George's arm and quickly interjected, "Let me clarify some things to you, Mr. Smith, and to you, Mr. Jones, who's obviously the one in charge here. Yes, it does seem you've got my friend George here by the balls. And I don't doubt you've probably got something up your pernicious sleeves giving you the ability to force me to resign as sheriff. It is abundantly clear to me that due to this situation, or these unexplainable events, something unsettling has alerted a person, or persons, within the secret halls of the CIA, or NSA, or God knows how many other unnamed government entities, probably including the one or ones you belong to."

Jeff continued, "You know I'm an Afghanistan vet and you're most likely carrying a copy of my and George's DD214 forms in your papers." Jeff pointed to Jones's briefcase before continuing. "You also know that George is an Iraq vet. So, I'm almost positive that you both know that we both know that your bullsh–t is what it is and not to be believed."

Jeff firmly stated, "There's something else going on here. We all know that when the government wants something, it gets it, and it doesn't give a big, fat SH-T how it's obtained, whether it's legit or illegal. Obviously, somehow on the incredibly short notice of only two days, you've been able to mysteriously change the Forest Service boundaries adjoining George's farmland along with replacing his original and legitimate deed with this trumped-up forgery." Jeff pointed his finger at the deed, still lying on the table, before hitting it several times with his forefinger.

"You and I both know that the omnipotent and all-powerful U.S. government doesn't do sh-t like this unless there is a reasonable solution, especially since you do not, in any way, want this discovery to be made public. Right?" Jeff asked rhetorically.

"So," he continued, "how will you shut us up if you go through with your threats? Scoop all of us up and put us in some deep hole in Calcutta or Siberia where we'll never be seen or heard from again?" Jeff swept his arm in a circle, "Or will you simply order your mercenaries to simply kill all of us and then cremate our bodies leaving no trace of us? I figure you've already decided how to dispose of our trucks and equipment!"

Finishing his long screed, Jeff patted his friend on the arm and continued to stare at Jones.

A deathly silence ensued. It was time to deal.

Jones shuffled his papers, placed them back into his briefcase, and looked up. "In answer to your question, Sheriff, I'm authorized to offer everyone here a way out of their predicament. Now, let's cut to the proverbial chase, so to speak. First, everyone here will be required to sign both a non-disclosure agreement, or NDA, along with a Top-Secrets Act document, both promising in various ways NEVER to write, mention, or orally discuss the events of the past several days. Each of these documents come with severe penalties that will cost anyone, and that includes everyone here, who breaks the terms of either document, a life in prison with no parole or visitors." He added, "There will be no trial. One day the offender will simply vanish."

"Secondly, Mr. Taylor," Jones droned on, "your NDA will include clauses that will prevent you from revealing the circumstances surrounding the loss of your farmland to the Forest Service. You will also accept certain changes made to your original deed. In return, the government will pay you $100,000 in non-taxable money for the loss of three acres of farmland. This is non-negotiable."

Jones continued, "Thirdly, Mr. Monroe, Sheriff, you had a little problem in Afghanistan while on patrol in Kandahar Province. The circumstances of that situation once revealed, despite the U.S. Army's previous decision not to prosecute, will bring about a secret court martial and years in prison. The government will agree not to prosecute, provided you agree to signing the NDA and the Top-Secrets Act. Otherwise"—Jones paused—"we can ensure that your job and good standing in the community will be totally and unequivocally destroyed."

Damn! Jeff thought as he stared at the two nondescript looking bureaucrats. *The f-cking Army already agreed to hush up that situation! Obviously, someone spilled the beans and my ass is now toast. These bastards have really got me by the balls! Oh SH-T!!! I had to kill those women and their kids. After we took them out, we found grenades on all of them. One of the older kids was even wearing and wired with a suicide vest. We had no other f-cking choice!*

Jeff nodded his head toward Jones, saying, "Okay, no problem. I'll be happy to sign."

"Finally," Jones concluded, "the remains of the creature you have discovered will remain top secret and we will be taking it with us when we depart."

Smith stood up from the table and walked over to the UC crowd which was standing on the other side of the monster's pit and explained everything in detail to them. They all agreed to sign the necessary papers, so Smith returned to the table nodding at Jones as he did so.

Jones then stood up, telling George and Jeff he would return in ten to fifteen minutes. He walked over to the Blackhawk, climbed in and shut the door. Some twenty-five minutes later, he emerged from the chopper and returned to the table. He was carrying all the documents that needed to be signed.

"Guess he must have some sort of fax machine, or printer in that chopper," George mused aloud as he and Jeff signed each document without taking the time to read what was contained in the numerous gobbledygook paragraphs set out before them. *Well,* he silently mused, *when you're f-cked, you're really f-cked.* After they completed signing the documents, Smith slid a check in the amount of $100,000 across the table to George, saying in the process, "Thank you, Mr. Taylor, for being so understanding."

George audibly harumphed, picked up the greenish-colored check, read it slowly and methodically, then folded and stuck it in his front shirt pocket, staring all the while at Jones.

"I hope," George said, "I NEVER see either one of you pissant f-ckheads again!" Both he and Jeff rose and walked over to the pit.

Smith and Jones then motioned for the archeologists to come to the table where they sat and signed each document presented to them.

After all the documents were signed and double-checked, both Smith and Jones stood up and nonchalantly looked at everyone gathered around the table. Jones spoke, "For obvious reasons, none of you will receive duplicate copies, but be forewarned, they, and many other duplicate copies, will reside in various government files somewhere should any of you decide to talk. You will regret to your dying day that you ever did. Do I make myself clear?"

Several of the archeological crew nodded while the rest had a look of absolute fear in their eyes.

George and Jeff, knowing how the nefarious and secretive U.S. government worked, said nothing, but they continued to stare at Smith and Jones as if they were poisonous tiger snakes from Australia that needed to be put down. Smith and Jones looked at everyone again before turning and walking toward their helicopter. After several steps, Jones raised his arm and pointed with his index finger toward the pit. Two commandos from each of the helicopters parked on the southern side of Shalako Creek, shouldered their arms, and jogged toward the pit. One team member grabbed a body bag from a compartment on the side of his Blackhawk and hustled over to the excavation site.

The wheels of fate continued to inexorably turn.

George and Jeff, along with the others, looked over at the excavation as the camouflaged commandos approached the pit encircling the smaller group. Two of the soldiers spread the body bag out on the rim of the pit and unzipped it, while two other commandos entered the pit as they prepared to pick up the bones.

With no warning whatsoever, there was a loud deafening hum in the air surrounding the encampment, along with a loud crackling of static electricity as myriads of streaks of light flashed in the sky. The unexpected flashes seemed to originate from out of nowhere as if they were lightning bolts mysteriously emanating from the cloudless blue sky. Following the beams of light, Golden Orbs suddenly popped out of the sky and became visible.

Each globe hovered three feet in front of each commando's face. Smith and Jones, who were about to board their Blackhawk, found themselves frozen in their tracks as two Golden Orbs took up a position between them and the Blackhawk. Two more globes appeared in front of each Blackhawk. With a high-pitched whirring sound, the

Golden Orbs shot a piercing light into every single commando's face, along with the faces of the two pilots in each helicopter. The two Orbs, shining their beams into Smith's and Jones's faces using some unknown means, forced both men to step backwards away from their chopper and turn around.

Oddly, neither Jeff nor George or any of the archeologists' crew had a Golden Orb appear in front of them.

When the soldiers attempted to either un-sling or shoulder their weapons, each man suddenly winced in extreme pain as a laser-like golden beam of light emerged from each Golden Orb and struck their eyes. The metal in their weapons turned instantly hot, forcing them not only to scream out in agony but also to drop their rifles. When the commandos tried to unholster their sidearms they ended up screaming again and dropping the various makes of pistols. They all watched in horror as their weapons, now on the ground, started to melt and shrivel up before their eyes, until the remains of all the armaments had totally disappeared. Next, a loud whistling noise seemed to freeze all the commandos and pilots in place along with the four commandos at the excavation site.

Smith and Jones were forced to turn around and were invisibly pushed backward toward the creature's pit until they were standing at its edge along with the rest of the civilian group. The archeologists, by some unknown beckoning, had been forced to move away from the table and now stood together on one side of the pit. While everyone wanted to be able to move about, they all found themselves strangely glued to the earth, unable to move their feet.

The humming forced every person in, or surrounding, the pit to mysteriously look downward. As they did so, a huge flash of light almost blinded each individual. A large Golden Orb, double the size of the rest of the Golden Orbs, floated in the air above the pit.

Next, everyone heard a loud "click" from the large Golden Orb.

A brilliant laser-like light beam appeared underneath the Orb as it hovered over the bones. The beam slowly moved up the body until it rested upon the creature's head. The Golden Orb increased the intensity of its beam, which not only widened but also flared into a reddish-yellow color as it started to slowly move back toward the feet. As it did so, the creature's bones disintegrated before everyone's eyes. By the time the Orb reached the feet and shut off its beam, the bones, now all the same size and shape, lay in thousands of infinitesimal pieces. The golden engraved plate, located behind the creature's head with the letter and numbers X-365-43, now lay crumpled on top of the shredded bones.

As the larger Golden Orb hovered at the creature's feet, everyone heard a distinct "click" and watched as a small one-by-one-inch hole appeared on top of the Orb, which then slowly rotated until the hole was directly above the shattered bones. Electrical static filled the air as the Orb slowly moved back to where the creature's head once rested. As it did so, the bones' remains, along with the crumpled golden plate, were sucked up into the air until no trace of the creature was left.

The large Golden Orb then rose about ten feet in the air. Everyone's eyes looked at it as it hovered above them for several seconds. Then, with no warning, there was a mysterious flash along with a "poof"-like sound and the Orb vanished into thin air.

With its disappearance, a deadly silence descended upon the encampment. The only people who could still move around were Jeff and George and the five-member archeological crew. Yet, as if by an intuited signal, they all continued to stand near the pit as they looked around at the frozen statues of Smith, Jones, and their military-type detachment. Even the Blackhawk pilots appeared to be paralyzed in their cockpits.

The ominous silence continued for over a minute. As it did, Smith, Jones, and their troops and pilots seemed to come out of their stuporous trances, but not one of them was able to move more than a foot or so from their previous position. Even the six pilots appeared somewhat dazed, and some force kept them from starting their Blackhawks in anticipation of leaving.

What the hell is going on? George wondered.

Without any warning, a loud sound coming from nowhere discernable shrilled and pierced the air, causing everyone to cover their ears and instinctively look upwards.

Another large globe, about two feet in circumference, mysteriously hovered about twenty feet over the astounded people assembled below. It was shiny, black in color, and a loudish hum emitted from it.

Then, to everyone's astonishment, a metallic-like voice pierced the sky.

"Earthlings," it intoned as they all watched the Orb in stunned silence, "you will immediately leave this place." It continued forcefully, "Pay attention! University of Colorado anthropologists, government spooks, and the commandos—it has been decided that parts of your memory will be erased. None of you will be able to recall anything about the events over the past few days. We have decided that all of you will be given certain selective altered memories that will intuitively put your minds at rest so that you will remember a logical chain of events that omit what you saw, or discovered, or heard."

"As for Sheriff Monroe and Mr. Taylor," it continued, "you both will be able to recall everything that has occurred here and will be able to discuss these events between you. However, we have implanted in your brains—for lack of a better or more understandable term—a 'stopgap,' which will forever prevent you from talking, or communicating in any way, to anyone else concerning these events."

The voice continued, "Also, Mr. Taylor, when you go to look at your farm's boundaries on any Forest Service map, you will see they have not changed. In checking your deed at the courthouse, you will also see it has been returned to the original."

Lastly, the voice said, "Sherriff Monroe, your military record, specifically regarding the events in Afghanistan, has been totally destroyed along with all the pertinent copies."

Both men looked up at the slowly rotating Black Orb and just nodded their acquiescence.

A soft yellow light beamed from the Black Orb and touched each person's face for a second before moving onto the next individual. The Orb then moved in front of each helicopter and beamed its light into the eyes of the pilots before ascending into the skies to a height of fifty feet where it continued to hover. A high-pitched hum came out of the Black Orb and caused every person—civilian, military, and aviator—to immediately touch the left side of their heads.

"All of you present," the Black Orb voiced, "have now been implanted with an infinitesimally small microchip. Should you try in any way to have it removed, you will instantly die as soon as any surgeon tries to enter your brain in an attempt to remove it. Also, anyone at your Capitol who was involved in this operation has now been similarly embedded and their memory gone."

The Black Orb spoke again, its yellowish beam turning on both of them. "As for you, Mr. Jones and Mr. Smith, you both will not be able to move until I release you." The Black Orb's beam lit up Jones's briefcase, forcing him to drop it. The beam then turned a brilliant red and zeroed in on the cheap government-issued faux-leather briefcase which burst into flames. Within seconds, nothing remained except grey ashes, which a sudden breeze blew away in a hundred different directions, leaving no trace of their former existence.

"The archeologists," the metallic voice spoke loudly, "are to immediately pack up and leave within sixty minutes. You quasi-military individuals, along with the two civilians, will depart within the next twenty minutes. Should you specifically fail to do so within that time period, all of you and your Blackhawks will vanish, never to be seen again. Not one trace of you will ever be found."

A deep silence permeated the air as each group, now released from the mysterious hold that prevented them from walking, hustled off to accomplish their tasks in the allotted time periods. It would take not less than ten minutes for the Blackhawks to be able to warm up enough to fly. Jeff and George just stood around watching everyone hurry about their business.

The shiny Black Orb remained stationary in the sky over the encampment.

Jeff turned to George and spoke, "Well, after all that and getting reamed in the ass by our wonderful sh–ty USG, George, I know I definitely need a f-cking beer! Want one?"

Despite his vow not to touch alcohol, George enthusiastically nodded and both men ambled over to the Flamethrower. Pulling down a ladder leading up to the truck bed where he kept his Yeti ice chest, Jeff climbed up and disappeared for a minute. He soon reappeared and then descended with two cold beers in his left hand. Back on the ground, he handed a beer to George and they both popped open the pull tabs at the same time. The two friends leaned against the front of the truck and silently watched as both groups of people readied themselves to leave. The three choppers, with all people on board, warmed up and departed within thirteen minutes. The archeologists hastily worked to pack up their belongings and were gone within the allotted time.

The Black Orb continued to rotate and then, shining its yellow light beam to encircle both Jeff and George, it disappeared, leaving no visible trace of its existence.

The two friends slowly finished their beer while they discussed the day's events. They agreed that there was some sort of unknown power out in the stars that was so technologically advanced that it could probably destroy the earth if it wanted to do so. Both men just shrugged at their conclusion and thanked God they were still living. Getting into the Flamethrower, the two men drove off, leaving the encampment area and dig site.

"How do you even try to explain the unexplainable?" George commented as they drove off in a cloud of dust. Jeff just shrugged.

But what really happened during those three days in June in Dead Horse Valley?

✗✗✗

The wheels of fate now began to inexorably slow down.

✗✗✗

Hello, Earthling! My name is X-3,687-945. I live on the planet Xanthos some 700 million light years from the earth. Our galaxy, not yet discovered by Earthlings or their unsophisticated probes, is named the Santoxian Galaxy after the discoverer of our universe and planet some millions of eons past.

The "3,687" in my name denotes the generation in which I exist since the creation of our world, and the "945" is the number of times my name has been used in my sub-family structure. My son's name is X-3,688-946.

We have millions of eighteen-karat Golden Orbs stationed throughout the entire solar system. Due to our advanced technology, these Orbs film everything on the worlds, stars, and meteors where they are stationed. They send a constant interstellar feed back to our home planet where our superlatively advanced

Tribex521Generation7BYX computers analyze each feed in .00000000001 nanoseconds and immediately notify us of anything suspicious.

If our Golden Orbs do spot anything untoward, our computers start to compile in Zano seconds, a recording on our Xerium877-47BJR Stryberizen discs which are indestructible and last over one hundred thousand Earth years. That enables us to take whatever offensive action is necessary.

Long ago, we launched actual astronauts—explorers who were members of our society. They were accompanied by our Golden Orbs to survey anything they found of interest in the area they were assigned to patrol in the solar system. They would then transmit the information back to us. We manufactured small ovate capsules with walls twelve inches thick to absorb any radiation our explorers might be exposed to as they traveled through infinity. We called these capsules "Eggs." However, we quickly discovered that upon exiting their capsules on certain worlds, radiation exposure killed our explorers in the most agonizing ways. Over time, once we had fully developed our Golden Orbs, the Eggs became superfluous, so we discontinued manufacturing them as our explorers were no longer needed.

In the early years of exploration, sometimes our explorers and their Eggs, along with the accompanying Golden Orbs, disappeared without a trace. Other times they were accidently killed. This is what happened to X-365-43. Millions of years ago during one spring, Shalako Creek was flooding. X-365-43's Orb recorded him leaving his Egg and stepping too close to the creek's turbulent water. With no warning, the embankment collapsed and X-365-43 was hurled into the water. Having never been taught how to swim as we have no water on Xanthos, he became entangled by tree branches floating downstream and drowned. By the time the spring water had receded, X-365-43 was completely entombed under five to six feet of dirt. Over the centuries, the level of dirt would erode and eventually the weakened creek's embankment would expose his leg and foot.

During this entire episode, X-365-43's death was recorded and transmitted back to Xanthos by one of his accompanying Orbs. Expedition management did not have the wherewithal to retrieve the body, much less unearth it. Those in charge decided to leave it in situ and instructed the Golden Orb to remain there, guarding the grave.

With our technological know-how, we were able to upgrade each of our Golden Orbs every two Earth years. The upgrades were transmitted to each Orb so that they could remain at their designated station without having to return to Xanthos and leave their posts unguarded. Those same Orbs have the ability to throw a cloak of darkness over an area and they are also invisible to most of the Earthlings' satellites.

So, for thousands of years, X-365-43's Golden Orb remained in place. As trees died, or were struck by lightning, the Golden sentinel merely moved to another observation station. When X-365-43's leg and talons were exposed after a violent nightly torrent eroded the bank where his body resided, the information and pictures were instantly transmitted back to Xanthos to our Tribex521Generation7BYX computers. This transmission put the entire techno team on "C-alert." This meant they needed to continue to monitor the situation 50/17 (our days are fifty Earth hours long and our Earth weeks are seventeen days).

Thus, when George first discovered the bones, pictures of him and his horse were transmitted to Xanthos along with audio if he were to say anything out loud. When Jeff and George returned the next day in the Flamethrower, and then several days later with the arrival of the UC crew, the master computer issued a "B-alert." Fifty Golden Orbs were immediately dispatched to X-365-43's grave site. The trip to Earth took them less than an hour of Earth time.

The Golden Orbs were programmed so that they could remain invisible while observing the archeologists. Their internal programs ordered them to set up a continuous grid system over the encampment with the sides of each grid located a hundred yards from the center of the excavation.

When the onsite audio picked up information that the Earthlings intended to excavate the body, the Xanthos Tribex521Generation7BYX computer issued a full "A-alert." Both the larger Golden Orb and the shiny Black Orb were dispatched to Earth posthaste. Due to their extraordinary in-built speed, they arrived at George Taylor's land in fifteen minutes and were also cloaked in invisibility.

Those individuals in the command center on Xanthos kept an eye on each Golden Orb's transmission non-stop. On the third day, when the Blackhawks appeared, millions of bytes of data were transmitted to each Orb and they were put on high alert.

The light beams from the Orbs, along with their high-pitched ultrasonic sounds, hums, and vibrations, will remain our secret and not for you Earthlings to know.

As the Xanthos commander, I issued their final orders and was the Black Orb's speaker.

Earthlings, as one of your famous radio personalities, Paul Harvey, said at the end of his broadcasts, "Now you know the rest of the story!"

The wheels of fate ground to a halt.

Acknowledgments

An author's job can be a lonely one without the help, encouragement, and input of family, friends, and research sources along with the publisher's input, proofreaders, and an exterior and interior book designer. When I sit down to write, I have absolutely no idea where my story is headed. I write the first sentence, and the ensuing words seem to flow out of my fingertips onto the page. I conjure up each scene as it flows into the next sentence, sometimes surprising me when the story takes an unexpected turn. At that point, it appears that I cannot type fast enough to put the words onto paper. That, especially, is what happened with "The Body," which I wrote in four days versus the two years it took for me to write "The Time Traveler."

First, the author would like to thank his publisher, Julie Castro, who has now published his previous three books, and now his latest, and fifth book. Julie is a fantastic editor who always has a helpful suggestion or insight to clear up discrepancies or to elucidate upon and untangle some of my convoluted sentences! Without her, there would be no book for you to read!

Secondly, a HUGE thank you to Stefan Hansen of Creative Instincts for his design of the cover along with the interior design and typesetting. This is his third work for the author. His artistry and imaginative vision are most appreciated, especially his ability to find the various images used in this book.

Thirdly, of course, no book can be published without the expertise of a proofreader who can catch printing mistakes even after the manuscript has been intensely combed over 10-plus times by both the author and publisher. I would like to thank Ashley Niro for her keen eye on proofreading the book and finding the mistakes I made. Her comments and editing suggestions made this a much better book.

Fourthly, I would like to especially thank my friend James Delarato, a couple's pastor at Scottsdale Bible Church in Scottsdale, Arizona, for his assistance and insightful input for my story "The Time Traveler." His advice concerning biblical references was of immense help with my being able to complete this story.

FINALLY, A BIG THANK YOU to my wife, Donna Nardi, who can find almost anything online. Without her encouragement, this book may not have ever seen the light of day and, especially the short story "The Body," which was written during the week of her birthday.

Of course, any errors or omissions are the author's alone. Any similarity to people living or dead is by coincidence only.

E. Tayloe Wise grew up in Charlottesville, Virginia. On his mother's side of the family, he is a direct (seventh generation) descendant of Martha Dandridge Custis, whose second husband was George Washington. He is the great-great-grandson of Virginia Governor Henry A. Wise. In May 1968, he graduated from Texas Christian University with a degree in geography, sociology, and anthropology.

The following month, June 1968, he volunteered and enlisted in the U. S. Army and was trained to be a combat infantryman—or in military lingo, an Eleven Bravo. He arrived in Vietnam on May 2, 1969, and was assigned to serve with the 1st Air Cavalry Division, Air Mobile. While with his infantry company, he operated in the jungles of Tay Ninh Province and saw heavy combat during which he became his platoon's medic. He was awarded the Army Commendation Medal for heroism along with three Bronze Stars, two of which were for heroism. He also was awarded the Combat Infantryman's Badge and the Vietnamese Gallantry Cross. He ended his tour as an aide to Major General E. B. Roberts, the Commanding General of the 1st Cavalry Division, and left Vietnam on April 8, 1970, after serving 342 days in country.

The author then worked in his family's commercial real estate business in Charlottesville before retiring in 1989. He was accepted into the University of Richmond's graduate school and earned a Master's Degree in history in 1991. He did post-graduate work at American University in Washington, D.C. In the late 1990s and the early 2000s, he taught Asian history at the University of Richmond. He has also taught Asian history in Richmond, Virginia, at the Shepherd's Center and the Osher Center, both open universities for seniors.

The author's book, *Eleven Bravo: A Skytrooper's Memoir of War in Vietnam* was published in 2004 and is still in print. In addition to his Vietnam book, he has also published:

Letters from Potsdam: Colonel John S. Wise's Impressions of the 1945 Berlin Conference (2022)

The Other Side: Mist, Mirrors, & Strange Tales (2022)

My Life in Reflection: 101 Poems of Love, War, Satire, & Death (2023)